IN MANY WATERS

We gratefully acknowledge the support of the Canada Council for the Arts and the Ontario Arts Council for our publishing program. We also acknowledge the financial support of the Government of Canada through the Canada Book Fund.

Cover design: Val Fullard

In Many Waters is a work of fiction. All the characters, situations, and locations portrayed in this book are fictitious and any resemblance to persons living or dead, or actual locations, is purely coincidental.

Library and Archives Canada Cataloguing in Publication

Brodoff, Ami Sands, author
        In many waters / Ami Sands Brodoff.

(Inanna poetry & fiction series)
Issued in print and electronic formats.
ISBN 978-1-77133-365-8 (paperback). — ISBN 978-1-77133-366-5 (epub).
— ISBN 978-1-77133-367-2 (kindle). — ISBN 978-1-77133-368-9 (pdf)

        I. Title. II. Series: Inanna poetry and fiction series

PS8603.R63I52 2017   C813'.6   C2017-900301-1
                                                   C2017-900302-X

Printed and bound in Canada

Inanna Publications and Education Inc.
210 Founders College, York University
4700 Keele Street, Toronto, Ontario, Canada M3J 1P3
Telephone: (416) 736-5356 Fax: (416) 736-5765
Email: inanna.publications@inanna.ca   Website: www.inanna.ca

MIX
Paper from
responsible sources
FSC® C004071

IN MANY WATERS

a novel by

Ami Sands Brodoff

inanna poetry & fiction series

INANNA PUBLICATIONS AND EDUCATION INC.
TORONTO, CANADA

For Michael

Es una casa tan grande la ausencia
que pasarás en ella a través de los muros
y colgarás los cuadros en el aire.
Es una casa tan transparente la ausencia
que yo sin vida te veré vivir
y si sufres, mi amor, me moriré otra vez.

Absence is a house so vast
that inside you will pass through its walls
and hang pictures on the air
Absence is a house so transparent
that I, lifeless, will see you, living,
and if you suffer, my love, I will die again.

—Pablo Neruda, Sonnet XCIV

PROLOGUE: LOST AT SEA

Aziza floated on her back. She stared into the sky, longing to float there. Its darkness looked warm, safe. Chill seeped through her cotton pants and blouse, her blood and bones, clothes a useless second skin. Chilled, yet melting into the sea, soon she would become part of it.

Her mouth was dry and she swallowed to quench unbearable thirst. Where did water end and sky begin? A breeze on her face, like a human touch. No stars, no clouds, just this black funeral shroud stretched smooth. If only she could drift up into that nothingness and not gasp for breath.

Aziza dozed.

Later, her eyes flew open, panic surging through her so she knew she was alive.

Black water licked her limbs. She remembered where she was, had no idea how long she'd been floating in the sea, no sense how long she could hold on. Aziza thought of Uncle Nuru strapping her into the life vest the moment she stepped onto his old wooden fishing boat in the middle of the night at the port in Tripoli. Uncle had to tie the straps tight, Aziza was so skinny. She'd always been thin no matter how much she ate, with long arms and legs, a swan-like neck, slender hands and feet. Like her father. Like Baba, she was strong; unlike him, she looked delicate.

Her father, Idir, had vanished from their home in Tripoli six months ago. After Baba disappeared, the terror grew. Menacing calls, death threats scrawled onto the front of their house. Her father's leather shop in the souk ransacked, their home set on fire, then Uncle Nuru's burned to the ground. They were not the only ones. Anyone under suspicion, anyone disloyal to Brother Leader Qaddafi, or accused of disloyalty — it didn't take much.

Stepping onto the wooden fishing boat, Aziza hadn't known if she was more afraid to board or to stay behind. Her legs straddled dock and boat; Uncle Nuru lifted her on deck, her body barely shifting the vessel as she sought balance. Uncle soothed her; she tried to be calm. Her cousins had already boarded: Afua, one year older than Aziza, more sister than cousin at eighteen, and Afua's little sister Dede, who'd just turned ten. Bassam, a young man Afua fancied, who cooked the best kebabs in the city and owned his own shop, was on the boat with his mother and three sisters, the girls fighting over a doll they'd snuck on board, pulling it by its plastic limbs until a leg snapped from its socket and they burst into tears. Bassam huddled them into his chest, promised to fix the doll like new. He was a sweetheart, Bassam, and the girls believed him. Maybe he would, could, once they were safe on shore. Anything was possible. Afua nuzzled up to him, stroked his cheek and the hair prickled on Aziza's forearms.

She was angry with her cousin; Afua was using her, and Aziza had to put a stop to it. But here, now? How could she say anything true on this crazy, crowded boat?

Their voyage started out well enough. The worn boat, meant to hold eight passengers, was crammed with two, maybe three times that number — family, friends, neighbours, strangers, too. Aziza tried to count all the people as they leaned shoulder to shoulder, limbs tangled, children squirming on mother's laps, wriggling through legs. She stopped when she reached twenty-one. It was too crowded to account for them all pretzeled together.

Aziza grabbed Afua by the arm. "Sunshine, I need to talk to you."

"Shush," Afua hissed. "When we get there." She beamed her wide open loopy grin, like a baby's first smile, and it lit up her whole face. "I got news."

"What?" Her voice went flat.

Afua circled a hand over her belly that had a smooth soft roundness where her T-shirt clung. Aziza covered her mouth with her hands and Afua peeled them away from her face. Aziza felt oddly responsible: she'd known before she admitted it to herself, they were that close.

Uncle gave orders and the passengers obeyed, everyone afraid of chaos. Aziza had hoped they might make it to Malta, an island of safety. They were all so sick of terror. Her cousin, Tella, Nuru's eldest daughter had travelled to Malta nineteen months ago when she was twenty-two, and was granted asylum. She'd found work, Aziza wasn't sure doing what. Uncle Nuru hoped they would be equally blessed. So they chugged on in open water, frightened and hopeful.

They had been on the boat for two nights when winds picked up and the sea went all choppy, tossing them about. Gusts of rain pelted down. Waves rose like hills, then mountains of foam and water.

The boat's engine sputtered, then failed. The men blocked leaks from one place, then another. Before long, more sprung open. The stalled boat was pocked with holes.

Men, women, and children pushed and shoved, keening, grunting, their panic like a bad smell. Aziza screamed, but couldn't hear her own cry; everyone was screaming.

A fight started up between two of the men. Aziza's neighbour Jamal was knocked overboard and his family, desperate, pushed and shoved in a frenzy to get to him. Aziza heard the cries of mothers and their children, people dragging one another under the black sea, as they clung together. From the sinking fishing boat, Uncle held the hand of Bassam's mother who'd tumbled into the waves holding her youngest girl, he held and held the mother's hand, tried to lift them from the sea, and in the confusion of a big wave, he lost them. Aziza watched some passengers leap into the waves, as if into the arms of their mother.

And then she was in the water with Afua and Dede. Aziza heard Uncle Nuru call out to them as they clung to the boat. When Dede's hands tired, Aziza clenched her younger cousin between her legs, her own hands on top of Dede's, holding them fast to the fishing boat, which sank slowly beneath them. Afua screamed for Bassam; in the chaos, none of them could spot him.

Afua called out, drifting away. Aziza tried to soothe Dede, to stay close, but the current forced them apart, until she could no longer spot either of her cousins. For a long while, she heard Afua yelling for help, Dede crying, then it was still.

Silence washed white over Aziza's head, engulfing her.

She found herself alone in the water. Black night rolled into white-hot day folding into night and then again the stinging sun, fierce as a bright, hot mouth.

What would it feel like to drown? You could drown at sea, or drown on dry land. You could drown in the dark or inside this hot living sun.

Night ... when, which? Aziza saw stars glittering. Not stars —lights. Far away they sparkled. She rolled onto her stomach and paddled slowly, her throat burning, her arms lead weights.

She tired quickly, bobbing in the sea, eyes on the lights, sure they would vanish if she floated on her back to rest, even for a second, afraid the tide would change and sweep her out to sea.

Aziza swam and rested in a rhythm, making her way toward the tiny twinkling lights, pinpricks in the darkness.

PART I: ORPHANS

1. ZOE

NOTES: *Three centuries of Jewish slavery on tiny, Catholic island of Malta. How did we survive?*

Zoe Braverman girded herself up for the journey across the churning sea as she travelled from Malta's northernmost tip at Cirkewwa to Gozo, a smaller island in the Mediterranean archipelago. She didn't like being *on* the water because you could end up *in* it. Just like her parents, travel journalists, both drowned seven years ago at a notorious surfing beach on Mexico's Oaxaca coast while on assignment.

On the ferry, a ragged wind tore through the deck and Zoe braced herself. Rifling through her satchel, she dug for the note that had sparked this journey, dredging it up from the gritty bottom of her bag.

April 9, 2007
Dear Zoe,
Your arrival in Malta is a blessing. I heard you will be living here for a time. You see, our island is small and most news finds its way to me. Your mother was dear and remains so. I raised her from infancy and stayed close in spirit throughout her short life. I always had Cassie's best interests at heart. I'm at peace with that, but there is no peace in her untimely loss. Cassie's death was a tragedy, but was it an accident? Surely you owe

*it to your mother's memory to find out. I urge you to
come see me soon, but of course at your own convenience. I believe in God and Fate.
Fondly,
Gisi Agius*

There are as many ways to truth as there are human faces.
Zoe believed this Talmudic saying. Maybe Gisi was the way
to the truth, or at least a byway.

Her note was written in pencil, a meticulous block-lettered
print on a scrap of paper, as if she were in a hurry with no
stationery at hand. On the back was an address and phone
number.

Zoe had kept the note in her satchel for the past couple of
months and it was tearing along its worn creases. She'd mem-
orized the words in their odd diction, childlike emphasis, and
scolding politesse: *See me soon, but of course at your own
convenience. God and Fate.* Well, which?

Zoe's Mom had spoken often of Gisi, but her old nanny
hadn't visited them in the U.S., and so neither Zoe nor Cal
had ever met her. As the ferry rocked, Zoe remembered the
fitful closeness she'd shared with her mother. Her bond with
her larger-than-life father who'd literally thrown her into the
water when she was just a child, so she would learn to swim,
was fraught. Now, she couldn't shake off sadness and longing.
Her heart was a knot.

Zoe lost her footing, as the ferry docked with a heavy jolt.
Taxis idled and she stumbled into one.

After the dry, dun-coloured dust of Valletta, Gozo was lush
with green table-top hills, steep valleys, and wild untamed
coastlines. She wondered how often her mother and her family
had come here. It was beautiful, so different than the narrow,
twisting streets of Valletta, hot wind winding through their maze.

Zoe gazed out the cab window as they drove along deserted
roads, each village a neat cluster of houses ringing their own

parish church. Cal would love it here, yet Zoe wasn't comfortable bringing him along, afraid of what she might uncover. He'd been deeply troubled after their parents' drownings, awakening into strange panic attacks and nearly delusional thoughts. He developed a twitch in his mouth, which he had to this day.

Zoe got out at Hotel L-Imgarr around two o'clock, a baroque, mauve-painted property at the edge of a cliff overlooking the harbour. In the white and pink washed lobby, she asked for Gisela Agius.

A quarter of an hour, then twenty minutes passed, Zoe fidgety and fretful, looking up every time someone ambled through the lobby, agitated when it wasn't Gisi. Finally, a short, plump woman appeared with salt-and-pepper curls that fell in loose ringlets around her flushed, shining face.

"Gisi?" Zoe held out her hand.

The woman covered her face as Zoe approached.

"Are you all right? I'm Zoe, Cassandra's daughter."

"Of course you are, dear," Gisi said, wiping damp, raw palms on her cotton dress. "Your eyes are the same green."

"Everyone expects them to be brown."

"Your complexion is darker than your mother's was ... but you gave me a start. The shape of your chin, the way you tilt your head, it's just like Cassie."

Zoe had heard this before. She glanced around the lobby, "Look, is there a place we can talk?"

"They are kind enough to give me a room behind the kitchen." She spoke quickly, out of breath. "I'll make us tea, we can have a chat there."

Zoe followed Gisi to her bare, unadorned room and made herself comfortable in a wicker rocker near the window as Gisi put on the kettle for tea and set out biscuits on a ceramic plate, glazed blue and gold with *Gisi* written in the centre of an iris. The plate caught Zoe's eye, the shaky letters of Gisi, the flower drawn as if by a child.

"That little plate, well, your mother made it for my birthday when she was six years old."

"It's lovely," Zoe said, tracing her fingers over the flower, then Gisi's name, imagining her mother as a little girl, growing up in Valletta under Gisi's care; apparently her own mother, Ruth, was prone to melancholy. Cassandra had been a Daddy's girl—lucky, in that way.

"Did my mom visit you here? With my dad, Lior?" Zoe knew they had been given assignments in Sicily and Europe, places within easy reach of Malta.

Gisi squinted her large dark eyes, frowning, then made an effort to smooth her features into a close-lipped smile. "She didn't come back to us much. My happiest times were when Cassie was growing up." She smiled to herself. "That was my real life."

As Gisi excused herself to go to the washroom, Zoe felt a visceral urge to slip the plate inside her satchel, clay that her mother had moulded. She folded her arms across her chest, tucking her fingertips out of sight and harm.

"What brings you to us now?" Gisi asked when she returned, lowering her considerable bulk into a chipped wooden chair with a fraying tapestry seat.

"I've finished most of my work toward a doctorate in history at NYU. I got a small grant to come here and do some research."

"Your grandpa would be so proud."

Zoe nodded. "I wish I'd known him."

For the past five months, Zoe had been digging persistently into her mother's family history in Valletta and her own lost roots. She'd felt orphaned during her parents' lives, nearly as much as after their deaths. What did she have of them? Their published articles? Her mother's photographs? Her father's writings? Bereft, she had to find out what she could on her own, unearthing whatever rocks, perhaps treasures, lay beneath Malta's earth, stone and sea.

As a breeze swept up from the harbour, Gisi began to talk

with little prompting. She had a round, sweet face with a determined chin and dimples when she smiled. Her skin was brown
and weather-worn, though it was hard for Zoe to discern her
age; perhaps mid- or late-sixties.

"I think of Cassie every day. That girl is part of me."

"She called you her *other mother*."

Gisi dabbed her eyes with a slash of tissue. "You must miss
her something fierce."

Zoe looked away. In truth, she'd missed her Mom when
Cassandra was in her very presence; how lonely and unreal
it had felt to miss her when she was right there … but there
was always the glimmering possibility of more. And then she
was gone for good.

Gigi's hand lightly touched her own. "How did you manage,
dear?"

With difficulty, Zoe thought to herself. "It's what I do,"
she said aloud. Her parents might as well have believed that
they were immortal, and life, eternal. There was no life in-
surance. Zoe sold their ramshackle house with her beloved
room above the garage, sixty percent still owed to the bank.
She rented a crummy apartment in a worn old house in the
cheapest part of town, so that Cal could continue in the same
school, then scrambled to get a bunch of part-time jobs to
cover rent and food.

"Keep your memories to comfort you."

A memorial service. Fifty or so people, most of whom Zoe
didn't know well or at all—distant relatives, work colleagues
from the travel magazine, *Arrive.* Cal home alone, waiting for
their parents to magically reappear. Hollow, that ghost-horror.
No bodies.

Survival—that was all Zoe could think about. At twenty-one,
she'd just entered graduate school at NYU studying history and
Jewish Studies. Cal was only twelve, in the eighth grade. She
had a bit of financial aid for school, but had to juggle several
jobs: teaching assistantships, tutoring, research for her pro-

fessors, waitressing. Cal was in her thoughts, was nearly *all* her thoughts. Zoe packed his lunches, helped with homework, signed permission slips, attended parent/teacher conferences. There was always a list of things to do, to remember, to take care of. Looking after her little brother gave Zoe direction and purpose; Cal was her compass and anchor, even her sail, a reason to get up each day. Only now and then did the disturbing feeling seep in of water filling her lungs instead of air. Her real profession was worry, making sure Cal was all right.

"It's odd, Gisi, she never took us back home—here, to Malta. Yet, she taught us to read and write Maltese. That was important to her. I would have loved to have come home with *her*. I went to that hotel, where her home—"

"The Port Pacifika."

"Back in January." Zoe told Gisi a bit about her visit to her mother's former home, now the auberge Port Pacifika in Pjazza Kastilja. A daughter disguised as a travel writer, she was given a tour of the place. She had no idea which room had been her mother's, or what was retained of the original house. It might have been any auberge. More than anything, she longed to know where her grandfather Menash had held Shabbat services, as their home had been the gathering place for the Jewish community on the island. Zoe's guide pointed out the former parlour, the living room, and the library, which were now elegant lounges, television, and reading rooms. What was once a conservatory had been converted into a twenty-four hour coffee shop. Most of the bedrooms on the upper floor commanded panoramic views of the island's mainland and the fortifications of the Grand Harbour, vistas her mother had probably woken up to each day.

"Did you see the library?" Gisi took the pot of tea, which had now brewed and poured out cups for Zoe and then herself, as the phone rang and Gisi went to answer it.

What a library: mahogany walls, books lined floor to ceiling. Zoe closed the door and sat alone. After a while, she perused the books: heavy coffee table volumes with black and white photos of Valletta and glossy colour ones of the Knights of Saint John, an art book with paintings of Gozo. She stood on a stepladder and stretched to the highest shelf, reaching for an elaborate engraved spine. An avalanche of books crashed down, one cutting her cheek. Stooping, she gathered the volumes. A cracked black leather book with yellowing pages caught her eye. A little bookmark fell out with scrawls in a handwriting she recognized immediately.

A Bible. Zoe opened to the flyleaf and saw her grandfather's name written in blue ink, large expansive letters, his signature imprinted into the old paper, like Braille. The book was full of notes, scribbles, and a list of his congregants.

Still on the floor, Zoe touched Nannu's name, felt the engraved image of his handwriting. The page, her fingers, his hand, were distinct points of light alive with presence, breathing with life.

She was stirred, and for a moment, whole.

Are you all right? The man who had shown her around was in the room with her.

I'm sorry. These books fell....

He returned shortly with a bandage.

Zoe's hands trembled, but she took the Band-Aid from him and spread it across her cut, as a buzzer rang from downstairs. *I'll put these back,* Zoe said, as the man left her alone in the library.

This was the room—Zoe was sure of it now—where her Grandfather Menash had held Shabbat services. Nannu's Bible was rightly hers. She needed it, had to have it for her work. While the man was out of the room, Zoe tucked the Bible into her satchel and then quickly replaced the other volumes.

Now, Zoe squeezed lemon into her tea and added a lump of sugar, as Gisi returned to her seat. "Pardon me, that was my husband. You were telling me about your visit to the old house."

"Gisi, at first I didn't know which rooms were which. But when I was in the library, I found—"

"What, dear? You know the place was sold with some of their furniture and belongings." Gisi poured cream and stirred several lumps of sugar into her steaming cup of tea.

"Yes." That could explain the presence of his Bible; perhaps there were other things as well.

Gisi nodded sadly. "It's hard for me to walk by there."

By the time Zoe was born, both of her maternal grandparents were long dead. She'd seen their photographs. It was possible there were some pictures of the original house among her mother's effects, and she made a mental note to sift through those again.

"So how do you like Valletta?" Gisi asked, sipping her tea.

"The city is oddly familiar. Of course, I've seen pictures. When we lived on a lake for awhile, I helped Mom build sand castles modelled after Valletta."

Before Cal arrived to join her, Zoe had used her grandfather's notes and her mother's photographs as a map to visit the sites that contained Malta's hidden Jewish history. At each place she discovered, she felt a deepening tie to her lost family. She attended Shabbat services and had begun to talk with some of the families about their stories. Like her own, many were descended from Jewish slaves.

"You'll have your memories always," Gisi was saying, "like a treasure box you can open whenever you choose." She set a small napkin into her saucer to soak up a puddle of spilled tea. "You know, your mother and I wrote to each other right up until her death."

"Do you have her letters?"

"Drink your tea, dear, while it's hot."

"I have your note ... which disturbed me."

"Well, perhaps we should begin at the end and then go back to the beginning. Your mother's letters worried me."

"Why?" Zoe's voice rose high, pulled taut as thread.

Gisi pressed her hands against the little table between them. "I have Cassie's letters saved," she said with proprietary firmness. "She loved you and Caleb, but never thought she was up to scratch as a mother."

Zoe listened to the waves lapping in the harbour, a gentle sound. "What did she say exactly?"

Gisi patted Zoe's hand that lay on the arm of the rocker. "Now take a deep breath. Have a biscuit." Gisi passed the plate which was filled with a variety of biscuits, some iced with chocolate, others jam-filled.

"About that note you wrote me," Zoe said suddenly. "Mom and Dad, they had their ups and downs...." Zoe reached for a biscuit, but the sweetness of the chocolate turned metallic in her mouth. She took a long sip of tea to wash it down.

Gisi leaned forward and whispered, almost a hiss, "She wanted to leave him, you know. I must get that out straight away."

Zoe felt a deep pain in her chest and her breath caught, short of full, short of empty. "What about her sister? Our aunt."

At the word "sister," Gisi blanched, her brows lowering over her dark eyes.

Gisi must have been her aunt's nanny as well; the girls were apparently close in age, according to the little her mother had offered. Zoe knew her grandfather's jewellery line *Cassel Gems* was named after both his daughters. The first part was for Cassandra, but what about the *el*?

Gisi shook her head hard. "She is long gone."

"What do you mean?"

"She left and never came back, which was best."

"Why? It must have been terrible for my grandparents, she was awfully young."

Gisi gazed at a point above Zoe's head out toward Malta. "For your grandpa, yes, he was fond of the girl."

"You mean his *daughter*. You know, Gisi, your note upset me."

"Well, you owe it to your mother's memory to find out what really happened. There are people in Puerto Escondido in Mexico who knew Cassie well. A boatman named Manuel, and a woman with several businesses in the town called Luz, who looked out for her, or tried to."

Zoe felt her face grow warm. "And my mother's letters—"

"Please don't ask me for those now, dear."

Zoe nodded, as her anger festered. This woman was maddeningly stubborn, talking in riddles. Still, Zoe jotted down the names of the two contacts she'd offered. They sat for a short while longer talking about her mother's girlhood in Malta, Zoe absorbing everything, but sensing that there was a shadow story that Gisi was keeping to herself. Maybe her search would draw her into her lost mother's fitful warmth and light, as it shone through clouds.

"It's late. I should go," Zoe said.

"You can stay here tonight."

Zoe was weary. With her parents dead and Gisi eager to indulge in pastel memories, she didn't know how she would ever penetrate to the truth. "I was going to look for an inexpensive B&B...."

"I won't have it."

"And you?"

"I live in the little fishing village nearby. My husband expects me."

Gisi showed Zoe into the bedroom alcove and left shortly after. Lying awake on the narrow cot, Zoe felt lost and alone, an aching sadness. In truth, she was adrift in her life, pushing thirty, a loner. Ashamed of her fears: water and cats who sprang baring sharp claws and teeth. Stalled in her writing project. Nobody really knew her—not even Cal—making her own secrets harder to bear, all too private. Some days, grief blew through her sudden as a harsh change in weather. She missed her mom.

Before she turned out the light, Zoe spotted a tiny rocking chair at the foot of the cot with her mother's name painted on the back. Hung over one arm of the chair was a string of bright glass beads, colourful and shiny as hard candies. Zoe looped the necklace over her head and then clicked off the light, stretching out and closing her eyes.

Her mother could be a delight, full of games and fun, as if every day was a wrapped-up-ribboned present to tear open. Upside-down dinners of pistachio ice-cream and chocolate cake, pyjama days. Long afternoons at Lake Isle before Cal was born, being a blessed only.

Zoe drew stories on her mother's back with her fingertips and Cassandra had to guess her message. The soft white skin of her mother's back shivered if her touch tickled, or contracted, when Zoe pressed too hard. She loved the smell of her mother's skin, patchouli and baby powder spiced with the faint scent of sweat. Cassandra took a turn at their game, holding Zoe in her lap, enfolding her in a slender arm as she "wrote" with the other hand. Zoe had her mother all to herself at those times, a pleasure so fierce it was a kind of fever.

Zoe slept deeply, awakening to find the mark of her mother's beads imprinted on her throat.

2. CAL

The Carmelite church bells knocked Cal out of bed before seven a.m., gongs nearly as loud as fireworks and scarcely more musical. When the clamour ceased, silence stretched taut as cat-gut. Cal stumbled to the bathroom, and by the time he flopped back onto his monastic twin bed, all was tranquil on Valletta's Mint Street, a narrow, steep lane that dropped precipitously down to the Mediterranean. Cal surrendered to sleep, waking up after ten to the strains of the Malta Symphony Orchestra who practiced in a nearby hall, the bellow of a tuba, the answering trill of the flute. (When he'd first arrived in Malta back in March, Cal slept right through the orchestra rehearsing Beethoven's Symphony No. 6, the roar, crash, and climax of the fourth movement in F minor depicting a violent thunderstorm, fitting background to his dreams.)

Cal rubbed crusts from his eyes and swung his feet to the floor, his calves imprinted with the iron bed rail. The flat was eerily quiet, empty. He put on John Legend's "Let's Get Lifted" and sang along to the lyrics, loving those smooth, restrained chords: *I've got something new for you/ when it gets you won't know what to do/ Relax, let me move you/ don't resist it's in the air/ just one taste will take you there....*

Downstairs, notes for Zoe's magnum opus were spread out on the coffee table, piles weighted with rocks she'd collected on the steep drop down to the sea. Groggy, Cal noticed that his sister's yellow notepads were also fanned out on the floor, as if she'd been in the middle of organizing her ideas.

He listened to the whir of the ceiling fan—it made an odd clicking sound in the emptiness—then called out a phlegmy "Morning Zo!" and was answered with silence.

In the galley kitchen, Cal found her note, slipped beneath the French press. Then he remembered she'd told him something about a research trip around the islands.

> *Baby Brother,*
> *I'm off to Gozo, maybe further afield. Could be gone for a couple weeks. Enjoy being king of Serena's castle. Btw, there's this guy, Max Ellul, I want to talk to. He's been away in Israel, but is due back soon. Try and track him down for me. Be good. Call or text.*
> *Zo*

Cal set up the French press and made himself a pot of industrial-strength coffee, heating up the pastizzi Zoe had left in a white sack, seeping oil. (She'd also stocked up the small fridge and Cal didn't know whether to be grateful or worried.)

He turned "Legend" louder, grateful there were no roomies to call him Mr. Blue and switch up to trap or synth, no Zoe to play her dreaded klezmer.

Well, he could use some time by himself. Freshman year at Rutgers had bombed. Biochemistry? *Shit, what had he been thinking? Not!* So what if math and science had always come easily to him? Instead of calculating equilibrium constants, Cal filled sketchpads with caricatures of his professors and fellow-geeks. Instead of studying for exams, he painted murals and built sculptures from garbage and recycled materials. His best friend Josh was taking a year off to bum around Europe, maybe Morocco, and had asked Cal to join him, but Cal didn't have the money. Going back to the Jersey apartment wasn't an option; Zoe had sublet it—they needed every penny.

When she asked him to join her in Malta, it seemed like the perfect opportunity, or the perfect escape.

Cal took his coffee out to the balcony, staring out at the brilliant wedge of sea. Cars beeped, church bells chimed (now that he was awake, their sound was nearly tolerable), neighbours shouted. He could smell bread baking, the sun warm on his face. Cal had expected Valletta to be an oven, but so far it had been comfortable; now the Maltese summer was settling in. The thick walls of their two-hundred-year-old building kept out the worst of the heat and the twenty-six-foot ceilings prevented the perennial head crash into rafters and doorways.

Waking up slowly, he realized it was cool being out from under Zoe's eagle eyes. Cal grabbed his sketchpad and a stick of charcoal, drawing an old woman dressed head to toe in black squeezing oranges and lemons at a stand. A group of boys played marbles, a mother pushed a stroller. When he was a baby, his mom pushed him in a stroller now and then, but it was Zoe who'd carried him snug against her middle in a homemade sling she'd actually saved.

Taking off was unlike her. Zoe's caution was as much a part of her as her black hair and green eyes. Cal had almost gotten used to his sister's magical thinking that if she fretted about the bad thing that *might* or *could* happen, she'd ward off catastrophe.

Well, catastrophe had already happened. And Zoe was the one who'd given him the bad news ... which he *would not* believe.

Dad was not dead, couldn't have drowned. He'd promised Cal they were going to swim Lake Isle that summer, a mile-and-a-half out, a mile-and-a-half back. Cal trained every afternoon at the Y pool; he was ready. Though Dad came and went, he kept his promises. No way the sea could have gotten the better of him. Dad was too strong, too mad and bad. And Mom wasn't gone, not dead, just out of it like she got now and then, always looking at life through a lens. She had amnesia, forgot who she was, who they were, where home was, the fact that he and Zoe were back in New Jersey waiting for them. Dad was trying to get her back to her right mind and one day soon, any day now, he and Zoe would wake up and find their parents right there with them making coffee in the kitchen.

Zoe had pissed him off, going into gear like a wind-up toy planning that bogus memorial service. Well, he wouldn't go. How can you memorialize people who are still *alive?*

When she got back home, Cal tried to tell her off, set her straight. He saw the black words print across the screen of his mind, but when he opened his mouth, nothing came out. His lips twitched, making shapes not sounds.

For months, even years afterwards, he awoke to see-through dreads. That's what he called the terror at age twelve. The feeling came on the cusp of sleeping and waking.

You have artist's eyes, Callie. Describe it to me.

I can't. Again the mute twitching mouth, like a frantic insect trapped inside his lips, not a part of him.

Try.

A void, not black, clear nothingness. Not falling, not floating, not here, or there. Nowhere. He could not feel his body, his arms or toes or tongue; there was no world.

He awoke into panic, his senses raw. After the see-through stuff, he was flooded with sensations: colours clanged, shapes were outlined in black ink. Ordinary sounds made him jump, clothes chafed his skin.

Zoe took him to see Dr. Nathan Rosenblum, a psychiatrist with a soft, deep voice and warm chuckle that put Cal at ease. Cal went to see Dr. Rose for several years, a comforting male presence who could almost always find the absurd comical angle in life's killer coaster, and he never resorted to name-calling, jargon, or labels. Over a matter of long painful months, Cal found his voice again and could talk to Dr. Rose about pretty much anyone or anything, but his tic remained a part of him, as did his camouflage, chin tucked into his palm, fingers spanned from lips to cheek, a hand covering a face, saving face.

Cal dumped his coffee mug into the sink and changed into shorts and a T-shirt from his dwindling clean pile, then strolled around the corner to the Manoel Theatre. The morning was fresh, sun turning the limestone buildings and fortresses rose-gold. It was like being inside the set for *Gladiator*. A salt-wind swept through the alley-like street, as Cal dodged a tiny sports car that sped past him right on the sidewalk. *Shit! That was close.* As he passed the statue of Our Lady of Mount Carmel, she seemed to ask, *When will you start your life?* And Cal shot back, *Lady, this is my life!*

Walking into the Manoel Theatre, Cal burst out, "Fucking Maltese drivers!" just as Serena, the theatre's administrative director and Zoe's friend, bumped into him, glancing at the time.

"Watch your language."

"Almost got clipped."

"Keep your eyes open."

"Seriously, Serena, what's up with cars on the sidewalk? Side*walk*."

"Has to do with double-parking, Cal."

"Well, yeah."

"We've got over 160,000 vehicles on a *very* small island."

"Got it. That explains cars cutting you up, butting in at roundabouts and corners, overtaking in zigzags and tunnels on congested, potholed, crappily-constructed roads. And did I mention double-parking?"

"*I* did. How are you, Cal ... this, well, not *morning* exactly."

"Sorry."

"I could use your help with the tour today, I'm expecting a crowd. You look like you need an espresso."

"Cappuccino, thanks." When you wanted coffee you got an espresso, a cap, or an instant Nescafe, no such thing as plain old Joe. Cal followed Serena into her office and folded himself into a ladder-backed chair, watching as she fixed his cappuccino. Serena had pert, measured gestures, ladylike. He reached across to take the mug and swiped a staggering pile of folders from Serena's desk, which swept to the floor with a slap.

"Shit. I'm sorry." He crouched to gather them into his arms, the cappuccino sloshing over the rim of the cup.

Serena collected her papers, piling them under a crystal weight. "What am I going to do with you?"

The only place Cal's long limbs obeyed him was in the water. Cal sipped his cappuccino as Serena offered him butter biscuits.

He waved her away and she handed him a napkin.

Cal swabbed a charcoal-stained palm over his face. "Wonder how long Zoe will be off on her trip."

Serena shrugged, the boxy brown blazer at odd angles with her shoulders.

"She talked about going back to some of the places your parents travelled. Sounds like they shared an adventuresome life."

"Not with us."

Cal remembered his boyhood room, the walls papered with maps; he and Zoe marked each place their parents visited with a coloured push-pin to see where it was, how far away. He loved globes, atlases. Once they pin-pointed a place, they tried to imagine they were there, too: the aqua sea in Portofino, the walled city of Valletta, the Wailing Wall in Israel.... Later, he and Zoe pored over the travel features, as if smelling the flavours of a delicious meal they couldn't share.

"You must have gone along with them," Serena murmured, "now and then."

Not now, never then. Cal was ashamed to admit that his parents never took them along, not once. It was weird when you thought about it. They claimed they didn't want to interfere with Zoe and Cal's routine in school, but that was pretty lame.

"I feel as if I'm saying all the wrong things, Cal," Serena apologized, her amber eyes soft. "I'm clumsy that way." Cal watched as she moved to a little cabinet in small, measured steps—constricted by her narrow skirt—and withdrew a huge ring of keys.

"Did you know my mom, Cassandra Paredes?" Cal asked with an urgency that took him by surprise. "That was her maiden name."

"That name intrigues me: Paredes."

"They weren't originally from here. So, did you know her?"

"In passing." Serena jangled the ring of keys over her wrist like a charm bracelet. "My mother was the woman who cleaned this theatre, Papa was an electrician. Your mum came from an influential family. Your grandpa Menash was the leader of the small Jewish community here and owned an international jewellery business. He and your grandmother Ruth were close friends with the Tayars."

"Who?"

"George Tayar was a well-known entrepreneur here in Valletta, managing director of Marks and Spencer in Malta, a philanthropist and arts patron. We'll talk more later, Cal. I've got a tour to run."

"You'd think Zoe would've taken me along, you know? I mean, what am I *doing* here?"

"Building and painting sets, Cal, for a production of *Macbeth*. It's called a job."

She took a long sip of water. "Papa hasn't been well. I want you to learn to do the theatre tour. I may need you to cover for me."

Cal smiled at her. Serena always called her father, Papa, as if he were Cal's papa, too; Cal could use a papa, never having connected much with his own. Except in the water ... where they were both at their best.

In certain moods, Cal saw his father's drowning in a different light, as if he'd died in his element. That didn't reassure him about his mom, though.

"What are you thinking?" Serena asked softly.

Cal felt the colour rise to his cheeks.

Serena smoothed her skirt and opened the door. A clot of visitors gathered in the hallway. Cal felt the buzz of anticipation, as he listened to the babel of languages: French, German—or was it Dutch?—English, and a smattering of Italian.

He peered over Serena's shoulder as she glanced at the headline in the Maltese paper "BOAT WITH 115 MIGRANTS ESCORTED TO MALTA."

Nearly every day since Cal had arrived, there was something in the news about migrants from North Africa surging onto the tiny island. The stories and images were harrowing: men, women, and children sardined into jerry-built boats, crammed onto rafts, their skin glistening with sweat, eyes wide with terror.

Yet, his disturbance didn't last long. In truth, Cal felt oddly distant from the crisis. He'd never seen or spoken to any of the migrants, nor had Zoe, Serena, or anyone at the theatre, as far as he knew.

He looked at the photograph, another frail fishing boat overloaded with sick, desperate-looking people. "Where are these people from?" Cal asked.

"Mostly Libya, some from Somalia, Nigeria, occasionally Tunisia, Algeria, Morocco, Egypt. We're the closest port of entry to the EU."

Cal scanned the article silently over her shoulder, as Serena said, "Twelve bodies were recovered."

"Twenty-seven more were found clinging to tuna pens," Cal read aloud, "attached to a Maltese-owned vessel in international waters."

"They'd been there for three days," said Serena. "The owner refused to let them onto his boat."

"Why not?"

"He claimed they might seize it."

"In their condition?"

Serena reddened under her café-au-lait skin. "I feel terrible for these people, but what they're doing is illegal, not a crime exactly, but.... We are so tiny and overcrowded here. One of the smallest, most densely populated countries in the world, Cal. Italy is no help, neither is France."

Cal just looked at Serena. "There are good reasons, from what I understand, why they left home. And they look pretty ill."

"The numbers ... last year—"

"*Numbers?*"

Louis poked his head into Serena's office, mop in hand. "Don't talk about what you don't understand," he said in English, and then switched to Maltese, which Cal understood; his mother had made sure of that.

"Bunch of dirty pigeons feeding on our people. Taking jobs away ... for half the price."

Serena blushed more deeply. "Cal, I don't have a solution. But I do have a tour to run."

Cal followed her out of the office and into the crowded hallway.

"Welcome," Serena said, making her way through the throng, grabbing Cal's arm to pull him up beside her. This was a first. "I'm Serena Siggiewi and this is Cal Braverman. We'll be your guides this morning." The group gathered around them like private school kids, in a uniform of sorts: starched sundresses for the women, except for the Americans who favoured shorts and tank tops, khakis and polos for the men.

"The Manoel is the oldest public European theatre still functioning within its original structure," began Serena in a vigorous, full-bodied voice Cal hadn't heard before. Sonorous, that was the word.

"What was the debut play?" asked a tall, blonde woman with an accent Cal suspected was Dutch.

"The tragedy *Meropa*," answered Serena without missing a beat, "by Scipione Maffei, acted by the Italian Knights. Let's pass into the foyer." Serena extended an arm to point the way, letting the group file out before her. "We're standing in the Bonici Palace, which was acquired by the Manoel Theatre two decades ago."

Cal felt as if he were inside a jewel-box, the foyer adorned with shell-shaped niches, glittering bevelled mirrors, blue, green, and gold curtains, glowing candelabras and a winking chandelier. Later, he would do some drawings, perhaps an oil pastel to get the colours just right.

"Let's climb the staircase," said Serena.

They filed up, everyone walking as if on ice, barely making a sound. Cal felt outsized, like Gulliver in the land of the Lilliputians, the staircase so narrow and shallow, he could barely fit even the ball of his foot onto each step.

Serena led them into the auditorium, which was spacious and air-conditioned. "Built on the initiative of the Grandmaster Manoel de Vilhena, the theatre's Latin inscription reads, *Ad honestatem populi oblectationem. For the honest recreation of the people.*"

Later on, there was a spate of questions, which Serena answered with her signature patience and grace. At last the tour group dispersed and Cal and Serena shared a quick lunch at the theatre café.

"Oh, I almost forgot to ask you," he said, buttering a crusty slice of bread. "Do you know a guy called...?" Shit, he should have written the name down. He gave himself a minute, drinking down his coke. "Max something or other?"

"Ellul?"

"That's him."

"Max is a fan. He attends all of our plays, as well as the concerts."

"Zoe wanted me to track him down."

"I can give him a call, try to set something up."

"Great. Zoe'll be happy."

That afternoon, Cal worked with a guy on his crew painting an old hollowed drum for the witches' cauldron. Biagio was single, and like Cal, from elsewhere—Sicily—living with a band of cousins in Valletta. Cal concentrated on the wide lip of the cauldron covering it thickly with off-black paint while Biagio put in dashes of grey and teal.

"So, I wanted to go for a run tonight, but Kola hurt her leg, so we have to stay in. I'm not sure what's wrong exactly. I'm kind of worried."

Cal couldn't remember much about Kola. "How did it happen?"

"Running too fast, overdoing it. My girl has to be the number one centre of attention. All the time."

"How long you two been together?"

"Three years."

"Impressive."

"You have no idea…. So I'm thinking maybe we'll go to a club this weekend, *Anonymous* in St. Julian's. You in?"

"For sure. I'm definitely down to meet some people."

"The women are gorgeous. And everyone loves to dance!"

Cal set up a fan and trained it on the cauldron. "I'm not much of a dancer … wait a minute, Kola?"

"What are you talking about?"

"Not the jealous type?"

"She won't be there, Dude."

"How you managing that?"

"They don't let *anyone* in with four legs."

Cal joined in the laugh at himself. No wonder he and Biagio clicked, they were both a bit out of it *and* animal-people. Shit, he had to listen better, get out of his own head. They finished touch-up on the cauldron and went on to the Great Birnam Wood backdrop, dense with brush and trees and a threatening sky of indigo, mauve, and purple.

"So what kind of dog is Kola?"

"Bracco Italiano. They're bird dogs, tightly wound, hyper. While I was working late yesterday, she opened up all the cabinets and ate two jars of peanut butter. You know how hard it is to get PB in Valletta? Trouble with a capital T, like Kola."

"You're one lucky guy."

After they finished for the day, Biagio invited Cal for a beer with the crew, but none of them hung out for long. It was incredible to Cal that some of the guys he worked with building sets for *Macbeth* were already married and settled with families; if they weren't hitched, they still lived at home with their parents. He liked them. They got along, and joked around, but they were from different worlds.

Cal wandered the Valletta streets alone, stopping in at several galleries, a museum, and a church, filling his pad with more sketches, none of which were any good. He felt lonelier than he had in a long while.

Walking back to the flat, he stopped in the laundry room to fish out some clothes he'd left in the dryer a few days ago. As he thrust his hand inside the humid warmth, he felt a sharp scratch drag from wrist to knuckle as a creature leapt out of the machine and perched on the window ledge. It was an orange tabby with a coat of light and dark orange swirls, and daubs of cream, as if he'd been tie-dyed. A gorgeous creature, though skinny, with a matted dirty coat.

"Hey fella, I won't hold this against you." He held out his hand and the cat crouched, ready to spring. "Steady, now." The signature *M* marked his forehead, as he stared at Cal with round, copper-coloured eyes. The tabby had no collar or identification and Cal felt a surge of possibility.

He brought his laundry upstairs and cleaned the scrape that wasn't deep, already drying up, then filled a bowl with cream and returned to the laundry room where he set it down, not far from the dryer. Cal didn't spot the cat around, but hoped he'd be back.

For years Cal had brought home frogs and rabbits, saved a bird who flew down the chimney, and begged and pleaded for a kitty, but his parents weren't keen. After their deaths, Zoe wouldn't permit it. Everyone talked about cat ladies, but he was a cat man. Cats were discerning and independent, they had few needs. They came to you when they wanted, you couldn't force or cajole them—fiercely affectionate or gloriously indifferent—they never pretended to like you and didn't give a shit if you liked them. Cal was in awe of these wonderful creatures.

He changed out of his work clothes, then jogged down the steep narrow lane to the sea, missing his dad, their night swims.

The wind was strong and Cal anchored his towel under a loose piece of Malta stone, slid down rocks and sea wall, plummeting into the Mediterranean. At the moment his arms met the water, he gasped with pleasure. His wrist stung a bit, but it felt good, cleansing. It was dusk and he could just make out the glimmering lights of Sliema and St. Julian.

The sea was bracingly cold, but within a minute, his body adapted and he swam and swam, first crawl, then backstroke, then breast, a bit of butterfly, floating and just gazing at the sky. There were no swimmers in any direction and at that hour he didn't spot any boats. Early June was still too cold for most Maltese to swim. The locals warned him against swimming off the sea wall, rather than bicycling to an official beach, or better yet, ferrying to Gozo, but Cal relished the risk, even more the solitude. With five years of summer jobs as a lifeguard, he was confident under most conditions.

Eventually he lost track of time and what had troubled him melted into the sea. When he finally pulled himself out of the water, his toe bumping a rung of the ladder, it was full dark.

Arriving back at the flat, relaxed, wet and dripping, Cal spotted the orange tabby curled on the bottom step, asleep. When he eyed Cal, he roused himself and followed him nimbly up the steps, and when Cal opened his door, the cat darted inside.

3. ZOE

NOTES: *You called yourself, primus inter pares, first among equals. Grandpa, were you a born believer? I struggle daily, hourly. I'm not the best person—then I listen to your voice.*

On the plane to Mexico, Zoe put on headphones and listened to Ravel, straining for calm. Back in Malta, she'd sold off her late father's gold Longines watch and onyx cufflinks to pay for air tickets and rustle up some extra cash. She tried not to think about that impulsive move just now, concentrating on the rich, evocative harmonies and instrumental textures of Boléro. The journey felt both drawn out and instant. The plane descended in swoops and she was in Oaxaca.

She chose the same route her parents had taken at least three times before: the bus from the city to Puerto Escondido—a fishing village and former coffee port—dense green, as they climbed into pine forests, then descended into tropical jungle, with pops of scarlet and yellow, the smell like steaming vegetables. Her parents had loved this part of the world and Zoe felt an eerie connection; she dreaded seeing the sea.

Stepping down from the bus into El Adoquín, she felt the heat and humidity in every pore, an animate presence. She walked along an isolated dirt road, her duffel over her shoulder, keeping an eye out for the Villas Carrizalillo.

Though Zoe preferred anonymity, the young woman at the

desk recognized her name, asked if she was related to Cassandra and Lior Braverman, and when Zoe nodded unwillingly, she gave her a comfortable room, called Puebla, at a special rate. "I didn't know your parents, but my father was fond of them. I'm so sorry for your loss. Let me know if you need anything."

Zoe wiped sweat and grime from her face, thanked her, and rushed away to settle in. In truth, she wasn't ready for long conversations, the whole song and dance of strangers' pity, which required Zoe to be their buffer.

Once inside her room, Zoe could hear the waves sizzling against the cliffs. The beach, Playa Carrizalillo, wedged between steep grey crags, had a gentler surf than the notorious Playa Zícatela, known for its lethal undertow and frequent drownings, where her parents had died. Zoe would have to gird herself up to venture there, oddly necessary.

Unnerved by the surf, she unpacked. Puebla was a romantic spot, perfect for honeymooners and Zoe took a perverse pleasure in being there alone: tiny kitchen, terrace, sea views with a winding, steep path down to the beach. Collapsing on the bed, she strained to imagine her parents here on their several visits, some for business, others to celebrate an anniversary. From her vantage point, their marriage appeared close but fraught. Even as their daughter, she was an outsider, unsure what transpired between them.

Changing into a white linen dress, Zoe strolled out to the restaurant on the terrace, El Cielo, to the shush and pound of the surf. As she sipped a margarita, she observed the others in the small bar and restaurant. An older French-Canadian couple were talking about Quebec City to an attractive younger pair whom Zoe overheard saying that they were from New York and lived in Park Slope; the conversation flowed from French to English to Franglais. At the end of the bar were three young girls, all in bikini tops and short-shorts revealing smooth, half-moons of buttocks. The friends spoke rapidly in Spanish, swishing manes of glossy hair.

Watching them, Zoe felt like a new breed, the Jewish nun. Though she preferred to sleep with men, she enjoyed looking at women, but could not remember the last time she had made love. (What a lovely, quaint phrase!) All of her "relationships" had been swift and painful. With the exception of Cal, people flowed in and out of her life with frightful frequency. Nothing adhered. The sad truth was, she had no time for love, only longing.

Soon the waitress brought Zoe another margarita and a platter of homemade tortilla chips. She prepared guacamole at Zoe's table using an earthen bowl and stone pestle, mashing fresh avocado to a green paste, adding chopped cilantro, chilies, onion, and tomato, the dip releasing its tempting odours. As Zoe watched her work, she felt the evening air against her skin, soft and salted by the sea.

By the time she dipped her first chip into the guacamole, Zoe was ravenous. Since leaving New York, she was always hungry, in every possible way, ready to eat anything that didn't eat her.

Zoe noticed only one other person eating alone and stole bird-like glances. He was clean-shaven with a head of thick silver hair that flowed over his collar. Unlike Zoe, he was armed with a prop, a little jewelled box, which he was trying to pry open. At the man's elbow was a compact metal case that unfolded into a set of tiny tools. He sipped from a glass of red wine as he worked to pick the lock of the miniature box.

The box was round, the size of a silver dollar, its inlaid coloured stones reminding Zoe of her grandpa's mezuzah that she'd found in the room above the garage when she was a girl. She stared stubbornly; he irritated her—couldn't he pick in private?

What was he going to unlock anyway?

She ate her shrimp fajitas, had half of her second margarita, and stood, swaying, thinking of her father, squeak of his office door, wedge of lamplight. Daddy, am I in your book? Zozilious! He smiled, swung her high above his head, then pulled her in against his chest. For a moment, she was crushed there in heaven, till he lifted her to eye level.

She was beside the man's table, holding her drink. "I'm just curious."

He stared at her with squinting intensity. He was younger than he'd appeared, no more than forty, handsome with high, sculpted cheekbones. Zoe watched him fold the tiny tools into their metal case, like a Swiss Army knife. Turning, he stretched out lanky legs.

"I'm obsessed."

"With...?"

"I found this at an estate sale in Mexico City. It's quite old, I think, perhaps from the nineteenth century. Bloody tough to open."

"At the dinner table?"

"Indeed, bad form, but...."

"You're obsessed."

"Right."

The Queen's English, not overly plummy. Lashy blue eyes.

"What's your interest in that box?"

"I'm an antiques man. And who doesn't love a secret compartment?"

Zoe sipped the salty-sweet tang of her drink, weaving, then bumped into his table, jostling water, which sloshed over its glass.

The man caught her at the elbow, her drink spilling. "Sorry," he clipped.

Before Zoe could think, he'd nipped the drink from her slick fingers, placing it on his table. With one arm in a shepherding sweep around her back, Zoe found herself plopped boozily beside him. She looked at him—too surprised to be angry—the stranger's blue eyes pinning her in place. He turned her wrist, gazing closely at her bangle bracelet.

He released her, waving for the waitress. The man ordered in excellent Spanish, asking for two coffees, then switched to English. "No, make that a double espresso and a strong coffee. Right."

Zoe was too drunk for embarrassment.

"Are you all right?"

"Hope so."

Soon coffee arrived, the espresso for him.

He sipped slowly, then turned to her. "I'm Bertram."

"Zoe." She knew she would have a headache in the morning, a bad one. Had to remember to text Cal.

"That's an intriguing bracelet, might I have a look?"

She extended her arm, but did not remove her bracelet. After her parents' deaths, Zoe had received a lacquered box of her mother's jewellery. Many of the pieces were engraved with Cassel, the jewellery firm created by her grandfather; Cassel, an abbreviated hybrid of both of his daughters' names, Zoe's mother, Cassandra, and her missing aunt, the one she'd tried to pry Gisi about. The gems were rich saturated colours and the designs his own. The platinum bangle she always wore was engraved with the first verse of the Shema in Hebrew, and when the catch slid open, a hidden compartment revealed a black and a white pearl, linked by a figure-eight. The verse comforted Zoe; whenever their mother was home, she'd sung the Shema with her and Cal right before bed, a rare family ritual.

Bertram slid open the catch. "Ingenious and lovely. I see we both like secret compartments."

"I never take it off."

"I wouldn't either. What does it say?"

"It's a Jewish prayer, a kind of centrepiece to morning and evening services." Great. That put a tight cork into the conversation.

After a few moments, Bertram said, "So what brings you to Puerto?"

Zoe didn't know where to begin.

"That bad?"

Those eyes again, penetrating and warm. She couldn't remember the last time she'd seen warm blue eyes, though it was not an oxymoron, she realized.

"No, not really." Zoe was sobering up, damn, how unpleasant. Well, speak she could, and speak she would have to. Conversation. "My parents loved this place and told me about it. You?"

"Vacation. Relax, swim … do a bit of surfing."

Zoe gazed down at the crashing waves, relentless, terrifying.

"Have you given it a go?" asked Bertram.

"Relaxing … or surfing?"

Bertram laughed, deep, confidential. "Both."

"I'm trying to decide which activity terrifies me more: relaxing or surfing." She wasn't usually this open, but it felt good for once. "So," she ventured, "you say you're an antiques man, what do you do exactly?"

"I own a shop, Time and Again, on the Upper West Side of Manhattan. We specialize in British antiquities, though I picked up this beauty, ah yes, I told you already."

"Let me know what's inside when you are finally able to open it."

"And your bracelet? Is there a story there?" He leaned in to examine the catch.

Zoe pulled her arm away. "Look, I've interrupted you."

Bertram's eyes narrowed and he gazed at Zoe again with that squinting intensity. "And what brings you here? You didn't quite explain."

"Well, if you must know," Zoe blurted out in a strident voice caused by the lingering effects of alcohol, "I'm working on my thesis."

"Yes?"

Zoe took a long sip of coffee and motioned to the waitress for a refill. Of course, she'd come to Malta to work on her thesis, and had no inkling her journey would take her not only to Gozo, but to the Oaxaca Coast of Mexico. Geography aside:

in truth, she was not writing, that was her shameful secret. She was blocked—Zoe disliked that word which smacked of traffic and road obstructions—rather than creative process. Of course, she'd amassed copious notes, had too many ideas, more than ideas. And quintessential questions. As if looking at her project under an X-ray, Zoe became aware of how many decisions, both infinitesimal and large, she had to make to write a single sentence, let alone a word. She worked words along her tongue, squirreled some beneath, like a new taste, an exotic hors d'oeuvre, identifying not only the meaning(s) of a word, but also its flavour.

Then there was the question, a semi-colon or a colon here, a period or a comma there. She had big decisions to grapple with, such as the scope and focus of her project: would it be about the hidden Jewish history of Malta or include more personal history, delving into her grandfather's role as a leader, her mother's life on the island? Where—and how—to begin? How to handle time? Where to make the incision in time? as one of her professors had put it. A clinical, ruthless image. Vivid. Writer as surgeon. Where indeed? Her proposal to the Emet-Shazar Foundation for Jewish History Fellowships had been cogent, while in truth her ideas were in flux.

When she'd tried to write in her squeaky swivel chair in the Valletta flat, she felt as if there was a keg of gunpowder packed tightly beneath her ass, and she blasted up, wandering about the ancient walled city.

"I'm afraid I've lost you."

Zoe shrugged. "I try to convince myself that walking around all day, then filling index cards with notes is a useful, seminal stage of the work." She heard Dorothea Brooke's admonishment to Casaubon: *And all your notes.... All those rows of volumes—will you now ... begin to write the book which will make your vast knowledge useful to the world?*

"Gluteus maximus in the chair no longer works for me," she shot out.

Bertram laughed. "Well, then, we have to get you out of that chair. So you can have some fun in Puerto."

He raised his espresso cup and she her mug and they clinked, as if they held wine. It was a relief to spill her guts to this stranger about her *magnus opus interruptus*.

"So you see, I'm spending more time avoiding the whole project."

"Yes, of course. Must be terribly hard. Why not try writing out here over dinner with the chatter and the waves around you, or even watching the telly. Trick yourself into writing, it's less momentous." He leaned in close and whispered, "Write in bed. Breakfast there, and if things get cooking, forgive the lousy pun, have lunch there as well. There are precedents, you know, Proust of course, Eudora Welty, I could go on ... it's quiet—usually—except for the noise in one's head ... that it's all rubbish."

Zoe nodded. She sure knew about the noise in one's head. "How do you know about that?"

"I read, ruminate. Occasionally, I contribute pieces to antiques journals. We've all got some of that noise."

"How do you prevent yourself from falling asleep...."

"Must keep your project exciting, I suppose. Do you have the luxury—or should I say the torment—of working on it full-time?"

She laughed, a bit rueful. "The torment." Of wasting full-time.

"Brilliant."

"Not exactly. Pressure! Know that song?" Zoe sipped her coffee as Bertram flagged down the waitress and ordered a plate of fresh fruit.

"I'm distracted," Zoe confessed. "Here I am, giving myself a little break." Which wasn't exactly the truth.

"Well done." The fruit came arranged like a flower. "So is this your first time in Puerto?"

"Yes, but it doesn't feel like it. My parents spoke of this place, I saw pictures...."

"Perhaps I could take you round. Tomorrow?"

Zoe felt a rush of pleasure, but found herself saying, "I have plans; besides, I don't want to put a crimp in your schedule."

"No crimp, no schedule. Whenever you like, if you like," he said, his words clipped. "Perhaps you prefer to wander round on your own."

She'd punctured the fizzy feeling, but they sat together a while longer listening to the waves. Then Bertram picked up his miniature tools again. "You must be quite tired."

Zoe took the hint, stood, and there was the pounding headache, in contrapuntal rhythm with the surf.

"Let me walk you back."

He took Zoe's arm, as she leaned into his shoulder for balance. Bertram suggested they take a swim, mentioning a day and time and she nodded, barely listening, thinking she'd take a couple of extra-strength ibuprofens and one of her big fat pretty pink sleeping pills—surely that cocktail would shut up the noise in her head.

4. CAL

No one came to claim the stray orange tabby though Cal checked lost cat ads in the papers and notified local shelters. He named him Tonio and used all of his earnings to have him checked out at the vet and to get his vaccinations. Though Tonio was scruffy, skinny, and abandoned, he wasn't in bad shape.

Valletta baked in the heat, parching even the wind that blew through the narrow streets, as Tonio cooled himself under the ceiling fan and devoured all the plants in the flat, retching up green. When Cal put out his food bowl, Tonio growled, nudging Cal's leg three times and then nibbling or biting his ankle. One day folded up into the next, as Cal built sets for *Macbeth* and read the play at night, Tonio perched on the arm of the couch, one paw on Cal's shoulder as he licked his scalp with a sandpaper tongue. His purr was like a motor, regular as the air going in and out of his lungs, and the blood beating through his body, which was filling out fast.

Late at night, the city stilled: no church bells, cars, or people shouting, only a wild, hot, howling wind. At midnight, Cal went to bed, Tonio climbing in with him.

On a scorching day in mid-June, Serena mentioned that Max Ellul was back in Valletta and would be at the theatre in the evening to pick up some tickets; he and Cal could meet up for a beer.

The theatre café was crowded when Cal knocked off work. He was coated with a layer of sweat and sawdust, but had no time to race home for a shower. Scanning the room, which was mostly full of tourists and a few locals, he spotted a man nursing a beer at the rear of the café, the only person sitting alone: oldish, maybe late fifties, with a full red beard and a yarmulke on his head secured with bobby pins. Despite the heat, he was dressed in a starched white shirt and black jacket. Cal should have just gotten the guy's email and passed it along to Zoe. Now there was no getting out of this.

Cal approached his table—man, this was going to be awkward—and the guy glanced up slowly.

Cal addressed him in Maltese, embarrassed by his halting words. "Hello. I'm Cal Braverman and I work for Serena. This is weird, but are you Max Ellul?"

The man gave him a full warm smile, "It's wonderful to meet you, Cal. I'm happy you found your way to us." He put out his hand and shook Cal's with a firm grip, then motioned for Cal to join him.

Cal pulled out the chair with excessive force and it clattered to the floor, diners glancing his way. He righted the chair and plopped himself down, screeching into the table.

Max asked Cal if he'd like a beer and ordered him a Gulden Draak, the same brand he was drinking.

"I just got off work," Cal sputtered, switching to English. "Didn't have time to get cleaned up."

Max shook his head. "No problem at all." He stared at Cal from behind his glasses, a look so intent, it made Cal skittish. The stare was puzzling, but Cal didn't say anything, too tired to think. The waitress plunked down his beer and he took a long thirsty slug; it was fruitier than he was used to, welcome after the long day of physical labour.

"It's a Belgian ale," Max said, holding his glass to the light, a deep mahogany beer with reddish glints. "Big malt sweetness, demands sipping."

Cal nodded, taking another thirsty swig. The beer had a cloying sweetness that coated his mouth like velvet, but he could taste the alcohol, which was a damn good thing.

"You're probably wondering why I wanted to meet up."

"Not at all. You see, I knew your family."

Cal shook his head. "I had no idea."

"Your grandpa was my mentor, taught me everything I know about the jewellery business. People like him don't come along often."

Cal listened, nodding slowly. He knew his mother had adored her dad, but to Cal, he was just a ghost. "We never got to know him. Or my grandma or aunt either." For so long, it had been Cal and Zoe, the two of them alone together.

"Yes, it's a pity. I have so many stories."

Cal nodded, glancing around the room. "It's actually my sister, Zoe, who wants to talk to you. Okay if I give her your number or email?

"Of course." Max jotted down the information, handed it to Cal, then sipped his beer. "Tell me, what brings you and your sister to Malta now?"

Cal told Max about Zoe's work, his aborted college career and his interest in art, which he hoped to develop while in Valletta. He hadn't talked this much about himself in ages.

"I hope you'll end up loving the island as much as I do. Your mother was inspired here. It's where she started as a photographer."

"Did you know her well?"

"Our families celebrated holidays together." He reached under the table for his leather briefcase, slipping out a large black and white photograph. "I brought this to show you. Here's both our families on Pesach. I think this was taken—" he flipped the photo over—"yes, 1966."

He laid the black-and-white photo on the table, turning it to face Cal, then stood up and came around to his side of the table.

Cal studied the picture for a moment. "That's my mom, right?"

"At thirteen." He shook his head. "What a beauty."

Cal recognized his mother's delicate heart-shaped face, large, wide eyes, and dimpled smile. She was petite, all dolled up in a white eyelet frock and shiny patent shoes. Beside her was a tall gangly girl with a prominent nose and full mouth opened wide as if she were cracking up. She was dark-skinned and dark-featured. Though everyone else was dressed formally, the girl had on bell-bottom jeans and an embroidered peasant top. Her thick, black hair rippled in a wild cascade over narrow shoulders. Both girls held up their second and third fingers in a V, Cassandra in the peace sign, the other girl, making donkey's ears behind Cassandra's head.

"Who's next to my mom?"

"That's your mother's older sister, Yael."

"Whoa." He'd never seen a picture of the whole family together.

"Next to your mother on her other side is your grandpa Menash, and beside him, your grandma, Ruth."

Max went on to identify the other family members in the photograph, which included sixteen people in all, Max's four brothers and two sisters, various aunts and uncles and cousins, while Cal thought about his lost aunt. "Sorry." He interrupted Max in his long rendition of family bios. "Do you know what happened to Yael? All Mom told us was that she took off as a teenager and never came back."

Max ordered another round of beers, while Cal asked the waitress for a glass of water. Max didn't answer right away, long enough for their second round to arrive. "I think Yael wanted to learn more about her personal history and birth parents—your grandpa adopted her from a Catholic orphanage in Marrakech—forgive me, I'm telling you something you probably already know. Yael felt she didn't fit into the family."

"How come?"

Max took a long pull on his beer. "We can be quite insular

here, even clannish. Yael was a strong girl, tough." He laughed
to himself. "A kibitzer, always playing pranks."

"I guess vanishing was more than a prank, right?"

Max nodded slowly. "I would love to know what became
of her."

"You're not the only one."

They finished their second beers, as Max told Cal more
about what life was like growing up in the fifties and sixties
in Malta, how Yael ran away to the neighbouring island of
Comino one weekend on a lark and didn't come back for two
nights, staying in a tent with God-knows-who, her family wild
with worry. When it was full dark, they said their goodbyes
and Max slipped the old family photograph into Cal's hands.

Talking with Max was weird, communing with ghosts, who
took on flesh and life, making memories, when it had seemed
there were no more memories to make. His mother and lost
aunt in black and white, his grandpa and grandma, a family.
He wished he could talk to Zoe face to face.

Before bed, he texted her and sent a picture of the photograph: Max MA. Pic fam w MIA aunt Yael.

Cal opened his windows wide and put the ceiling fan on high,
played with Tonio and a piece of string. Finally clicking off the
light, Tonio nestled in the crook of his arm. The flat was still
very hot and Cal tossed and turned for an hour, before giving
up on sleep. It would take a while for the place to cool down.

Agitated, he left the flat and jogged down the steep hill to
the seawall. Ignoring the ladder, he lowered himself against a
sheet of rock, his arms spread-eagled, his feet losing purchase
in a shallow niche, so he slid down scraping his chest, thighs,
and inner arms, the pain oddly bracing. Cold water folded
over him, engulfing his body, his scalp prickling with pleasure.

Swimming underwater in long cleansing glides, Cal didn't
want to surface. When his lungs were about to burst, he plum-
meted up, just his head showing dark and wet as a seal. He saw
the moon, the sea shimmering into fish scales. Plunging under,

Cal let his mouth fill with seawater; surfacing, he sprayed a geyser into the night.

He swam far from shore, then slowed his pace, switching from crawl to breaststroke. The quiet of the night was broken suddenly by a splashing. When he looked toward it, he saw a spot of phosphorescence.

There was a moving shape, a human cry.

Cal cut through the water, and as he drew closer, he spotted a wild thrashing in the sea. Speaking words of comfort, he had no idea what, he reached for an arm. Long hair brushed his face like seaweed. A girl grasped for him, then clutched his neck, slipping away.

Cal rolled her onto her back, her eyes wide, yet dull, terror and exhaustion all mixed up. Thank God she had on a life-vest. He encircled one arm around her slender chest, so he could tug her to shore. She held onto his arm, her grip tight as a vice.

Slow and steady, Cal glided in toward shore, using the strength in his legs, sculling with his free arm. The girl craned her neck to look at him and he whispered to her that it was all right, she was going to be okay, to just rest. Dark ropes of seaweed curled around their legs and the girl cried out; Cal shook the tangle free, kicking hard in a rhythm. He took a deep breath, a long glide and felt a surge of energy. He would not let her go.

5. CAL

MEMENTO MORTIS

Dad, remember you and me in the water, any water? Remember how it sucked on dry land, how you looked past me? Unless you were pissed off. What did I do? Didn't matter if you were in one of your moods. You'd stare me down until I looked away, afraid of you. Big blustery guy, bushy black brows, hail-fellow-well-met-routine. Called me Buckaroo, Chip, Monkey, Bright Eyes, Kid, Buddy. Any name would do. What, shit, you couldn't quite place me? Except when you were in a rage. Then I was Caleb ... but sharing your beautiful Blues after you knocked off work—Bessie Smith and Muddy Waters—and in the water, I was Calley. If I was already in bed, you'd lift and carry me down to the lake. When I opened my eyes, I saw the black water, the dark warm, like a person. You were the dark, you were the water. I rode your back as if you were a porpoise, smooth, sleek, faster than anything. We'd travel the world like that. You whooshed me making a wake, threw me hard into the air, catching me after I cannonballed. I wasn't scared. Loved that grey-green-water-world. You were out there with me tonight, Dad. In the water, you know my name.

6. ZOE

NOTES: *Why is Yael left out of our family history, the family liturgy? What's her story?*

The next morning, Zoe was wobbly, but after coffee, a banana, and a couple of extra-strength ibuprofen, she faced the day.

She read Cal's text, her heart quickening as she clicked open the cell phone photograph he'd sent her. Yael. Zoe was eager to hear more details from her laconic brother and wanted to see the original family photograph. Of course, it fit: Cassel Gems, named for her mother Cassandra, and her missing aunt Yael. Odd, that Zoe's grandparents had given her mother the name of a tragic Greek goddess and her older sister a Hebrew name, meaning strength of God. Apparently, Cassandra's mother had chosen her name, and Zoe guessed that their father had chosen the sister's. Yael's name made perfect sense, now that she thought about it, given Nannu's faith.

The walk from the villa to the tiny administrative office nearly did Zoe in; the heat and coastal humidity were terrible and she struggled with each breath, as if inhaling vapour. At the office, Zoe asked the young woman on duty about the lagoons of Manialtepec, which she'd seen in her mother's photographs: flora mimicked reptiles and reptiles melded into rock, tree, water, and weed.

"My mother always went with a guide ... Manuel—"

"*Por supuesto.* Manuel Fuentes."

"So he's still around?"

"I will call him for you."

"Oh, and there's something else." Zoe explained that though she was very comfortable here, she'd need to find a more affordable place. The young woman made a few more calls and found Zoe a room in her cousin's house just down the dirt road.

"*Muchas, muchas gracias.*"

"*Mucho gusto.*"

Two hours later, Manuel Fuentes came to collect Zoe at the entrance. He was a strongly-built man with close-cropped hair, sharply hewn cheekbones, and a long upper lip. Dressed in a khaki shirt and pressed, pleated pants, he had a slightly formal, old-world manner. Zoe settled into the backseat of his mini-bus, which rattled on the dirt roads of Puerto, a knife stabbing through her skull with each jolt. Her dinner last night, the encounter with Bertram and his tiny jewelled box, seemed part of some dream. He was dishy; that's what her mother might have said. Now and then, these British locutions had popped out of Cassandra's mouth. Made sense, given that Malta was part of the British Empire during much of Cassandra's girlhood—until 1964—and her own mother had been English.

At the spongy shore of the mangroves, Zoe stepped into Manuel's powerboat and they chugged through the lagoons as birds, reptiles, and succulents loomed in and out of the mist, a dreamy landscape torrid as her mood. Trees with soft greyish roots cascaded into the slow-moving river like plaits of hair. Manuel let the boat drift, as Zoe studied birds and plants through Manuel's binoculars, imagining her mother seeing some of the same sights. What different lives they'd had, Zoe rooted at home, caring for her brother, her mother and father out exploring the big wide world. Now, it was her turn.

Now and then, a slimy reptile skittered up rocks or trees, then froze. Manuel started the motor and they crossed to where river met sea, docking at a deserted beach.

Zoe spotted a small, weather-beaten shack and an old man missing most of his teeth; he was shirtless with brown, crinkled elephant-hide skin. There were two hammocks set up in a patch of shade and Manuel suggested they take a break.

He unpacked provisions, which Zoe accepted gratefully. Sitting in the hammock, she nibbled bread and cheese. "Have you worked here long, Señor Fuentes?"

"Since I was a young boy, Miss. Please, call me Manuel."

"I'm Zoe."

"It is always good to end on something sweet."

Zoe took a fig. "My mother loved this place, she spoke of it often. Maybe you remember her ... Cassandra Braverman?"

"Por Dios."

"It's okay."

"I was saddened by your parents' sudden deaths, a terrible tragedy."

Zoe struggled to extricate herself from the hammock, which entangled her limbs like a spider's web. She found a rock and sat down.

"My mother told me about this beach, I saw photographs."

"Her photographs made you see *las cosas* in a new way, so different than what you find in a travel book. I took her out often. She spoke *Español* and we had many long talks."

They sat for a while, listening to the surf, the old man gathering shells, his mangy dog beside him. Zoe nibbled the chewy sweetness of the fig. Finally, she punctured the quiet. "And my father, did you take him out too?"

"Solamente una vez."

"Why just once?"

Manuel shrugged. At last he said, "Your mother preferred to go *sola.*"

"Yes?" Her voice sounded plaintive in her own ears. Could

she create memories from scratch now that her mother and father were gone, by reinhabiting their life? Her beleaguered project embodied that hope, that longing.

"I'm sorry," Manuel said, "we should speak of happier things."

"I have questions. My mother—what did you and she talk about ... on your excursions?"

Manuel waited a long while before answering and Zoe couldn't read the expression in his impassive eyes. "*Por supuesto,* the beauty of the lagoons, the birds we saw, the reptiles and flowers. Cassandra drank it all in ... with the pleasure, delight should I say, of a child."

"So, you're saying she was attached to Puerto."

"Yes, she had close attachments *here.*"

Had they been *lovers*? It was hard enough communicating in English with other Anglophones, but the capacity for confusion and misunderstanding when one person was not speaking his native tongue was vast. Zoe changed tacks.

"Did my mother mention her sister?"

"Now and then." Manuel's full lips parted, as if he were about to speak, then stopped himself.

"What?" Zoe asked.

"She did mention *una hermana* she loved very much, but lost—"

"*Lost?*" Or dead? If Yael was lost, she could still be found, unless she didn't want to be found. "How?"

"Cassandra told me that they were once like twins, *comprendes*? It was such a sadness to Cassandra when her sister left. Because they became strangers."

"But why? Do you know if the sister is still alive?"

Manuel shook his head slowly. "I am sorry, Zoe, that I do not know more. We must return now. I am scheduled to take a family out on the boat this afternoon."

"Can we talk more tomorrow?"

"I am full tomorrow and through the weekend, but your

mother had a close friend, here. Luz Milagros. Did she speak to you about Luz?"

"She mentioned the name." This was a bold lie, Zoe winced inwardly.

"Luz owns two businesses in Zícatela. Cafecito, a place for coffee and sweets popular with *los grin*—the tourists and surfers—and a restaurant, easy to remember because it is named after her family, *Los Milagros,* and this place sits right on the shore at Zícatela. A ring-side seat, if you will, to watch the surfers."

Ughh. What a nightmare. A memory struggled to surface but vanished like silverfish. "My mother did mention Cafecito and the other restaurant. Something about a squid speciality?"

"*Sí, sí.* Luz will be happy to see you, Zoe. Please tell her that I suggested it."

"*Bueno.*" As Zoe rose from the rock, the old man returned and handed her a collection of shells, a bit of seaglass, and a piece of driftwood shaped like a dolphin.

"*Muchas gracias Señor.*" She would give these treasures to Cal. Suddenly, she missed him, fretting like the old days ... but he was okay, fine. Later, she'd call, or better yet, text. Cal preferred texts. In her pocket, she found a handful of pesos and gave them to the old man.

Back on the boat, Manuel was quiet and Zoe stored up her questions. They passed an older couple, their skin black as bark, who had caught three fish. Manuel bargained, then paid for their catch.

"*Por mi familia,*" he said proudly, "my wife, she will make a beautiful dinner tonight."

When they arrived at the hotel, Zoe touched Manuel's shoulder lightly in thanks, hoping that this chain of people who had known her mother might lead her back to Cassandra, now just a ghost.

7. CAL

Cal reached the familiar seawall and felt with his feet for the ladder. How in hell was he going to get this girl up onto dry land? She stared at him, her hands clenching his wrists tight as handcuffs. He scarcely thought it possible for anyone to hold him as firmly as she did now.

The silence of the night and the now tranquil sea surrounded them. He'd have to get help. He would need to take her to the hospital.

Cal grasped the ladder with his one free hand and managed to slide the girl in front of him, between his legs, murmuring to her all the time, scarcely knowing what he said. He coached her up the ladder, lifting her hand to the highest rung she could reach, curling her fingers around it, then squeezing them tightly beneath his own hand, as if she were a small child. Once he had both of her hands gripping a rung of the ladder, he planted her trembling feet one by one on the bottom step, nudging them with his own feet; weak, she let go and fell back against him. Cal tried again, getting her hands around the next rung, supporting the girl between his own legs and arms. Slow, steady, one rung at a time, they ascended, resting between each step.

Cal wasn't sure how long it took them to get up the ladder, perhaps twenty minutes or more, but at last they reached the top of the seawall. Cal laid the girl out on a flat rock, watching her thin chest rise and fall. He unfastened her life vest.

They both rested, breathing hard. Then Cal lifted the girl into his arms, one arm supporting her back, the other beneath her knees, carrying her off the rocks onto the narrow Valletta street. Though she was very thin her sodden body was surprisingly heavy. He would never make it, had no phone to call for help. "I've got to get you to the hospital," he said.

The girl flailed wildly, babbling in her mother tongue. Arabic? He wasn't sure. She tried to break free, but Cal grabbed her tightly around the waist.

She struggled, punched and kicked.

He braced himself against the blows. "Hey, you need to warm up. We'll go to our place."

She mumbled something he could not understand,

Cal squatted down, guiding the girl onto his back, putting her arms around his neck, his hands linked beneath her knees. Her arms which had seemed limp a moment before as they draped over his shoulders now gripped him hard around his neck.

He moved her hands to his chest. "Got to breathe."

Cal jostled her higher, and she clung onto him with her arms and hands and knees. Slow and steady, he made his way up the steep hill to his flat, having no idea what to do next.

Cal lay the girl down on the couch. Her whole body shook, as she mumbled to herself. He should call an ambulance. He was afraid to, afraid not to. He'd been hearing about the detention centres for migrants—no better than prisons—and didn't want to deliver this girl straight into one.

Cal's heart pinged like a pinball in a machine, must focus on what he knew: EMT, good old Boy Scouts, though he'd quit at age ten. He brought down a thick terrycloth robe of Zoe's and laid it across the foot of the couch. "You need to take off your wet things." He pantomimed his words, uncertain if she spoke English or was even well enough to understand language. "Put on this robe," he gestured, "I'll make you some hot tea."

Her eyes looked dull; she was barely moving.

Cal slowly reached toward her, she swatted him away.

Her show of strength reassured him. "I'll be back."

Cal put the kettle on to boil, set out milk and honey, then went to look for a blanket. Grateful to find a woollen one stashed in a closet, he scrunched it up into his arms and brought it downstairs, laying it over the iron banister, as the kettle whistled.

Cal brewed tea very strong, adding plenty of hot milk and honey. He brought the mug to the girl and laid it down on the coffee table, relieved to find her wrapped inside Zoe's robe. He tried to comfort her murmuring, "It's going to be okay."

She was shivering hard, her teeth chattering and he returned with the blanket, swaddling her inside of it. She was so slender, she was nearly lost in its folds. As Cal wrapped her up, he could hear her heart beating slow and heavy inside the thin cage of her chest, her breath against his cheek. Cal wrapped a comforter around the blanket in a double-layer. He found a knit cap that he'd worn over on the plane, a relic of New York and New Jersey winters, and gently pulled it down over the girl's head, covering her ears—keep her head warm, that would help.

Her large, dark eyes stared out at him, the pupils melting into the irises; her lips parted, and for a moment, they just looked at each other.

Cal took the mug of tea from the table and helped the girl to sit up, supporting her narrow back, and then doled out spoonfuls of sweet milky tea. Her head moved to his hand, her lips parting, as she greedily sipped.

Tonio sprang over, rubbing back and forth against Cal's legs, then nipping his ankle.

The girl finished the last spoonful, slurping loudly, and Cal brewed another mug for her. When she had drunk that down, he heated up a can of chicken noodle soup and fed her tablespoonfuls of salty broth with little chunks of chicken and tangles of noodles. She startled him by reaching into the bowl with her slender brown hand and scooping clumps of noodles in a tight fist, then directly into her mouth. Cal took a deep breath: she was going to make it.

When Cal smiled at her, the girl whispered, "Thank you," her voice hoarse, cracking with effort. She repeated the phrase in what he now recognized as Arabic.

Her English startled and reassured him; he knew only a phrase or two of Arabic, suitable for tourists, from a friend at college who was from Dubai.

The effort of the meal both satisfied and exhausted her and she lowered her head onto the pillow, closing her eyes. Soon Cal heard the gentle saw of her breath, as she curled knees to chest, arms encircling her head, as if to shield it from a blow.

Cal watched over the girl in a vigil, anxious that she might take a turn for the worse, or awaken into panic, remembering his own terrible time, the see-through dreads, the muteness. Each year, with more distance and time, he felt a bit more solid, but understood how anyone could break. Cal fixed himself a pot of coffee and sat close to the couch, Tonio in his lap. After several hours, he hovered somewhere between sleeping and waking. Soon he spotted the pink-tinged dawn and the deafening church gong vibrated through his raw nerves and burning muscles.

The church bells startled the girl and she jumped awake, crouching like prey. Cal moved toward her, but stood still when he saw the panic in her eyes.

She screamed.

"Shush, shush," Cal murmured, anxious that someone might hear her; but no way, the deafening gongs shielded their privacy.

When the clamour stopped, Cal approached the girl and told her what had happened, how he'd found her in the sea. "It's okay," he reassured her, "you're safe now."

She seemed to calm down a bit, pushing her back up against the head of the couch, glancing around the apartment, bewildered. Tonio came over and nestled against her leg.

"You're in Valletta, on the island of Malta," Cal replied.

"Malta, yes?" She bent down and stroked Tonio who curled on top of her feet.

"That's it. I found you lost at sea," he repeated, as calmly and quietly as he could. "Out there alone in the water."

The girl nodded slowly and Cal noticed that her eyes were wet. Moving slowly, he handed her a box of tissues; she swabbed roughly at her eyes and cheeks.

Cal wondered about the others—she must have been part of a group—but was afraid to ask.

They were quiet for a while. When she looked up at him, he said, "I'm Cal. What's your name?"

"Aziza," she mumbled softly.

"Where are you from?" he asked, bolder now. "Where did you start out?"

Aziza took a deep breath and exhaled slowly. "Tripoli," she said, and the sound of the word, perhaps her home, brought forth a rush of tears. Cal didn't know how to help; he stood by the couch, awkward, then sat on its edge and put a gentle arm around her shoulder. She stiffened, then relaxed into him. Cal sensed that her response was impersonal, almost a reflex; he might have been a wall welcome in its strength and immobility. Cal let her weep, just sat and waited for her to cry herself out. There was so much more he wanted to know, but it would have to wait. When Aziza quieted, he pulled the covers up to her neck.

"Rest a bit. I'll make some breakfast."

"Could I have a wash?" Her voice was a whisper.

"For sure. My sister is away, but she'll have some pyjamas or something."

Aziza smiled faintly at Cal, as he set off to plunder Zoe's closet. He found a pair of old sweats and two t-shirts and laid them at the foot of the couch.

Her eyes focused on a green T-shirt which she snatched and balled up, throwing it onto the floor with a violence that took him by surprise. Tonio thought it was a game and pounced on the shirt, pushing it this way and that, chewing it.

"What's wrong? Don't like green?"

She shook her head hard. "It is the colour of the Devil's book."

He had no idea what she meant, but knew not to press her just now. Cal led Aziza to the shower, then went into the kitchen and set out food and water for Tonio. He cleaned out his litterbox, then set to work making breakfast. Soon the small kitchen was fragrant with sizzling butter, frying eggs, and the nutty scent of fresh coffee. As Cal cooked, listening to the sound of water rushing in the shower, he thought about how sheltered he'd been, despite the early loss of his parents, how static his life was, how little of the world he'd had a chance to explore. Well, the wider world was literally washing up on his shore. Glancing out the window, Cal watched people going about their morning business: shopping, sweeping the streets, doing errands. He'd have to get out of work today.

It was early yet, but Cal didn't want to reach an actual person at the theatre. He dialled Serena's number, grateful to get her voicemail—*stomach flu, double-ender, no visits!* TMI, but he couldn't have her dropping by. No doubt, she'd be extra busy at the theatre, and later on, with Papa. Cal was not an experienced liar, but he gave it his best shot.

The table was laid, the breakfast set out, the aroma even better now that the toast had popped, as Aziza appeared in Zoe's sweats, which were baggy and too short on her willowy frame. She seemed to glide across the floor, as if she were moving through water.

Aziza was tall, at least five foot nine or ten, Cal guessed, with reed-like arms and legs that reminded Cal of an undersea plant. She had a narrow oval face with the mournful beauty of a Modigliani, her black eyes widely spaced, her mouth small with full lips now chapped and scabbed from her journey.

Cal could see from her dazed look that she was still in shock, but shit, she'd made it through the night: breathing, walking, talking, eating. He'd figure out what to do next ... later. Cal had never taken care of anyone before; he'd been the son, the brother, the baby.

Aziza folded herself into a chair and Cal served her breakfast, watching her eat, taking pleasure in each bite she swallowed. She took birdlike bites of egg and toast, which only seemed to remind her of how starving she was, and soon she shovelled the food into her mouth without pride or embarrassment. Her long black hair, curling with wet, dampened the front and back of the sweatshirt and Cal went to find her a dry towel, which she quickly wrapped around her head in a turban.

Cal guessed that she was about sixteen or seventeen, and with her dark eyes and hair, her smooth café-au-lait skin, she might blend in here, until she opened her mouth.

Aziza was quiet now and Cal thought about turning on the TV or radio—maybe there would be news about her boat, the other passengers—but she was calm and news was rarely good. Cal poured Aziza more coffee and she helped herself to cream, plunking in four lumps of sugar.

"Quite the sweet tooth," Cal said, and she scrunched her dark brows together. "You like sugar."

"Yes, I like sweet. Most people like sweet."

Cal added four lumps of sugar to his coffee, as Aziza watched him with a faint smile.

"We are both sweet tooth. You and me."

They sat in silence for a while, the moment of communion vanishing like vapour, as Aziza's sadness settled back in, a dark weight.

"Do you feel like talking?" Cal knew he was being clumsy, but threw his offer out there anyway.

Aziza pushed her plate away. She sighed, but it caught in her throat, turning to a raw cough.

"Do you want me to get a doctor?"

"No!" She jumped up from the table so fast her coffee cup

sloshed, then crashed to the floor. Aziza shook her head wildly, then wrapped her arms around herself.

Cal turned on the radio and quickly set it to an R&B station he liked. He took Aziza by the arm. "Careful! You're barefoot! Sit in the living room while I get this cleaned up."

She backed away from him, her eyes suspicious, as he set to work. He put up more coffee, joining Aziza in the living room where Tonio perched on the arm of the couch.

"How you doing?" he asked softly.

She put out her hand and petted Toni.

"He likes you," Cal said.

She smiled.

"That's Tonio. *He* adopted *me*. Did you have a cat back in Tripoli?" realizing too late that this was not the best question right now.

She stared into space. "I come to join my cousin, Tella. She land here nineteen months ago. Her boat have over forty people, all from Libya. Last we had heard Tella was doing good, but the others we don't know."

Maybe that would help Aziza's status in Malta. Truthfully, Cal had no idea, he didn't know how these things worked, but he could find out.

"We lost touch with Tella. Last we hear she is living an honest life, an open one." Aziza smiled, revealing an over-bite that made her lips appear even fuller.

"Coffee's ready."

"Don't be using all your good coffee on me," Aziza said. Was it a teasing tone? That reassured him for the moment.

Cal smiled at her, as he handed her a mug. Aziza took it, looping her fingers through the handle.

"Do you know where Tella is?"

Aziza shook her head. "We lose touch, so don't know what is happened. Tella, she a trained nurse." There was a sad, faraway look in her eyes. "Can you help me find my cousin?"

Cal let out an old man's sigh. "This island's small but crowded with people." That was the crisis, no room for the flood of migrants. "We can try, for sure."

"Who is this we?"

"I have an older sister, Zoe. You're wearing her clothes."

Aziza coloured under her light brown skin, her shoulders tensing within the baggy sweats.

"She's away now, but when she gets back—"

Aziza grew agitated, her knee pumping. "And when is she to come back?"

Cal was embarrassed now and shrugged.

"I wonder if I make the wrong decision," Aziza said. "I think I should go to Canada when I have the chance."

"Canada?"

"Montreal. Do you know this city?"

"We have some cousins who live there, supposedly, but I've never met them. What's your connection to Montreal?"

"I have a job in Tripoli as a mother's helper for a family, the Fortier's, who are from Montreal. The father, Roger Fortier, he is a doctor and also working to prevent landmines. They treat me like their daughter, even if they not my blood. Roger teach me to swim along with his three children. The family are speaking French, English, and Arabic. I learn from them many things."

"I can't believe you made it to shore. That's a feat."

"I feel the water, it drag the flesh from my bones. But I hang on, hang on."

"How many were on your boat?"

"It was too many," she said. "My Uncle Nuru's fishing boat, it better than some. I know of nineteen others on a dinghy made of rubber, no better than a child's play-toy. It go pop! Like a balloon. I hear it from my boat.

"Our boat take in water. Everyone panic, the women they screaming and dragging each other under. My Uncle Nuru hold his girls high, reaching for me too. I try to help Dede, but the sea be too strong, the current pull us apart. I don't know what is happened to them all." Aziza started to tremble again, her whole body shaking.

"I'm sorry," Cal said.

Aziza's shivering grew worse and Cal wrapped his arms around her, but felt her pull away, so he bolted up in search of another blanket. In Zoe's room he found the one that buttoned up like a warm coat, a souvenir their parents brought back from Tlingit. Cal wrapped the blanket around Aziza, showed her how to fasten it closed, and in a while, her shivering slowed, then stopped.

"I don't know what is happened to Baba—"

Cal touched Aziza's arm lightly. "Maybe it's better not to—"

"All over my country is big letters, by the road, in the square, at the souk."

"Billboards?"

"ALL LIBYANS ARE QADDAFI. I fear he put Baba behind the sun." Aziza held her head in her hands, covering her face, and wept in harsh choking rasps.

Cal put his hand lightly against her hunched back. When she looked up, he handed her water and she drank it down in shuddering gulps.

"Rest now," Cal said softly, as he cleared up their breakfast.

When he returned to check on her, she was rocking back and forth, warm inside the blanket cocoon.

Always, he'd been drifting, dreaming, standing in place. Now he had this newfound stranger to look after. He'd help her find her cousin, or reconnect with that family in Montreal. So much to work out. Cal felt as if he had stepped back into the water, feeling it rush past, his hands aching with the cold, fishing in the current for gleams.

8. ZOE

ZÍCATELA, MEXICO

NOTES: *Jewish community all slaves, seventeenth and eighteenth centuries, captured by Order of St. John. Made up merchant class, vulnerable to capture. Nearly impossible to escape from this island. Dig up first-person accounts?*

Zoe heard the surf before she saw it, the roar and hiss, hot as steam through a kettle. Playa Zícatela, a strip of grey, gritty sand, possessed little poetry. Cacti bristled, debris and driftwood—shaped like refuse—littered the shore. Limp kelp and seaweed tangled in foamy pools, like the hair of the drowned.

A damp wind swept off the ocean and Zoe zipped her sweatshirt to her chin, pulling the hood over her head. Waves were supposed to be soothing, but their endless rumbling, the sea's sucking force terrified her and made her ashamed; she'd spent a lifetime disguising fear as distaste.

You didn't have to be Freud to figure it out. When Zoe was a toddler, her father hurled her over his shoulder into the fireman's carry, methodically walked out into deep water at Lake Isle, and chucked her in. Water burned the inside of her nose, choked her throat and lungs, stung her eyes. He plucked her out and held her to his chest, chuckling. Zoe never quite forgave him for that scare, but her lifelong fear was perverse revenge. Her parents' drowning deaths only made her terror burrow in more deeply.

Zoe was cold and hungry when she found Los Milagros, settling at a ringside table, so she could torment herself watching monster waves. There were no bathers, but the surfers were out.

She ordered a half bottle of wine and the fish special, girding herself up to locate Luz. The *veracruzaña* was just how her parents had described it, tomatoey and spicy, the fish both tender and dense. Shameless, Zoe used the last bread roll to swab her plate of sauce, which pleased her waiter, as did her Spanish.

As she sipped coffee, Zoe stared out to sea. The Pacific glittered and fumed. A woman surfer balanced inside the enormous crescent of a wave that looked about twenty-five feet high, arms extended for balance, fingers tickling the inside of the barrel, as a huge letter C folded over her head, rushing her along on the wildest ride of her life. Zoe shivered involuntarily as the surfer glided into shore. Water was deceiving with its hidden power that could gnaw away rock.

After paying for her meal, she asked the waiter about Luz and he directed her toward the kitchen. Zoe stood in the doorway as a young dishwasher ran what appeared to be used drinking straws under the tap, cleaning them with bare hands. A woman hovering near the oven spotted Zoe, then scolded the boy, tossing the used straws into the garbage. She was a little spitfire with auburn hair that took on a purplish cast in the kitchen light. The boy, sheepish and defensive, answered that they always cleaned the used straws this way. The woman quickly stepped out of the kitchen, shut the door tight, motioning Zoe into the hallway.

Zoe explained who she was and absorbed the shock of recognition in the woman's eyes.

"If you can wait ten minutes, we can speak alone," Luz said.

After an hour and three more coffees, Luz led Zoe out of the restaurant to a beach house not far from shore, where they could hear the steady crash of the waves.

"Can I offer you anything?" Luz asked. "A coffee?"

"I'm on caffeine overload."

"*Que?*"

"Do you have tea, something mild?"

"Sí, sí." Luz filled the kettle.

Zoe sat on the couch as Luz brewed tea in a little porcelain pot. As she poured out a cup for Zoe and then herself, the scent of steaming mint leaves filled the room.

"I think of your mother every day," Luz said. Her voice was light with a precise, staccato rhythm, as if she were taking a bite out of each syllable. "I am so sorry."

"Thank you," Zoe said, her reply equally clipped. She was numb from hearing the same sympathies nearly in the same words albeit from different people.

"When your mother and father visited, this area was a secret hideaway known mostly by surfers." Luz stirred sugar into her tea, her hands small and brown, with long nails polished candy apple red. She had quick, deft movements, her hands like little birds alighting here, then there, while her body remained still. Zoe's mother had always observed everything and everyone so closely and Zoe had absorbed the habit, a quick entry into people.

"Your parents came, oh, I have lost count, more than a half-dozen times. Each year, I got to know your mother better. They rented one of my cottages very close to the sea. It has a screened-in porch where your mother liked to retreat during the heat of the day."

"Can I have a look?"

"It is rented now," Luz replied, her face closed.

"Oh, okay."

Luz seemed to sense her frustration. "Perhaps later, I can show you the cottage, the tenants may not mind." She touched Zoe's shoulder lightly with her fingertips. "I will ask them for you."

"Thank you."

"Your mother talked always to me. I learned her life in one

piece and then another, but she was, how can I say this in *inglés*, a fragile soul, but if she was upset, offended...." Her laugh ran up and down, a musical scale; she had small, pearl-white teeth that stood out brightly against her caramel skin.

"She didn't talk to us about you."

Luz shrugged, dismissive. "I see you understand," she said mysteriously, her full lips smug. "When she was upset, your mother would simply disappear. Very distressing to those of us who love her. She possessed many sides, like a jewel."

The present tense of *love* was a jolt. Zoe thought of her grandpa Menash, her own conviction that the dead are real, that they speak to the living. It was her truth, why not others?

"How did you meet my mother?"

Luz sat quietly, sipping her tea, as if gauging whether she could be open or not. "Well, I heard strange sounds coming from the cottage, your mother was laughing wildly. I admit I listened, concerned about whether to call *la policía*."

"But she was laughing."

"A laugh like a scream."

Luz retreated into private memories. "Your father was a difficult man." She said this as if to herself.

Zoe's limbs tensed, anger so sudden it took her by surprise.

"He spoke in a low deep voice when he was tormenting Cassandra. That is how he gained control. He kept calm; his calm in those moments was evil."

Zoe stood up, tea sloshing over the side of her cup. She knew her dad wasn't perfect, but she wasn't ready to hear this weird stranger catalogue his failings. "My father's dead. Have some respect."

Luz let out that horrible musical laugh again.

"I guess I'll go."

She caught Zoe's arm, her fingers curled with their varnished talons—sharp claws and teeth, like a preying feline. "Within a family, there is..." She paused for effect, casually sipping tea. "Loyalty. Please sit down."

Zoe slowly lowered herself back onto the couch, but sat on its edge, poised for flight.

"Your father liked to hear your mother tell him about her childhood, everything. He wanted to possess her, even her memories, to re-live her experiences, the good, bad, and the ugly, as you say."

"I say?"

"An expression." She divided the second word into three staccato syllables.

"The first day that I met Cassandra, your father was doing his special *game.*"

"Please don't malign my father."

"*Malign,* what is this word?"

"Trash talk him, after his death."

"I am sorry, but I am only speaking the truth. I will try to round its edges. Your father did give Cassandra a hard time."

"I think you've got it wrong."

Luz stood abruptly, her body martial in its movements. "I have said too much."

She rose and refilled their cups with tea, then went on. "*El núcleo* that most of us are fortunate enough to possess, like the pit of a fruit, your mother she had instead a space. *Que pena.* And being a Jew in Malta ... for her it was so very *complicada.*"

"What did she say exactly?" Zoe had discovered that her mother couldn't fully embrace the faith and devotion that had guided Zoe's grandpa, but before her sister left, she'd enjoyed the sense of community. God was the problem. She struggled to believe. But so did many people.

"Some days, when we spent a long while talking, she asked me to call her Chaya."

"Her Hebrew name."

"She used this name with people with whom she felt ...safe. Her father whom she loved so very much, your *abuelo* Menash, he called her Chaya."

Zoe had rarely heard her mother use her Hebrew name,

which was beautiful both in its sound and meaning: life. Yet, she'd heard her grandpa call her mother Chaya in the tapes she'd unearthed in her secret place above the garage. Notes and tapes and photographs for the project father and daughter began together after Yael's flight, perhaps as a way to heal.

"And when you don't have that pit of strength," Luz went on, "well, *pues,* I don't know if you can create it *de nada.* She loved you, but being a mother did not—"

"My father loved us as well." A burn of acid in Zoe's gut. Did she want the truth? Or to protect her parents' memories? She couldn't have both.

"Everything, it was about him, no?" A deep groove of parallel lines appeared between Luz's brows. "Everyone should not be parents."

"He was my father."

"*Perdón, Díos Mío.*" Luz took a sip of mint tea.

"Why do you need to beat up my dad's memory?"

"Cassandra was my friend. I knew your father through her eyes and I could say, my ears. They fought. Perhaps I am telling you something you know, as their daughter?" Her brows peaked in challenge.

At home her parents lived side-by-side, cool and separate lives, though Zoe remembered fights between them when she was small. There was also more passion then, perhaps.

"I could hear them. And the sounds frightened me." Luz's fingertips fluttered through her short auburn hair, then alighted on her cheeks, as if giving herself a caress. "So I would pass by, stop in at their cottage. Your father did not like my appearance there."

She expelled a short bark; clearly she had a whole repertoire of laughs. "Some days, he hated me," Luz went on in her soft, flutelike voice, pronouncing each syllable, as if it were a note of music. "At others, I even dare to admit, Lior was afraid of me." When Luz spoke of her father, she was tensile, ready to spring, cords of muscle visible in her neck.

"Why would he be afraid of *you?*"

Luz's eyes flashed at her. "Because I was there. Watching. On to him, as you Anglos say."

"We are not a collective."

"Lior did not like our friendship, which stood between them, but she could not have survived—*Por Díos*—without me."

"Well, she didn't."

Luz sat erect, her chin raised, looking past Zoe. "Neither did he."

Shit, Zoe hated this woman.

Luz leaned toward Zoe. "Your mother did not exist for Lior, except as a decoration, an … ornament, such as you would hang on the tree at *Navidad.*"

"We don't celebrate Christmas. We're Jews."

"*Lo siento.* It is just an expression. And some Jewish people, do enjoy to honour all holidays, including Christmas."

"Whatever."

Zoe was hot, the damp humidity gathering under her arms, between her breasts. Her face was slick and she reached for the bandanna that she kept handy to swab the Puerto sweat from her face and neck. She missed Malta's salt wind and dry stone heat.

"Let's go out there," Luz suggested, motioning Zoe to a screened-in porch, where the sound of the waves pounding and sucking at the shore was much louder, as a damp wind blew. "It will be cooler."

Zoe sat on a wicker loveseat, trying not to allow one part of her hot, sticky body to touch another, as Luz folded her small limbs into a rattan rocker, cradling her tea between both hands.

"Often your mother would come and visit me when your father took his siesta," she said. "Or when he had a surfing lesson. We would sit in this room and talk for hours, drinking tea, as you and I are right now. She would tell me everything. Because she wanted to, not because I told her to." Here, Luz stretched her shapely arms wide. She was quite beautiful, her body with its fine-boned grace, that flickering light in her eyes with their amber filaments, her pouty lower lip.

"Nothing was too private, we had the connection that only two women can have." Her gaze was far away, out to sea.

Zoe felt the hot, wet wind pick up, lashing into gales. The sky lowered, steel-grey clouds massed, banking up around the house. Then all was silent, but for the waves, the air an eerie iridescent purple. Luz didn't seem to notice.

"It's odd," Zoe started, as she felt the first drops through the screen. Then the rain crashed down and it was too noisy to speak, even think; Zoe peered out into wavy walls of rain. Lightning flashed, there were cracks of thunder, then the pock and clatter of hail hitting the roof of the house.

Zoe stood suddenly, Luz rousing slowly from her reverie, letting rain beat against the porch, wet swaths gusting through the screen. "It does not rain much here in Zícatela, but when it does...."

"Don't you think we—"

"The day of their deaths there was a terrible storm, much like this. Before the storm hit, your parents took a break to surf. There was no warning of that storm, no forecast. I think they were having a difficult time that day, more than usual, and your father believed a break would refresh them both."

Luz motioned, palm down, "*Venga*," and Zoe followed her into the kitchen.

"Wait here," she commanded, disappearing into the recesses of the house.

Zoe soon heard stairs creaking above her head. She waited; ten minutes expanded into fifteen, perhaps twenty. Then the rain stopped all at once, like turning off a faucet. Zoe heard the sea, its waves unrelenting, and a fresh breeze blew, cooled by the storm.

Zoe ventured out of the kitchen and wandered about the house. Behind its modest façade, the place expanded into reasonable family-sized proportions, as if it had been hollowed out. Several rooms branched off from a central living space with elegant couches, a bench and bar stools. A staircase to the floor above bisected the living room.

Zoe crept upstairs, the wooden steps squeaking underfoot. At the landing, she found a long hallway adorned with black-and-white photographs. Zoe was startled to see that many depicted her mother, some where she wielded a camera and was photographing an object or person just out of view, while an unseen person photographed her.

Her mother looked happy. The beauty was in her absorption: doing her photography. Her hair was wild, her eyes focused deeply on what she was shooting. One could only wonder what her subject was and this gave the pictures a haunting mystery.

Zoe looked at picture after picture. The concept might have seemed contrived if someone had described it to her, but the photographs were alive, kinetic. She wondered who had taken them ... Luz?

Zoe wandered into a little room off the hallway with a divan stacked with silk and linen pillows and a sea view. In a corner was a shrine, a small fountain with pebbles below a tiny platform, enclosed within a glass shadowbox. There was a lock of coppery hair tied with black hair and a photograph of Cassandra and Luz, Cassandra sitting in Luz's lap, her arm around Luz's shoulder, Luz's arm snug around Cassandra's waist, their cheeks touching. It felt transgressive for Zoe to imagine the camera, the person behind the lens. Who was it that was looking? Maybe Cassandra had set her camera on a timer and taken the pictures herself. In the shadowbox was a gold locket Zoe's mother had always worn with a Hebrew blessing inside, engraved by her father. There it was, under glass.

Zoe closed her eyes, as if the brief blackness could dissolve erotic speculations and images about her mother and Luz.

"What are you doing?"

Zoe jumped. This woman was like an evil cat, slinking up without warning, ready to spring, baring sharp teeth and claws.

There was a gleam of disdain in Luz's eyes, her lower lip curled in contempt. She came so close that Zoe could feel the heat of her breath. Luz shut the door to the small room, then turned a lock, and all at once Zoe was terrified of her.

"Zoe, you should not wander about someone's house un-invited."

"I'm sorry. I didn't know what happened to you. I waited and waited." Her words came out in a rush.

"You should have waited longer. You Americans are so impatient."

Zoe imagined Luz could hear her heart slamming inside her chest. Up close, she had a spicy scent to her skin, musk and sweat.

Zoe looked into her face; Luz's lips were slightly parted, as if she were ready to speak. Then she unlocked the door, moved aside, and the spell broke.

Zoe bolted past her and jogged down the stairs. The woman was a witch, she had to get out of here! She ran out of the beach house, gulping air.

"Zoe!" Luz called out. "Please wait!"

The waves still pounded, Zoe saw that the surfers were going back out to sea, the sky luminous after the storm. Luz stood on the front porch. "Come in for a moment, I want to show you something. This is what took me so long."

Zoe turned toward her, cautious. "I'll wait out here."

"You have to learn to trust," Luz murmured, her eyes and voice coaxing. "If you want to find your mother."

"Find her?"

Zoe inched up to the entry of the haunted house.

Luz placed a kind of aluminium suitcase on the front steps, her head bowed. "I have your mother's mementoes. We knew each other a long time, over many years. You see, she left some of her things at my cottage between trips. I saved what I could."

Luz raised her head, her voice shook as she spoke. "I promised your mother ... that if anything ever happened to her, I would—"

"What?"

"I could not bring myself to destroy this part of her."

"Have you gone through what's in here?"

Luz shook her head. "Not everything. I am not ready yet."

Zoe felt a wave of relief that she would possess something of her mother, all to herself. For once. She reached up and grasped the aluminium case from the steps. "Rightfully, this is mine," she said with finality. Zoe lifted the absurd looking case and walked away from the house, thanking Luz with a quick wave, before heading along the beach towards Puerto.

PART II: SISTERS

9. ZOE

I am alone by myself. Like usual. It's so hot I can't breathe. Is it like this in Malta? I'm out in the yard, yanking off dandelion heads. Dad's posted a sign in front of the garage.

KEEP OUT!

I kick that sign high into the hedge, hold my breath, racing up the crumbling brick steps that lead to the room above the garage. The door is jammed tight. I press it with my shoulder, then sit on the railing, hammering with my heels. I bash that old door again and again. At last, it opens with a screech.

I am inside here with you.

My secret place is big, windows on three sides and crammed with old junk—clothes no one wears, books no one reads, paintings no one looks at—unwanted things, all forgotten.

It's musty and hot in here, so I force a window open and wedge a book thick as a brick into the sill. At last a breeze blows through.

Nannu, I declare this place my private tree house, ours, where I can talk to you whenever I want. We'll be inside and outside at the same time.

In a corner is a crate labelled, *Abba,* in Mom's handwriting. Inside are notebooks, dozens of photographs of Malta from summer of '69.

I open a book, *Our Family History,* with pages of your notes and begin to read.

Our ancestors were from Paredes. We took our name from

the little village where we lived in Portugal, not far from Porto, on the right branch of the River Douro.

A world of terror. Daily massacres by mobs of fanatical Christians, threatened with murder and extinction. Our faith rooted in our hearts. We formed a secret society.

Inside Jews: Marranos, conversos. Saved from death by converting to Catholicism. That was our public self. In private, we continued to practice Judaism. We had inside selves and outside selves, inside names and outside names, split right down the middle.

At twelve or thirteen, kids were told the dangers of being openly Jewish and parents explained the different names used by their family. We can only imagine what it must have been like. Judaism was a crime.

It was not always so. During the early Middle Ages when Jews lived in Portugal in a relatively free society, they used first names from the Old Testament: Abraham, Moses, Isaac. Later, those Hebrew names and the Hebrew language were forbidden, but we secretly transmitted them among our families. Our inside names.

Though our family survived as Marranos in Portugal, our ancestors Moishe and Sarah emigrated to Malta in 1823, to practice our faith openly. A gift.

Nannu, listen. Outside I'm perfect little mommy to Cal, but inside, I wish it was just me, Mom and Dad and me, like it used to be.

Outside I pretend our family is normal. Inside I hear Mom and Dad fighting, their voices sharpened like instruments.

Outside, I act like Mom and Dad are around. Inside, I know they are gone, away. I am alone by myself.

Outside, I pretend I'm good. Inside, I know I'm rotten as bad fruit.

I open another one of the crates, Nannu. It's filled with your books and other precious things. I find a mezuzah, shaped like a key. *Shin-Daled-Yud* is carved into its case: *Shomer Daltot Yisrael, Guardian of the Doors of Israel.*

Grandpa, was this mezuzah on your door in Malta? Can I keep it? Will it keep you close to me?

I find your prayer book. You've written notes all over in any white space you could find.

Prayer opens the heart. Yud hay vav ha. *The One who is was will be.*

For next Shabbat service: discuss holiness in time. How we are linked more deeply to time, than to places or things.

You mean, like you and me.

In another box, I pull out a little cassette player and a dozen tapes. Some are your sermons for Shabbat, each labelled with a date. Others from 1969 must go with your notebooks and Mom's photos for the project you both started about the sacred, secret sites in Malta and the island's hidden Jewish history. She talked about it, now and then. How it went unfinished, abandoned, with your death.

I pop one of the tapes into the recorder and press, *play.* Your voice fills the room, deep and soft with sandy pebbles running through. There is no then and now, no here or there. You are right here in the room with me, speaking in my ear.

Nannu, I listen to sounds, not words. There is grit in your voice and sometimes it breaks, the sound wraps me up inside it like a warm soft quilt. My eyes sting, hot, then wet.

Nannu, you are here with me and I am there with you. I can talk to you and you will speak to me.

You say, listen: *Think of God's name. Four Hebrew letters: Y-H-V-H which sounds like breath, air passing in and out of the lungs. Was, is, will be.*

That is us together as it should be. I'll come back to our place every day, Nannu.

Stay with me. Hear me.

10. CASSANDRA

Cassandra sat on one arm of her father's recliner, Yael draped over the other side, her long skinny legs stretched across Papa's thighs, dirty heels resting in Cassandra's lap. The Passover seder was over, the guests gone, leftovers put away, the washing up completed.

Their mother came in and served each of them a glass of iced tea, folding herself with lithe limbs onto the couch, knees curled to chest.

"I have everything I need right here," Papa said.

Cassandra rested her head on his shoulder, which was strong and warm against her cheek. She adored him so much it hurt, and liked to believe, she was his favourite.

"I feel like a stuffed turkey," Yael said. "Why does every Jewish holiday involve so much food?"

"Not every one, Spidey. You've forgotten Yom Kippur, the fast. Striving to be a better person."

"I'm not such a bad person, Papa! It's always one Jewish holiday after another. There are just *too* many of them." Yael glanced at their father with a mischievous smirk.

Cassandra helped her out. "And we can't even skip school."

"Well, if you girls want to attend Jewish school, I can arrange it. Ship you off to London."

"Really?" Yael sat upright. "I would love to get off this island."

"But Jewish school, Yaya?" Cassandra taunted. "I just can't see you following the rules of the Torah."

"Can't we worship in our own way?"

"Fortunately, you can," Papa said. "Here. Now."

"So do we have to celebrate *every* holiday?" pressed Yael.

Papa nodded, smiling, his dark eyes resting on Yael, then Cassandra. "We *are* rich in holidays, it's a mitzvah. Why wouldn't we want to celebrate? I don't like to compare one festival to another, but in truth, Pesach is my favourite."

"Why, Papa?" asked Cassandra.

"Because of the food, silly," offered Yael.

Their father tickled Yael beneath her knees until she jumped, giggling. When she settled down, he said, "No, not just the food, the story. Think about it. Pharaoh, King of Egypt, fearful of our people's power, decrees all Jewish babies killed. Moses is put in a basket and set afloat on the river by his mother and sister Miriam. None other than Pharaoh's daughter finds him, saves him, raises Moses as her own. So a Hebrew child becomes Prince of Egypt. When he grows up, Moses kills an Egyptian guard when he sees him beating a Hebrew slave. Then Moses flees to the desert and is chosen by God to free the Jews."

"So he grows up a secret Jew," Cassandra said.

"Yes, dearest. Like our own family who were outwardly Catholic, but practised their true faith in secret. Now we can be open with our beliefs. Today, for us, it's community that matters."

"Papa, save your sermons for Shabbat!" pleaded Yael.

He chuckled. "Okay, Spidey." He patted Yael's bony knee, turning to their mother. "Your brisket was too good, Ruthie. And the kugel, I should have skipped my second helping."

"We should take a stroll," Ruth suggested, running pale fingers through her blonde bob. "There will be a lovely breeze, now. We used to go every evening."

Papa only moved to sip his tea. "Six kilos for me by the time we finish our second seder with the Elluls tomorrow night." He patted his paunch.

"Menash," Ruth said. "I would love to go to England with

the family next year. I never seem to get home."

"Home?"

Cassandra saw blotches rise in her mother's fair skin, a sure sign of anger held in too tight. "Perhaps I have two homes," Ruth said. "It would be good for the girls to spend some time in my part of the world. They have family in England."

"We'll discuss it dear."

"That's what you always say."

"We never go anywhere," Yael complained.

"I'm needed here, my darlings."

"And perhaps I am there," Ruth cut in, an edge of bitterness in her voice. She stood abruptly. "I miss rain, I miss green, our garden after a shower. I even miss the mists and grey. And the sea."

"You are surrounded by sea right here, Ruthie."

"Not the North Sea and the Irish Sea and the Celtic Sea."

"We'll talk tonight, Ruthie. Perhaps we can make a family trip this summer."

He stood and kissed their mother on her forehead. "I'm ready for that walk, Ruthie. Girls?"

Cassandra looked at Yael and they shared a signal, a slight flicker of their eyes as they met each other's gaze. They had other plans. Gisi had the night off, so they would have the house to themselves. Now *that* was a mitzvah.

Cassandra pulled Yael into their parents' bedroom, and then into their mother's dressing area, and finally into her walk-in closet. They faced each other and Yael bowed her head, murmuring. "Bless this *sanctum sanctorum.*"

"Let us pray," Cassandra touched the top of Yael's warm head, thick with black tangled hair.

Together, they riffled through their mother's clothing, grabbing whatever suited their fancy, tottering in heels, jangling with bracelets, pocketing spare change, forgotten lipsticks, intriguing ticket stubs from evening purses.

Yael yanked down a mini-dress, holding it in front of her body, Cassandra gazing at the two of them reflected in the mirror. The dress was silk: cream with bold blocks of fuchsia, purple, and mauve. The pop art colours were striking against Yael's nutmeg-coloured skin. "You look amazing."

Yael's laugh was wild.

Cassandra swept her sister's hair off her neck, twisting it into an updo.

Yael frowned at her reflection, hissed, "*It's as if her features were arranged by Picasso.*"

If only Cassandra could erase those cruel words. Once the sisters overheard a friend of their mother's saying this about Yael, the friend's laugh like ice tinkling in a glass. "She had one too many at the benefit lunch for the Manoel. And that bitch actually loves Picasso."

Yael pressed the tip of her nose upward, as Cassandra gently swatted her sister's hand away from her face.

"Ask Ima to borrow it for the dance."

"Are you crazy?" Yael pulled the dress even higher on her brown thighs, tugging at the material that gathered loosely at her waist. Cassandra looked at her sister's eyes, enormous in her oval face. Her brows were thick and dark, meeting over the bridge of her nose like children's drawings of gulls. She had a high, broad forehead and a prominent nose. Growing up, people who did not know the family stared from Yael to Cassandra and back, then from Yael to Ruth and Menash, trying to figure out where this gangly black child came from. Cassandra wanted to shout at them.

Her father told both his girls the story of how Yael came to join their family. Cassandra was nearly sixteen now, and had heard not only her father's version, but her mother's, their nanny Gisi's, Yael's own, and had fashioned her own tale. Cassandra felt as if she were present when it all happened, and in a way, she was.

Her parents, Ruth and Menash Paredes, believed they could

not have children of their own. They had spent years trying, had undergone the usual battery of tests with the best doctors Valletta had to offer, as well as several London experts, but no definitive cause was found.

Several times a year, Menash took trips to Marrakech to buy gems; Ruth rarely accompanied him. On one of these trips, just before Hanukkah in 1952, he came home with a child in white swaddling. The baby's eyes were squinched shut and she was screaming, her face purple and wet with fury. Menash rocked her tenderly up and down as Ruth peeled back the soft blanket to expose the baby's dark brown face. The infant cried even harder. Cassandra could almost hear her parents' exchange.

Where did you find her?

After dinner with Zev, we stopped in at the orphanage. Well, Yashem had plans for me. I fell in love. We are parents at last, Ruthie. What shall we call her? She's a fierce beauty.

I don't know. Whatever you wish.

Yael.

Ruth was unknowingly pregnant with Cassandra, and when Yael was what they guessed to be around nine months, Cassandra was born.

Cassandra looked at Yael in the mirror. "Gisi could shorten the dress, take it in at the waist."

"Ima would never let me wear this."

"You know *she* would never wear it. I have no clue what it's doing in her closet."

Yael shrugged, turned this way and that, admiring her reflection. "Don't ask me."

The sisters loved all the new fashions: the hot pants and miniskirts, the maxis in batik and tie-dye, the vinyl and space-age metallics. They liked boys with long hair, paisley shirts, and high-collared Regency jackets. Pink Floyd was their band and they made fun of the twist.

Yael sat down at their mother's vanity and Cassandra made

up her sister's eyes with smoky shadow and long fake lashes.

"Whoa, look at you! Well, do you want me to ask Ima for you?"

Yael shook her head.

Cassandra persisted. "Max Ellul would love you in that dress, Yaya."

Yael snorted, but a big toothy grin lit up her face. "It's you he's into."

"Max is not for me."

The girls heard Gisi's footsteps in the hall.

"Quick!" hissed Cassandra, tearing the dress up and over Yael's head, her thick black hair tangling in the collar. Once their nanny had passed by, the girls slipped back to their shared bedroom out of breath, nudged shoulders, then hips, wild laughs rising in unison.

Late that night, Cassandra and Yael stepped out onto the balcony that opened from their bedroom, the rest of the family asleep.

"Look up," she said to Yael. The stars glittered in full dark, sparkle and brilliance against velvet. Cassandra needed her sister's presence to experience the world, to share everything.

"If you could click your heels and go anywhere, where would you go?" Yael asked.

"You mean like Dorothy?"

Yael nodded.

"Well, it wouldn't be Kansas."

"I'd like to ride atop an elephant in India," Yael said. "Or travel up to the Arctic and see the midnight sun, feel snow, maybe spot a polar bear. Snow must be incredible. Soft, but cold, melting on your skin."

"An ice-covered ocean, can you imagine?" Cassandra said.

"Or Kenya, lions and tigers and boas, oh no! Better yet, giraffes or a zebra."

"Don't forget elephants. They are very intelligent, have their own language."

"Who says?"

"I read about it in an elephant book."

Yael rubbed her eyes. "My lids hurt. Did you have to pull those suckers off? I'm sure I lost some of my own lashes in the process."

"Like ripping off a Band-Aid."

"Must be a better way."

The girls changed into long cotton nightgowns and got ready for bed. Cassandra pulled back the counterpane and slipped beneath the sheets, Yael sliding beside her. They sighed in pleasure at the touch of cool, clean linen. The night wind blew through the open window, ruffling the curtains, blowing the girls' hair across their cheeks.

"Do you want me to braid your hair?" Cassandra asked Yael.

"I like it loose. Mum always did it too tight. I grew up with a constant headache."

"Do you think we'll ever leave the island?" Cassandra's voice was plaintive.

"*I* will."

"We should go together at the same time."

Yael didn't say anything, so Cassandra rushed in to fill the gap opening between them.

"Tonight, let's dream the same dream. Where shall we go? If we imagine it as we fall asleep, we can be—"

"The Arctic. I'm thinking of snow, you imagine the midnight sun."

Cassandra curled up knees to chest and Yael spooned her rail-thin body around her sister, her knobby knees pressing into Cassandra's calves, long arms in a protective sweep around her. Sleep came all at once, like a swoon, as snow swirled, melting on the sisters' lashes and hair.

11.

The next day, Cassandra came home early from school with a migraine. Without thinking, she opened her mother's bedroom door to tell her she was sick. Ruth straddled a man, her head thrown back, bob swinging over neck and shoulders. Her expression was startling, one of transport.

Cassandra stood in the doorway, mute. She saw thick thighs furred with black hair, calloused feet, dirty heels. The raw smell of sweat and sex nearly choked her. The man raised his head.

Cassandra recognized his face.

Her mother swivelled around, her bare skin translucent. She leapt off her lover's lap like a panther and yanked on her silk robe.

Blood rushed up behind Cassandra's eyes; her head was thudding so hard, she felt it in the soles of her feet. The man tore the sheet from the bed, wrapped it around his body, and strode out of the room. Cassandra could not look, could not look away. She was sure now, it was Zev, her father's "friend." A short time later, mother and daughter heard him leave the house.

"Come in." Cassandra stepped into the bedroom and her mother bolted the door.

"I'm sick, Mum."

Ruth pulled her daughter's head in against her chest, a rare moment of physical intimacy. "Please sit down. I must speak with you, then you can rest, sleep. I'll get ice, a washcloth."

Cassandra pressed her palms against her throbbing head, as her mother took her firmly by the shoulders and sat her down. She took Cassandra's chin into her hand and moved her eyes so they met her own.

"Please look at me."

Cassandra did what her mother told her to do, a somnambulist.

She spoke quickly, a harsh whisper. "You must not tell your father."

Cassandra felt nausea thickening her throat.

"I need your word." Her mother put her long fingers on either side of Cassandra's shoulders and squeezed hard.

Cassandra lurched out of her grip. "You're hurting me."

"You see it would be a double-wound for Abba. He and Zev ... Menash and I go..."

"I'm sick."

"You and Yael have each other, you and Abba are close, Yael and Abba are even closer, working together."

Cassandra flinched. *She* was Papa's girl.

"Gisi adores you. I am always the odd one out."

Cassandra shook her head hard to erase what she'd seen.

"Your papa is a good man, but he's not perfect. He has hurt me, too."

Cassandra stared her mother down. "So, it's tit for tat. So to speak." She laughed hysterically, shrill and furious, squeezing her eyes shut until the room spun like a carousel gone crazy. When she opened them, her mother's slender body was crumpled, belly concave, narrow shoulders hunched, chin drawn into her chest. Cassandra felt a rush of pity for her, a germ of truth in what she'd said.

"How could you do this, Mum?"

Her mother's hands trembled, but Cassandra couldn't bring herself to comfort her, as if her own body and emotions were frozen.

"Please don't tell Papa, Cassandra. It will only cause more hurt. I'm finished with this mess."

"Fine. You have my *word*, my *promise*. For Abba's sake, not yours. You make me sick."

"Please darling, let me get you settled."

"No." It hurt Cassandra to wound her mother, even when she detested what she'd done.

Cassandra left the room, slamming the door, despite her headache. In the medicine cabinet, she found acetaminophen with codeine and took two pills. She drenched a washcloth with cold water and lay down in her darkened room, the pounding going on and on, until blackness enveloped her.

The following morning, something was wrong, as if a toxic poison had infected everyone. Cassandra's mother greeted her with silence and her father looked into his lap when she entered the room. Yael, who always ate a stevedore's breakfast was nowhere around. Later, when Cassandra asked her father about the darkroom he planned to build for her sixteenth birthday, he told her he couldn't spare the time. This was weird, so unlike Abba who'd seemed as eager as Cassandra to turn an old storage room into a darkroom.

That night, when Yael was soaking in a bath, Ruth came into the room and bolted the door. Her eyes were red and swollen; she clutched a wad of used tissues, wringing them into bits.

"Doesn't a promise mean anything to you?"

"What?"

"I gave in to Zev, because I—"

"Mum, *please*, no details."

From the shadow of her cleavage, her mother drew out a note, handing it to Cassandra. The note was written in Cassandra's hand, a tiny block print nearly perfect as type. She wrote her *i*'s and *j*'s without dots and her *g*'s and *j*'s ended in a straight line.

Abba,
It hurts me to see you betrayed by Ima and the man you call your "best friend:" Zev Tabat. I came home

sick from school and walked in on them. Together.
In your bed. I'm so sorry, Abba, but I can't keep this
ugly secret.
Love, Chaya

Cassandra couldn't speak. Then she said, "Mum, I didn't write this."

"You gave me your word!" her mother cried out.

"I keep *my* promises."

"Cassandra, this is your handwriting."

"I didn't write that note."

"Don't lie to me."

"I'm not."

"Who then? Gisi has arthritis, she could not write this. I know I've caused pain, but you've magnified it with your self-righteousness."

"Me?"

"Yael was in school. She knows nothing of—"

"Get out of my room."

Her mother bowed her head, and for a few moments, didn't move. Then she unbolted the door with trembling hands and left the room.

Yael emerged from the bath, her dark brown skin damp and glowing, her hair dripping, until she twisted a towel around her head into a turban.

"What the hell."

Yael looked away, out the window.

"How could you?"

Yael wheeled around and stared straight at Cassandra, her black eyes cold as onyx. "How could *you* make that promise? Don't you love Abba?"

"More than you!"

Yael dropped the towel onto the floor into a crumpled heap, then tore her dressing gown from the closet, wrapping her body in white terrycloth.

She plopped down on one of the twin beds, making it bounce. "I came home early, too, earlier than you in fact." Her voice was light and breezy.

"How come?"

"I wanted that dress. For once, I was going to look, well, not beautiful—that's your department—but striking. I can do striking. I was in the walk-in when I heard her come in ... with Zev. I shut myself in there. I was there the whole time. It was like a porno."

Cassandra rushed at Yael, covering her mouth with her hand until she felt the pressure of Yael's teeth against her palm. It would be easy to squeeze the living breath out of her, to snap that skinny neck. She kept on until she looked into her sister's eyes, which were wide and terrified, the same eyes that gazed into hers every day of their lives and something broke within Cassandra, her hand loosening. Only Yael could bring out this violence in her.

Yael choked, panting like an animal.

"You scare me, changing minute by minute."

Yael's dark eyes flinched uncannily like their father's.

"You have to tell Abba that you wrote that note."

Yael stared at the floor. Cassandra watched her sister collect herself; Yael was good at that.

"You've got to make this right."

"What does it matter? Making this *right*? No one will believe me ... and anyway, who wrote what is not the issue. It's that Mom was fucking about with Dad's best 'friend.'" Yael combed her wet hair, working to untangle knots.

"I'm going to stay with a friend," Cassandra said, "until you tell Abba the truth."

"Have a good stay. I will love having the bloody room to myself."

Cassandra told her mother that she would be staying with her friend Sarah for a night or two. Gisi gathered her into her arms and helped her pack her bag. For the moment, it was comforting to be enfolded in Gisi's plump arms, as she was as a child.

"That *sister* of yours, so-called, is never up to any good and—"

"Stop Gisi, my head is starting up again."

"When you get home, everything will be set to rights. *Trust* me."

That word felt like a curse.

12.

The hot Malta sun drenched Cassandra's room, turning it golden, the beauty of the day lost on her. Yael was gone. Was she hiding, one of her many pranks? Growing up, she'd folded her lithe body into impossible spaces: curled knees to chest inside cupboards, under silks in their mother's hope chest, crouching on the rooftop; once, she crawled inside the chimney and another time, she slid down a man-hole, exploring Valletta underground.

No, this was no prank. Yael had left a note. Cassandra plucked it from the dresser and flopped back onto her bed to read it.

> *April 27, 1969*
> *C—*
> *I need to find out who I am alone. Without you. To get away to truly see me.*
> *Love, Yael*

Cassandra could picture Yael, her black hair wild, scribbling the note standing up. It was written in her large, loopy hand, her real writing. She could see Yael even when Yael was not there.

So, her sister didn't care about finishing secondary school or saying goodbye face-to-face, or bothering to tell them where she was off to, and when or if she'd be back. Cassandra went over everything she could remember, trying to make sense of it, talking to Yael in her head, writing a response to that maddening note, though she had no address where she could send it. Her anger and hurt clenched her heart, too upset to think about what Yael meant.

Gisi's voice broke into Cassandra's thoughts, warning her that she was going to be late for school. All Cassandra wanted to do was sleep and sleep.

She padded softly into the kitchen still in her nightgown, where her parents sat at the table, poring over another letter. Cassandra felt weird, awkward with both of them, thanks to Yael. She'd fixed things good, so that both of her parents felt betrayed by Cassandra. They glanced up, her mother's green eyes worried.

"What does she say, Papa?"

"I'll read it."

Cassandra stood behind her father as he read Yael's letter aloud.

> *Dear Papa and Mum—*
>
> *You have given me a home, a loving family. I will always be grateful for those gifts. For the longest time, I've felt desperate to get out into the wider world. With all that's happened, I need to go now.*
>
> *Let me explain. Papa, you've always taken great pride in your family history, now mine in part. I know our family were Marranos, their true selves and faith a secret. My own history remains secret from me. Still.*
>
> *I need to find out who I am, where I came from. I'm nearly a woman now. I know I don't always act like one, but getting out on my own will be the best remedy both for me and our family. I'll be forced to grow up.*
>
> *I've saved enough money from birthday gifts and jewellery sales to live for a while. Please don't come after me. I'll let you know I'm safe.*
>
> *Love, Yael*

"Should we go after her anyway?" her mother asked. She held her coffee cup aloft, shielding her face in curls of steam. "She's never had any common sense."

"Ruth, she's a smart girl."

"A girl, yes." Her hands trembled and coffee sloshed over the rim of the mug. Gisi appeared and wiped it clean; she left the room, but hovered in the doorway. "Menash, Yael is young, quite wild."

"My daughter—"

"*Your* daughter?"

"Yael knows where to find us." He lowered his head into strong, square hands, hiding his face, as if he didn't trust his own words.

Her mother glanced up, running her eyes over her remaining daughter from head to toe. "Cassandra, dear, please get dressed. And brush your hair. You look like a wild animal."

"Ruth," her father warned. "Not today." He sipped his coffee. "Yael wants to get out into the world. I did too when I was her age."

"At least after graduation," said Ruth. "She may need that diploma some day."

"Yael has a gift, her jewellery designs are one-of-a-kind. In time, some day—"

"Some day? I'm worried about today."

Cassandra glanced at Gisi, who appeared from the doorway to refill her parents' coffee cups.

"Gisi, thank you," said Papa. "We have everything we need for now."

Gisi nodded. "I'll make a shopping list, Mrs. Paredes," she said, and left the trio to themselves.

"You seem awfully calm," Mum accused Papa, her green eyes cloudy as beach glass.

"Panic never helps," he said, stirring cream into his coffee. Papa looked down at his untouched eggs and toast. Then he began to eat with a vengeance, as if his food were to blame, not stopping until he had dipped the last corner of toast into a pool of yolk. He wiped his mouth and beard with a slash.

"Where are you going?"

"To work."

"Not yet. Please."

"Mum!" Cassandra interrupted, hating to see her mother get desperate.

"Yes, Cassandra?"

"Don't be pathetic."

"What did you say?"

"Nothing. I said nothing."

"Ladybug, off you go now," her father's voice was firm, tugging her hand, so she would bend down and give him a kiss goodbye. "Get yourself ready for school."

Cassandra shook her head, coppery ringlets shining in the light.

"Your Ladybug and your Spidey," Ruth murmured. "Look what Spidey's done now. Ash, spiders eat ladybugs."

"Enough, Ruth."

Her father pushed himself up from the table, his chair clattering to the floor. Cassandra went upstairs, dressed mechanically, and fled to school. Anywhere was better than here.

For several weeks after her sister's flight, Cassandra could barely get out of bed. When Yael had been gone for two weeks with no further word, Ruth coaxed Cassandra from bed, fed her breakfast on a tray, and tried to distract her with talk. After her mother left her room, Cassandra went to the full-length mirror and stared at her own reflection. She was in pain, yet her creamy skin and gold-green eyes seemed to mock her spirit.

Papa barely looked up when she knocked and then entered his shop, head bent over a design.

"These are Yael's," he said, his voice clotted with phlegm. "I may go ahead and make these filigreed earrings with carnelian, as she envisioned it, and the bracelet, a link of bloodstones."

At last, he looked up at Cassandra. "Chaya."

Her father stood up and took Cassandra in his arms. He smelled of strong coffee and pipe smoke, as well as a cologne the sisters had chosen for him, like fresh-mown grass. Cassandra breathed in his scent; she couldn't stand for him to shut her out.

Abba was a bear of a man, and burying her face in his thick black hair, now peppered with grey, scratching her cheek against his full beard, smelling his aftershave, Cassandra felt like a little girl again. She found herself breaking down, and it was a relief to cry, to let go.

"Sit, Chaya. It's not your fault."

She couldn't think what to say, could not bear any more lies.

"No more of this madness."

He sat down in the big swivel chair and pulled her into his lap, as both she and Yael had sat during their girlhoods, each sister on one knee. Cassandra let her calves dangle, swinging them lightly against her father's, as she lay her head against his warm chest.

"Abba?"

"Hush now, Chaya." He gently stroked her hair with his broad palm, so hypnotic it almost put her to sleep.

"Abba," she persisted, lifting her head and turning to look directly into his eyes. "I didn't write that note, the one about Mum."

Her father was very still and Cassandra couldn't read his thoughts.

"Tell me you believe me, Abba."

Her father cleared his throat, then let out an angry, "Accch!" which softened into a resigned sigh. "You know, it doesn't matter now."

"What do you mean?"

"I've lost Ruthie, Zev, the schmuck!" He swept a hand through his wavy hair. "Ima feels she's lost you, as well as Yael. And she loves you, Chaya, so much. If only you could understand her way of loving."

Cassandra let out a horrible snort, her mouth a smirk. How could he worry about her mother after what she had done to him? "Abba, I need to know you believe me."

"I do."

"Will you try to find Yael?"

"I received a postcard from her today. I showed it to your mother and I will show it to you, too. We can let the air out of our chests, now."

"A postcard?" Why not her, why had Yael not contacted *her*?

Her father reached across his desk and retrieved it. There was no return address, a Marrakech postmark the only indication of Yael's whereabouts. As Cassandra read the brief note in Yael's large, loopy hand, she couldn't stop the confusion, hurt, and rage that knotted in her chest.

Abba, I'm rambling around the city of my birth. I'll write when I can. Want you all to know that I'm fine, not to worry. I long to create something beautiful, perhaps useful, thanks to you. Love, Yael

"So you see, Chaya, she's well and will stay in touch."

"With you."

"All of us."

"After what she did—"

"Ladybug, maybe it has more to do with Yael and what she needs to do right now." His eyes looked acutely uncomfortable. "We all make mistakes, do wrong."

He sat up straight, lifted Cassandra gently off his lap, and stood her up. "Someone has a birthday coming up. Sweet sixteen! We have a darkroom to build, now don't we?"

Cassandra spent the better part of that Sunday making plans for her new darkroom with her father and every day after school, they worked together with a local handyman to set it up. Despite all that had happened, she was excited by the prospect.

Nine years before, she'd grabbed Papa's Rolleiflex, a black and silver magic box. Cassandra loved its shape and shine, the eye and crank, its secret compartments and power to stop time, preserving an image. She was seven.

"Here," her father had said, placing his hands over hers, showing her how to peer inside, snap a picture, then wind the film. Papa let her shoot a photograph of an emerald he had cut himself. Later, she took charge of his catalogue, photographing raw uncut stones—clear quartz, jade, lapis lazuli—as well as Papa's finished designs.

When her sixteenth birthday arrived at the end of May, it was a hard day for them all, but they celebrated as a family with a home-cooked meal, a cake, and the unveiling of the darkroom. Cassandra's parents presented her with a new camera, a Leica M5 Rangefinder. There was no word from Yael.

Cassandra still didn't understand her sister, the person she felt she had known best, but she focused on her photography. She spent hours in the library and found the work of Hungarian photo-journalist Martin Munkácsi. His *Three Boys at Lake Tanganyika*, showing the trio caught in silhouette running into a wave, stunned her. The picture caught the joy and grace of their movement in a moment. Her idol soon became Henri Cartier-Bresson and his book *Images à la Sauvette (The Decisive Moment)* her bible. She took her camera into the street.

Abba was interested in documenting the Jewish community in Malta, its near-hidden history, and the sacred relics that existed beneath and behind what most people noticed. Perhaps they could produce a little catalogue or monograph. What's more, he hoped to incorporate elements of the relics into new jewellery designs. They had a project.

Cassandra finished out the school year indifferently, taking photographs around Valletta, and even on Gozo and Comino, instead of doing homework; sometimes her father went along. Cassandra's mother returned to her charity work and her parents seemed to come to a truce; Cassandra saw a new tenderness and care with which they treated each other.

Late one night, when Cassandra came down to the kitchen to make herself a cup of tea, she overheard them in the nook, sipping cocoa and talking in low voices, before they were aware of her presence.

"You didn't have to do that, Ruthie," her father said, cupping her chin.

"It's nice when you notice, Ash."

"Don't let's turn around, Ruthie, when we have so much ahead."

Cassandra crept back to her bedroom, wondering what her parents were talking about, surprised to find Gisi waiting for her. "I made you some warm milk, Cassie. Have a little milk and a biscuit. It will pop you right back to sleep."

Cassandra took the steaming mug and thick shortbread biscuit and propped herself up in bed, looking over the day's prints.

"I have something for you, Cassie," Gisi went on, her voice sly.

"What is it?"

"Give me a moment."

Gisi left her bedroom and returned a few minutes later carrying the aluminium case that Yael had used to show her jewellery samples.

"She left that behind? I guess she wanted to travel light."

Gisi sat in the chintz armchair and snapped open the case, pulling out a book with a beautiful marbleized cover in the pinks, mauves, and purples that Yael was especially fond of, the colours of the dress she had coveted.

"What is it?"

"Looks to be a little diary."

"How did you get that?"

"She left it behind," Gisi answered tartly, avoiding Cassandra's eyes. "As I said, it seems to be a sort of journal, though of course I didn't read it. I thought *you* might want her things, you two being thick. You can hold onto them for her until she comes back."

"I doubt she's coming back, given how she left."

Gisi ran her plump veined hands over her dressing gown. "I don't have the gift of prophecy."

"Put that back inside the case, Gisi. I need to sleep. I've got a lot of pictures to shoot tomorrow."

Gisi handed the aluminium case over and Cassandra shoved it roughly under the bed.

"Get your rest now, dear."

Cassandra rose, shut her door tightly, and bolted the lock. For a while she sat up, the night black outside her window, the street quiet. Then she leapt out of bed, dragged the case out, and laid it on the bed. Snapping it open, she held the diary in her hands. It was quite small, but thick. Cassandra didn't even know her sister had kept a diary and she thought she had known everything about Yael. Her hands trembled as she held the lovely book, but she couldn't bring herself to open it. Not yet.

Cassandra didn't believe that Yael would have purposefully left the diary behind after taking the trouble to keep it. The aluminium case, maybe, it was cumbersome, but the diary she could have easily slipped inside her purse or suitcase. Did she leave in such haste that she forgot it? Cassandra knew it wasn't beyond Gisi to have snatched the journal, that woman was a snoop. Anything seemed possible: Cassandra had lost faith in her own judgment.

Agitated, she took a sip of warm milk. And then she had a terrible thought: was it possible that Yael had left the diary behind on purpose for her to read? Or could she have written it with that purpose in mind? She opened the diary, then snapped it shut. No, it wasn't possible; Yael was impulsive, not calculating. Cassandra was frightened about what the diary might contain, that it might stir her too deeply. She thought of burning the pretty little book to ashes without reading it. To make it not be. She knew reading it would hurt and she hurt too much.

Cassandra put the diary back inside the aluminium case and slid it into the deep bottom drawer of her dresser, straining to shut her thoughts about Yael inside there as well.

She stepped onto the balcony that opened from the bedroom. The stars appeared one-by-one, glittering brightly. If only Yael was here, Cassandra might have enjoyed their brilliance, but now they seemed too perfect, their sparkle cold and distant.

13.

Cassandra spent her summer doing more photographs in Malta, and on Gozo and Comino, holing up for hours in her new darkroom. Being on the island without Yael made her see her everyday world in a new way and now she had a fresh purpose.

When Yael was around, they'd experienced everything together, though Yael's spirit often dominated. She'd conducted races down the Armoury Corridor in the Grand Master's Palace, leading Cassandra to the coastal cliffs, insisting they lean out over the precipice, their arms spread like wings. Now, Cassandra studied each statue and savoured the shape of the cliffs from below, instead of risking her life at the peak.

What a relief to be done with school! A summer free to immerse herself in photography.

Cassandra strolled the steep, narrow streets of Valletta, more like crevices carved between flats of Malta stone. She loved the dry heat and yellow sun, the hot dusty wind that blew through alleys and passageways, the warm biscuit of Malta stone, which turned golden at midday. Her camera was a welcome weight. The concentration she needed to take a good shot set her free; she was no longer the object of the world's assessing gaze, she was doing the looking. No one bothered her, the camera created a firm boundary. She savoured her aloneness in the crowd.

Cassandra focused and shot, a rush of pleasure as she worked. She thought of Cartier-Bresson's words: *"There is a creative fraction of a second when you are taking a picture. Your eye must see a composition or an expression that life itself offers you...."*

She loved the phrase *"that life itself offers you."* It was all about remaining open, available.

Some days, Valletta was a *plein-air* museum, others a fortress, with walls, castles, look-out towers, and sentry posts built across the city's bastions, architecture that had imprisoned Yael. Here and there, Cassandra spotted the symbol of the eye, carved into buildings and boats, orbs that seemed to spy on her as she spied on her world.

Cruise ships took port in Grand Harbour and disgorged multitudes of passengers. One broiling hot July day, a ship from Japan docked, the passengers dressed in azure T-shirts with *Il-Belt*, or "The City," printed across their chests. Each tourist carried a camera and they descended like colonies of blue ants. Cassandra photographed them, taking their photographs.

On Sundays, she set out with her father to explore. Cassandra admired her father's devotion, not only to Judaism, but to everything he did. If only she could believe, all might be well. At each Shabbat service, she prayed with Papa that Yael was okay, wherever she was, and that she'd return to them one day. Prayer was hard; faith felt beyond her now.

Papa took her on the short journey to Comino; from afar, it looked like barren rock with patches of stunted shrubs. Once on the islet, its garigue bloomed into a mosaic of wild flowers, cliffs visible for miles.

There were only four people actually living on the rocky isle, Abba told her—two brothers, their aunt and a cousin—all descendants of Cutajar's farming community and their home was now a natural preserve, overrun by wild rabbits, rats, and snakes, not to mention snails, beetles, and ants.

"Chaya, do you know the story of Abraham Ben-Shmuel Abulafia?" Papa asked, as they sipped from a thermos of iced tea. She shook her head. Sharing a picnic of Gisi's home-baked *imqaret* oozing with date filling, he told her about the Jewish visionary and Kabbalist who proclaimed himself the messiah. Born in Saragossa, Spain, he dreamed of dissolving the differences between Judaism, Christianity, and Islam, and set out to Suriano to convince Pope Nicholas III to heed his ideas and ease Jewish suffering. "Well, Chaya, the Pope sentenced him to death by fire. With the pyre prepared, the Pope died of a heart attack. Abulafia had to escape or would be executed, so he lived out his days right here on the isle of Comino where he wrote Kabbalistic and philosophical works including his *Sefer Ha'ot,* or *Book of the Sign.*

"He proposed that Palestine be merged into a Jewish state. I have his writings. They inspire me like Cartier-Bresson inspires you."

"Why?"

"His teaching from mouth to ear."

"Which means what exactly?"

"We become nothing but an ear which hears the universe. Abulafia practiced various meditation techniques to lose himself in the infinite, in God."

"Papa, I believe in what I can see."

"Of course, you're a photographer."

"Were there other Jews in Malta during Abulafia's time?"

"About a third of our people were Jewish, then. They lived independent and prosperous lives. Many owned land, and they worked as doctors, merchants. The situation changed in the second half of the Middle Ages when the Edict of Expulsion forced all Jews to leave the country, or convert and give up nearly half of their possessions."

"The Knights' rule was not a good time for us, either, but nobody teaches us that dirty little secret in school," Cassandra added.

"Jews were slaves. The Knights took passengers of merchant ships hostage—many were Jews. Free Jewish people visiting Malta had to enter through the *Jews Sallyport,* not much of a welcome."

"I've seen it in Valletta."

"Napoleon's seizure of Malta was a blessing—for us. On the road to Egypt, he conquered the island and applied the laws of the French Republic, abolishing slavery. Jews were free again and our community could rebuild. Valletta became an important stopover on the road to the Middle and Far East. Jews from Gibraltar immigrated here and established businesses. Soon others followed from North Africa, Portugal, Turkey, and England."

That afternoon, they visited the ancient walled city of Mdina, six miles west of Cassandra's home. Abba showed her the sign marking the old Jewish silk market and Cassandra shot it from several angles, one picture with her father standing in front of the red door.

At Mdina's Cathedral Museum, they pored over deeds and other documents written by Jewish notaries in Maltese with Hebrew script, the earliest known Maltese language texts, Papa told her, dating back to the fourteenth century. "Mdina was our capital, then, with a vital Jewish community."

All summer long Cassandra travelled around the island with Abba on Sundays, waking up early to beat the heat, guided by his maps and notes. She'd lived her whole life here and had never been aware of all these relics, some paradoxically hidden in plain sight, and felt like a sleuth, an excavator.

They went to Gozo early one morning. At last, they reached the southern temple of Ggantija in Xaghra. Near the inner apse, her father stopped. "Chaya, look at the ground under your feet."

Cassandra made out the two-line inscription, ten words, seven in the first line, three in the second.

"*To the love of our Father Jahwe,*" her father translated for her. "When the Phoenicians occupied Malta, about 3500 years ago, the first Jews landed on Gozo—they were Israelite mariners from the seafaring tribes of Zevulon and Asher. This sign is proof they were *here*."

They stopped awhile, as Cassandra took photographs and her father made notes. She saw the link between past and present, her community's tenacity and strength. It wasn't the same as believing in God, but it was belief in resilience.

At Marsa cemetery at the southern tip of the Grand Harbour, Papa showed her decorations resembling Torah finials topping the gabled, stone gate. "Before World War II, many Jews fleeing the Nazis came to Malta. We were the only European country not to require visas of Jews escaping German rule."

"Something to be proud of—finally."

Papa nodded.

Exploring the Jewish dead, Cassandra wondered how they'd lived.

"This is the only Jewish cemetery we still use," her father said as they walked around, studying the graves and inscriptions.

"Our family arrived here early in the nineteenth century, seeking a life with greater freedom than they'd had in Portugal. Moishe and Sarah came in 1823. They had eleven children!"

"What did they do?"

"The Paredes were fish merchants. I didn't follow suit." He chuckled softly. "They had a thriving shop in Marsaxlokk filled with fresh catch brought in straight from the sea. And they started a cannery. They fared well. I'll show you our plot."

Cassandra studied the simple headstones, all engraved with Hebrew blessings, some adorned with torah finials, menorah, or Stars of David.

"For the longest time, in Portugal, they'd led a double life. Living that way takes a toll on the spirit. Being split down the middle."

"Is this their grave?" Cassandra gazed down at a cracked headstone, decorated with a large Star of David.

"Yes, you can just make out the dates. Moishe lived to ninety-two, rare for that time; Sarah passed away at seventy-five. They are buried together, their children and children's children alongside them. Chaya, I want to be buried here."

"Don't think of that now, Papa."

"Come."

She and Papa stood beside the grave of Moishe and Sarah with its large, weathered stone. They each looked around for a rock to place on the grave. Neither of them mentioned Yael's name, but Cassandra sensed that both of them were thinking of her.

As they packed up to leave, her father pulled a postcard from his pocket. "Here, let me read this to you."

Cassandra felt a wave of grief blow through and nearly level her. She closed her eyes.

Her father put the postcard down on the Paredes headstone. "Are you all right, my love?"

"Papa, at times I imagine Yael is dead!" The words just came out of her mouth before she could stop them. Cassandra found that if she let herself believe that Yael had died, she could preserve what had been good between them. Her father drew her into his chest, the postcard fluttering to the ground. When she opened her eyes, Cassandra spotted the Marrakesh address. She picked up Yael's postcard, scanning the brief note.

Dearest Papa—
I'm safe. Hope you and the family are well. Please pass on my message with love to Mum and Cassandra. Yael

Cassandra needed Yael far more than Yael needed her. That was clear and this truth, painful.

"She tells us nothing, Papa."

"She sends word that she's fine."

Cassandra strained to harden herself, not to feel so much.

He kissed her and they parted ways, Papa to return to work, Cassandra to retreat to the Upper Barrakka Gardens to cool off and think about all her father had taught her.

The gardens were lush with ficus trees, palms, and Aleppo pines. Cassandra was nearly out of film, but took a few final shots, photographing the bronze bust of Albert Einstein that graced the arched stone walls. She found a quiet bench in the shade at the central fountain; thankfully, she saw no one she knew.

Looking up, Cassandra spotted a stranger gazing intently at her, eating gelato. When he caught her eye, he approached and sat beside her on the bench. He was sleek and polished-looking with dark aviator glasses and a blue-and-white-striped shirt.

"That looks good," she said in Maltese, surprising herself.

He answered in English. "It *is*." He filled his spoon with a mound of chocolate gelato and held it out to her. Without thinking, Cassandra ate. The cool, rich melting chocolate was so delicious it made her mouth gush, her teeth ache. Without speaking, the man handed her the cup of gelato and she took it, taking a few more spoonfuls. While she ate, he reached for a canteen. He stood slightly, pulled out a pack of cigarettes, shook one free, and offered it to her.

"Not a smoker," she said in Maltese and he chuckled. "You understand Maltese, do you speak a little?"

Clouds covered the sun and he pushed his glasses to the top of his head. "I get by," he said, lighting up, squinting fine grey eyes as he inhaled deeply. "I'm pretty good with languages. Fluent in French, Spanish, Hebrew, Yiddish, working on the Maltese." He stretched out lanky legs.

"Hebrew and Yiddish?"

"Years of Hebrew school. Picking up languages comes in handy for a travel writer." He took a long drag on his cigarette. "Should quit," he said. "Should do a lot of things."

"Shouldn't we all."

"I'm Lior." He extended his hand. His were large, like her father's, but with long, slender fingers. Cassandra saw him studying her camera, rather than her—unlike the boys she knew—which pleased her. He was not a boy, perhaps about five or six years older than she was, putting him in his early twenties. He caught her eyeing the canteen and offered it.

"Didn't plan well in the water department."

After Cassandra had her fill, she handed the canteen back to him, her fingers numb with cold. "Lucky you came along."

Lior smiled at her. He was unnervingly handsome in a meditative way with clear grey eyes, highlighted by thick black brows, and a head of glossy black hair that flowed over his collar. His nose was straight and narrow, his cheekbones high and sharply hewn.

"So," he said, "do you have a name?"

"I'm Cassandra, but my father calls me Chaya."

"*Life*, lovely. I'm greedy about life."

"Wish I could feel that way."

He drew his brows together. "You don't?"

"Depends when you ask me. Your greed sounds like a good thing."

He shrugged, studying her face. "It depends. So Cassandra/ Chaya, how do you explain this double-naming?"

"Oh, my mother likes Cassandra—she's British—and my father favours Chaya. She won out, since my father chose—" She caught herself, not wanting to talk about Yael.

"Yes?" He waited patiently, stubbing out his cigarette.

"So they both got their way."

"What should I call you?"

She felt her ears heat up and spread to her cheeks; she hated blushing, it left her feeling naked. "I like both names."

"So Cassandra-Chaya it is, then."

"Complicated. And pretty ridiculous."

He laughed deep in his throat. "Cassya." Lior intoned the newly created name, as if he were a rabbi and this was her baby naming ceremony.

"Well." At first, she felt a rush of pleasure, then heard the new name as a combination of her own and her lost sister's. More than anything, she needed a fresh start, a new self.

"So what are you doing in Valletta?" she was abrupt, eager to change the subject.

"Oh … well." He drew out a hard-backed composition book

and showed her pages of notes. "I'm in the process of writing a column for *Malta Today*, covering the listings—cultural and political events. I'm doing the weekly "Discovering Malta" column."

"Where are you from?"

"Brooklyn." He raised his brows. "New York."

"Obviously."

He shook another cigarette out of his pack, lit up, inhaled.

"So, as a home girl, maybe you can show me around the *hidden* Malta." He blew smoke into rings. "What's your project with the camera?"

Though he had fed her gelato, shared his water, and was the most fetching man she'd ever met, Cassandra was not ready to share the nature of her project; it might lead to other revelations.

They sat in awkward silence, watching a small flock of birds alight on a palm, bending its leaves under their weight, pigeons feeding off crumbs, and locals and tourists walking the paths, their limbs slow and fluid in the late afternoon heat. The sun was going down, soon it would be twilight, and with luck, a breeze would pick up.

"Well," he said, standing, and Cassandra felt a quickening; she didn't want to lose him just yet. Up until now, she'd had no interest in boys, because that's what they all were. And she had been full, consumed by her closeness with Yael. She couldn't think of her sister.

"I can show you around a bit," Cassandra said, speaking too fast. And then she offered, "Believe it or not, I'm still finding out more about this island."

He gave her a warm smile, bowing his head for a moment, so his hair rushed forward. "A photographer."

"If I could do nothing else, I'd be happy." She stood, too, and saw there was a big discrepancy in their heights. He was about one meter, ninety. Lior packed up his knapsack, and at the last moment, handed her his canteen. "Take it—if you're going to be out a while."

Cassandra was heading home, but wanted something of his.

"How shall I find you ... Cassya?" They both laughed, as he brushed a lock of hair from her eyes. Lior pulled a pen from his pocket and handed it to her. Cassandra took his hand, flipped it over, and wrote her phone number on his palm, pressing down so the numbers would be indelible, at least for a time.

14.

Cassandra raced home, her body alive with the possibility of entering a wider world. She rarely met anyone from outside of Malta.

Before she knew it the summer was over and secondary school began again. So that she wouldn't have to return home after school and face her mother and Gisi's inquisition, Cassandra brought her camera and kept it safe in her locker. She was only half-present and went through her classes like a somnambulist, just getting by. Her studies, the teachers, the other students existed outside and apart from what really mattered: Lior, her photography, Abba.

Lior began to appear at the school gate, which caused a frenzy of gossip. Cassandra kept herself aloof; she was just biding time, she would get her secondary education certificate and then begin her real life. Of course, Abba hoped that she would continue her studies and take the matriculation exam for university, but Cassandra had other plans.

Lior whisked her off and they went about the island, visiting places she had walked by her whole life but barely noticed, experiencing them anew through Lior's eyes. They made trips to Mdina, to the ancient Neolithic temples, talking about the history, politics, and religion of her home; since she'd learned so much from Papa, she could teach Lior. While Cassandra took photographs, Lior scribbled notes in his hardbound books or talked into a tiny pocket tape-recorder. By the end of September, he had spoken to his editor at *Malta Today,* and after the editor looked at Cassandra's portfolio and chatted with her about her family history in Valletta, he brought Cassandra on board. She would do photographs for both the listings and for Lior's weekly column, "Discovering Malta." A real job! Cassandra was elated that she could actually do something useful in the world.

After a long day working together, Lior wanted to swim, and once in a while, Cassandra joined him. It was nothing for him to leap from craggy rocks into the Mediterranean, or slide down the seawall into the water. Like most Maltese, Cassandra usually only swam when the weather was unbearably hot at the beach in summer, but Lior would swim any time, any place, during any season.

One Monday in late September, with their column as an excuse, Cassandra cut school and she and Lior took the ferry out to Gozo and Ramla Bay, with its red-orange sands leading to a swath of crystal-clear water. The beach was nearly deserted.

Cassandra sat with her legs tucked up to her chest on the big beach towel they had unrolled, as Lior bound into the blue-green sea, his arms, legs, and chestnut-brown. He was beautiful to watch as he pulled himself through the water, arms moving in rhythm, legs kicking up fountains of foam.

He gestured for her to join him and she stepped slowly and shyly into the sea, and he gathered her into his arms and rushed her through the water, tucking her against his chest with her legs wrapped around him. They stayed at the beach until late afternoon and then Cassandra went back to Lior's flat on Triq Santa Lucija.

Lior's doorway had a mezuzah, while his door-knocker was adorned with the golden Maltese cross, and she smiled at the coexistence of sacred objects. The apartment was a studio, containing just a bed, a kitchenette, and small pine table. The bathroom could barely fit both toilet and shower stall.

"Welcome to my castle."

Cassandra felt chilled after their swim, her thin cotton sundress clinging to her wet skin, but didn't want to go home yet.

Lior looked about the room, spotted a sodden towel under the bed, disappeared into the bathroom and came back with a small worn one. "This is the best I can do."

Cassandra vanished into the bathroom, ran the water and stepped in, jerking the cheap plastic curtain closed. Warming herself under the stream, she thought, *I'm alone in a man's apartment.*

She towelled dry and quickly changed back into the shorts and T-shirt she'd brought to the beach, wishing she had something nicer.

Lior had set out a bowl of salted nuts and bottle of red wine, La Vallette, sweeping his hand in a flourish to indicate the humble spread. Cassandra settled on a wooden stool.

"I've gotten good feedback on the column," he said. "Lucky I ran into you."

"I was getting a bit rancid here, ready to rot."

He chuckled his low laugh, then poured each of them a glass of wine. La Vallette was a bit rough around the edges, according to Abba, who called it plonk, but who cared? Cassandra drank hers down quickly.

After her second glass, her body felt light, her head an untethered balloon. Outside his window, it was twilight; soon it would be dark. She found herself getting chatty, spilling everything about her project, and part of the story about Yael, the nasty trick of the letter mimicking Cassandra's handwriting, her sister's flight. Their entire story, the nearly unbearable closeness she'd always felt for her sister, the oneness, Cassandra kept to herself.

She started to talk lightly, but found she was crying. Cassandra stood up, embarrassed. "Sometimes I wish she were dead. Or I was."

Lior stood and pulled her head into his chest. He stroked

her hair, dried her face with his own against hers. His cheek was warm, a bit rough. She felt dizzy and sat down on the bed, their hips touching.

"You're lovely. That green light in your eyes." He kissed her and she felt his kiss radiate from her lips spreading throughout her body. She lay back on the small, thin mattress and he covered her with his body, caressing her gently, kissing her neck and shoulders.

"I wish—" Always that word, so weak and pale, yet with its own strong current.

His mouth covered hers so she couldn't speak and she felt him hard and pressing into her, an ache flooding her pelvis, limbs, and chest. He pulled down her shorts and panties in one motion and lifted her flimsy tank over her head, reaching around to unfasten her bra. He was quick, expert.

"Please turn off the light."

"I want to see you."

Cassandra closed her eyes and heard him shedding his clothes, felt his nakedness, his warm skin, his body lean and strong, but with a softness on the underside of his forearms, his inner thighs. His buttocks were high and round, all muscle. She stroked him there, laying her hand in the crease. He used his palms and fingers to map her out, that lightning current of connection between her lips, her breasts, and Cassandra spread her legs, laying herself open. Lior drove into her now, his long black hair brushing her face, her throat, her breasts, and she cried out in pain and pleasure as she felt the sharp spurs of his hips burrowing into hers; he kept on and on, placing one hand under her buttocks and then shoving two fingers into her mouth, and she felt herself smash and shatter, losing herself. When he came he lifted her off the bed, pressing her against him and she thought she might break in two.

Both of them breathed hard, letting the ceiling fan cool their skin.

"Cassya," he said. "My own Cassya." She let out a sigh of pleasure, as he held her in his arms; they dozed.

When they awoke, he asked, "Would you like more wine? A cup of tea?"

"I have to go."

"I'll walk you," and as they strolled he encircled her within both arms, as if he would always protect her.

Some weeks later, her father called her into his study after Sunday breakfast. "Come here, Chaya."

She obeyed and sat down on the couch.

"We don't talk anymore."

"Abba, I'm sorry I haven't been going over the photographs with you, I know there's lots to do, but—"

He shook his head, his dark brown eyes stern, melancholy. "It's not the photographs, or the project, Chaya. Do you realize, you missed Shabbat services yesterday morning. Where were you?"

She sputtered, off guard. She didn't want to lie to her father, could not bear it. She said nothing because she had nothing to say.

"Well, what do you have to say to me?"

"I'm sorry, Abba."

"This is our time together as a family, a community. We're small."

So was their family now.

"I'll be there next week, Abba. I promise." The services did provide an anchor for her that she missed. "What will you speak about, do you know yet?" She was thinking about Yael, how she still missed her sister so much, sharing everything that happened.

As if he reading her mind, he said, "You know, I've had no word from Yael lately. At first, there was a postcard every couple of weeks. A line or two. Then she sent a note once a month with very little news. Now nothing."

Cassandra felt a strange compression in her chest, hated being held hostage to his pain. She had too much of her own.

"Will you be at Shabbat services next week?" her father pressed.

"Yes, Abba. Of course."

He drew her in and kissed her forehead as he had done when she was a little girl.

As fall drew into winter, Abba grew unwell. He was slower and less busy with his jewellery making, his Valletta shop, Cassel Gems, and his international business. He told Cassandra and her mother he felt a weight in his blood. When he climbed the steep Valletta streets, he confessed that pain knifed through his chest, his breath coming in ragged bursts.

Cassandra called Dr. Azzopardi.

"So I've got a bum ticker," Papa said following a thorough medical workup. The doctor prescribed an armamentarium of medications, a special diet and exercise regimen, and saw Papa more often for check-ups.

As Hanukkah came and went, Papa withdrew. Hanukkah was the time of year when he had brought Yael back from Marrakech to join their family and Cassandra guessed he was thinking of her, as they all were.

Though Cassandra was shy, reluctant to bring Lior home to meet her parents, she invited him to the townhouse for Shabbat dinner. To Cassandra's shock, her mother donned the form-fitting pop-art mini-dress that Yael had coveted and that had set off the chain of trouble. It sickened Cassandra now. Would she ever be free of reminders?

Abba was cool and formal toward Lior, an alien politesse one moment, an artillery of questions the next: his background in New York, his family, his education, his plans for the future. It was a great relief to Cassandra when the evening was over and Lior returned to his flat, safe from her possessive father, who could not bear to lose another daughter.

That evening, her father knocked on Cassandra's door when she was about to go to sleep and sat on the edge of her bed, as he had done so many nights of her girlhood. He sat silent for a while, as Cassandra waited.

"It takes a long time to know someone," her father said, his voice deep and steady.

"What are you saying, Abba?"

"You are still so young and he is already a man."

"What, Abba? Say what you mean."

His voice was low, clotted with feeling. "This Lior, he seems as if he will bend others to his will, that he will mould and shape them like soft, wet clay, and if—"

"You don't know anything about Lior." Cassandra felt frustration and anger well up in her chest. "You met him once. Once!"

"True. But I have an instinct about people and a bad feeling about him."

"You should hear yourself. You sound crazy. You don't want me to have a boyfriend! Whomever I bring home will never be good enough for your precious Chaya. For God's sake, Abba, he's Jewish!"

"You're too young to see a man, Chaya. You're still just a girl." Her father looked into Cassandra's eyes.

Cassandra's heart felt like cracked glass.

He cleared his throat. Shifting on the bed, its springs popped under his weight. "Chaya my love, be careful." He sighed deeply and murmured under his breath. "I wish in my own life I had taken more care, I—you have a keen eye, Chaya. Be sure not only to look, but *see*."

"Abba, I'm very tired. No sermons now."

"Understood. Goodnight my love."

He reached down to kiss her on her cheek, but Cassandra turned away.

Papa moved slowly from the bed, his knees stiff, and as he left her room, Cassandra was struck by how old he looked, his husky build, which usually exuded vitality, now worn and weighed down.

Cassandra continued to see Lior, but rarely brought him home that fall, winter or spring. Abba's health deteriorated in a rapid spiral and one day in early June when Cassandra went in to bring him a cup of coffee on a Sunday morning, she found him still asleep at eleven, his face turned to one side, his eyes open: flat brown discs. She lifted his hand, lifeless in hers, and cried out. Cassandra wrapped her arms around Abba, embracing him as tightly as she could. Neither Gisi nor her mother could pry her free.

That night, after her mother made arrangements for Papa's funeral and burial, Cassandra and Ruth sat at the kitchen table, the two of them alone together. Though their relationship had been strained at times, they knew they had only each other now. Her mother took Cassandra's hand in hers.

"We must contact Yael," she said. "A telegram."

Cassandra nodded, in shock, talking to Papa in her head.

Ruth rooted around until she found an address on Yael's last postcard, a boarding house in Marrakesh. "We'll put 'Get Answer,'" she said.

Before the funeral, an answer came back via telegram. "*Sorry Papa's death. Heart love with you.*"

Over a hundred people attended Papa's funeral service, but Yael was not among them. As they sat shiva, dozens of friends, colleagues, and neighbours passed through the house, sharing memories, telling stories about Menash Paredes. The house was filled with food, talk, even laughter, yet Cassandra felt like a sleepwalker. Within one year, she had lost the two people she had loved most in all the world, and she felt a void in her heart that nothing would ever fill.

When the official mourning period ended, silence fell on the nearly empty house. Lior was often with Cassandra during this time and her mother grew fond of him, but Cassandra thought and dreamt of her beloved Papa. Night after night, mother and daughter talked of the future, what they would do. Staying in Malta was painful now, but leaving was hard, too.

Three weeks after Papa's death, a letter came from Yael. Cassandra opened it and read it to her mother.

Dear Mum and Cassandra—
I was so sad and sorry to hear of Papa's death. He's always been a great support to all of us. I learned so much from him, and in many ways, he's made me who I am. I've started a new life and can't come back to Malta now. My life, my world is changed. I'm doing what I am meant to do, learning every day, looking forward, not back. I hope Papa would approve. I know this time is hard, painful. My thoughts are with you.
Love always, Yael

They sat together for a long while, not knowing what to say. Finally, Ruth spoke.

"At least we know she's okay."

"That's what Papa always said."

"She's gone on with her life, we must try to do the same, darling."

Cassandra felt an iron hand on her chest. She wondered if the weight would ever lift.

That fall, Lior was offered a job in New York City on a travel magazine and asked Cassandra to join him. Cassandra and her mother hashed things out day after day, going round and round in circles. It was difficult for mother and daughter to part, as they were the last two members of their family in Malta.

"What do you want to do, darling?"

"It's hard for me to leave you now, Mum."

"Don't fret about me. I have a little family left in London.

You know how I've missed England." She laughed ruefully. "I kvetched enough over the years, for all the good it did."

"So you'll go back?"

"Yes, the prospect comforts me a little, but I will miss you so much. We will write often and visit back and forth for holidays."

Cassandra nodded slowly as she took her mother's delicate hand inside both of hers.

And so arrangements were made to sell the townhouse. Cassandra helped her mother with all of the details of the changes to come. In October, they both packed up, said their painful goodbyes, and left Malta.

Cassandra boarded her flight to New York leaving behind the island of Malta, the only home she'd ever known. With Yael gone, her father dead, and her mother settling in London, Cassandra didn't know if she would ever return to Malta, and if she did, it might be a lonelier place than any foreign country in the world.

Cassandra was quiet on the flight, as Lior took notes, each in their separate worlds. She gazed out the window as they flew over the shimmering sea, wondering where its many waters might take her.

PART III: IN LONELY LANDS

15. AZIZA

I stand at the seawall. Stare out on the water, blacker than sky, still as death. Baba, the sea shows no sign of what it's consumed. Our boat, Uncle Nuru, my cousins Afua and Dede, an unborn baby, Bassam and his mother and sisters ... neighbours and friends and strangers. I shiver; the water scares me.

Baba, where are you?

I wished you were on the boat with us, but am so grateful you were spared that fate. You're not here, not there, please Baba be somewhere.

I miss Afua, though she'd been using me lately. Sunshine told Uncle she was with me and snuck off to see Bassam. Again and again, I hid her little rendezvous, but inside something sour festered.

What was it? That I didn't protect her? Baba, Afua was with child when she died.

As girls we had a game, Sunshine and me, we called it Black Sun. Daring each other to do all kinds of mad, bad, crazy things. We hated Jamal Fakhouri, the baker on the far side of the souk. Though the man made sweets, he was nasty, kicking Afua when she touched a cake, slapping my hand, just for looking. Fakhouri was fat as this world with a sleeping sickness. Black Sun, Black Sun, what can we do, just us two? We dared each other to sneak a special ingredient into his recipe. I gathered fine white sand, and while he was dozing, poured it into his mixing bowl. We watched him make a sand cake, collapsing in giggles. Black Sun, Black Sun, what can be done, just for fun? We hid teacher's glasses during lunch, so she couldn't do the math lesson, and on my twelfth birthday we swam without a stitch of clothes in the middle of the night. Black Sun, Black Sun, what can we do, us lucky two?

I miss Afua, cousin, sister, best friend. While she stayed bold to the end, something happened, changed in me, maybe after Amah got sick. No more Black Sun. I was jealous because Afua still had fun, did as she pleased. The girl had a boyfriend who was smart and good-looking and kind and made the best kebabs in our White City ... but I liked Bassam, too. That was, is, my sad little secret. It's my fault that Afua became a mother far too soon. I tell you so much now that you're not here.

Baba, where are you? Close enough to touch, your leather mules slapping as you round the corner, you turn to shadow, then silhouette. I follow you; I am your shadow.

Tripoli bakes in stillness. Brightness is everywhere. White waves of desert, our sandsea.

We're home in happier times. I brew tea, slice bread, set out jam and honey. Outside our window, the glue tree glimmers green in the early light, sticky stuff oozing from its joints. The orange tree blooms with plump bright fruit. Together, we walk to the souk, the sun so fierce, I could fry sfinz, your favourite pastry, on the pavement. You hold my hand and call me Ghazala. I run ahead in bounding leaps, your gazelle.

Our shop: inside an arched bay, the ceiling dark strips of fabric. So many stalls in the passageway: one with spices, a second, scarves, a third, baskets.

I know all the shopkeepers and some spoil me because I'm your girl. We want for nothing.

I sweep our shop, blades of light piercing through the fabric ceiling. Dust sparkles, as I wind belts into coils. You pretend they're snakes, tickling me, twisting one around my legs till I jump, laughing.

I set out every size of your *babouchen*, leather slippers in tidy pairs, some adorned with sequin flowers. I arrange pouches, purses, and satchels on hooks. You say everything is okay, but I know you're scared. Your best friend Kalil Malik disappeared last week. I loved to watch you play cards or dominoes on the balcony, smoking, drinking tea. Kalil, like you, read political books, poetry, and novels. All forbidden.

A boy saved me from the sea. The same sea connecting you and me. Who is he?

I found a key on a peg, pocketed it, and set out into the night.

The fresh air calms me. A skinny dog creeps out of an alley and I pet his matted fur and gaze into his crusty eyes, then stare back out to sea. Baba, you were like a little boy swimming and splashing for hours to cleanse the grime of the souk.

I climb back up the hill, pace the streets, peering into windows. Afraid someone is after me.

I find a church. Ivory candles burn before shrines of Jesus and Mary. I go to an empty pew, bow my head, and pray.

In Libya, prayer flew away from me with black flapping wings. At St. Marks, guards watched. Inside and out, outside in. We had to walk lightly, smell the air, inhale fear along with incense. Everywhere were giant pictures of Qaddafi—he followed us, all Libyans—everywhere. BROTHER QADDAFI, OUR SOULS BELONG TO YOU.

Baba, I will never forget the car that followed us to St. Marks. Black as a beetle. Three men tumbled out smoking and talking in low voices, watching. You insisted we attend Sunday services as usual. The men ate sandwiches dripping grease and meat. The next day, the same men appeared at the souk. You were out buying leather.

Where is your father? When will he be back?

I served them tea in glasses, wet beneath my clothes, a cold, dank sweat. They helped themselves to your cigarettes and touched the *babouchen*, marking the soft leather with greasy fingers

At last they left, toppling a display of satchels, so they fell into a discarded heap, like a dead beast.

I leave the Valletta church. Back on the street, it's getting light. I see the huge dome of another church. This city is rich with churches.

I remember where I come from. The sun rises over the city. Baba, where are you?

16.

A man grabbed her by the wrist. Aziza yanked away, then recognized the boy who had saved her from the sea. As sun washed over the city of Valletta, the nooks and crannies of the medieval buildings came alive: a lion guarding a fort; a pigeon nipping the long beard of a man frozen inside a niche; a single eye drawing Aziza into its black hole. A candy-coloured bus trundled by, and Cal pulled her back to his flat, his hand encircling her upper arm.

He shut and bolted the door. Anger hardened his eyes into green glass. "You can't go wandering around the city. It's not safe."

She clasped her hands together; they felt dry and chapped, the nails ragged. She'd been talking to Baba. Remembering home so clearly she was there, both happy and fearful.

"I woke up—you weren't here."

She lowered her head, eyes downcast. Sitting inside that beautiful church had nourished her soul; the calm within the cool, dim-glowing sanctuary let her escape from her dark, racing thoughts and soothed her heart; there she felt close to Baba and Amah. There was no way to explain any of this to Cal.

"I know it's hard to be cooped up in here, but that's how it's got to be for now. The government doesn't take well to refugees. You could be arrested. Taken to a kind of jail."

"Jail?" She was not a thief.

"It's best to stay quiet until we get your status settled. Understand?"

She nodded, slowly following Cal into the living room where she sank down onto the couch, exhausted. His cat came over and leapt up beside her and she pet him over and over, such a beautiful creature with orange and cream and reddish-brown swirls, such soft fur, a comfort. Cal perched on the arm of the couch, his leg bobbing up and down, a hand covering his face. He mumbled something she didn't understand.

"I'm sorry, what did you say?"

"Can you tell me something about your situation in Libya?"

It was hard to think about it now, her family and their life, as if it belonged to another place, another time, a different girl. But she would try, she had to explain herself somehow or she'd remain a stranger. How else could he help her?

"My mother pass on when I am fifteen. Six month ago, Baba's leather shop was destroyed, our house set to fire. Baba vanish. He was taken in the night. We hear nothing, don't know what is happened, but—"

"But what?"

"He read wrong books, have friends under suspicion. He don't paint our shutters green. He don't paint our walls green." She hissed, almost spit out the words. "He won't take down our family pictures to put up the big picture of Brother Leader."

Cal looked puzzled, then understood her.

"Qaddafi," he said. The notorious Green Book; green, the colour of the "revolution."

"My mother she was always afraid and the fear twist her into strange shapes. We all breathe fear along with air. A storm, even when the sun is shining."

Cal nodded, as Aziza went on. For the moment, as Tonio licked her wrist and fingers, she felt comfort in telling him her story "There was a tale my family convert from Islam to be Christian. But we was always members of the Coptic Christian church."

"I guess there aren't too many of you in Libya."

Aziza nodded. "My grandparents come from Alexandria, Egypt. When my parents were young, both families move to Zelten in Cyrenaica, where they find an oilfield. My grandfathers get good work in the oil refineries. My parents, they grow up together." The thought made her smile and she looked wistful for a moment.

"But they don't agree. My mother she want to stop going to church if it be against Qaddafi. She paint our world green, but Baba he say no."

Aziza buried her face in her hands. When she lifted her head, she swallowed over and over, as if a stone were stuck in her throat.

Cal went into the kitchen and poured her a glass of cold water. She was quiet for a while, then went on. "My parents they move to The White City before I was born. My father, he never want to work in the oil refinery. He learn leather-work from his uncle. My father, he had his own shop in Tripoli's medina. He make beautiful leather *babouchen*—his work very fine."

Aziza lowered her eyes. "Before my mother die, she make Baba promise to send me to Cairo for safety. But I am not permitted to leave Libya. At first I am happy. Baba have only me."

Cal was quiet. Finally, he murmured, "I'm sorry, Aziza, you've had it so tough."

She shrugged, dismissing him.

Anyway, what are *babou*—"

"*Babouchen?* Leather slippers, many wear them to pray. Our family, we was under suspicion."

"Because of the religious conversion rumour?"

She nodded slowly.

"Shit. I've got to get to work in a few hours."

Aziza was more agitated than she had felt in the street with the sky above them.

"Let's put our heads together."

She narrowed her eyes. "We cannot make two heads into one."

He laughed, his long limbs loosening, and she was sure he was making fun of her.

"It's just an expression, Aziza."

She gazed out the window, as the sun rose high over Valletta. Soon the working day would begin, sunlight baking the city. What would she do, where would she go? She could not just sit around this flat day after day. Cal seemed kind, but how could she know for sure? It was difficult to really trust anyone; people surprised you with their darkness. She had seen it on the fishing boat, and back in Tripoli, as men stalked her family. There was a different darkness in her mother, sparked by fear. Refusing to go to church, urging Baba to paint their walls green, burning a journal or book Baba was reading to discuss with Kalil over a beer. Amah withdrew into silence, marked by the humming fridge, the ticking of the clock, the call to prayer from the mosque. At times, she burrowed in so deep, Aziza couldn't find her. Even when she was right there.

"I'm sorry," Cal said, approaching her. "I don't mean to upset you, just thinking out loud here."

She nodded, padding into the kitchen.

"Can I make you a cup of tea, an espresso?" he asked.

"Tea, please," she said, perching on top of a stool, pulling knees to chest, wrapping her arms around herself. At home, she enjoyed brewing tea for Baba, pungent with mint and sage, holding the pot high to make as much foam as possible. The stool was tiny, its seat barely large enough for an average bottom, but she felt safe curled into herself, small and compact.

"I'm going to do espresso," Cal repeated. "I can't believe I've got to go into the theatre soon. I'm a zombie."

"I am sorry."

"It's not your fault."

They were both quiet, as he made tea for her, espresso for him, the noise of the machine and the whistling of the kettle a comfort. A kettle, a lovely cat, homey and normal. He was lucky. Soon Cal set a miniature cup and a large mug on the table before them. He rustled around and found biscuits, then butter and jam.

"Help yourself, don't be shy."

She was hungry and took two biscuits, buttering them thickly, then adding strawberry preserves. She sipped her tea, which was milky and sweet. Since he'd lifted her from the sea, Aziza never felt full; no matter how much she ate, a part of her was hollow.

"I need to find my cousin," she said at last. She was thinking about how on a clear day, looking out to sea from her home in Tripoli, she could see Malta, like one of these biscuits floating in the sea.

"Tell me about her again. There was so much going on—"

"She is my Uncle Nuru's eldest daughter and she came to Malta over a year-and-a-half ago. Tella was twenty-two, then. We received a few letters, a card or two. Tella was doing good. It give us courage to make our journey."

"Where is she living?"

"She say on Gozo."

"Gozo's not a big place."

Cal pushed a piece of paper and pen toward Aziza. "Write down her full name for me. Does she share your last name?"

"Her last name is Mezwar."

"Anything else you remember? Write it down."

Aziza jotted down everything she could think of about Tella, while Cal went to get dressed. She strained to recall facts, details. Tella had described the beauty of the small island of Gozo. Aziza thought she remembered Tella writing that she was helping a woman, a family around the house, or was it in a small hotel? She was not sure; back then, her mind was on helping Baba in his leather shop and caring for Dr. and Mrs. Fortier's three children who were like wild animals.

Soon Cal returned to the kitchen dressed in loose white pants spattered with paint and a raggedy T-shirt. "Anything coming back to you?"

"I remember some things...."

"Every little bit helps." He sat on a stool, sipping espresso, huge fingers looped through the handle; the tiny cup looked to Aziza like a child's toy.

"I wish my sister were here. She's been on the island longer, might be able to help."

Aziza stiffened, worried about what this older sister might think, finding Aziza in her flat, wearing her clothes. With her brother. "No, I—"

"What?" He seemed angry now, impatient.

"I have a worry," she whispered, "about your sister."

"Zoe's cool."

"I see the face of the woman in the street. How she look at me. Like I am a criminal or—" She knew the word, whore, prostitute, but could not bring herself to say it.

"Which woman?" Cal drained his cup and poured out a second.

"The woman in the street with tiger eyes." She had seen Aziza and Cal together walking back to the flat, watching, her lips parted, eyes startled and severe.

Aziza noticed Cal's cheeks turn pale, but he laughed, not a happy laugh, a nervous one.

"That sounds like Serena, my boss. She lives near where you were wandering around and works right around the corner. Serena gets up very early to go to church. "Look," Cal went on, his brows drawn together. "This is why I'm asking you to stay here for now."

"Shut inside this place?"

"Yes, shut up, I mean *in* ... safe." He said the last word slowly, as if he didn't quite believe it himself. "Serena is a good woman, but we have different attitudes. I'm new here, though my mother was Maltese. I'm no expert on the law, but I've been reading up on your situation in the news, on the net."

"The net. What is this?'

"Internet. On the computer."

"Oh, yes."

"I have to be straight with you."

Straight, Aziza wondered, a line?

Reading her confused expression, he said. "I mean honest. I'd like to help you gain asylum here. I'm sure Zoe will want to as well, but Serena, some people born and bred in Malta are going to be less ... sympathetic."

Aziza sipped her tea slowly, making it last. "I am simply another person in the world."

"Exactly. But you need to be cautious." He reached for a recent newspaper article he'd clipped and showed it to her. "Here's a map of Malta. You can see how small it is. It's pretty crowded. Not much land, lots of people. Many Maltese believe that it's tough to take in so many more."

"But we cannot stay in our country, our lives are in danger."

"I understand," Cal said. He glanced down at the article: *One person arriving illegally is like 953 in Italy, 1129 in Germany, average number of arrivals is about 45% of Malta's annual birth rate.*

"If we find Tella and I go and live with her, then I will be okay, is that right?"

Cal looked away and his face, so open and kind, shut against her.

Aziza drank the rest of her tea, spooning a clump of sweetness from the bottom of the cup.

"Got to go. At suppertime, we'll talk more, make a plan.... Tonio will keep you company."

His voice trailed off, and without glancing back at her, he strode out of the flat, as the bolt of the lock slid shut with a threatening thunk.

Aziza sat alone in the empty flat apart from all of the life bustling outside. Valletta was full of noise and people. Now and then, she heard sharp, loud blasts, like gunshots, which made the walls and floor of the flat tremble. Glancing out the window, she saw women doing their shopping, men smoking and chatting in clusters, glancing at newspapers, children playing; soon there was the comforting chime of church bells.

Exhausted, she lay down on the couch and fell into a deep sleep, dreaming of her mother, frail and in pain from breast cancer, looking up at her with dark eyes, reaching out a hand to Aziza, her only child, her daughter, begging her to leave Libya, to go to Cairo, or Malta. Aziza heard gasping and then a choking, felt a hand on her forehead, then her head, stroking, as a voice spoke over her mother's wails. "It's okay, Aziza. I'm here."

She awoke with a start, her body streaming with sweat, her face drenched. The black silhouette of a man leaned down over her and she sat up so suddenly, she bashed her head against his, bright spots spinning behind her eyes. Aziza screamed and he covered her mouth with his hand, whispering low.

She began to thrash, but he contained her. "It's Cal. Aziza, you had a bad dream, that's all."

He released her and got up and went to the kitchen.

Aziza moaned, still recovering from the nightmare. She heard the sound of the tap, water running in a hard fast stream, then the squeak of the fridge. The crack of ice, the clink in a glass and she remembered where she was, overcome with grief. Alone.

Cal handed her a glass of water that she sipped slowly. Aziza crunched ice chips, the cold shards sharp against her tongue and the roof of her mouth.

"I heard you, I thought you were choking," Cal said softly. "And then I realized you were …crying … in your sleep." He kneeled down by the couch beside her.

Aziza thought of her mother and began to weep, wide awake now, as Cal stared at her. Sometimes she could not visualize her mother, Chardae. Fragments swam up: the lovely arch of her black brows, the dimple in her chin, her full hips and soft hair, which she could not tame, but they were scattered jigsaw pieces which never quite formed a whole. She grasped at fragments, feared losing Amah completely.

Cal extended his arms toward her. "I'm sorry," he murmured, "I'm so sorry."

She cried for a while within his arms because they were there, he was here.

"Guess what?' he said smiling. "It's the middle of the night again, our time, I guess."

Aziza managed a smile for him. He was good, kind. She knew she was fortunate that he had found her, and yet at times, she wished she had perished along with the rest.

"I'm looking into asylum for you, how it works, other possibilities too."

"What can I do?"

"Wait. *Quietly.*" He went about the apartment, showed Aziza where she could find CDs, gave her the TV control. "I've got books, magazines." He went to gather a stack for her. "Plenty of food. I'm going to try to go back to sleep or I'll be fried. You do the same."

Aziza tossed and turned the rest of the night. When she awoke, the flat was quiet. She put on classical piano music and flipped through magazines looking at pictures, too anxious to read. Time passed slowly, as if each minute expanded, torturing her with its empty bubble. She watched the clock, waiting.

At three in the afternoon, Aziza spotted a woman approaching the flat. She darted away from the window, leapt upstairs, crouching in the sleeping loft. From there she heard the loud ring of the doorbell. It was the same woman she had spotted earlier, Cal's boss, after her. Aziza crawled under the bed, like an animal in its cave. The ringing went on and on, insistent, worse than the blasts she had heard before, which Cal explained were "feast bombs," celebrating Catholic saints. All at once there was a hard rapping on the door. Even from the sleeping loft, under the bed, Aziza could hear it. The pounding was hard, angry, insistent. Aziza covered her ears, squeezing tight; she cowered, waiting. At last there was silence. She hid a while longer, worried that the woman might still be outside, ready to pounce.

Finally, Aziza crept out from under the bed, coughing from dirt and dust. On Cal's night table she found guides, maps, schedules for buses and ferries. She felt safer up here in the sleeping loft but she had to move quickly.

Inside the sister's closet was a satchel and Aziza slipped in a tourist guide and schedules for bus and ferry. She took underwear and a pair of cotton slacks, a pair of shorts, and several shirts, some with short sleeves, one with long. There was a sweatshirt with a hood and she stuffed that in as well.

Aziza spotted Cal's wallet, just tossed onto a side table, gaping like a fish's mouth. Feeling dirty, wincing, she stuffed bills and coins into an inside zippered compartment of the satchel, then scribbled a hasty note.

Cal, thank you for everything. I am going to look for Tella. Aziza

She left the flat and kept her head down, walking as she consulted the Malta guide, the bus and ferry schedule, like any other tourist.

No one bothered her, or paid her any attention. Aziza found her way to the bus stop, which was not far from Cal's flat, and she waited with a small group of others, some speaking Maltese, others English, and a couple who were having a conversation in French. She understood snatches, thanks to the Fortier's, the Montreal family she had au-paired for in Libya, who had begun to teach her French using their children's grammar books. She'd learned English from her father, who had studied it in school, and practiced both tongues with the Fortier's who spoke both French and English perfectly.

Aziza wasn't sure how long she waited. At last, she heard the bus lumbering up and stepped into the orderly line. Taking her turn to buy a ticket, she boarded. Aziza kept her eyes on her guidebook all the way to Cirkewwa, at Malta's northernmost tip. When she glanced up, an elderly lady with an enormous straw sunhat and billowy dress smiled at her from across the aisle.

"Quite bumpy isn't it? If I'm having trouble now, just imagine how I'll be on the ferry!" Her laugh was girlish, though she appeared to be well into her sixties.

Aziza forced a smile, hiding behind her guidebook.

"I see you have your *Lonely Planet,* they are always good, don't you think? And also Victor Paul Borg's *Rough Guide to Malta & Gozo*, you are well equipped for your visit," the woman went on. "Victor is a friend of mine in London, actually, but of course you know he grew up on Gozo, roaming the beaches and playing hide-and-seek among the Ggantija Temples!" Out came the laugh again, like bubbly sweet soda. "Oh, am I bothering you?"

"No," Aziza said carefully. "I, too, become a little sick on buses, so I am trying to keep to myself."

The woman foraged around in an enormous pocketbook, drawing out a small tin, as if she had struck gold. "*Ouala*! You must chew on an Altoid, do you know they have ginger now? It's just the thing for a queasy tummy." She snapped open the little box and held it out.

Aziza had no choice but to reach out and take one of the candies and pop it into her mouth where it melted and burned. She coughed, wanted to spit the nasty thing out when the lady wasn't looking.

"There you go," the woman said, beaming, her mouth bright, red and shiny as new plastic. "That's why they call them *curiously strong.*" She stuffed the tin back into her bag. "We two should sit together on the ferry," she announced. "Look after one another."

Aziza felt a welling anxiety in her chest, like a moth flapping wings against a window. The woman kept staring at her, so Aziza said. "You are kind, thank you." Before she could lower her head back into the guide, the woman cocked her head and peered at Aziza, as if she were a strange specimen trapped and frozen under glass.

"May I ask where you're from dear? I can't quite place your accent."

"Excuse me," she said, "I need to move to the front. It's my ... stomach."

The woman drew back, as if she had been struck. "Well, then. Off you go."

Aziza found an empty seat behind the driver. Across the aisle was a mother with three young children, too frazzled to pay her any attention; for the moment, she was safe. She would avoid the older woman on the ferry, but there would be others. Strangers might address her. As long as she remained calm. Calm. She loved the sound of that English word which sounded just like its meaning. She chanted it to herself *calm, calm, calm*, her lips forming a soothing hum.

At last, they arrived in Cirkewwa and Aziza put away her guidebooks, went straight to the ticket booth and purchased a one-way fare to Gozo, as if she were any other Gozitan, taking a half-day in Valletta for shopping. She felt a pang, having robbed Cal. If everything turned out all right, she would repay him.

A large crowd was boarding the ferry and Aziza lost herself in all the people and stepped on board. She found a seat, turned outward to the view of the Gozo channel. The ferry began to pull out from its port and Aziza felt her stomach leap. If she could find Tella, her cousin would advise her on the proper steps to take to gain asylum, help her to find honourable work, and make a fresh start. She forced herself to hold on.

As the ferry chugged along, the wind chilled her, and Aziza reached into her bag and pulled out the sister's sweatshirt, zipping it to her chin.

For the first part of the journey, Aziza enjoyed herself, taking in the view, a barren chunk of limestone with patches of stunted shrubs between Malta and Gozo, then sculpted cliffs; she heard another passenger say that isle was Comino. If only Baba could see it, be here with her. They chugged along and Aziza felt brave enough to sneak a glimpse at the other passengers. Many were sipping from steaming containers of coffee or munching on snacks, and she was tempted to go buy herself a warm drink and something to eat—she had money—but then thought better of it. She might run into that lady from the bus who would attach herself to Aziza like cling-wrap.

"You look rather chilly."

"Hello," Aziza murmured, as if her fear had summoned the woman.

"Join me for a cup of tea below?"

"I'm afraid my stomach can't take it. But you go on. Please."

The woman glanced at her strangely, that examining look. "I'm Matilda Winpenny."

Aziza didn't answer.

"And you?" she persisted.

"Ramla."

"What an interesting name. Where are you from?"

Aziza tried to think quickly. "Montreal," she spurted out.

"Oh, a lovely city ... but dear, I meant where are you from *originally?*"

"I am going to the toilet now," Aziza said, and fled to the washroom. Inside, the smell was awful: urine, a whiff of excrement, and she was back on the wooden fishing boat, crushed between unwashed bodies. The acrid stench sucked into her nostrils, crawled down her throat into her belly, as her mouth watered full with nausea.

Aziza buckled over, holding her belly, as someone rapped on the door. The banging went on. There were shouts, a keening of gulls, and Aziza was on the boat with Uncle and her cousins, women, men, children pushing, shoving, keening, grunting like animals.

She vomited whatever was in her stomach, and then retched up a thread of blood, the brilliant scarlet that gushed from Dede's palms as she clung to the fishing boat, and Uncle Nuru struggled to drag her back up on board.

Aziza put Dede between her legs, put her hands on top of Dede's until they were cramped and aching, as her cousin Afua drifted away, the boat sinking beneath them.

Aziza burst out of the toilet, screaming. She ran through the ferry, her arms wild, yelling in Arabic to look for Dede, Afua, her Uncle Nuru. A man approached her and bound her within his arms; wild with panic, she thrashed and kicked, trying to escape.

Aziza ran to the rails of the ferry, leaned over, watched the black water heave and foam. She screamed and screamed until she had no voice, clawed herself up on the railing, the ferry rocking and pitching. Her foot slipped and she scraped her knee and shin, saw blood oozing from her skin. Determined, she climbed the railing again, she had to get off the boat, her fingers curled around the bars so tightly her knuckles whitened, when she felt herself lifted away, a stranger holding her under her arms. She tried to kick, to scream, but had no strength, no voice.

All around her, people huddled, speaking a tangle of languages, barks of orders, babies crying.

Aziza closed her eyes and felt the boat lurch, then stop. People surged all around her, but she couldn't get away.

Announcements came over a loud speaker in a language she didn't understand. Aziza heard the wail of an ambulance, opened her eyes and saw the flashing scarlet lights, men in white, the whine of a police car, men in uniform.

Loud voices clashed around her. White-clothed men walked her off the ferry and lifted her into a screaming ambulance that sped away.

17.

Aziza didn't remember her time in Gozo General Hospital in Rabat, but a day later—or was it as long as two?—she was herded onto a rickety mini-bus crowded together with other ill-looking women, rattling through dry, sooty roads. As the bus lurched to a stop, billows of dust blinded her. When the air cleared, Aziza saw a pock-ridden expanse of packed dirt crowded with tents, and a compound of concrete block barracks. The compound was filled with swarms of people, as officials dressed in the uniforms of soldiers, shouted orders at them. Aziza was too frightened to speak.

She and a group of women were escorted by uniformed guards to an area with three thin walls and no ceiling and told to remove their clothes. One woman started shouting in Arabic, "No, I will not do it!" She was immediately removed from the area by a male policeman and Aziza worried what would become of her.

Though it was high summer, the holding cell was cold and Aziza shivered, goosebumps sprouting on her arms and thighs. She started with her sandals and slipped those off; they barely stayed on anyway, too small for her long, narrow feet. She felt ashamed of her heels, which were black with grime and dirt, where the sandals failed to cover her feet. A woman dressed in military garb watched her with a dull stare and snapped at her in English, "Get on with it. I have hundreds to process," then gave Aziza the small courtesy of turning away and chatting with her colleagues in Maltese. Now, Aziza had to shed something else. She wished Afua were here, Sunshine would know how to get around this bitch.

Aziza unzipped her sweatshirt and shucked it off, then began to lift her T-shirt up from the plane of her hips, but stopped, remembering that she had nothing on underneath to cover her breasts, so she pulled down the T-shirt and dragged Zoe's khaki pants to her ankles and stepped out of them, standing in white cotton panties. She turned to the woman, who commanded that she take off her T-shirt and she did so in one clean rip, like tearing off a bandage.

The guard patted her up and down and Aziza closed her eyes, the humiliation only slightly less painful if she did not have to meet the woman's stare.

"You can dress now. Your identity number is 4735."

Aziza dressed quickly, though her clothes now seemed soiled, as the guard told her to surrender her belongings. She handed over her satchel; inside was everything Aziza now possessed, which actually belonged to Cal and Zoe.

Several different guards took Aziza and the other women who had arrived in the mini-bus to one of the tents outside. Aziza counted twenty beds, which also functioned as cupboards because there was so little space. She was still shivering and noticed one small heater in the tent.

After a few minutes, a male guard came, and for no apparent reason, escorted Aziza out of the tent and into one of the barracks. She was taken to a room teeming with women, some pregnant, or with children, others quite elderly, all waiting together in a confined space.

An official handed her several sheets of paper filled with tiny writing, as well as a pencil, and asked her to fill out the documents. Aziza leafed through the pages, so anxious, the black type seethed like a colony of crawling ants, nothing made sense. Then she realized that the forms were written in English, a language she understood.

Aziza sat on a stool and pored through the documents, which were long and complicated. Others milled about, some pacing, scarcely ten centimetres between them; she and the other women *were* the ants. She felt a caged creature's scream rising in her throat, but tamped it down, forcing herself to be calm. There must be a way to contact Cal, to find Tella.

She had no idea what time it was. There were two small windows and they were locked closed, a grey light filtering into the crowded room. She was hungry, but didn't know when a meal would come, or if she and the others would be fed. There was no clock anywhere or a calendar or anything that could help her know where she was in time, how much was passing.

Aziza slipped off Zoe's sandals, as they had made blisters where their too-short backs cut into her feet. She swept her soles back and forth on the concrete floor, which was gritty with sand and sticky with some nasty residue, the sand making her think of the sea, not far, wherever she went on this lonely island, her own home both near and far.

Aziza's bottom started to ache, so she crossed her legs under her, trying to make sense of the forms. When she looked up, a small group had joined her with their forms, a teenager about her own age with an oval face, delicate features, and a mole at the corner of her upper lip; a short, stout elderly lady with a cloud of grey hair brushed away from her scalp, like a big silver sun; and a woman who appeared to be with child.

The pregnant woman spoke to her in Arabic. "I don't understand these forms. I don't know English."

"I do," Aziza answered in her mother tongue. "I can try to help you. I'm Aziza, from Tripoli." In the middle of this foreign country, speaking Arabic felt like an echo of home.

The women exchanged names; they were all from Libya, except for the pregnant woman who was from Somalia. Jedira was the woman with child, the girl her age was called Silya, and the old lady, Riuza. Aziza felt a small measure of comfort to learn these women's names and to share her own, as they had been given only identity numbers, as if they were not quite human.

"So you are with child?" Aziza said tentatively to Jedira. "Won't that make them give you some special care? If not for your sake, at least for the baby?"

Jedira's dark eyes welled, and Riuza and Silya shot Aziza toxic looks.

"That's a question you should never ask," scolded Riuza. "When you don't know a woman's situation."

"I'm sorry," Aziza said, stung, looking from Jedira to the other women, feeling stupid, ashamed. She was just trying to find a thread of connection.

Jedira began to weep and Riuza handed her a handkerchief and put an arm around her shoulder. "Have a good cry," she coaxed, "cleanses like a spring rain."

Jedira rose and Aziza saw that she was a tall, statuesque woman, her features sharply hewn and her lower abdomen swollen.

"I crossed the desert, and when I reached Tripoli, my pregnancy was almost at term," she said. "Before boarding the boat, I bought brand-new scissors and hid them, making sure they stayed clean. I knew I might need them.

"We were seventy-nine people on our boat, squashed together, barely able to move a muscle. The second day on board, my pains came. A man and a woman, perfect strangers, helped me deliver my baby girl. The man held my arms and the woman cut the cord, using my scissors. I held onto my daughter tightly, fed her from my breast. I called her Ghnima."

"Reed," Aziza said, "a beautiful name."

Jedira smiled to herself, remembering. "She was a long baby, going to be tall like me.

"Each time the boat swayed, I was terrified Ghnima was going to fall overboard. You see, I bled badly, haemorrhaging after the birth, and people stripped off their clothes to help stop the gushing. I was dizzy, had no strength, afraid I would die and not be able to care for my baby girl. Everyone looked out for me and Ghnima. They became my family, these strangers.

"For the next five days, we had little food and water. My breasts went dry. I could not feed Ghnima. She screamed, then became listless. Everything happened so fast in the middle of the sea. I could do nothing. My baby girl died in my arms."

Jedira began to shake uncontrollably, her legs, arms, even her head. Aziza and the other women huddled around her until the older woman Riuza gently pushed them away and rocked Jedira in her arms. After a while, Jedira's trembling stopped, her tears dried, and Riuza lay her down on her cot, where she slept for a while covered by a thin blanket.

Riuza shook her head and whispered. "I can't imagine anything worse for a mother."

"Do you have children?" Aziza was usually not this forward, she waited for things to come out naturally in their own time, but longed to get to know these other women, even a little. Not to be all bunched up, each one locked inside herself.

Riuza nodded. "Kids and grandkids. I've got a son and a daughter. My boy has twin sons going to turn three next month. My daughter has a baby girl, six months old. They are going to join me. Now, they are biding their time."

The others went quiet, gathering in a corner farthest from the door to examine the forms. Aziza acted as interpreter and tried to understand the pages and pages of technical language. The concentrated focused attention she needed to complete the forms and help the others gave her a modicum of strength and kept panic at bay. "We will continue tomorrow," she said. "Each day, we can do a little more."

"I think it's tomorrow," Silya added, "but I can't keep track. A volunteer from the Jesuit Refugee Service comes by. I hope it's Maria. She plays with the children, brings us sanitary towels; she can help us with these forms."

"She is working to get us out of this hell-hole," Riuza said.

Jedira sat up on her cot, then threw off the thin blanket,

and came over to join their group. "There are others trying to help," Jedira volunteered, "a group of them come. They pray with us and bring news."

"How long you been in here?" Aziza asked, dread threaded through her voice.

"I've spent thirteen months in detention," said Silya. "It's this waiting that is going to kill me. I'm young and strong and need to put my mind to something."

"I'm old and need to as well," said Riuza. "The boredom is going to kill me, not being able to do anything for myself, or for others. I've waited nine months for an interview. I have one coming up, but I can still do more time, months in detention, even after I have my interview. This is what others tell me who are still prisoners here."

Aziza worried what days, weeks, and months in this place would do to her spirit. "What about visits? If we know people here in Malta, can they come see us?" she asked.

Jedira shrugged. "I don't know a soul on Malta."

Aziza was slick with sweat, but cold, shivering. "How do we get in touch with people? People we know here, who could help us?"

"We have access to the phone in the evenings," said Silya, "but there is a rush. If you are making a local call, it might be possible to get through. We can only use the phone for a short period and there are always dozens waiting."

"Can friends, relatives, call the authorities for us? Aziza asked. "People who could help?"

"I have a cousin in U.S.," said Jedira. "Queens."

"Whew, hoo!" Riuza whistled through her teeth. "Sounds fancy."

"Queens is in America, part of New York. She wrote to me that she called the authorities asking for me, she gave them my full name, Jedira Uksem, but the person on the phone had no idea who I was, nobody knew my name because we have only identity numbers."

Aziza was shaking now and the older lady Riuza took a thin blanket from her bed and wrapped it around her. Aziza thanked her and willed herself not to cry, not to fall apart; it would do no good. Her head and neck ached; she longed for one of Amah's homemade pillows. Chardae loved to sew pillows, embroidering the fabric with pictures of wildlife. A gazelle with a striped buff coat, white rump, and ringed horns, a sand-coloured fennec fox with enormous ears and thick paws. When she could no longer help Aziza's father in the souk, Chardae worked on her pillows day and night. Their home was filled with them, all shapes and sizes, in an assortment of fabrics. Colours and comfort and rest. If only Aziza had one now to lay her head down, the pillow with the gazelle, on a background of blue and gold. She was Baba's ghazala. To survive in here, she'd have to will her mind away. To sleep, rest, think, to gather whatever strength she had left.

Aziza pulled the ends of the blanket tightly around her, and tucked her legs, knees to chest, her feet frozen into numb blocks.

Jedira was running her hands through her long, black hair, slick as liquorice. "I want to get my hair off my neck, I can't stand it like this!"

Riuza went to her and stroked Jedira's hair with her strong, square fingers. "Sit down, girl. I'll braid it for you. I'd give both feet for *your* hair."

Jedira laughed and sat on her cot while Riuza settled behind her cross-legged and got to work, parting the long black silky hair into sections, working with quick, deft movements. When she finished a braid, she took something out of her pocket that looked like a spool of thread, cut it with her teeth, and tied up the braid.

"How'd you get that?" Silya asked, marvelling at the spool.

Riuza winked, nodding, her head framed by her halo of silver hair. "I have my ways, nothing is going to stop me."

Aziza smiled at her. "Can we write?" she asked suddenly. "Can we contact people?"

"Yes," said Jedira. "We can write letters."

Aziza let the air slowly out of her chest. "Where do I get paper, a pen, an envelope, and stamp?"

"Come," said Jedira. "Maria gave me a supply, I keep it under my bed."

"Wait a minute, girl!" Riuza said, quickly finishing a braid and tying it fast with thread. "You going to mess me up." Jedira sat still until Riuza finished the section she was working on, then took Aziza's arm and walked slowly, wending her way around the crowded beds, leaning back on her heels with the weight of her lost baby until she found her bed. She stooped down, one hand on her back, and Aziza said, "Let me," scooting under the cot and reaching with one long arm, her hand scraping the floor until she felt the contours of a cardboard shoebox and drew it out.

Jedira gave Aziza some sheets of lined paper from a pad, a stubby pencil, an envelope, and even a stamp. Such riches. She hugged Jedira, went to her cot, and began a letter to Cal, her only friend in Malta.

18.

To Cal,

I am sorry. I am sorry for taking your money. I am sorry for taking your books. I am sorry for taking your sister's clothes. I am sorry for not listening to you. Sorry, sorry, sorry, does it mean anything?

I don't know what day this is. I started to write the first day I arrived in Detention, but was not permitted to go on. More days have passed, I'm not certain how many. The first five, I make a point with a pencil on the inside of my wrist to mark the days, but my friend Riuza stop me, because my black punctures make an infection. Now I am using the wall, but I missed time.

I am working with a group of women in my barracks to fill out forms, so technical and confusing, they put up a challenge. My goal is to finish next week with the help of Maria, a volunteer from the Jesuit Refugee Service. Once the forms are complete, I have hope of an interview. When I have this interview, I don't know. I wish after my interview, I will be granted asylum in Malta and be able to join my cousin Tella.

Can you help me, Cal?

Can you find Tella and inform her of my situation?

Can you get me out of here? I am in a Detention Centre called Lyster Barracks in Hal Far, where we are in two compounds, one area with tents and one with what they call Hermes block. When you write to me, be certain to put my identity number

on the envelope. 4735. I hope it is a lucky number.
  I wait for your reply.
  Aziza

July 3, 2007
Aziza,
  *I am trying to locate your cousin, Tella. So far, no luck. I'll
keep looking for her. Get in those forms, as soon as you can.
I've gathered some facts. First, the "good" news. You fit the
conditions of a person who should be granted asylum. From
what you've told me, you are a Christian, but are being accused
by authorities in Libya of converting to Christianity from
Islam, which is punishable by death. Am I getting this right?*
  *Now the bad news: detention lasts as long as it takes for
asylum claims to be processed, evaluated and decided upon.
It can take 5-7 months, sometimes 10, to be called in for an
interview; the limit is a year. Even people in your situation
can wait that long.*
  *I am trying to get help. My sister may have ideas. It's touchy
with Serena, my boss at the theatre, like I've told you, but at
heart, she's a good person.*
  Do your forms. Try to take care of yourself. Just hold on.
  Cal

To Cal,
  *I rejoiced when I received your letter. I feel as if I have a
life rope now, as you were my life rope in the sea. I am not
a criminal, but am being treated as one. Today, the toilets
overflowed and the floor is covered in dirty water and worse.
It stinks. My friend, Riuza, an older lady who is kind, became very sick with an infection in her lungs. Her stomach
is bad too. So they take her to the hospital, where I hope
she will recover. But I don't want her to have to come back
to this toilet. I miss her. My mattress is damp and I don't
sleep. My body is craving air and sun. We see nothing out of*

the cracked dirty windows. I have a trick where I take my mind on a voyage. Back home in the hot bright sun under our plum tree. Drinking tea on the balcony with Baba, a sea breeze cooling our faces.

Here day is night and night, day. I will die if I stay. Some do, already have.

Any news of Tella?

Aziza

July 7, 2007

Aziza,

I know you're strong. I felt it when I dragged you from the sea, the way you grabbed me and hung on, how you fought me off when you thought I might check you into the hospital.

I've got to be straight with you. I'm afraid I can't get you out of there on my own. When Zoe arrives back in Valletta, I will get her help, but I don't know if we have the power, the influence, and the whole business may take too long. That's my sense after doing my homework. Five months, seven, a year in that hell-hole—no way.

I've got to tell you something. I finally found a Tella on Gozo, working at a small hotel ... but she says she's not your cousin, that she doesn't know you. I'm really sorry, Aziza.

Here's the thing. Even if I track down your cousin Tella, and she has been granted asylum and wants to help you, I'm not sure how much that would speed things up for you within this crazy, mixed-up process.

I'm remembering you told me you worked for a Canadian family. You said they were in Libya for a while and you were an au pair or something? You told me they went back to Canada ... was it Toronto? Montreal? I can't remember now. Sorry.

Can you send me their full name and address? I will contact them on your behalf. Maybe they can do something.

Cal

To Cal,

Who was this woman called Tella? Maybe it was my cousin and she afraid of saying so. Your letter got my heart beating too fast. Can you tell me more? Where was she from? What she look like? She is lying to you. That bitch!

I want to scream.

The Canadian family they called Fortier. The father is Roger, a medical doctor. The mother's name is Anne and she is a trained nurse. Montreal is where they from. They have three children—two boys—Patrick and David. Patrick is going on eight, no probably nine by now, and David is twelve. Their oldest is Caroline and she must be thirteen by now.

I can't remember their street, but it have a flower in the name. They said they live near the centre city but not inside it. Looking behind me, I see I make a mistake not going with them when they ask. But I have to stay with Baba, my Uncle, and cousins.

After what I am going through in here and the other people like me, I am thinking I do not have a future in Malta.

Go back to Tella. Get the truth out of her!

Find the Fortiers. Please. Maybe they my last hope.

Aziza

July 11, 2007

Aziza,

I have good news. I found the Fortiers, the right ones. You wouldn't believe how many Fortiers there are in Montreal! I kept at it, making call after call till I found the right family. I've spoken to Dr. Fortier, Roger, on the phone. I talked to Anne, the mother. They're fond of you and really concerned about your situation.

Aziza, the Fortiers want to sponsor you, to bring you to Canada. Montreal. Frankly, I think this is your best option.

Dr. Fortier is in touch with the Maltese authorities and with Immigration Quebec, which has a special program for refugees and for victims of persecution in their own country. He's on your case. Refugees like you are admitted after having lived in a camp, like you, and because they were victims of persecution in their own country and their lives were in danger, your situation exactly. Resettlement in Quebec is your best hope.

When Zoe gets back, I know she'll want to help. Maria from the Jesuit Refugee Service is working hard to speed things up. Don't despair.

Cal

Cal, my friend,

Of course you know I have no papers, no passport. I do want to join the Fortiers. How can this happen? Do you know how long it will take?

I am still breathing, but not kicking.

Aziza

July 13, 2007

Aziza,

Yes, it's possible. I hope it will happen. Dr. Fortier is working on getting some kind of temporary travel document for you, given your circumstances, so he and his family can sponsor you to come to Canada.

I need to try to get you a copy of your birth certificate. Write me your full name, date of birth, where you were born, and the names of your parents. Also, it would be good to have the name and address of your church and your priest in Libya, so we can get proof that your life was in danger for religious reasons.

It may take a while, but I'm pretty sure it will be shorter than waiting for asylum. Trust me on this one.

Think Canada. Montreal. Snow, have you ever seen it? It's beautiful.

Cal

19. ZOE

NOTES: *An ancestor of ours attended the College of the Company of Jesus in* XVII*th C. Asked his name, he answered: "Which one? My inside or my outside name?"*

Zoe's phone rang, startling her out of her thoughts as she flipped through an old notebook of Nannu's. It was Cal on the line and his tone worried her. He was okay, but a friend was in trouble, though he wouldn't get into specifics on the phone. Zoe made arrangements to fly out the following day.

In the meantime, she sat on her bed in the little room and kitchenette she was now renting down the dirt road from the hotel, that weird aluminium case resting in her lap, its planes cold, edges sharp. She still felt high following her second dinner with Bertram, a round of margaritas, and another long chat, which she vaguely remembered touched on her various fears: cats, water. How she couldn't cry. What was she thinking, turning herself inside out for a stranger? Well, the release felt good, bracing, and she understood why people resorted to rushes of confidences on trains and planes, and to unsuspecting diners at adjacent tables. At least it distracted her from the disturbing encounter with Luz.

She steadied the case between her thighs, pressing her thumbs hard against its latches. The case was locked and Luz, no doubt, possessed the key. Zoe cursed Luz, then herself for being a bloody idiot, as Bertram might say.

Zoe searched her room, opening bureau drawers, scanning the floor, looking for something narrow and sharp: a penknife, bobby pin, even a paperclip. No luck, so she asked her host, Alma, to borrow a screwdriver. Though Alma gave her an odd, suspicious look, she found one that looked perfect: small and sharp.

Back in her room, Zoe shut the door and put the case up on the kitchenette counter. She fit the screwdriver in, jiggled it in the lock, and monkeyed around for ten minutes or so. Trying a different angle, she felt the metal release of the lock. Zoe pressed her thumbs against the latches and the aluminium case sprung open like a clamshell, its insides spilling out over the counter and onto the floor: letters, photos, and objects from her mother's past. She was on hands and knees retrieving everything when Alma called up to her in Spanish that there was someone to see her. A moment later, there was a rap on her door.

"What!"

"It's Bertram."

Shit. The beach, her fears, Bertram had promised a swimming lesson today, and drunk as she'd been at dinner, Zoe had agreed. She'd forgotten about the whole silly business. This was her penance for getting up close and personal with strangers, even ones as beautiful as Bertram.

Zoe went to the door, opening it partway, hiding behind it.

"So," he said, "have I been rightly stood up?"

He was dressed in pale blue trunks and a gauzy cotton shirt, the type Mexicans peddled to tourists on the beach. Though he tried to smile for her, she could sense his disappointment.

"The day is perfect. We practically have the beach to ourselves and there's a breeze, though the water is calm. Not a usual combination here."

He sounded nervous. Well, so was she. "It's not a good time for me. I've got something—"

She saw the contraction in his eyes, the colour of Larimar

stones. "Well then, we can arrange another time," Bertram said, his voice too chipper. He glanced at the spill of objects scattered on the floor. "I see you're getting sorted. Are you comfortable here?"

Zoe nodded, "It's fine. And cheap, which is what matters," gathering her mother's things in both arms and tumbling them back inside the case, lowering, but not closing its lid; the contents would have to wait. She'd spent a good deal of her life putting lovers off. At twenty-eight, she had yet to have a relationship that lasted more than six months; her last boyfriend dubbed her a runner. True enough. Right now, she couldn't figure out which possibility spooked her more, facing the sea, or sifting through the contents of the case.

"Give me a minute."

"Take your time."

In her room, Zoe pulled on a black maillot and slipped a sundress over her head, grabbed a towel, and joined Bertram.

Together, they walked down the dirt road back to the hotel and then descended the steep, winding stairs that led directly onto the beach.

"This would be a kind of paradise ... for most people," she said, half to herself, half aloud.

Bertram put his hand on the small of her back as they walked abreast to the bamboo trellis. He lifted his shirt over his head, and after a moment of shyness, Zoe pulled off her dress and left it in a heap, tossing her towel on top.

The sea appeared tranquil and Zoe watched the gentle shushing surf, the blinking sparkles rushing toward her, then receding, rushing, then receding; they mesmerized her, then made her afraid, like bits of shattered glass. These sparkling shards had sucked her mother in and under, and even her father who had been such a strong swimmer. The sea sizzled with menace.

She remembered her first "swim" again. Often, it came back to her in nightmares. She was happily building a sand castle with her mother at Lake Isle, fashioning it after the city of Valletta through her imagination, since she'd only seen pictures. It was one of those times when she felt close to her mother, nearly in love, as they laughed, sand filling their laps, the miniature city theirs alone. All at once, her father burst in on their perfect miniature world, lifting Zoe about the waist. Later, she would find red imprints on the soft skin of her belly that turned purplish-blue. He marched down to the water's edge, flipped her upside down and over his shoulder into the fireman's carry. She kicked and screamed, pounded his back with tiny fists. There was a leap in her belly as she was flipped upright and hurled into deep water. A brutal slap, then she plunged under into a dark grey world, sinking, sure she would die. At last her father's arms were around her, surging her up through water to air. She was four years old.

Zoe felt a light hand on her shoulder. "It's going to be all right."

"What if we get into trouble?" she asked, as he started to make his way down to the shoreline. "The sea can change."

"I'm here."

"There's no lifeguard."

"I am a lifeguard, worked countless summers doing it in Cornwall."

Bertram reached for Zoe's hand and they walked down to the water's edge. The rush and pull of the waves made her recoil.

"I can't do it." The feeling surged up again, the grey viscous water sucking her down, not being able to breathe, see, be.

"Let's get our feet wet." Bertram stayed calm, his eyes steady. He tugged on Zoe's hand, pulling her gently down to the water's edge. "Let's just sit awhile."

They sat facing the sea watching the roll of waves.

"Just let the water wash over you. Get comfortable with it. Makes a treat, doesn't it?"

Zoe laughed. She loved the way he spoke; it charmed her, those British locutions. The surf came in, frothing, its foamy edge tickling her feet and hands, which burrowed into the moist, wet sand. The wave washed over her thighs, then drew out.

They sat for some time, the waves rushing in and covering Zoe's feet, calves, thighs, sometimes reaching her waist. She leapt up, her body sucking free of the moist sand. Bertram coaxed and settled her back down. "Right."

"Bertram, I know *how* to swim, my father made sure of that. I had some lessons as a kid. I can do crawl, breaststroke. I'm not very good, mind you, but I can do it. I'm not happy even in a pool, but the bigger and darker and more infinite the body of water, well...." Zoe began to build a gothic castle, dribbling wet sand into towers and turrets.

"Let's go out a bit."

"I'm happy right here."

"Quite."

They had a laugh together, the sound muffled by the rush and whoosh of waves. "I'm going to get knocked down, pulled under."

"I won't let you." He looked at her steadily and she felt a sudden firing of desire, which was stronger than her fear of the waves, or a part of it.

"Let's go in now," Bertram said, "farther out."

He swept his arm around her waist, and as the wave pulled, he let it bear them both out; laying Zoe on her belly, he kept one arm around her. Strangely, the physical motions of his strong hands positioning and protecting her brought back her father, but a gentler, kinder version of him.

"Let's swim parallel to the waves," Bertram said. "Do your breaststroke."

He let her go and immediately a huge wave broke over her head. Underwater, a roar in her ears, panic; she couldn't surface.

Bertram grabbed her about the waist and her head emerged, as she breathed in deep and hard, her lungs burning. He tugged her in, lifting her high each time a wave broke, so that her head managed to stay above most of them.

When they were in shallow water, he let her go, and she

found her feet, running out of the sea.

Bertram stepped out after her, shaking his head, his silver hair gleaming.

"That wasn't so bad now, was it? You survived."

"Barely."

"Tomorrow, we'll have another go."

"I can't. I've got to get back to Malta." All through the day, Cal's anxious voice simmered just below the surface.

"Is everything all right?"

Zoe felt a visceral wave of panic. "I don't know. My younger brother's there alone. Supposedly, he's okay, but a friend's in trouble."

"I'm sorry. Can I help?"

"Thank you," she said, resting her hands on Bertram's shoulders. "I want to stay in touch with you."

Bertram pulled her into his chest and they hugged tightly for a long moment, Zoe beguiled by this man and longing to know more of him. She couldn't remember the last time she'd made room for such a feeling.

Back in her room, Zoe collapsed on the bed, still in her wet bathing suit, patches of sea salt coating her skin and reached for her mother's aluminium case, spreading its contents out on the coverlet. Then she peeled off her suit and wrapped herself in a robe, studying the papers, photographs, and objects one by one. A beautiful little diary caught her eye, small enough to fit in the palm of her hand.

Its stiff covers were time-worn, the corners bent and frayed, but the pattern and colours were still beautiful, traditional Italian marbleized paper in tones of pink, mauve, purple, and cream.

She opened the little book and ran her fingers over pages and pages of writing in Maltese, a large, loopy scrawl that looked difficult to decipher in places as some entries were crossed out and written over, or erased, with a new thought recorded on top of old smudges. It would be slow going at first, though

Zoe's nine months living and working in Valletta had refreshed her fluency. The first entry was dated in April, 1968, and was quite short.

As Zoe read it, she felt a tingling in her blood, like the vibration before sound. The diary was Yael's.

20. YAEL

Given to me by Abba, April 5, 1968
Fl-aħħar. Kollha tiegħi stess xi ħaġa.
Abba gave me this diary today. He bought it in a Sicilian shop that specializes in marbleized papers and handmade books, promising another when this is filled ... it's so fat, I know I'll have it for a long time. At last, something of my own.
Waħdu. I ħtieġa li jkun waħdu.
Alone. I need time to myself....
Need to write when Cassandra's not around, hide my book. Her motto: what's yours is mine.
Writing is not for her, looking is. Can't see her sitting all alone, by herself, with herself. I'm in one of my hiding places—Prince Alfred's Courtyard behind Pinto's Clock. What a grandiose object! Makes me laugh. Four dials: time, day, month, and phases of the bloody moon! I have hiding places all over Valletta, secret places at home.
Cassandra is out shopping for summer dresses with Ima and Gisi, their pet. Mum invited me but her eyes spooked me. There's hurt, anger, whenever she looks at me. Never would have adopted me if she knew she'd get pregnant anyway with a beautiful baby girl who looks just like her. I'm too dark, too skinny, with a humongous schnoz. A spine that sticks out through the skin of my back, a chain Cassandra rubs bone by bone, her lucky charm.

July 7, 1968
I'm happy hiding, writing in my book, or when I'm with

Abba. C hides behind the camera—untouched.

Maybe I'm lucky. If someone loves me, they love me for me. If someone loves C, they may love her green eyes or perfect skin, the graceful line of her jaw. How will Cassandra know if someone loves her for her ... or just her perfect image?

Biex ikunu sbieħ, anki għal jum!

To be a beauty, even for a day! Just to see what it feels like.... Here's the thing: when we're together, I'm beautiful, too ... or more ugly by contrast. Which?

I see her! She's come looking for me. Upper Barrakka Gardens, behind Les Gavroches.

July 29, 1968

Abba is up north in Canada—Montreal—seeing cousin Ezra Goldberg. The guy manages some big fancy jewellery store called Birks. I've got various cousins up in Canada, none of whom I've met. Abba talks about Nathan and Zipporah Bernstein who distribute his jewellery to Eaton's and other department stores. I begged him: let me come! Fold me into your big red suitcase. I'm good at bunching myself up, making myself small. "No, Spidey, wish I could, but you need to stay in school." Screw school.

School is not necessary or relevant for me. I want to make jewellery, do my own designs, like Abba—I can learn everything I need to know from him. In school I'm just passing time.

Cassandra is popular. I am tolerated ... by association.

More and more I've been thinking and wondering about where I came from. What it's like in Morocco. Abba found me in a Marrakech orphanage, but I don't know why my mother gave me up, or even who she is or was. My father, too. I'm curious, need to find them. It's weird coming out of a void, but I can be whomever I want to be. Cassandra's not so lucky. Expectations of her are huge.

I don't like wanting what she has.

I want, I need, I, I, I. I jagħmlu *myself* kultant morda.

When we were little, I loved sharing a lunch box, a schoolbag, a room, a bed … at this point, I've had it. Enough.

We do have the best talks, late at night. Ima, Gisi, even Abba, have no idea what we discuss: our private dreams, the boys we're in lust with, the feeling. I taught C how to get the feeling climbing ropes and it's become an addiction for both of us.

August 9, 1968
Dejjem flimkien. Iż-żewġ minna bħala waħda.

Always together. C says she wants the two of us to be together always. I'll design jewellery, she'll do photography. Living as a dynamic duo is NOT *for me. I'm antsy, suffocating on this tiny island. All I've known is this lonely land surrounded by water. Hemmed in. Got to get out of here, but how, when? Abba's got those cousins up in Canada. I want to see snow, bet it's beautiful. Both cousins are in the jewellery business and have good connections.*

Papa speaks now and then of having grandchildren. It's weird, I see them before I see a man, their father. I do want to have kids some day. C is 100% positive that she does not *want children. Why? Why not? I don't get it exactly.*

She can't stand the idea of pregnancy, says, having a human (hopefully) growing inside her. Halved and doubled—it's a science fiction nightmare when you picture it, she tells me. No, it's a miracle.

We are halved and doubled. And you love it. You and me and me and you.

September 3, 1968
Abba is back from a trip to Marrakech. He showed me the gems he's going to work with. They're beautiful in their rough form and beautiful after he cuts them. He gave me a piece of black tourmaline, for luck, which I keep inside that aluminium

*case he found for me to show my pieces around to clients. I
feel like 007!*

*Abba is glued to the television, listening to reports about
the Vietnam War. Americans are protesting and Abba is also
against the conflict, as we all are. War begets war, no beginning
and no end.*

Sept. 19, 1968

*Tomorrow, after school, Max Ellul will be coming to Abba's
workshop. Abba is training him to cut raw stones and gems.
We'll learn together.*

*Red hair, freckles, eyes that change colour like a mood ring,
from green to brown to blue. Magic eyes.*

*Last time we were all in the shop, he admired some of my
designs, one for a pendant that I engraved with a two-line
inscription that is known as the first sign that the Jewish
people landed on Gozo. I've written it like the original, in
the Phoenician alphabet, "To the love of our Father Jawe."
This inscription is near the inner apse of the southern temple
of Ggantija in Xaghra, on the ground under your feet. Abba
took me there when I was very small, only three years old.
The pendant is shaped into a menorah.*

*I get nervous around Max and am afraid I'll cut my finger
off with one of Abba's tools. Does Abba see how much I'm
crushing on Max?*

*I hope I'll have a boyfriend soon, I hope that it will be
Max. Cassandra says she has no time for a boyfriend and
no use either.*

*The pendant I made is beautiful, if I say so myself. I used
eighteen-carat gold and the menorah is studded with rubies
for the flames. If you think of a menorah as a tree, my en-
graving is on the trunk. Hanukkah is coming and I could give
the necklace to C. Not sure. I could sell it, put it in Abba's
catalogue, or keep it. Cassandra. That's who I made it for; its
beauty suits her.*

Oct. 3, 1968
Abba's passion is to keep our small community strong. The Catholics tolerate us; many are friendly. I haven't felt prejudice here for being a Jew, but being black does not go over so well, especially as I am in a family of white folks. Strangers don't know what to make of us, of me. They need a story.

Am I a Jew? Because I was raised by Jews?
I don't fit in with our cosy little community.

Wonder what faith my blood parents are—or were. Morocco is mostly Moslem, so I suspect my parents are too. Will I ever find out? Lately, I'm obsessed. It's not a question I can ask my family. It would hurt Abba and turn Ima against me even more.

Sometimes I feel she's embarrassed to have me as her daughter since I don't look like her biological child. Don't act like it either. When I can't be bothered to take a bath, or wear the same jeans and T-shirt two days running, that alone drives her spare. Yet I know she loves me. I feel it, like sun through clouds.

April 11, 1969
Jiena fl-imħabba.

Nearly every day now, Max comes to Abba's shop and we work on designs. Some days C is with us, too, photographing for Abba's catalogue. I love when it's just Max and me.

Abba brought back the most beautiful Berber beads from Marrakesh. Silver filigree inlaid with triangles and circles of coloured enamel: blue, gold, and green. Max admires them, and we both had the idea to make them into cufflinks.

I can describe a design I see in my mind's eye and he knows exactly what I'm talking about. We can bounce ideas back and forth. I can lay my head against him, in the crook between his shoulder and chin. We fit.

Ughh. 45 RPM love song alert.

I'm so freaked out when I'm around him—like I'm going to throw up.

We eat lunch together at school, sit next to each other on Shabbat, Abba leading the service unless there is an official rabbi visiting from Israel. Abba calls himself first among equals, because he is not a rabbi himself. Every now and then, I lean in and whisper something sarcastic into Max's ear. But he believes. Not a good tack.

April 15, 1969

Today was the pits. I don't want to re-live it through writing, BUT need to get the poison out of my system. At lunch, Max sat with C and me, but settled beside her. Could not keep his eyes off my witch of a sis. On her come-hither green-for-go eyes.

… But C doesn't care!

I hate her.

April 17, 1969

Għandi tama darb'oħra.

Shred of hope. Max and I had a talk. He fears his father who wants him to become a rabbi because this "calling" is not for him. I told him about my wish to find, or at least find out about, my blood family. He gets me.

We have a spring end-of-school dance, Spring Fling. Cheesy for sure, could anything be more lame? But I want to go with Max.

Could be a blast. We'll dance all night, then jump into the Med off the seawall. There's an after-party and a breakfast.

I need Max Ellul to take me to the Bloody-Stupid-Spring-Fucking-Fling.

April 20, 1969

This afternoon Ima has her fundraising meeting for the Manoel. I'm going to check out her walk-in closet with C. C thinks I look great in the pop-art mini, its pinks and purples are my colours. I definitely want to borrow it. Stuffed

*the thing into the way back. Not safe. Crumpled it onto
the floor, where Ima will never find it, and hopefully, Gisi
won't bother to notice when she's cleaning. Good to know
C's on my side.*

April 22, 1969
Boghod. Habi.

Hiding. Down at the seawall. State of shock.

*Today Ima was supposed to be at a meeting and it was
Gisi's shopping time, so I cut school while my class was off
on a field trip.*

*I'm in the closet, so to speak, Ima's walk-in. Flipping through
hangers like a madwoman and still can't find The Dress. Then
I remember: crumpled on the floor. So while I'm crawling
around down there, looking, I hear Ima laughing and a man's
voice. They're laughing and talking and holy shit! Coming for
the bedroom.*

*I slide the door closed, crouch down behind Ima's racks
of dresses. It's hot and stuffy in there, but I try not to move,
even breathe.*

*Can't believe what I'm hearing. Ima is saying something
about it being okay, the house is empty, the girls are at school,
and Menash won't be back till late.*

*"Come here," the man says. I recognize his voice, but I'm
not sure. But they've got more important stuff on their minds.*

Their laughter again.

*The quiet and heat is too much inside the closet. I hear the
clop of a shoe, the click of heels, a whoosh of silk, tear of a
zipper.*

*The headboard creaks, I hear them murmuring. There is the
barest rustling, maybe the sheets? Then their breathing, panting
like dogs. Low, quick, Ima moans, he coaches her in hoarse
whispers. I hear the wet slap of their bodies, then a terrible*

banging, as if someone's head or fist were slamming against the headboard and the door to the bedroom opens with a little click, then a whine.

Silence. It's C. I recognize her step.

A loud squeak and rustle, heavy thuds. The man leaving?

"Come in," Ima says. Lighter steps follow, the slide of the bolt.

C says she's sick with a migraine. Ima is in a panic, makes Cassandra promise not to tell Abba about what's gone on with Zev. So it is Zev. C gives her word.

April 23, 1969

C didn't tell me anything, kept it all inside. She took meds for her migraine, slept and slept. I was shell-shocked, sad in a way I've never felt before. Like I'd lost something, we all had, that we could never get back. I wanted to talk it all over with Cassandra. But she withdrew.

Sometime in the middle of the night, Cassandra woke up. I could feel a current running from her nerves into mine.

C undid the buttons on my nightgown one by one. The nightgown fell away. I was awake, naked, but didn't stop her. I let her touch me, my belly, my flat chest. She took my nipple into her mouth until it rose inside her lips. I couldn't stop her, or myself. I thought of Ima, Zev. I'd heard them all worked up, rousing me, everything ruined, our family.

My eyes squeezed tight, a burning between my legs, and I touched C until her back arched and her belly rose, our breathing fast, sharp, until we both got the feeling.

Cassandra sealed her hand over my mouth, her lips over my lips.

Her hands, her lips caressed every part of me—planes, nooks, hollows. I pulled her hair hard, bit her lip. Cassandra's fingers plunged inside of me. I couldn't resist her. Didn't want to.

When we lay still, quiet, Cassandra murmured over and over. A promise or a threat. We'll always be together Ya-Ya. Always. The two of us. You and me.

I belonged to her.

I couldn't sleep. My hands and feet were shaking, but the rest of me felt heavy, nearly dead.

Then the shame oozed in, or was it out? Hot, sweaty, a stink to it. I'd have that bad odour about me always. Hidden inside, or maybe others could smell it on me.

When I heard C's slow steady breaths, I untangled myself, went to my desk, took out my pen, and wrote a letter to Abba about what I knew, who I'd seen: witnessed. I became Cassandra. Wrote in her hand. (It was too easy.) Broke the promise she'd made to Mum not to say anything.

When I finished the last sentence, my fingers tingled. I was myself again. I could forget about what I let happen between me and C.

I crept downstairs and left the note for Abba.

Back in our room, I swept clothing, toys, and books off the second bed, slipped into it and fell asleep. I tista 'tieħu n-nifs.

I could breathe.

April 24, 1969

Cassandra's taken off for a bit. I should feel guilty, but don't. Abba should know what's going on in his own bed, and Mommy Dearest deserves what she gets.

Frankly, it felt good when Cassandra's perfect little handwriting flowed out of my pen. Miss Perfect. Perfect in every way. If only people knew....

April 25, 1969

I can't sleep. I'm tossing and turning, so I'll just stay up. Write it all out. I was looking forward to having this room, this bed to myself. C is staying with her friend, Sarah. Looking forward to spreading my arms wide, stretching out my legs, turning over fast, feeling alone. At last. But I have my thoughts, which are not good.

I'm thinking over everything that's happened in our family. How we can't turn back, how the future won't be just more of the past.

I'm wondering if I'll ever have a normal life, a boyfriend. Wondering about so many things. What if I hadn't said anything to Abba about Mum shagging Zev, Abba's best "friend." Cassandra would have kept her promise to keep Mum's secret. I would've told Cassandra that I was hiding inside the closet and saw and heard everything that she did.

If neither of us had told Abba, we'd still have each other. What then, then what, what if?

April 26, 1969

I'm trying to picture what life is going to be like when C comes back home. Nothing will be the same. Can anyone forgive and forget? Even if I confessed my betrayal, there would still be Mum's, and everyone would despise me anyway.

April 27, 1969

Awake again. Insomnia is pure torture. It's hard for me to think about my sister, now. Me and C, C and Me.

April 27, 1969

I've had no sleep for several nights, running from crazy. I want Cassandra home and yet not. Gisi's knocking.

* * *

My clock says three a.m., the whole family, except for me and Gisi, are fast asleep. C still at Sarah's.

Gisi burst in on me a few minutes ago.

Writing a book?

I need to get some sleep.

She sat her fat bottom on my bed so close I could smell her breath, sweet and rotten as the insides of a spoiled fruit. She told me to leave home, go far away and not come back. The woman is a wicked snoop who sees and knows everything. About everyone.

When she left my room, I was shaking.

I need to get out of here. Start somewhere new. I've been desperate to leave Malta anyway. I've got money: savings from birthday gifts and my jewellery pieces. Enough to last maybe a year—if I'm careful and go somewhere cheap. I know Abba loves me. If I need money or help, I can turn to him. I pack up, scrawl a quick note to C, and one to Mum and Dad. Can they ever understand? I'm a prisoner on this lonely island. Enough. Off on my own at last. Free.

PART IV: THE OTHERS

21. CAL

A military guard brought Aziza into the visiting area, a windowless room with a cracked concrete floor, veins of grit and sand wedged into its fissures. As much as he'd tried to prepare himself, Cal was not ready for the sight of her. He looked away for a moment to arrange his features, if only for her sake. She was all sucked out, her once proud posture concave, shoulder blades like wings, the spurs of her hips sharp through torn cotton pants. Her smooth caramel skin was now ashen and blotched. It was painful to see her dark eyes watery and bloodshot, purplish crescents notching the delicate skin beneath them.

When she spotted Cal, she opened her mouth and a long spiralling sound like the cry of an ambulance spewed out of her with a life of its own. The guard steadied her and whispered something into her ear and Aziza immediately covered her mouth, a gesture all too familiar, Cal's own.

He caught a glimpse of his face reflected dully in a random rectangle of stainless steel nailed into the wall, relieved to see he had on his ordinary everyday expression. Just outside graceful, historic Valletta was this parallel world, several circles of hell with thousands of prisoners. Too easy to pretend these "centres" crammed with humans didn't exist.

The guard led Aziza to a plastic chair behind a metal table and Cal sat facing her on the other side. He wanted to speak, to say something, anything.

"What are you doing?" Aziza's voice was cold, flat.

Some days he had no idea, playing with Tonio who was growing plump and pampered, listening to Legend and Common and Mary J., creating fake backdrops of woods and castles with rubber knives and ketchup blood and foil crowns and papier mâché heads, and swimming and swimming farther out each day or night until he could no longer think or feel his body, but also staying on Aziza's case, investigating the best way to get her the hell out of here. Connecting with Roger and Anne Fortier in Montreal about sponsoring her—surely her best chance at freedom—hashing out the bureaucratic details, though they couldn't rely on just one option.

"I'm getting help."

Aziza looked away. "Why?"

Cal could hear cacophony from the adjacent rec room, the blare of a TV, children shouting and crying, people babbling, the blare of orders through a microphone. All the other Others.

Having lifted Aziza half-dead out of the Mediterranean, Cal felt responsible for her, yet half-capsized himself. If he could only help her, one person.

"I talked to my sister last night. I expect she'll be home soon. I know her—she'll want to help you." Not that Zoe had any special pull or powers.

Aziza's hands fluttered like trapped butterflies. "I took her things, she will hate me. I am not a thief."

Cal shook his head. "None of that matters. Don't even think about it."

"I don't know what to think about."

Cal pulled his chair as close as he could, the metal table edge pressing into his belly. "This. I talked to Roger Fortier in Montreal and he's filed an application with Immigration Quebec's Refugee Service. He's sending documents for you, so that you can obtain temporary travel papers."

"Is this really to happen?"

"Yes. Aziza, listen. Documents will arrive for you care of the authorities, in order for the Fortiers to sponsor you, and to get those travel papers. Fill out the sheets with your full name, date and place of birth, and the same information for your mother and father. Don't forget your address in Tripoli. Did you always live there? The names and addresses of your schools, dates you attended. Say what happened to your father, what you know, and what you don't know. Write it all down. Okay?" His voice came out firm and strong, as if it belonged to another guy.

Aziza nodded.

"Like I said, help is coming. We hope you'll have a place with the Fortiers in Montreal. Keep your mind on that."

Aziza smiled slowly. "I received a letter, then a phone call from Dr. and Mrs. Fortier. They are hopeful I will be able to join them but—"

"Yes," Cal broke in.

"But how long will this take? I don't know how much longer I can hold on inside here."

Cal looked at the guard who was picking his fingernails and drinking a cup of coffee out of a styrofoam cup.

"I don't know exactly," he said, "but I'm trying to find out. I'll call you with any updates and I'll visit again if I'm allowed to. Hang on."

They sat for a short while longer, Aziza asking Cal again about what he was doing and about Zoe's trip away. Cal could see how it both drained and heartened her, this new effort to make ordinary conversation, a moment mimicking normalcy. He remembered that same feeling when he first went to see his old shrink Dr. Rose. A capsule of safety within the see-through dreads and the world too bright, too harsh, outlined in ugly black ink and coloured in with blinding hues.

Soon the guard called an end to the visit. Aziza stood and Cal took both of her hands in his, hers dry as bark. "Soon," he whispered as they led her away, and he stepped outside gulping hungry breaths of Malta's fresh salt sea air.

22. ZOE

NOTES: *Marranos, conversos. Jewish families like ours borrowed names from the animal world: Leon (lion), Carneir (sheep), Lobo (wolf); some from trees (Pinheiro, pine), or Oliveira (olive tree); even geography, Serra (mountain range), Rios (river), Vales (valleys). Within the same family, members used different names from each other. Inside/Outside names, Inside/Outside selves.*

Flying over the ocean, Zoe dreams of a girl. Thin and green, tough as seaweed. Arms and legs flung wide, she plunges beneath the surf, a live pulse like gills beneath her skin. Starfish, seasleeper. All colour, life, and motion above. She rises, breaks the surface, soars into bright air. A bird heading who knows where.

Zoe awoke from her dream and sat very still crushed against the plane's window, stirred by being this fishbird, this birdfish.

It was already July and walking back to the flat very late, she realized she had been gone for just over two weeks, though it had felt like an emotional journey of months and years. Letting herself in, a fusty stink assailed her senses.

Cal rushed into the foyer and gave her a bone-crushing hug, then lifted her into his arms which had become strong and sinewy with muscle, no doubt from building sets at the Manoel.

"Sorry I've been an outlaw sis," Zoe said. "You sounded really upset over the phone. What's that smell?"

Zoe dropped her bags in the foyer and shook out her aching wrists, collapsing onto the couch and closing her eyes for a moment. When she opened them, a creature sprang into her lap and crouched there, making strange yowling sounds. Zoe felt her entire being harden from the outside in, as if she had been dipped in plexiglass; she dared not move a muscle or flutter an eyelid.

"What is *that*?" She was petrified, spaces yawning between each word. Her skin prickled as if it had fallen asleep and was coming back to life again.

"You mean *who*. Tonio, my cat."

The cat, more like a baby tiger, with light and dark swirls of orange, copper, and cream, jumped roughly out of Zoe's lap and stalked over to Cal who stooped to caress him, burying his face in the cat's plush fur.

"Is this a joke?"

"He's not going to hurt you."

"What's he doing here?"

"Tonio was homeless, abandoned, followed me into the flat. He was starving, Zoe, and no one came to claim him. I've taken care of everything—he's up-to-date with his shots and we've got a really great vet—vets are among the nicest humans I've ever met, by the way."

We've got a vet? She couldn't fucking believe this. How dare he? Zoe grabbed her bags and stomped up to her room, stowing the aluminium case and its treasures in a wide drawer, covering it with stacks of tops. When she came back into the living room, Cal was playing with the cat, throwing a toy shaped like a mouse, watching him pounce, again and again.

Alarmed, she looked around, didn't see her well-organized piles of notes that she had left just so, everything needed to be in its place or something vital could get lost, and once lost, it could stay missing, gone for ever. "Where is my work, my notes? I had everything in order under special rocks I found by the sea."

"I had to move your stuff. Tonio likes to play with, well, just about everything." Cal laughed, then threw the mouse toy again and the cat caught it in mid-air and began to gnaw its rubber flesh.

"I stacked all your notes and put them inside your night table upstairs."

Great. Now it would take hours, maybe days to sort out her notes and even her thoughts. Her piles had been systematic, organized the same way her ideas existed inside her head. Now it was one big jumble. How would she ever find her focus?

"Put him in his crate. Now."

"Tonio doesn't have a crate."

"Well, get him out of here." This was her place and he was her guest. How could this have happened in a matter of weeks? Cal taking over.

He lifted the cat, snuggling it against his chest, and carried it upstairs to the loft bedroom. Zoe heard the door click shut and could finally let the air out of her chest. Her terror subsided and she let him have it.

"Cal, what the *hell* were you thinking?"

He shook his head, oblivious, his lips making that weird twitch he got when he was anxious or upset.

"I'm allergic!"

Cal's lower lip curled, his eyes squinting into slits. "Are you having a reaction now?"

"Fuck you. I'd call this a reaction. Cats live twelve to fifteen years!"

"It's one of the many things I love about them. Tonio will be good for both—"

"I'm not a cat person."

"Could have fooled me. Seriously, Zo, maybe you'll become one. Tonio and me, we've become very attached to each other. There are lots of studies—cat owners are less likely to die of heart disease and have a decreased risk of non-Hodgkin's lymphoma."

"Good to know." She paced the living room, exhausted and wired at once, rancid from the recycled plane air, stale from the invasion of Cal and cat.

"Pet owners have better self-esteem, are more fit, less lonely, more conscientious, extroverted, less fearful, less lonely, anxious, and whatnot."

"*Whatnot*? You said, 'less lonely' twice." So he was putting a sheen on the situation with a whole bunch of verbiage. "This whole place stinks!"

"I'll clean out Tonio's litter box. You know, I've had more pressing problems, lately, and I really need to talk to you about something urgent. The cat, the litter box, well, as Dad used to say, it's not a priority for right now."

Zoe went into the kitchen, opened the fridge and took out a half-finished bottle of Sauvignon Blanc. She poured herself a big glass and sat at the kitchen table where she could not hear that bloody cat yowling to be let out.

Cal came in to join her. "Give me a minute." She sat gulping wine as he cleaned out the litter box and put out fresh water and cat food. "I want to let Tonio out now. You need to get used to each other."

Zoe objected but he went upstairs anyway and released the feline prisoner. She strained to control her fear; it made her terribly ashamed, but it was visceral and instinctive. Tonio trotted into the room like he owned the place and went to his food bowl.

"It's okay, Zoe, he won't bother you."

"So what's going on?"

Cal opened the fridge and helped himself to one of the many bottles of beer crammed in there in lieu of nourishment. Then he told her how he'd found a girl floating in the sea, barely alive, that the small battered fishing boat on which she'd journeyed from Tripoli to Malta had capsized in a storm and that she was the sole survivor. This young girl, Aziza, was hoping to find asylum in Malta, but was now incarcerated in one of the island's detention centres, warehousing the tidal wave of migrants from North Africa.

"I hid her here for a while," Cal said, nursing his beer.

He was unbelievable, her brother, Mr. Saint and Saviour par excellence. "Was that before, or after, your cat rescue?"

"Stop. Did you hear what I just said?"

She sat very quietly for a moment, taking it all in.

"I've been reading about the crisis, these so-called centres. Why didn't you tell me sooner?"

"It wasn't phone fodder. And frankly, you seemed pretty busy yourself."

So much had been going on that they each had been keeping to themselves.

"I really need to find out more about our family—I have lots to tell you, but all that can wait." Zoe took a long sip of the wine that was crisp and slightly fruity and went straight to her head, since she'd eaten so little on the trip back home.

"Apparently, there are four 'open' centres run by the government," Cal explained, "and six closed centres. The three larger ones are managed by the military and the three smaller ones by the police. There are about a dozen or more centres run by the church and a number of NGOs. Aziza is stuck in one of the worst places, The Lyster Barracks, run by the army. Overcrowding, poor hygiene, a couple of functioning toilets. I just visited her there."

Zoe shook her head as the cat went under the table and brushed Cal's legs, raising the hair on the bare skin of Zoe's forearms and calves.

"You have no idea. Some migrants have been locked up for five years, from what I've learned. In '05, they set the limit at eighteen months, but after that time, asylum seekers are just transferred to another centre. Open, whatever that means. They don't get a work permit."

That evening, Zoe sat with Cal as he made calls to a half-dozen people he knew in Malta who were working on behalf of migrants, as well as to other contacts, whom those people recommended that he talk to. He phoned leaders at the Jesuit Refugee Service who were aiding migrants in the Detention Centres. Later on that night, Cal contacted a human rights lawyer that was a good friend of Zoe's in New York, both of them not registering until it was too late that Cal had woken him up in the middle of the night, as New York was six hours ahead of Valletta time. Groggy as he was, the lawyer promised to contact an immigration specialist he knew in Quebec, and to get back in touch with Cal the following day with advice. Cal told Zoe about Aziza's one contact with that Montreal family she'd worked for in Libya.

Well, while she'd been off on her mission, her little brother had grown up—fast.

"I'm tempted to talk to Serena," Zoe said. "She's connected to virtually everyone here on the island. And she's become a friend."

"Not a good idea—I know Serena's views on the migrant situation. The Fortier family is her best option ... but I have no idea how long it's going to take."

Zoe finished her wine and poured herself a second glass, grabbing another bottle of beer for Cal.

"I want to know what you've been up to," he said.

Zoe needed to think about everything that had happened here, and in Mexico. She had uncovered a good deal and was still absorbing what she'd learned about her mother and her lost sister, Yael, some of which she wanted to share with Cal, but now was not the time.

"It's awful what that young girl is going through. Not to mention all the others. Let me know what I can do." She was still pissed off about the cat, but proud of him.

Now she was desperate to unwind a bit; the wine would help and so would some good music. She got up, her body stiff and aching from travel, and opened the computer to her music. "You have to listen to this, Cal, it's from the Klezmer festival

in Israel, dozens of great bands, about six hours of music."
She turned it up top-volume and the cat skittered under the
couch, cowering. Perfect.

"Noooo!" Cal held his fingers in his ears.

"Mom liked this music, so did your grandpa."

"You're making stuff up."

Zoe got up and danced and swayed to her beloved Klezmer,
wineglass aloft, hoping the scary cat would keep away from
her for now.

23. CAL

Late summer and early fall passed with little progress for Aziza, though Cal now visited her once a week to keep her spirits up. Then, on Halloween night, Cal received a call from Dr. Fortier. At last, he was successful in getting Aziza admitted to Quebec by sponsoring her to work for his family as an au pair. He'd finally obtained a temporary travel document for her, as well as an airline ticket from Malta International Airport to Dorval in Montreal. Aziza would be escorted from the Detention Camp straight to the airport on November nineteenth under police supervision.

Cal shared the news with Zoe and then immediately called Aziza. She wept on the phone. When she could get words out, she said, "I feel like I am dug out from quicksand." She and Cal stayed on the line a bit longer, but Aziza grew anxious, afraid that there would be a hitch in the plan, that everything would not run smoothly, and she would remain incarcerated. Cal struggled to reassure her, but in truth, he shared her fears, scarcely able to believe in good news.

The night before Cal was to meet Aziza at the airport, he packed the clothing and essentials they'd bought for her into a duffel, while Zoe filled a small cooler with sandwiches, fruit, cookies, and juice. Cal was agitated and Zoe didn't seem herself either; sleep was out of the question, so they stayed up all night, chatting and drinking tea, while Zoe avoided Tonio. She seemed less terrified, but certainly wasn't bonding with the cat, either. Well, he'd be patient.

"Do you want me to go with you?" Zoe asked. "If you'd rather see her off on your own, I understand."

In one way, he longed to be on his own with Aziza, if only to say goodbye, and yet they wouldn't have any privacy, as she would be under police guard. If something went wrong, he'd need help.

"Come."

"Of course." She put her hand on his knee which was bobbing up and down of its own volition. "Now can you stop that jouncing and twitching, you're driving me crazy. We should try to get some rest, if not sleep."

Early the next morning, Cal and Zoe grabbed the duffel and cooler and headed to the airport. Cal held the one-way plane ticket to Montreal, provided and paid for by the Fortier family, who would meet Aziza at Dorval airport.

Aziza entered the airport flanked by two policemen. She looked much the same as she had on his visits to the Detention Centre, bone thin and ashen, her eyes with a lookout's gaze, darting and alert. When she saw Cal, she lit up, a lightning rod energy in her limbs, as she tried to come toward him, but the policemen restrained her.

Cal went over to the trio with Zoe by his side.

"I have Aziza Odissan's plane ticket to Canada. Can I talk to her a minute?"

"Until she boards the aircraft, she is required to be under police supervision to ensure that she leaves the country."

"I'm sure she'll be fucking thrilled to get out of here."

"Cal." Zoe squeezed his forearm so hard, she left the red imprint of her fingertips on his skin.

Anything Cal had to say to Aziza, he would have to say here, now, among this group including the two policemen, his older sister, and everyone else gathered in the hangar-like waiting and ticket area.

"We have some things for Aziza," Zoe addressed the two policemen. "We're local friends from here in Valletta. We've packed some clothes for her, a bit of food for the trip."

She tried to hand the duffel and cooler to Aziza who smiled at her, mouthing "thank you," as one of the policemen intercepted and took both.

Cal looked directly at Aziza, willing the rest of the crowd, even his sister, the world, to fall away. "You're going to be all right now. Just like I promised the day I pulled you from the sea." He scarcely knew what he was saying; he surely didn't feel that powerful.

She nodded, barely strength to move her head, which looked like a heavy flower on a fragile stem about to bend and break.

Despite the presence of the police guards, Cal moved in and hugged Aziza as she reached up and embraced him, still strong enough to press painfully against the back of his neck. It unnerved Cal how much her hug hurt and he let her clamp him with all her might until she was drained of force and the police guards tugged her away from him.

"Write to me," Cal said, "when you get settled. Ask the Fortiers to set you up on email, okay?"

"Please call us Aziza—after you rest up—so we know that you arrived safely," Zoe added. "Come to think of it, you'll be too tired, so ask Dr. Fortier to call us for you."

"I will," Aziza said. "Thank you for everything. And if you see Tella—"

Cal glanced away, then forced his gaze back to Aziza. "You've got a new life waiting."

Cal and Zoe lingered until Aziza was escorted through security and to her gate. They couldn't see whether she was able to claim and keep the duffel of clothing and cooler of food. As long as she got away, that's what mattered. Cal was reluctant to leave, to go back to the flat. The plane would not take off for another hour-and-a-half, and he insisted on waiting until it roared down the runway and rose into the sky. Away.

24.

The next day, Cal holed up in a storage room at the theatre, holding Macbeth's severed head between both hands. How light it felt, with the perfect expression of aggrieved surprise; he and Biagio had worked for days to get it just right. Bins held body parts—hands and legs of brightly moulded plastic, coloured glass eyes—doublets, hose and hooded cloaks, kumquat-size rubies and emeralds on heavy chains and studded foil crowns. Cal sat on the floor and spread out a white cloth set with a cannibal's feast. He plucked Macbeth's head from the centre of the "banquet table" and held it aloft.

Are you lost?

Macbeth's severed head nodded.

I was lost and then I found Tonio. Or Tonio found me. Lost and—

"Cal?" Serena stood in the doorway.

"Yes!" Cal grabbed sheets of tissue paper and wrapped a leg that began at the knee and ended with a foot, an odd shade of fleshy pink.

Serena glanced down at his installation.

"You like my *objet trouvé*?"

"Appetizing. Think you can get this lot cleaned, wrapped, and stored today?"

"Absolutely."

"So your friend got off all right up to Canada?" Her arms were crossed and her glasses down around the bridge of her nose.

"Hope so." He kept his head down, playing with a pair of golden glass eyes. He was lost and relieved now that Aziza was gone; though it was for the best, he missed being a part of her life. He couldn't look Serena in the eye, and though it made no logical sense, he blamed her in part for what had happened to Aziza. "Who the hell knows what will become of the hundreds of other migrants ... no, how about thousands?"

He got to his feet, leaving his ghoulish installation as it was.

"Cal," Serena said softly, "why are you angry at me?"

"Have you got any idea what goes on in those *centres*? Nice word...."

Serena closed her eyes slowly. The histrionic gesture made Cal's rage flare, gas to flame.

"It's a horrific problem, I know, but I don't have a solution. Our tiny island can't handle these floods of ... people. If only—"

"I think we maybe better not get into this discussion." Cal knew he sounded indignant, self-righteous, as though the situation was everyone else's fault but his own. Zoe had strong opinions, too, but she was more measured and realistic.

"Cal," she said, "there won't be as much work around here ... we're having an orchestra concert this coming Christmas, not a play."

"I get it."

She touched his shoulder lightly and he stiffened. "I'd still like help with the tours and I have some odd jobs for you, once you finish organizing the props and costumes from *Macbeth*."

Before Cal could answer, he heard Serena's heels clicking away.

That evening, Zoe was poring over some letters and photographs that she had spilled out onto the coffee table in the flat.

"How's it going?"

When she saw Cal looking at her, she loaded everything back into an odd-looking aluminium briefcase, the old-fashioned kind with a combination lock that no one used anymore because everybody carried a laptop. "What is *that*?' he asked pointing to the case and its contents. "You look like a character out of *Goldfinger* or something."

She laughed. "That's way before your time, Little."

"Don't call me Little, midget. What is it?"

Tonio stalked over and began licking the smooth cold surface of the case.

"He loves this thing," Zoe said, laughing.

Well, maybe Tonio was growing on her, she certainly seemed less terrified and the phantom allergies had never materialized. This was good, really good.

Zoe leapt up from the table and came over to him. "Anne Fortier called and Aziza is safe in Montreal."

Relief washed over him, a kind of joy. "Did you speak to her?"

"Yes, I just said—"

Tonio brushed Zoe's leg and she surprised Cal by reaching down and petting his orange swirls in an offhand way, perfunctory, but progress.

Of course he meant Aziza, not Anne.

"Oh no, I didn't speak to Aziza. She was sleeping. I bet she'll be doing a lot of that for a while."

Cal nodded, surprised by how much he longed to hear Aziza's voice. It was strange how he missed her, given how little they knew each other. He felt hollow with her gone, though grateful she was safe. Finally.

He went to boil water for tea. Once settled in his room with a big mug of English breakfast and Tonio snuggled in his lap purring like a machine, Cal started on a letter to Aziza. Except for his brief notes to her in detention, he couldn't remember the last time he had indulged in that ancient art.

At the theatre, Cal had more free time and wanted to do some painting. When he asked Serena if she knew anything about dirt cheap studio space, she surprised him by leading him to an empty store-room on the top floor of the theatre that wasn't being used and had decent light.

"You can work in here," she offered, as Cal cut his glance away. He'd felt at odds with Serena during the past few months, though rationally he knew it was unfair to single her out with blame for the migrant crisis in Malta, well, Europe for that matter.

"You're too nice to me."

"True."

Before Aziza's arrival on Malta, Cal had worked on his art casually, haphazardly, sketching and drawing in the cracks between his theatre commitments, his beers with the guys, his swims. The results didn't matter much; in fact, he worked hard not to want anything too much. Now, thanks to Serena—and Zoe—he could immerse himself in his art. The prospect both excited and terrified him. What if he was no good?

During the cooler fall and early winter months, Cal spent his free time in the newly-appointed studio painting and experimenting with mixed media. When he began in November after Aziza's departure, he felt tentative, the art critic's voice hectoring him inside his head, *that he wasn't it, just shit, didn't know what he was doing, doing shit*, but once immersed in a canvas, the static stilled, at least for a while.

He was thinking about Aziza all the time and wished he had a photograph of her, yet he had a nearly photographic memory of faces, of bodies. At the same time, his experiences with her—rescuing her at sea, caring for her in the flat, learning a bit about her life, working to free her from detention—began to seem surreal, as if they had happened in another time, in an other place, to a completely different person.

Nonetheless, he visualized her late at night when the city was asleep and found if he concentrated deeply, he could conjure the specificity of her features, her expressions, the way she stood, walked, even slept, and that a photograph might hinder the depth and breadth of these images by freezing them in time, making them fixed, static.

Cal filled a large sketchpad with drawings of Aziza in the sea, at his flat, wandering Valletta. After a few weeks of sketching, he moved to canvas and oils. His first piece was of her floating barely alive in the Mediterranean. Next, he did an impressionist piece of the fishing boat and the crowd of migrants packed onto it as it began to take in water and sink. Then there was a series of bodiless faces and faceless bodies inside the Detention Centre, which he had to paint through what he had heard and read and seen from mostly outside the compounds, except for his brief visits.

He wasn't happy with any of this work—except for some of the sketches—and these paintings embarrassed him, so he destroyed them all. Thankfully, no one had seen the work but him. However, he kept his drawings of Aziza and some of his sketches of Valletta.

During the fall, Cal walked for hours around Valletta, collecting junked mirrors, old wire hangers, mineral water bottles, even old nails from construction sites. He liked the edges of shattered mirrors, the weight and twisted shapes of nails, the translucent beauty and glossy colours of empty water bottles. He started to work with these found objects that had heft and a lonely beauty, though no more use in the world. He attached dozens of discarded bottles in greens, blues, yellows, and quartz-like white, shaping them into a linked chain that wrapped, leaned, and twisted into knots. The final shape was an enclosure with a circumference of twelve feet, suggesting links and chains.

He hammered the nails into an old puppy crate, which he then suspended from the ceiling, and converted into a light fixture.

For several weeks, he wandered Valletta collecting discarded cell phones. When he had hundreds of them, he built an interlocking modular system of dead mobiles, which made a totem pole nearly reaching the ceiling of his studio.

He'd always loved mosaic and wanted to try his hand at one, though on a larger scale. On his rambles around the city, he gathered broken bits of seawall and sea glass. Back in his studio, he built a simple wooden base fifteen by nine feet, and filled it with sand, then began shaping the shards into shattered faces in jigsaw pieces.

This piece consumed him for several months and working on it gave him a reason to get up each day and to rush back to his studio after he finished the tasks Serena had given him. As he set the intricate glass pieces into place, he put on Mary J., "My Life," *If you looked in my life/ And see what I've seen... /If you looked in my life/ And see what I've seen....* He was happier with this particular piece than he'd been with his paintings and sensed he'd found his métier.

Cal was in contact with Aziza via email (letters took too long to write, send, and receive), and every couple of weeks, he made a long distance call to Montreal. He tried to introduce Aziza to Skype, but it spooked her, even made her paranoid; she was convinced that if they could see each other on their screens, so could others. After all she'd been through, it made perfect sense. Their voices alone were good and talking to her without the threat of crisis hanging over them was new, though their conversations were awkward, with long silences.

"The children, they are improving my French," she said to him on a windy winter night, actually six p.m. his time, midnight, hers. "I have this very long way to travel."

"It's a beautiful language."

"Yes, beautiful, but so very hard to make right."

"And to write."

"The children love to correct me, especially Patrick and Caroline. It is their greatest fun and pleasure."

"The more languages you know, the better," Cal said, feeling stupid, not knowing what to say. He felt that a conversation was occurring beneath their words, that what they said didn't even matter so much because their true selves, their real lives and feelings vibrated beneath their voices. He wanted to show her what he'd been doing, particularly his floor mosaic.

"There is something I need to ask you."

His lips worked making shapes not sounds and he instinctively covered his mouth with his free hand.

"Tella? You did find her, yes?"

Cal cleared his throat, took a deep breath, stalling. "Yes, I did. She's okay, but frightened after everything she went through—you can understand that—given your own ordeal—"

"What is this ... or deal?"

"Sorry. Tough time, after what you went through, maybe you can understand her fear. Tella, no doubt, was afraid of being locked up in detention ... or being sent back to Libya. Sometimes people who we trust are...." He couldn't go on with any more platitudes; he felt idiotic.

"Not as large as we make them?"

"Exactement."

There was a long pause, the crackling line, both separating and joining them.

"I wake up and am in the sea," she said, "floating," her voice a thread across the line. "And then I am back in the desert walking and walking on hot white sand. Sometimes, I don't know where I am."

The blood rushed in his chest; if only they were face to face. "I wish I could see you," he said.

"Maybe some time you will come up to Montreal," she offered. "It is such a beautiful city and I love the snow, but I am not so usual."

He'd fantasized about a visit, could hardly believe she'd suggested it, and forgot to answer.

"So you are not liking this idea?"

Both he and Zoe were leaving Valletta at the end of the year, returning to New Jersey. As for visiting Aziza, there were trains from New York City to Montreal; it was fairly affordable and the long ride appealed to him. "No, no, I like it. Sounds like a plan."

"For in the future some time, to see how I am getting on. Soon we will be celebrating Christmas."

"Yeah, should be beautiful with all that snow."

"And you?"

It took him a while to respond, as his mind was on a possible visit, then he realized she was waiting for his answer. "Yeah, no. We'll be celebrating a holiday called Hanukkah. We'll be lighting eight lights. Actually, nine, if you count the *shamash*, the assistant candle used to light the others."

"Cal are you still there? So you will be lighting?"

"Yeah, it's the Festival of Lights. We'll be lighting maybe while you're lighting. Who knows? Well, maybe not at the exact same time exactly." He took a deep breath; why did he sound so ridiculous when he talked to her? He couldn't listen to himself anymore. "We'll do it."

25. ZOE

NOTES: *Mom told me Grandma said she was "British to the bone." You write, how can you go forward if you never turn around? Nannu, speak to me.*

Bit by bit, Zoe returned to her work in Valletta. Yael's diary had opened a startling window into her mother's bond with her lost sister. Yael was real to Zoe now, at least as a teen, but the diary was written thirty-nine years ago; if Yael were alive today, she would be fifty-six years old.

Zoe wanted to meet Max Ellul, Yael's old crush, and her beloved grandpa's protégé. As he had known her aunt around the time she'd fled Valletta, perhaps he'd have a clue as to where she'd gone and what had become of her.

Thanks to Cal's meeting with Max, she had his phone number and tried to call several times, but got no answer. An older couple Zoe had befriended during local Shabbat services told her that he ran a business in the heart of the craft village, so Zoe ventured out to Ta' Qali on a windy November day while Cal was busy at the Manoel Theatre in his studio.

Ta' Qali consisted of an odd cluster of ex-RAF Nissen huts on the road to Mdina, near the football stadium. A fellow craftsman pointed Zoe to a large central stall, presided over by a broad, bearded man and a lanky teen with glowering eyes and a scowl to match, dreaming of elsewhere. Max Ellul, most likely, maybe with his son.

Before introducing herself, Zoe took a look at the wares displayed inside the half-cylinder hut, as well as on the surrounding patchy lawn: models carved of globigerina limestone shaped into *kenur,* the traditional stone hearth for making stews, and for *luzzus,* the local wooden boats, as well as a selection of jewellery. A series of pendants displayed against burgundy velvet caught Zoe's eye.

The man lifted a mahogany box out of the jewellery case to give Zoe a closer look at the pendants: they were quarter-size discs with Hebrew letters carved in ebony and short messages engraved on their gold backs in Maltese: *tenaċità, immaġinazzjoni,* and *devozzjoni.*

"These are beautiful," she said. All three one-word messages spoke to her: tenacity, imagination, devotion.

The man looked as she imagined Max Ellul might: powerfully built and well-preserved with a neatly-groomed roan-coloured beard and a full head of red hair beneath a black silk yarmulke. Behind his wire-rimmed glasses, Zoe couldn't help noticing his hazel eyes, a brownish-green that day, reflecting the olive of his button-down shirt.

Magic eyes. Zoe remembered Yael's phrase from the diary, feeling the distant past collapse into the present, as it did every time she listened to Nannu's voice.

The man removed the burgundy velvet cushion from the wooden box in which the pendants nestled. He lifted one out and asked if Zoe would like to try it on.

She nodded.

"May I help you?"

"Thanks," she said as he fastened the clasp around her neck in a swift movement without grazing her throat. Reflected in the counter's mirror, Zoe studied the ebony carvings of swirls and spirals and the Hebrew letters which stood out against the gold setting; when Zoe flipped the pendant over to read the inscription, she saw that he'd chosen *tenacity,* just what she needed right now, though *devotion* would have been her pick.

"Are you on holiday in Malta?"

Zoe answered in Maltese, finally introducing herself.

Max came out from behind the table displaying his wares. "Why didn't you say so? I met your brother, Caleb, this summer. We had a beer together. What took you so long to find me?"

When Zoe first arrived on the island, Max was away in Israel, and by the time he returned, she was off in Mexico. Zoe breathed out in a long sigh. "I'm here now."

Max laughed. "Now is good."

"I know you knew my family, my grandpa, and my mother, of course—"

"Jonah!" Max called out. "Son, I need you to take over for a bit."

The teen slouched over, his features a surly mirror of his father's and told him he could stay for an hour, then had to take off.

"Come Zoe, do you have time for a chat?"

"Of course."

"There's a place nearby with good coffee."

Max led the way to the periphery of the craft village to a small café called *Gulepp* and quickly ordered two espressos and a plate of pastries. They sat outside on ladder-back chairs, the din and crowds a short distance away.

As the waitress set out their water, and then the espressos and pastries, Max shook his head, lowering his eyes. "I was terribly sorry to hear of your parents' deaths."

Zoe nodded her thanks.

Max placed a jam pastry on her plate with broad, strong hands and Zoe remembered from the diary how gifted he was in cutting gems and making jewellery, although he'd clearly expanded his offerings.

"I loved your Nannu, he was like a father to me. You see, I wasn't close to my own."

Zoe busied herself cutting her pastry, cautious about revealing how much she already knew.

Max sipped his espresso. "My father saw me as a rabbi, *his* dream. Your Nannu saw me for who I was and could be. Sounds corny, I know."

Zoe was moved by his words and wanted to learn more, to hear stories, anecdotes that she could squirrel away as treasures. And yet, Max *did* become an unofficial rabbi, the first among equals, following the same calling as Nannu. Zoe let silence open out between them before she confessed, "I feel as if I know him. I realize it sounds crazy, but...."

They were both quiet for several moments. Then Max said softly, "The dead can inhabit us."

Zoe knew this if she knew anything at all.

Max sipped his espresso and took a healthy bite of pastry. "I have to admit *I had it bad* for your mother." The bare skin above his beard turned ruddy.

Zoe managed a smile for him. "And my aunt had it bad for you." The words walked out of her mouth before she could stop them.

Max put his tiny cup back into the saucer with a click. "How do you know this?"

Zoe scrambled for a white lie; she was no good at it. "My mother told me." She waited a few moments before going on, sipping her espresso and taking a bite out of the plump pastry, so stuffed with jam, it oozed onto her lips. Embarrassed, she wiped her mouth with the napkin. "But she didn't speak much about her sister, she never wanted to talk about why Yael left. It was too painful, I guess."

Max nodded. "They were inseparable as girls. I saw a good deal of your whole family for years. Our family attended services led by your Nannu and he mentored me in the jewellery business. I was a little flea."

"Did you hear anything about Yael since she left Valletta?"

Max took a long while to answer. "Something unexpected happened ... years ago."

Zoe's heart beat faster. No one, except for Yael herself—

through her diary—had offered anything fresh.

"After your Nannu passed away, I received a small package from Yael with a little note. She sent me a pair of cufflinks she'd made from Berber beads. Your grandpa had brought them back from a trip to Marrakesh when we were teens working in his shop. Both Yael and I had admired the beads and thought they'd make beautiful cufflinks, but we never got around to it—your grandpa kept us too busy. So she sent them to me as a memento. I was touched."

Zoe was astounded. She hadn't heard of anyone whom Yael had been in contact with since her disappearance in 1969. "Was there an address? Did you get in touch with her?"

Max sipped his espresso. "Yael left no return address. The package was sent from a post office in Marrakesh. Of course, I wanted to thank her, but I couldn't find a contact address or phone number. And then life took over."

Zoe wondered if Yael was still in love with Max after she'd fled Valletta. "Any news since?"

"Sadly, no. She sent that thoughtful gift thirty ... oh, must be thirty-seven years ago. That was the last I heard from her."

Zoe had scoured the internet for information on Yael Paredes and had come up nearly empty, save for a few references to her mother's family in Valletta. There was no news of a death, few references to a life, odd for such a seemingly charismatic person.

"Did Cal give you the family photograph, by the way?"

"Yes, thanks so much."

Max ordered a second espresso and refills of water. "Yael had so much curiosity, an adventurous spirit. I hope she still does. She confided in me once that she wanted to learn about her origins, see the world. We're small here. A girl like her, well, she felt hemmed in on our island. But tell me, what brings you to Malta now? Your brother mentioned a project."

Zoe told him about her studies, the fellowship, her ideas for her thesis, and Max took it all in quietly; he was a good listener, rare these days. She wanted to meet and talk with more of the Jewish families who went way back on the island, work up some oral histories, see how they compared with her own family's story. "I have a list of my grandpa's congregants and I've met with some people here, but I wonder if you could give me an introduction to others."

"Of course, why don't you and Cal come to Shabbat dinner with us?"

"Sure. I'll drag my brother along."

Max smiled. "Good. I look forward to having you both." He wrote out the address for her.

"There's something else," Zoe said. "I have piles of photographs my mother shot of sacred Jewish sites on Malta. Nannu made notes, and tape recordings." Her voice broke when she mentioned the tapes. "I visited some of these places when I first arrived, but got side-tracked. There are more I need to see before my time runs out here. I'd love to know anything and everything about my family—there are so few of us left. I wonder if you could possibly go along with me, as a guide."

"My pleasure."

They wandered slowly back over to Max's hut, where his son couldn't wait to get away and join his friends, while Zoe realized that she was still wearing the inscribed pendant.

"I need to give this back to you. I'd like to choose one for my brother Cal, as a Hanukkah gift. "The one inscribed with *immaġinazzjoni.*"

Max waved her away, insisting that she take both pendants as gifts, her family had already given him so much. They made a plan for the following Sunday to visit some of the sacred sites together.

That Sunday, Max and Zoe took a *dgħasa* from Valletta to Vittoriosa to visit *Il Triq tal-Lhud,* or *Street of the Jews.* In the notes for his monograph, her grandfather had said that Jews were held in Vittoriosa slave prisons during the seventeenth century, but were allowed to leave during the day to carry out trade nearby on this street. Now, *Triq tal-Lhud* ran into the square near the Church of St. Lawrence and was called Old Governor's Palace Street. Max helped Zoe find the tiny alley just off of the street, which bore the original name, *Triq tal-Lhud*. Her mother had photographed the sign. Now, the alley was packed with tourists and Zoe felt hollow, watching them snap pictures and shop for little trinkets, miniatures of the Knights of St. John who had captured and enslaved the Jews.

In her mother's photo, the alley was vivid, breathing with life. She spotted a small tailor's shop, a barber's, and a bakery.

"Here," Max pointed to a souvenir shop, "was where your Grandma Ruth's grandpa worked as a tailor, and there—he indicated the bakery—was my grandpa's dry goods store."

"Wait a minute, Grandma Ruth was from England."

Max chuckled, clearly uncomfortable. "Your Grandma Ruth was sent away to British boarding school and later settled with cousins outside London, but her extended family were Maltese—to the bone. Forgive me for saying as much, but your Grandma Ruth was a bit of a snob. She goes back further on this island than your grandpa's side."

Now, Nannu's entry made even more sense, about not going forward, without looking back. "Do you know more about my Grandma Ruth's ancestry here?"

"A bit. Sometimes people like to write themselves a new story."

Zoe opened one of Nannu's notebooks that focused on the Jewish slave community on the island and read Max what he'd written:

The slave prison was a square building where the Jews lodged at night. They had all sorts of trades: barbers, tailors. A stout fellow was bought for 120 or 160 scudi. One rich Jew was sold in the market for 400 scudi, and supposing himself free—he had a passport from Venice—struck the merchant who bought him. He

received fifty blows, his head and beard were shaved,
a great chain clapped onto his legs.

"My people, and apparently some of yours, were trying to escape to the Levant from the persecution of Pius V, and fell victim to the Knights. They survived that slave prison. And here we are now, standing here."

They smiled at each other in a moment of communion. She would write about the Jewish community in Malta, linking it to her own family's history, including Nannu's writings, sermons, and philosophy, and her mother's photographs. Her project would link past and present. History, yes, but a personal story, she'd breathe life into dusty, distant facts.

"Years ago," Max was saying, "in medieval times, one-third of Malta's population was Jewish." Zoe felt a tingling in her fingertips as Max showed her the sign marking the site of the old Jewish silk market at 3A Carmel Street, next to a scarlet door.

"Look at these," she said, taking some of her mother's photographs from her satchel. "She took a few shots, from several angles. Here is my grandpa in front of the red door."

He was beautiful as he gazed directly at her with a prophet's dark glowing eyes and the beard to match. His black brows grew over the bridge of his nose and he had thick curling hair threaded with silver, a strong, square jaw. His build was large-framed and sturdy.

She and Max studied the photographs, which both arrested and freed time. Zoe was transported back to her mother and Nannu, as they were propelled forward to her, inhabiting the same moment.

Later, Max took Zoe to the Jewish cemeteries that her mother and grandfather had visited together, using Cassandra's photographs and Nannu's notes as a guide. Just outside Valletta, on the road to Floriana was a neglected Jewish burial site, overgrown with weeds. Most of the graves were of infants and children. Zoe was thinking about how far-flung Jewish people were, both tenacious and fragile. Nomadic, but able to survive like tough plants growing in cracks of concrete.

After lunch, they travelled to the Marsa cemetery at the southern tip of the Grand Harbour. Zoe and Max walked through the gabled, arched stone gate decorated with Torah finials. Here, they found the graves of the first Paredes family who had come to Malta from Portugal to practise their faith openly. Her mother had photographed the graves and inscriptions and her grandpa had written as much as he was able to uncover about them. They found several generations of Paredes at the burial site, and at last, Nannu's grave. (Her grandmother had chosen to be buried in London.) Zoe asked Max about Nannu's funeral, strained to imagine his burial, the cluster of mourners, the thrum of voices in Hebrew and Maltese, the voices of family and friends and neighbours and colleagues, and of course, the close-knit Jewish community on the island. She felt a cool breeze off the sea.

She knelt before his headstone and read the inscription, written both in Hebrew and Maltese, a line she had discovered one lonely afternoon so many years ago in that magical inside/outside room above the garage.

When you imagine Him near, that's when you will find Him.

The inscription spoke to her, as a connection to spirit, wherever you might find it, to Nannu and all of her loved ones who were lost, missing, gone, or dead. Her parents both gone, their bodies part of the sea. She understood how the body became a shell, even a prison, and death a release of the soul and spirit to a new journey. She longed for the souls of those she loved, living on.

Max recited Kaddish, the prayer for the dead.

Barukh atah Adonai....

Zoe remembered the meaning of prayer to Nannu, *to become the words.*

She joined in, thinking of the first time she heard her grandpa's voice—time stopped—and he was right there in the room with her, the presence of Nannu in her life, a kind of miracle. Her eyes burned, then streamed, her face hot and wet. For the first time in as long as she could remember, she cried.

"*Barukh atah Adonai eloheinu melekh ha'olam, dayan haemet.*"

Zoe felt that she would give anything for a moment with her grandpa, to feel the warmth of his hands. She knelt on the ground, searching for a stone. She found a black one, round and smooth, glinting with a single vein of mica. A stone, we put a stone. *We are here.* She placed the stone on Nannu's grave and left with empty hands.

26.

NOTES: *Piles of scribblings taking shape at last. No longer drowning in notes and paper, like Casaubon. A Jewish history of Malta through the lens of my family's story. Use Mom's photos to illustrate, Nannu's sermons, notes, as primary texts. A window onto the larger Jewish community. Nannu, I'll complete the project you and Mom began.*

As December drew to a close, Zoe and Cal prepared to leave Valletta. Zoe planned to celebrate Hanukkah on the island, as they'd done each year at home for as long as she could remember, often the two of them alone together while their parents were on the road. It was up to her to make Hanukkah special for Cal while he was growing up: telling the story of how the Maccabees' single vial of oil, enough for one day, miraculously lasted for eight.

Zoe always prepared latkes from scratch, the whole house redolent with the scent of crisp, browning potatoes, onions and oil. She made jelly donuts, thick with powdered sugar and bursting with jam, and surprised Cal with small gifts: a dreidel, a paint box, a snorkelling set, and handfuls of gelt, gold wrapped, coin-embossed chocolates. They sang songs and played dreidel, betting for gelt.

Leaving Valletta was going to be tough, as Zoe still had much to learn. She hoped to return to Malta before too much time and distance filled in the spaces between her life at home and the work she'd begun here.

Rummaging around in her suitcase, she found the small menorah she'd packed, which had been among her parents' effects. Zoe dug up some silver polish and set to work cleaning the tiny candle holders. She didn't know if she'd be able to find Hanukkah candles small enough to fit into the miniature holders, so Cal suggested they improvise with birthday candles.

Together, Zoe and Cal stood before the tiny menorah, as Zoe lighted the *shamash* and they sang the prayer together, then lit the first light. It comforted her that Jews all over the world, strangers, would be sharing this ritual. Nannu's words came back to her, *holiness in time,* as Tonio bounded up on the counter, attracted to the flame, like a moth to light. Cal cradled him and set him down out of harm's way.

"I have a Hanukkah gift for you," Zoe said, handing Cal the pendant with *immaginazzjoni* engraved on its back.

"This is cool."

"I hope you don't mind," Zoe pulled out her own necklace from beneath her t-shirt, as Cal gave her a hug, pulling her into his chest. "Max Ellul makes them. Thanks for finding him and going to Shabbat dinner."

"Yeah, you owe me. Which brings me to, well … we have a decision to make." Cal picked up Tonio and stroked his fur, enviably comfortable with the capricious creature. "I'll take total care of him, do vet visits. If I go away, I'll line up a cat sitter. You don't have to do *any*thing."

In truth, she'd sort of gotten used to the cat, working her way around him, bit by bit less fearful. A kind of aversive exposure therapy. And she could see how much Tonio meant to Cal. Reading her ghost Aunt Yael's diary brought home just how painful it must have been for her mother to lose her sister; it must have been hard for Yael, too, though she wouldn't admit it as a teen. How could she if she was so intent on flight? Zoe didn't know what she would do without Cal. "Just don't expect me to fall in love—with Tonio."

He shot her a smirk. "Anyway, I'm going to give you a piece of—"

"Your mind?" She laughed at him, couldn't help herself. "Your ... heart?"

"How about, art. Gimme a bit more time. And I'm going to have an open studio before we leave. Just so folks can see what I've been up to."

Well, they both needed to talk about what they'd been up to, more and more, little by little. Zoe placed the delicate *hanukiah* in their Valletta window, so passers-by could see the flames dance.

PART V: HOMEGROUND

27. CAL

On the train to Montreal Cal slept, dreaming of Lake Isle. To coax him out of the water, his mother promised the swings. She pushed him so hard, he saw himself whirling over the top of the pole, spooling around it, but there he was: caught fast. Cal never knew when she'd catch him—one swing, seven, or ten—their little game. When he woke up, he thought of her rhythm of catch and release, spotty presence, escape guaranteed.

Cal left the train groggy, riding the escalator up from the platform into the station. There he looked around for the Canadian cousin he and Zoe had tracked down. He spotted a tiny, elderly woman bundled up in woollen coat, scarf, and cloche hat holding a sign with his name emblazoned on it. Now this was a cringe-worthy first.

After he introduced himself, the woman reached up and Cal had to twist sideways in a deep-knee bend, his cheek crushed against his cousin's powdery neck, a pair of trembling arms fastened around his back in a hug.

At last, he felt her arms loosen, and with a sudden cramp in his knee, he stretched back up to his full height.

"Mrs. Bernstein...."

"Call me Zippy."

"Um ... it's good to meet you." He looked down at this stranger and relative, a little old woman with a puff of cotton-candy hair peeking out from her hat, her head thrust forward at him, her pink mouth pursed into a satisfied close-lipped smile.

"Come, dear. Hope you won't mind my old beater, but I refuse to buy a new car when I don't need one."

Cal followed her outside into the agitation of swirling snow to an ancient silver Chrysler. The car failed to let out a beep when she didn't buckle up; its body shook and rattled as she sped through the winter storm, cursing at drivers and weather, lurching up the drive of a washed pink brick house set atop a steep hill with a view of the city spread below, all twinkling gold and silver lights.

Once inside, Zippy took Cal's outerwear and unpeeled her own winter layers in brisk, determined movements, her elegant house enveloping him in its sudden warmth. She was swaddled in a fuzzy blue sweater dress to match her eyes, her body stooped and thin, but for pendulous breasts. She barely reached his armpit. Cal hadn't been around many elderly people; she was a novelty.

"You get your height from Menash," she said, her words lightning quick, as she stored gloves, hats, scarves, and lined up boots.

Cal went blank for a moment and she tapped his shoulder with surprising force. "Your grandpa."

"Never met him. My dad was tall, too."

She nodded in staccato rhythm. "So you finally made your way up to us. You could have picked a better time." She pointed out the window at the whirling white.

"Nice change."

She let out a gutsy laugh, bigger than she was. "Let's go up to your room."

"Thanks for letting me stay."

She flung a tiny gnarled hand in a slapping motion. "Family is family."

He'd heard that one before. The house was huge, a hundred years old or more. It was cool being up on the rise with Montreal spread out below. He dumped his backpack on the floor and checked out the four-poster bed with its cream comforter.

Though he loved sleep, he worried about that fiddly bed. Of course, it would creak, maybe collapse; he didn't even dare sit on it.

"You have a nice place here."

"It's hard to leave." She gave him a wink. "Hard for other people to leave, too."

"Oh, don't worry about me. My sister's expecting me back in a couple weeks. And I have a cat who's probably missing me."

"My Torty died this past summer."

"I'm sorry."

"I'll show you pictures."

"Cool. I've got lots of Tonio on my phone." Well, there was at least cats in common.

"So your sister must be taking good care of him."

Actually, he'd gotten a friend to cat sit Tonio, he didn't quite trust the two of them alone together just yet.

"You should have brought Zoe along—there's always a neighbour to watch your kitty. You two need to branch out, let the family in."

"My parents were not great about keeping in touch," Cal said, digging in his backpack for his toothbrush.

Zippy didn't answer for a moment, maybe avoiding his minefield. "These days, I always have a guest or two and I love the company. Whenever I go anywhere—or used to—for my business, I was always happy to come back home." She smoothed the nap of her dress, then patted her legs. "You must be hungry."

Cal shrugged. "Always."

"I baked you some muffins, gluten-free. I don't want to miss out."

She put a trembling arm around Cal's back and nudged him toward the staircase. "I'll make a pot of tea, we can schmooze."

Downstairs, they sat on stools arranged around the kitchen counter, as snow slanted down so densely it was difficult to see beyond its white mesh screen. Zippy brought a teapot to the counter; she covered it with a crocheted cosy and came back with delicate cups that matched the pot. From the oven, she pulled out a tray of muffins, as big as softballs, smelling of cranberry, orange, and butter. Little pots of jam and cream appeared next.

"We'll have them the English way. Do you like clotted cream?"

"I've never tasted it."

"Take." To his surprise, Zippy held the pot of cream out to him, inviting Cal to scoop some out with his finger; the smooth thick cream melted slowly against his tongue.

She poured the tea and moved the pitcher of milk and bowl of brown sugar lumps toward Cal. "I've got lemon, too."

Cal felt clumsy holding the tiny perfect teacup; it was so delicate, he was afraid he might drop and break it. Zippy held out the plate of muffins and Cal took one, slicing it in half, and spreading it thickly with cream and jam.

Zippy watched him eat. "It's nice to have a man around. I think of my Nathan every day."

Cal couldn't speak for some moments, his mouth full of muffin, which he washed down with a few slugs of tea.

"When did he pass away?"

"It's been a long time, now, but I talk to him every day. Can't help it," Zippy murmured, vaguely looking through Cal. She nodded twice, then said, "So, you are looking at schools in Montreal?"

"Art schools, yeah."

Zippy smiled at him.

"What do you know about Concordia's Fine Arts program?"

"I've attended vernissages of graduating students. I hear the program is good ... and you have family here."

Cal reached for a second muffin and Zippi nodded approvingly. "You need to fill up those long legs!"

"I'm also applying in New York. The School of Visual Arts in the City and Pratt in Brooklyn."

"Keep your options open," Zippy said, sipping tea with lemon. "But of course we hope you'll come up north if it suits you."

Cal looked around, wondering who the "we" referred to exactly.

"I'm sorry you and your sister didn't get in touch sooner. I certainly tried with your parents...." she waved away her comment, no need to lay on the Jewish guilt. "We attended the memorial service for your parents—you probably don't remember us—you were surrounded by people."

He wasn't there. Cal's lips twitched and he covered his mouth, still painful to remember that time, afraid of tumbling into reliving it. He and Zoe had lived a pretty reclusive life ... but now there was Tonio, good old Tonio to keep them company. He couldn't stop the evil chuckle that rose from his chest.

"What's funny? Did I miss something?"

He shook his head. "Just thinking about something else."

"Now this evening—"

"I'm really sorry...." This was bad, here he was freeloading at his elderly cousin's house and he'd made plans. "I'm seeing a friend later." He realized that this sounded rude. "Would you join us?" How weird would that be? She'd never go for it.

Zippy waited, alert.

"We might check out a gallery in Old Montreal, an opening of a Concordia student, actually. There'll be a crowd." Or they might blow that off and just go out to eat.

"Good for you," Zippy said. "Mix and mingle. Find out everything you can, I'll be cosy here." She drew her chin into her chest, a sudden, sharp movement.

He was afraid he'd offended her. "My friend, she's not from here."

"A she. Your girlfriend?" She slapped her left hand with her right. "I have to stop being an old busybody!" Zippy sipped her tea and nibbled away at the browned cap of the muffin. "So, how do you know her?" Zippy pressed, cocking her head and leaning toward Cal.

Cal laughed, his face heating up. He put his hand over Zippy's little freckled one and felt it tremble slightly under his, like a grounded bird.

"There I go again," Zippy said. "What time do you have breakfast, Caleb?"

"As late as possible. It's Cal—Caleb makes me feel sort of weird." Sad, actually. His mother loved to call him Caleb, and now and then his dad, when he was serious, disappointed or angry. Even though it meant no good, the formal name made Cal miss his parents. Though he hadn't seen them in a consistent way, there was always that chance while they were still alive.

"Would you mind if I jumped in the shower?" he asked. Then added, "It's nice to find a new relative."

"I'm hardly new."

"You know what I mean."

She began to rise from the stool, with considerable difficulty, and Cal helped her up. He gathered plates and cups, carrying them to the sink, then loaded the dishwasher. He had to pick up Aziza at seven and was incredibly nervous. They hadn't seen each other for several months, under terrible circumstances, while she was in detention and under police supervision at the airport. Best to ditch the gallery plan. He'd bus to the Fortiers' house and they could walk to the restaurant, talk while they walked.

28. AZIZA

Aziza finished her duties for the day, though taking care of the Fortiers' three children, Patrick, ten, David, thirteen, and Caroline fourteen—and helping around the hectic house—was a job without edges. Over a cup of tea in the kitchen, she told Anne that she had dinner plans.

"So where are you going to eat?" Anne asked, looking directly at Aziza, her eyes the colour of Libyan honey. Thinking of bees, of honey, of the sidrah tree, as snow swirled, made Aziza miss home.

"I'm not sure."

Her thoughts were tangled and Anne waited, but Aziza couldn't look at her for long. She was grateful to the Fortiers; the work here was good, it helped to be busy, but grief and terror still swam up when she least expected. She thought of Cal finding her near death, and then following her internment, another kind of death. Twice he had seen her broken, twice he'd saved her. The weight of gratitude veered toward shame, an obligation she could never repay. Aziza couldn't imagine ever sharing a normal friendship with him. There was so little common ground.

"What are you thinking, Z? Tell me."

Aziza shook her head, still surprised by the shortness of her hair, which she'd shorn to chin-length with one of the kids' craft scissors, striving for a new look, a fresh start. Shorter in the back, slanted forward framing her face, she hadn't done a bad job of it. But could she truly start fresh? She'd met others here who wanted to be born new with no before-life. That wasn't who she was. Looking back was both pain and pleasure. She would never forget Amah and Baba, that would be like cutting off a limb. Baba might be alive somewhere. Aziza hoped and prayed he would come back to her, some way, somehow. To look ahead was both exciting and scary, maybe bad luck. You look too far into the future, Baba said, and you trip on a rock just under your feet, and so she lived in an odd, eternal present.

Anne waited, patient.

"Please forgive me, Anne. I am thinking of home."

"Aziza, there's nothing to forgive. Do you want to talk?"

Aziza shook her head.

"So, know what you're going to wear tonight?"

Aziza shrugged.

"Let's go through my closet, okay?"

"Must we do so?"

Anne laughed and got up to hug Aziza. "Come ... bring your tea."

Aziza took her tea into Anne's bedroom, the duvet rumpled into a creamy cloud. There were gilt-framed paintings on the walls by an artist who decorated his women with peacock feathers, and the darkly polished bureau was cluttered with crystal bottles of perfume, scattered jewellery, coloured candles, and so many creams and lotions Aziza had no idea what each one was used for.

"I don't want to take the clothes off your back, Anne."

"I have too much. In fact, every couple of months one of the racks in my closet collapses. I think it's a sign."

"I don't want to dress up all silliness."

"Just a sweater and jeans or cords."

"What is 'cords'?" Living with the Fortiers for the past two months, both her English and French were improving. Anne often spoke English, Roger, French. The whole family was bilingual, skittering, lightning quick, between the two languages, the kids resorting to a mix, which Anne called Franglais. Still, she had so much to learn.

"It's short for corduroy—a kind of fabric—good for winter, cosy." She pulled out a pair of slacks the colour of red wine, ribbing in the fabric. "These won't fit you, you're much thinner than me, but I bet Caroline has a pair that'll work."

"Only if it's all right with Caroline. She may not want to loan me a pair of her cordor…" Aziza could hardly pronounce the word.

"No matter. Let's have a look at my tops."

Anne was off today and looked relaxed and beautiful to Aziza, swathed in a midnight blue robe of velvety fabric. The sprawling brick-and-cement-block house with its comfortable clutter, soft woven rugs, and worn wood floors, its ceramic vases filled with fresh flowers, the tall gold and walnut clock which ticked like a heart, loud enough to be heard throughout the main floor, stunned Aziza. As did the whole neighbourhood which everyone called NDG. She'd never seen such abundance lived in so casually, without notice or care. Each object was a treasure to her, and yet the family barely noticed these things any more than they noticed the noses on their faces.

Aziza didn't want to borrow Anne's clothes; Anne was considerably shorter than Aziza with full breasts and wide hips, a nipped-in waist. She looked ripe, perfect. In Libya she would be a goddess.

Anne went to her crammed and messy closet and Aziza followed her, squeezing in beside a painted cupboard stuffed with sweaters, varied as candy in their colours.

"How do you make a decision what to put on each day?" Aziza asked.

Anne's hands fluttered, useless at her sides. "I know, it's too much. Please take some things.…" She pulled out several stacks of sweaters and laid them on the bed. The high, soft piles tumbled into heaps and pools of fabric.

Anne opened up a half-dozen sweaters, so Aziza could look at them.

"Go on Z, pick something."

Aziza finally chose a cream-colored pullover with a full wide collar. The fabric was soft and warm, yet light.

"Try it on," Anne urged.

Aziza was shy and self-conscious, uncomfortable dressing or undressing in front of anyone, even more so after her experience in detention.

"I'll go check on the kids. They're downstairs watching *School of Rock* for the hundredth time. What is it about repetition? Anyway, Z, would you show me how it looks on you?"

Aziza nodded slowly.

When the door to Anne's bedroom clicked closed, Aziza was enveloped by quiet. A bubble of laughter rose and burst from below, the children's voices happy, carefree. Aziza swallowed to get rid of the sour, rancid taste in her mouth. Resenting the kids made her small and mean; how could she begrudge them a life they were born into? Their mother and father both alive and healthy.

Many mornings she awoke lost, in confusion, so exhausted she could barely get out of bed. During the night, she crossed the desert, sinking deeper into white-hot sand, which turned into sea, where she thrashed for her life, then floated, huddled on a raft which turned into a cot inside a crowded cell. She was forever in between, never anchored to a place.

Aziza went back inside Anne's closet, where she felt less exposed. With a sharp tug, she pulled her grey sweatshirt off. She wanted to feel the sweater against her skin, shivering as it floated down over her body. It did not chafe or itch, the fabric was too fine.

Moving to Anne's mirror, Aziza stared: the cowl neck folded over and framed her face, revealing her collar bone and a bit of her shoulders, the creamy white setting off her dark hair and eyes and olive skin. She wasn't used to the notion of clothing as enhancement, for her and her family, it was merely functional; the sweater was too precious.

As Aziza gathered her clothes, she spotted a pair of *babouchen* shoved to the back of Anne's shoe collection. Crawling on hands and knees, she slid them out, held them to her face, the smell of the leather rich and warm, alive as human skin.

Her father had made these. He'd sold many pairs just like them, each set beautifully crafted, some the colour of chocolate with the heel set inside the shoe, others like the pair he gave to Anne, caramel-hued. They were soft but durable, moulding to the shape of one's feet. Her father had made a pair for Roger, and for each of the Fortier children.

Their shape, their scent, their feel, brought Baba back; she was inside the souk, the *babouchen* displayed neatly on wooden planks, arranged by size and colour, then the sandals; belts coiled neatly on nails, sleeping snakes.

There was a soft rap and Aziza turned quickly, rushing to return the *babouchen*. When she opened the door, Anne stood there.

"You look lovely."

Aziza hardly heard her. She knew that she couldn't return home to Tripoli, but she needed to find out what had become of her father. A few neighbours, and some friends, still lived in Tripoli; she would contact them, ask Anne and Roger for help—they knew how to get things done. Before Aziza could ask Anne for advice about her father, Caroline appeared in the doorway.

"Wow. You look amazing Z." She had her mother's fair skin, but her father's dark hair and eyes, and was a striking young girl, tall and slender for her age.

"I'll lend you my skinny black cords, if..."

"No ifs, Caroline," Anne scolded.

"If," Caroline continued, unfazed by her mother's warning, "you let me do your makeup."

"Now you know Aziza doesn't wear makeup."

"There's always a first time," snapped back Caroline.

Aziza smiled at Caroline. "It is a deal," she said.

Waiting for Cal to pick her up, Aziza remembered him as huge, tall, strong, and grown-up. When he carried her from the sea, it was like a second birth, but the person who greeted her at the door with a tentative smile was boyish, skinny, and awkward. A touch in greeting was out of the question.

As she left the house, Aziza glanced back and saw the three children against the golden glow of the upstairs window, watching. Aziza and Cal left quickly, dawdling for a moment on the street a few houses away from the Fortiers.

"Do you want to bus or walk?" Cal asked.

Aziza waited a long time before answering. The snowy night was beautiful, but she was still not used to the cold, the crowds on public transport, which brought back the Valletta bus to the ferry and then—she stopped the images and racing thoughts with all her might—thinking of snow, white flakes fluttering like butterflies. Now, here. White was the colour of Tripoli, her home, The White City, white-hot, and white was the colour of Montreal, cold winter white.

"I want to walk."

"It's an amazing night."

Aziza felt his arm around her back for just a moment, before he curled it through her arm, fastening her hand close to his bony hip. Aziza let the air out of her chest, his touch relaxing the tension between them.

Aziza was relieved that the restaurant was casual, full of families as well as couples, noisy and warm, fragrant with the smells of butter and garlic, parmesan and tomato sauce. The waiter suggested tortellini stuffed with mushroom and cheese, which Aziza ordered, while Cal had spaghetti and meatballs. They drank a lot of wine and she told him a bit about her life in Montreal with the Fortiers, while he shared his plans to go to art school. The tortellini was delicious, rich and heavy.

She found that she felt more shy in person than she did writing or emailing, where she could be both alone and together with him. Actually having him right here, across the table from her, where she was warm and well fed and not in any kind of crisis was new.

Cal ordered cappuccinos and a sweet she had never tried; he fed her a chunk of the cylindrical pastry stuffed with a white cheese. The thin pastry crunched against her teeth and the sweet cheese, both smooth and grainy, dissolved thickly against her tongue. She was full enough to burst.

As they were finishing up their meal, he said, "I've got a crazy idea."

She smiled at him. "What is it?"

He covered her hand with both of his. "I'm staying with my cousin Zippy and I noticed that she has this toboggan in her garage."

"What is a ... to-bag-an?" Aziza thought her English was pretty good, and getting better, but there were still so many words which were foreign. When she had more time, she thought about taking a class, but which would she attack first? French or English? Both needed improvement.

"It's a big wooden sled with no runners, you know, skis, on the underside. You ride it down a mountainside in the snow. Better yet, I'll show you."

"Oh yes, a sled." Patrick and David went sledding with their dad and Aziza wanted to try it. "When are you making this plan?"

"Tonight. You game?"

"What game?"

"Tobogganing."

She was eager to take her mind away from worry over Baba and missing home. "Yes, all right."

While they waited for the check, Cal called his cousin Zippy to let her know that he would be stopping by and going into the garage. "Just so you know I'm not a burglar," Aziza overheard him say, unfamiliar with the word burglar, making a mental note to look it up later in her English dictionary.

An hour later, they were trudging through a woodsy trail surrounded by snowy pines. Cal took Aziza's hand and she breathed in the absolute silence, but for the occasional hoot of an owl, the whoosh of the wind through pines as clouds of snow blew in bursts of cold around their faces.

She stood close to Cal in her fluffy white sweater, parka, boots, mittens and tuque, which Anne had bought for her to survive her first Canadian winter. The wind-driven swirls were sharp and cold at the top of the hill and she wrapped her arms around her chest.

Cal kneeled in the snow and held the toboggan in place for her, showing Aziza how to sit down with her legs extended. She was scared and excited at once, watching the others race down the hill in the snow-lit darkness, perhaps a handful of sledders, lone fathers with a child or two, a couple, a family. Cal sat down behind her and she felt the snug fit, his lean chest pressed against her back, his long legs surrounding hers.

"Ready?"

Aziza's throat felt tight with her own held breath.

The toboggan stuck for a moment. Cal put his gloved hands on the ground, rocked a few times hard, rocking her with him, and they were off, flying down the mountain. For a split-second, Aziza watched the sledders below, heard their cries of pleasure, then squeezed her eyes shut.

The toboggan made a barely audible shush, like the ocean. Plunging down, Aziza's heart rose with a live flutter, leaving her weightless. Freefalling. She screamed, her face tingling. Slowing, they glided into the flat plain, the ride pure joy.

"Again!" she said to him. "I want to do—go down again."

He grabbed her hand and they ran up the hill, as Cal dragged the toboggan.

They went down again and again, perhaps a half-dozen times, though Aziza lost count. On the last ride, the toboggan swerved to the right, and at the base of the hill they smacked into a snowbank, tumbling into a drift.

Aziza found herself buried in white powder, Cal nearly on top of her. He rolled off of her, and she sank into the drift. She struggled to get her feet under her, but her boots dug in deeper; she was up to her thighs and began to panic. She closed her eyes and a scream escaped.

"It's okay, Z," Cal said.

Her eyes flew open, and she saw him standing above her on some hard-packed snow beside the drift, covered in white dust.

"Help me!"

"Hold on a minute."

He took her hand and pulled, but it was like a child tugging her; she was held fast by the deep snow, buried in cold quicksand.

"Wait a minute."

She would drown in snow, instead of sea.

"It's going to be okay, Z. I'll get you out of there."

A tall, broad shouldered man approached them with two small girls. He spoke to Cal in French, asking if he could help.

"*Oui.*"

Aziza closed her eyes. Distantly, she heard Cal and the man speak in French, softly, but with determination. She felt herself fall backward into the drift, nearly buried, and then there were strong arms beneath her knees and around her back, under her arms, and all at once she felt her boots suck free of the snow and rise to the surface, as she was lifted, like a baby, from the white sea. Meant to live.

29. CAL

Cal loped and slid through the snowy streets back to his cousin's house, pulling the bright yellow toboggan behind him. He remembered to call Zippy to tell her he would be home by twelve-thirty; she'd be in bed, but he had a key.

This city was beautiful at night. Hives of golden flakes beneath the glow of the streetlamps, tall and bent as sunflowers. Cal wanted to capture and hold onto these northern images. He felt a freshness to life here, a direction that had just begun during his time with Zoe in Valletta. The toboggan slid along on a layer of packed powder, light, quick. The trees were black bones, the stone buildings ledged with snow, chimneys chugging smoke. He would do some sketches tomorrow, perhaps it would lead to a sculpture or installation. They didn't have winters like this in New Jersey.

Cal could hear Aziza's voice in his head, see her smile, feel how she curled her fingers into her palm so he could enclose her hand within his. She was both tough and fragile, a rare mix he hadn't encountered before in the girls he knew. Cal promised to bring his portfolio to dinner when they got together next, and he was wondering which drawings to include, though his best work were the sculptures and installations he'd made in Valletta; he could show her photos of those.

Walking, even in all this snow, he was getting hot and unzipped his parka. Funny, how nice snow could feel when you were in a good mood, full of wine and pasta and garlic bread.

Cal knew he had to turn up from Sherbrooke to Zippy's house. It was hard to make out street signs, but when he saw the large park, the library, he headed uphill. He knew Zippy was high on the hill between Westmount Avenue and the Boulevard. Cal made a couple of random turns trying to remember his way, the toboggan rolling over in a fierce gust from the mountain. He was full of his own thoughts when a person darted out of an alley.

Cal jumped; he stepped backward away from the intruder, slid and fell, landing on his ass, losing hold of the toboggan that careened downhill, crashing into a tree.

"Are you all right?" a woman asked. Dressed in an enormous scarlet cape, she reached out a gloved hand. He waved it away and got back to his feet. Cal raced down the hill after his toboggan, and dragged it back up, where the stranger stood in his path.

"You sort of came out of nowhere." He pulled the toboggan up beside him like a dog on a leash.

She laughed, a deep throaty sound. "So you've been out sledding. What a night for it." She gazed at the sky, letting flakes melt against her upturned face. Her skin was the colour of nutmeg, a sharp contrast to the scarlet cape and hat.

"Are you Caleb Braverman?"

"Who are you?"

She laughed again which pissed him off. "What's funny?"

"Are you Caleb?"

"I asked, who are you?"

"I came from my cousin's house just now. She wanted to turn in for the night and asked me to go out and look for you, afraid you were lost. I certainly got turned around a lot when I first came here. She mentioned you were walking from NDG. Walking in this weather and tobogganing to boot—excuse the lousy pun—you'll fit right in."

"Are you going to tell me who you are?" Cal was surprised by the edge in his voice.

"Sorry. I know this is odd. I'm a relative of yours. Let's go back to Zippy's. We can talk there. You must be freezing."

"Not at all," he lied. Cal was weary and cold, in need of dry clothes and something hot to drink. That was all he could think about for the moment, so he fell into stride with her.

30.

Cal entered his cousin's foyer with the woman in the red cape as the quiet of the old house drew in around them. He shucked off his jacket and couldn't wait to get out of his wet clothes.

"I'll be back." Tip-toeing up to his room, he flinched each time the stairs creaked under his weight. He longed for a pounding hot shower, but that would have to wait until the woman left the house. Cal was tempted to put on pyjamas, but decided on sweats and headed downstairs.

He found her in the library on her hands and knees building a blazing fire in the stone hearth. She wore loose black pants, her sleeves rolled up to reveal slender sinewy arms. Her hair was loose and long, black with threads of silvery white, striking against the bright red of her sweater and bark-brown skin.

"Let me take care of that," he offered, bending down to pick up a log from the canvas sling which held a neatly-stacked woodpile.

She waved him away. Crouching to adjust a log with bare fingers, she rocked backward and pointed at the floor-to-ceiling bookcases. "You'll find the complete works of many of the Victorians, Zippy loves those novels. Are you a fan?"

"Well, I like some of Dickens. I haven't read many of the ... Victorians. He found himself scowling, and strained to arrange his features into a more neutral expression. Intent on the fire, they watched it catch into bright, hot spears.

"Ahh, that's good," she said. She pointed out the window to a large deck, two greyish tarps. "I built those cribs for Zippy. Stacked the wood, chopped it too." She smiled to herself, full lips closed.

"Yeah?"

"My winter sport."

Cal couldn't stop the smile, which twitched, then spread across his face.

The woman stared at him, then shook her head hard, as if to shake off a dream. Then in a brisk, workmanlike voice, she asked, "Are you a skier, Cal?"

"Never learned."

"Likewise. But if I could get that axe out right now," she glanced at him for effect, then let out a low chuckle. "Ah well, we'd have the Westmount police over here in a jiffy. Zippy's neighbours had to have a tree cut down last November and I spent a week chopping it into logs. There is nothing like bringing down the axe, hearing that thonk."

She was a bit off, maybe just a show-off. "You seem quite at home here. What's your connection to my cousin Zippy exactly?"

"She's my cousin." The woman stood up, tall and lithe.

"How so?"

"I'm going to have a glass of port. Can I offer you one? Or would you prefer tea, or … hot chocolate? Zippy usually keeps plenty of heavy cream in the fridge, I could whip some."

"Port is good." No way he was going to succumb to his urge for hot cocoa.

She made her way to a well-stocked liquor cabinet, filling two crystal glasses with port. Cal sat on the couch as she settled herself in a leather armchair. She crossed her legs under her and sat very straight. She was fit, strong, ready for anything. Anywhere from forty to sixty—he couldn't tell.

The fire snapped and sizzled, the grandfather clock ticked, and the comforting sounds of the old house drew in around them, a whistle of winter wind rattling the windowpanes, the creak of a heavy door.

She took a sip of port, nodding with pleasure. Her dark eyes were large and fine, her nose prominent. Cal tasted his port, its warmth coursing down his throat, blossoming in his chest and stomach. He nodded with pleasure. Better not get used to this.

"It's funny how life turns out," she said. "You can be very angry at someone and pitch an axe, severing your bond. Even if you want to make amends later, to bridge—well, it becomes … too difficult. Or you keep missing each other."

Cal went to the fire, standing before the flames.

She smiled at him, staring at him far too long. She had a full wide mouth and her eyes looked nearly black, something oddly familiar in her features. Cal flicked his eyes away, warming his hands over the fire. From behind him, he heard her voice, talking as much to herself as to him. She joined him, poking a log as it fired off blue-edged sparks. Cal turned to watch the gust-driven snow.

"Odd, isn't it, where we find ourselves," she murmured.

It was past one o'clock in the morning. Cal was hungry, tired—wanted food, then bed.

"I always believed that I would have children," she said, as he turned and made his way wearily back to the couch. "I wanted them, though my sister became the mother."

He got it, all at once. The photograph of the skinny black teenager making donkey-ears behind his mother's head. Dark and thin, strident and impulsive, according to Max Ellul. Doing whatever, whenever. It fit, *she* fit.

"Cassandra had you and your sister, Zoe." She went to him.

He nodded slowly, stunned. Cal remembered the vague outline of the story, how his mother's sister had fled home as a teenager. He knew little more than that.

"As a girl, I was called Yael."

Now, he was confused again.

"My name is Elle Yunes—I changed it as a young woman—

not long after I left Valletta. I'm your aunt." Her words were earnest, a firmness and urgency in her voice, as she sat down beside Cal on the couch.

Her presence unnerved Cal, her features larger and stronger up close.

Changing her name underlined what he and Zoe had figured out, that she had wanted to cut ties, preferred not to be found. She took a sip of port, then placed her hands flat on the coffee table. Cal noticed the strength in her dark brown arms, their reach. All that wood chopping.

"We were like twins," Elle said suddenly, "and yet not."

He coughed, a short bark, increasingly perplexed, uncomfortable.

"Cal, may I call you Cal, or do you prefer Caleb?"

"Cal." He nodded, his head bobbing.

"Your mum felt we were two halves of a whole. We finished each other's sentences, were always together. But I—" She stopped herself.

Cal sat very still. The fire burned, its crackling and the occasional pop of a log the only sound in the room. He remembered the time he had fallen into an open sewer grate in Montclair. He'd been running backward to catch a ball and then found himself up to his neck in a black hole, smelly water reaching his chest, his leg broken. Strangers called EMS and they hauled him out and placed him on a stretcher. Zoe met him at the hospital; he had an excruciating spiral break. His parents were away on one of their far-flung assignments. He was seven years old, Zoe just sixteen. The fall, rush of darkness, came back now. Blackness, rank smell, dirt, fear. Pain so bad he vomited. His shock was like that now.

Elle placed her hand on top of his. "I don't know what you'll make of this, Cal, but I think of your mum every day. And I suspect until her death, she thought of me too."

She drew into herself, folding her legs under her, crossing her arms. A log rolled to the edge of the fireplace, its edges soft and grey, its underside smouldering. Elle rose from the couch; crouching, she added a new log and some kindling. With a poker, she prodded the fire into orange flames. She stood staring into it, not speaking.

After a long awkward silence, she said, "When I left home, I was seventeen years old, out for adventure and ready to fly away. How old are you Cal?"

"Nineteen."

"There, maybe you get it. If you don't know where you came from, how can you figure out who you are? I didn't expect to never see my family again."

"But that's what happened."

"You know, I tried to contact your mother a number of times. I wrote to her, care of the magazine, *Arrive*."

This was news to him. "When exactly?"

She took in a long breath. "Ten years after I left home, I mean Valletta, when I was twenty-seven, your mother twenty-six. Perhaps it was too little, too late. I was ... I thought a letter, first—"

"So...?"

"I never received a reply from her."

"Are you sure she got it?"

"The magazine confirmed they had forwarded it. I figured she wanted nothing to do with me." Her face went stony and blank, hardening against him or the memory of his mother.

He got up abruptly; the room was beginning to feel confined and overheated. "You said several times."

"Cal, come and sit down."

They sat with enough space for another person between them. The wind keened, the sound almost human.

"In my late thirties. I could no longer stand being estranged from Cassandra, your mum. I felt remorse for what I'd done—" She stopped short, waved away her uncompleted words. "I missed her, when I let myself." Having asked him to sit, she stood and poked the fire, which rained scarlet sparks, then went to refill her glass of port. He held out his empty glass and she refilled it, before sitting down on the couch.

Cal concentrated on each sip—port was delicious stuff, wished he could indulge more often.

"I can be impulsive, it's bad and good. I guess, our strengths and weaknesses are all knotted up together."

He'd never thought much about that, stayed quiet.

"Anyway, when I was thirty-seven, this was twenty years after I left Valletta, I knew I needed to do something. The anniversaries of my flight, leaving my sister, my family, were terrible for me. I had to make things right. I discovered that your mum lived in Montclair, New Jersey, not too far from our cousins here in Montreal. At least four times a year, I went into New York for my business, so on one of those trips—it was April of 1990—I showed up at your house."

Cal calculated that he would have been almost four, Zoe, twelve. "I don't remember you."

Elle nodded. "We never met. I spotted a tricycle out front, a swing set and jungle gym in back."

Was it right in their own backyard that Mom had swung him on the swings? Not in Lake Isle after all? Memory played all kinds of tricks, he'd have to ask Zoe.

"I loved the look of your house, pale yellow, tiger lilies growing in clusters. Ramshackle but homey and so many windows. You had a great room above the garage with windows on three sides. I wondered what you used it for, storage? A studio of some kind?"

Cal's mind was on his mother swinging him, higher and higher, catching him in her arms. Letting him go.

"I appeared on your doorstep, rang the bell. Your father came to the door. He was an imposing man—you see, I'd never met him. Tall and strong—I see where you get your height, your broad shoulders. His eyes were cold. At least when he saw me standing there. Before I even introduced myself, I knew he knew who I was. He wasn't happy to see me."

Cal sipped his port, looking at his aunt as she spoke, all this new to him. His dad had never talked about Cal's aunt, wasn't too interested in keeping up family ties.

"I didn't hear any sounds within the house," Elle went on. "The silence was strange. I introduced myself, though didn't need to. I asked for Cassandra, my sister. Your father told me she wasn't home. I asked him when she'd be back and he didn't reply. I offered to wait.

"'Think you can unring that bell?' your father bellowed. 'You need to leave. Dante reserves the seventh circle of hell for people like you—who betray a bond of love and trust.' Know that one?"

"So you left, gave up?"

She laughed deep in her throat. "You don't know me, Cal. I'm stubborn. When I feel resistance, I push back. I wasn't so easy to get rid of. Finally, losing patience with me still standing on his doorstep, your father told me to leave my address. I did, as well as my phone, email, fax, the name of my jewellery boutique. I wrote it all down for your mother, hoping she would get in touch with me."

His aunt stopped speaking and buried her face in her hands. "Nothing," she murmured bitterly. "I wonder if your dad ever told her about my visit. If he gave her my address."

Cal had no clue. "So you tried once."

"No. I called the house several times after that trying to reach my sister. She never picked up herself and didn't return my phone messages. Again I wrote to the magazine where they worked. I was persistent."

"My mom never told me about any of this. Neither did dad."

She crossed her legs under her and wrapped her arms around herself, as if for warmth. "I assumed your mum didn't want to see me."

"You were the one who left. You caused a lot of pain, I guess."

Elle nodded slowly. "I'm not going to make excuses for myself. For who I am, for how I've been. It's too easy."

"Yeah, it doesn't change anything."

"But listen, Cal. I never believed that I would never reconnect with my sister, that we'd be permanently estranged. Of course, I didn't let myself think about it. Life gets in the way, we're all so busy, frantic not to leave open any chink for ... *what?*" She sipped her port. "Cal, our papa, your grandpa had an expression, *divine time.*" She let out a bitter laugh, almost a bark. "Not that I'm a believer, but I did feel there would be a *right* time, a season, that Cassandra and I would meet again. Perhaps by chance ... or that Cassandra would forgive me and eventually look for me. But the meaning of life is that it ends. Kafka. A favourite.

She could be irritating.

"I never let this truth sink in. Now I'll never forget it. My sister's death caught me up short."

Cal looked up at her. "My folks died seven years ago. You already knew about us by then. Way before."

"I should've gotten in touch, but your mum had made a decision not to open that door. I wanted to respect her wishes, maybe I was afraid, but all that changed when you," she touched Cal on the arm and he tensed up, startled by the sudden contact, "when you came up here to Montreal. As my father, your grandpa would have said, it was meant to be. Divine time."

Finally, she lifted her hand from Cal's arm and he felt the tension drain from his limbs; his mind flitted in a dozen directions.

"Is your sister here too?" Elle asked.

He shook his head, frustrated by her non-sequitur.

"Cal, I'm sorry. I know this is a shock." She glanced at the clock. "You see the time?"

It was one-thirty a.m.

"You probably want a hot shower ... a bite to eat. I should get home, I have an early start tomorrow."

"You're very elusive."

"It's just that I feel I should talk to your sister, too. Will you contact her, maybe we could arrange—"

"A big old family reunion."

She winced.

"Thanks for ambushing me, Auntie Yael. Oh, I mean, Elle." He felt contempt drip from his voice.

"I'm going now," Elle said abruptly. Cal stood and she surprised him by wrapping her arms around his shoulders. He stiffened, unable to give in to her embrace.

31. ELLE

Elle wandered the city in the snow, as if it were a map of the dead, her sister, father, and mother all gone now. Meeting Cal felt like an end and a beginning, his presence bursting through the silent white wall that had existed for decades between her and Cassandra.

Elle remembered Cassandra's refusal to have kids—that was her notion as a teen—her vow that she and her sister would be together forever. In a way, they were. Elle was free to wonder, to fill in who Cassandra had become, what they might have had, if they'd been able to forgive one another. There were reminders of her everywhere: A stranger with her sister's build would cock her head at the same angle or hold a camera, as if it were a baby and Elle would see Cassandra. Now she saw her sister in Cal.

Walking in the cold, she remembered pressing her knees into Cassandra's calves, stretching her thin arms around her younger sister in a protective sweep, enfolding her. Her absent presence everywhere and nowhere.

Elle looked through the swirling snow, a layer lifted by the wind, glistening, the bare branches, furred bones. The city was deserted and the night silence moved her. She had built a life here, a successful jewellery boutique, had gotten to know her cousins who were wise to keep a safe distance. Her nephew and niece—how odd those words sounded in her ears—were all grown up now. Elle knew every time that she looked into

Caleb's eyes—no he preferred Cal—she would feel both pleasure and pain, her nephew newly found, her sister within him, lost and found.

32. ELLE

MEMENTO MORTIS

Cassandra, it's between dark and dawn and I'm trying to sleep. Fall asleep, what an oxymoron! You realize you've fallen when you awake from a dream, a velvet black sleep. The more I strain to woo sleep, the more wakeful and anxious I get. C, I'm in menopause, you never lived long enough for this particular female hell.

The holidays are my busiest time at La Pierre Éternelle, my jewellery boutique. At night I make lists in my head, not much of a soporific. Yet Papa would have been so proud: both local and international demand for my handmade pieces displayed on metal sculptures of hands, wrists, necks, ankles, and feet.

Cassandra, I have a whole mess of sleeping aids, both natural and heavy-duty RX. Should I knock myself out … or get up, brew tea, and talk my heart out to you? To fall or not to fall, that is the question.

Remember when we first heard the term "hot flash." Wow, it sounded sexy. Hot flash. What could be bad? We envisioned unbearable urges, sparks of desire.

I'm brewing a cup of Lapsang Souchong, the scent smoky as a campfire, your favourite. I'm hooked. Forget about insipid chamomile. Like you, I prefer a tea with heft. I fuelled myself with a cup on the afternoon I wrote Papa the note in your hand. I grabbed the pen and notepad, shaping your handwriting, your words flowing out. Now, years later, I understand that being you was the only way I could commit my betrayal without doubts, fears, regrets, remorse. (That all came later.) What a sense of power I felt—and my high spirits carried me away from the only home I'd known.

Cassandra, I had to get away far, fast. Gisi threatened me. Not too many people scare me, but that woman did!

I packed essentials into a suitcase, sliding it under the bed. I'd been making sketches of cufflinks fashioned from Papa's beautiful Berber beads and took a pair with me, for good luck. Found my passport and birth certificate in Papa's desk drawer and discovered that I was born in Marrakech to a woman named Bakka Yunes. Papa never mentioned my mother's name, just that he'd found me in a Catholic orphanage called Sacré Coeur. I assumed he didn't know who my father was, or why my mother gave me up.

I was Yael, then.

In a leather satchel, I stashed my birth certificate, passport, and wallet, as well as my diary and pen; I planned to write down everything I learned about my origins. This diary was one of the few things I possessed that was mine alone. I cherished it.

I may have slept a few fitful hours that spring night in 1969, though I can't recall sleep, only that I woke up before dawn and wrote you a short note and one to Mum and Papa before fleeing the house.

I took a cab to the airport, boarding a flight to Casablanca. On the plane, I saw my diary was missing. I'm sure while I was asleep, Gisi stole it.

C, we'd both heard the sounds of planes taking off and landing, had listened to that distant roar. As the plane built up speed on the runway, I put my head back against the seat and shut my eyes, feeling the lift in my belly with take-off—I was inside of that roar now—ten thousand metres above the earth, held aloft by nothing I could see or understand. It was thrilling.

I gazed out the window and glimpsed the landscape of our childhood, Valletta's golden fortresses and castles, now mere playthings, the sea pressing in around the island city. The middle and aisle seats were both taken by businessmen and neither one took any notice of me. Thankfully.

In Casablanca, I boarded a bus for Marrakech. Outside my window, I saw the wild surf of the Atlantic, darker and rougher than our Mediterranean. We rode through sun-baked villages, littered with stump-like shrubs. Rocks protruded from the earth like weathered gravestones and shepherds herded sheep and cows. Some had donkeys or camels, the men in robes of tan or white, pointed hoods over their heads, like magicians. Here and there were crumbling stone houses, low cement sheds. Cactus and succulents grew wild. As I made my way to Marrakech, I caught sight of the Atlas mountains, their craggy peaks snow-capped. C, we'd never seen mountains before. I was awed by their beauty and power. It was my first glimpse of snow, too. (Except in our dreams and fantasies.) I loved it.

When we arrived at the bus station in Marrakech, I collected my suitcase and stopped at the information desk, asking in French for directions to the orphanage. The woman was kind enough to draw me a small map.

Once outside, I was surprised by the dry comfortable temperature—I'd expected extreme heat—but it felt like the high twenties. I shucked off my shawl and started to walk, following the little map.

Cassandra, I was afraid to find the orphanage and yet longed to. Growing up, protected inside our family within the walled city of Valletta, I felt far away from my personal history. Yet all of my life, I knew I was different. I needed only to look at you or into the eyes of any passer-by who froze me with a cold stare, or worse, a condescending smile, as if he or she could see straight to my naked core.

C, I tried to cross the street but traffic was crazier than in Valletta. No signals. Bicycles, scooters, cars, motorcycles, and calèches whizzed, buzzed, and clopped by in every direction. I took my life in my hands, crossing. Marrakech was completely flat, and wherever I strolled, I spotted the minaret of the Kout-oubia Mosque. It was nearing sunset. The call to prayer rang out over the rooftops, a sound of such clarity and longing, it seemed to emanate from both inside and outside of me. C, you knew exactly where you came from, a knowledge I didn't have yet. Was I born Muslim? Who was Bakka Yunes?

There were palm trees, what looked like a castle, orange-billed storks perching on its ramparts, and far below, vendors pulling camels. The houses were all a shade of pinkie-peach.

The medina was surrounded by a high crenellated wall, pierced by towers and dotted by more than a dozen gateways, also a red-tinged peach. Ah, The Red City. I entered a teeming sprawl of tiny covered streets and alleys, some protected from the sun by makeshift lattices. Men in short rounded skullcaps, similar to Abba's *kippah*, displayed their wares. The colours, the smells! Mountains of dried fruits, nut-and-sesame candies, pottery and leather ware, engraved brass plates and shiny silver teapots, embroidered silks and linens, baskets and hand-woven carpets, jewellery and burlap bags spilling spices, dried leaves, and herbs. I could go on. I was tempted by some beautiful chunks of amber to use in future designs, but had to make my savings last; I didn't need more weight.

After wandering the souk for a half-hour, I found myself in a large central square. I smelled grilled meat and spicy lamb sausages as hundreds of gas lanterns lit up billows of steam. A woman in a white headscarf grabbed my arm, offering to decorate my wrists and hands in henna. I thanked her and walked on, following the sound of wailing flutes, where several snake charmers lifted the lids on their cobras. It was a live show, Cassandra. A circus! Dancing musicians in blue costumes, fire-eaters, acrobats, and jugglers, whirling dervishes and minstrels. A man seemed to be pulling someone's tooth, another writing a letter for a customer. A group of herbalists displayed dried plants, ostrich eggs, live iguanas, and coloured powders that promised youth, beauty, and a magic cure for whatever ailed you. Surely, you visited Marrakech for one of your many assignments. If things had turned out differently, we might have compared impressions.

By the time I was ready to look for the orphanage, the sun was nearly gone, the desert air cool. My only familiarity with orphanages was through literature, Dickens and the Brontës. You know more than anyone: I've never been the self-pitying sort, so when I imagined being an orphan, I was inside my own fairy tale. As special as you, my dear sister.

I girded myself up before visiting Sacré Coeur, now or never.

I found it hidden on a quiet, secluded block. The building was of white limestone with a large crucifix adorning the arched entryway.

I rang the buzzer, then walked in, rolling my suitcase. A young woman sat at a pine desk; she wore a head scarf and a long dress over loose pants. She said something to me in Arabic, no doubt some version of, *Can I help you?* and I addressed her in French.

"I think I was born—I mean my parents told me that I was brought here as a new-born—and then adopted. I'm seventeen now, so it would have been in 1952. I'm from Malta."

I felt a thickness fill my throat and changed tacks. "I want to find out anything you can tell me about my parents, my mother especially."

I pulled out my birth certificate with my mother's name on it: Bakka Yunes.

"Are you all right?" The woman asked in French.

Words failed me, so I handed over my birth certificate. I heard a sudden burst of children's voices and a bustling of activity, then an adult voice speaking slowly and firmly.

The woman glanced at her watch, "It's seven o'clock. The children are going to bed, now."

"So early?" What if one of them was not tired, or afraid of having a nightmare, or wanted to play, a liberty a parent might grant. It was weird, strange.

"Yes, that's the schedule." The young woman smiled. "The early bedtime works best for our routine and for the Sisters, of course."

I glanced past the woman into the hallway and saw several nuns shepherding a group of children to the washroom. Cassandra, the orphanage was immaculate and orderly. I could hear children, but they were not boisterous, and honestly, I wondered what would have become of me if I had grown up here, instead of with Papa and Mum. I asked for a glass of water.

"Of course," said the woman, rising to get a small paper cup and filling it at the water fountain. "You seem tired," she added. "Why don't you take a seat," she motioned to a small, hard-backed chair.

Gratefully, I slumped into the chair, which offered little comfort.

"If you were brought here as a new-born, we should have a record. I can check for you." She walked in a smooth fluid motion, almost floating, and disappeared into the long corridor.

I realized how tired and hungry I was, smelling the remains of the children's supper: I conjured up mashed peas, some type of chicken, applesauce, all mixed with the sharp ammonia and bleach of cleaning fluids. Awful.

I heard a clamouring as the children kneeled to say their prayers and the varied voices, the deep contralto of the nuns, below the clear high sound of the children almost made me cry. All at once, a real cry of a baby knifed through the melodious chant, and all too quickly, the infant's voice was silenced.

I waited. Some twenty minutes later, the young woman returned.

"I'm sorry," she said. "We have no record of you here."

I took a minute to speak. "Are you sure?"

"I've checked quite carefully. We keep good records. I'm sorry we can't help you."

Words came out in a rush. "My father said he found me here

as a baby. Can you check again? There must be some mistake!"
The story of my birth was a comfort, the foundation of my
being. To have it threatened shook me up.

The young woman remained calm, but firm. She told me
she was leaving soon for the night. I asked for a phonebook
or whether she could find a number for me before she went
home. A moment later, she found Zev's phone number and I
jotted it down.

The woman placed a hand on my shoulder and offered me a
bed for the night. C, I was so drained, with no energy to look
for a café and a room. I took her up on it.

The next morning, I set out in search of breakfast, arranging
to pick up my suitcase later. At a small street side café, I bol-
stered my strength with strong coffee, working up my courage
to contact Zev. I recoiled at the memory of him and Mum. I
imagined Zev naked, apelike.

I finished breakfast and went to find a phone. Zev picked
up on the first ring, his voice deep and clotted with phlegm.

C, I couldn't find my voice, as Zev cursed, about to hang up.

I spoke up, first in Maltese, then switched to English. I explained who I was, that I was here and needed to speak with
him face-to-face. Now it was Zev's turn to be silent. C, I could
hear his heavy breath on the line.

"Are you still there?" I asked.

"Yes, I am." At last, he named a restaurant at the Jardin
Marjorelle where we could meet for lunch.

I set out for the new town. Guéliz spread out around Avenue
Mohammed V, a more peaceful neighbourhood than the old
town, the buildings and hotels painted a uniform pink, the
streets wide and airy, lined with orange and jacaranda trees.
I walked north until I found the little garden, designed by the
French painter Jacques Majorelle, an oasis in the city. I strolled
among the palms and profusion of plants from every corner of
the world in rotund pots painted an intense blue, bright green,
or lemon yellow, cooling myself at the fountain and sparkling

lily ponds. I thought of you, C, being such a visual person, how this place would have charmed you.

When Zev arrived at the garden cafe, I recognized him but saw immediately how I'd coarsened him in memory. He was tall, strapping and dark, with a fine head of thick hair that waved over his forehead. Zev stood erect; his eyes were deep-set and intelligent-looking. I admit, C, I couldn't help noticing that he was handsome, even distinguished. There was nothing ape-like about him.

Zev took charge, securing a corner table, ordering for us both. He seemed on edge, avoiding my eyes.

Our salads arrived. Steaming platters of couscous, topped with lamb, vegetables followed, and a stack of fragrant, crusty bread.

Zev nodded to me as he dug in, using the bread as a utensil; I copied him. Neither of us spoke for some minutes. Finally, Zev wiped his mouth and looked up.

"I'm surprised to find you here."

My words flooded out. "I have questions, so many, but first you must promise me—"

"What happened with your mother—"

"Stop."

Zev's eyes expanded.

"I need you to promise that you will *not* contact my family."

"Yael, be reasonable. They must be frantic, worried."

"I will write them. Can you give me your word? Or else, I'll leave right now—"

"Please, Yael." Zev flashed a slight smile, his teeth well cared for, like the rest of him. "No threats."

"Okay."

"Well, then, you have my word."

"For what it's worth."

"Your father was my closest friend."

"*Was.*"

"Let me explain—"

"Spare me."

"What's said between us, stays between us." His brow creased. "What brings you to Marrakech? Are you here to crucify me for my sins?"

I took a long, slow look at Zev. His brows were dark and thick, set straight across deep-set eyes, which made them unnervingly intense. "Tell me again what that word means?"

Zev looked into his lap.

I gave him an evil stare.

Zev ordered green tea with mint and pastilla. When the round pie came to the table, he cut me a giant wedge.

"It's a Moroccan delicacy. Pigeon cooked with onions and saffron, then almonds and spices, the pastry coated with sugar, cinnamon, and egg yolk. Taste."

C, I took a bite, had never tasted anything as delicious, both sweet and savoury, creamy and crunchy.

Our tea arrived in a pot with a long, curving spout. Zev poured it from a height into stencilled glasses, so the tea had bubbles in it. He offered me hard sugar cones and we drank in silence.

"You worked with my father, I guess you were sort of a close friend … before. Anyway, I don't know how much you know about my life. I'm adopted. A stranger on the street can see that."

Zev listened, his eyes on mine.

"I came here to see where I was born."

Zev nodded slowly.

"You see, I've lived my whole life on Malta. I've only travelled the shortest distances. It's funny about an island, how you feel both free and hemmed in."

"Yael, I know what you mean, Malta is a special place."

"It will always be home, I suppose. And then not."

"What do you mean, not?"

I felt heat crawl up my neck. "Well, I was born here, for one thing. It's only natural to wonder where you came from."

"How do you like our mint tea?" Zev asked, his eyes and voice softening, kindly.

"Very much."

"You will enjoy the ritual if you stay awhile. I'll teach you how to make it, how to pour. We like our tea with bubbles, they add to the flavour."

My smile was a grimace. Me and Zev, Mum's lover, making plans. Then I realized, we were both rebels, both traitors, bound by our betrayals. Zev had little chance of repairing his relationship with Papa and I believed, then, that I couldn't return home.

"I went to the orphanage," I blurted out. "Where Papa found me. He told me you were with him at the time. It was odd, they had no record of me."

When I looked up, Zev slumped onto his folded arms.

"What is it?"

Zev raised his head, a dark flush to his olive skin. "I'm ashamed of what happened with your mother. I've always felt sad for her, she's more fragile than she appears."

"My mother?"

"She's been through a good deal. At times, I felt caught in the middle."

"What do you mean?"

Zev pressed his lips together. "You have a connection to the orphanage, Yael, but you are not an orphan."

For once, I didn't know what to say.

"You have both a mother and a father, well, you had a mother and you have a father, still living. Let me step back. There is no easy way to say this, Yael. Your mother was a woman named Bakka Yunes."

"I know. Her name is on my birth certificate."

"And there is a connection to the orphanage. Your mother worked there as a cook for many years until her death, which was late in 1952."

"The year of my birth."

"That's right. She died when you were five months old. Bakka had ovarian cancer; it progressed quickly. She knew that she would not be able to care for you."

"So she put me in the orphanage? You say I have a father, still living ... who is he?"

"No, she didn't put you in the orphanage, Yael. Bakka contacted Menash and asked him to take you back to Malta and care for you."

"What are you saying?"

"Menash Paredes is your biological father, Yael. I know he wanted to explain, but this was not something he felt he could reveal. I don't believe in secrets, despite ... despite my own-- Yael, your father and Bakka were very much in love, but your father led a divided life, he was split right down the middle."

Stunned I thought of Abba, how he always spoke of our ancestors being split down the middle, possessing inside and outside selves, leading divided lives. Papa made such a big deal about having an open life, a unified one.

"You resemble your father, Yael, as well as your mother. Bakka had beautiful skin, much like yours." He smiled. "Your mother was a lovely woman. She always put others before herself. Bakka would have made an extraordinary mother, had she been given the chance."

I felt the din of voices around me like the hum of insects, pressing in, insistent. Zev was still talking, but his voice had become senseless babble. I held onto the edge of the table.

Zev came around to my side and put his arm around me. "You're in shock, it's understandable. I know I've taken a liberty here, but I believe you have a right to know the truth. I only wish ... never mind, wishing does no damn good."

I shook off his arm and Zev returned to his side of the table.

"Why would he do this? My father?"

Zev shook his head. "You know, he loved them both, I suppose, still loves your mother. He was heart-broken when Bakka died, but then he had you, and as far as I know, he has been true to your mother since." Zev looked down, taking long sips of water. "He was my friend, I need to say was, because of what I've done, but I didn't approve of his behaviour ... any more than—"

"You're both scum."

Zev laughed despite himself.

I wondered, Cassandra, if Abba would have ever told me the truth, if I'd come back home.

"How did they meet?" I asked. "How in the world did my father, a jeweller in Valletta, meet this Black Moroccan woman who worked as a cook in a Catholic orphanage?"

Zev smiled more broadly now, his face relaxing. "It's a good story. Your father lives inside his head, dreaming up new designs, meditating upon Jewish history and philosophy. While on business here, he didn't step down properly from the curb, and almost fell flat on his face into the street, crazy with oncoming traffic. You see what it's like here! Bakka was right there, caught him before he fell."

"Was she a large woman? Strong?"

Zev laughed. "Statuesque perhaps, but slender and quick as a whippet, built rather like you, Yael. She caught him, saved him from being killed. They both stepped back onto the curb and got to talking."

Now, I wanted to walk, which we did for another half-hour inside the gardens. When we left, Zev offered me a place to stay, either in his home, or in a Ryad run by a woman he knew. I chose the Ryad and spent my second night in Morocco there, my life changed forever.

Cassandra, I soon changed my name to Elle Yunes to honour my mother. I ended up staying in Marrakech for eight years. Though it's hard to comprehend, I helped Zev in his jewellery business and he continued the education Abba had begun. I made a pair of cufflinks with the Berber beads I'd brought along with me, based on a design Max Ellul and I came up with together as teenagers in Papa's shop. After Abba's death,

I sent them as a gift to Max who'd adored Papa. By then, my old crush had cooled into fondness and nostalgia for my old home and friends and childhood.

You see, Zev, too, wanted to make amends and did so through mentoring me. Later on, I accompanied him on a few trips to Montreal, where I met our cousins, Nathan Goldberg, and Ezra and Zippy Bernstein.

At twenty-five years old, I began a new life in Montreal. By then, Abba and Mum were both dead.

One thing I've learned, shame is as powerful as rage or fear. All three ruled me once. Cassandra, my fist was clenched so tight against Abba, Mum, Gisi ... that when I finally opened my cramped fingers, my hand was empty as air.

I wonder: did you ever receive my letters? Did your husband tell you that I came to your home? Did you get my messages? Did you choose to stay away?

Dear sister, I've met your son. You have a beautiful boy ... no! Cal is a young man. In him I see you. I hope to meet Zoe, your daughter. You live on within them.

33. AZIZA

Aziza was late and quickened her pace, wind drawing tears from her eyes. High, crusty snow banks flanked the streets, salt scumming her boots. The day was dark, damp: filthy. The northern winter, enchanting while new, now made her weary. Nights, she dreamed of the desert, its waves, a dry white sea.

So she could wander about and keep warm, Anne introduced her to the Underground City: *Ville Intérieure*. It fascinated Aziza, tunnels stretching out for kilometres across the city where one could eat, shop, sleep, even hide. Now and then during her time off she wandered through the hot bright labyrinth, huddling over a coffee, watching passers-by, straining to imagine their lives. Who were these people? Where did they come from? Would she get to know any of them, any *one*? In time, as Anne reassured her, would she form friendships, build a new life, have a real home? In Libya she felt as if her family had lived underground, but not in safety.

Now, she slogged through the St. Henri streets, searching for Toi Moi et Café. The sidewalk narrowed, became a crevice, squeezed between snow banks. A group of boys clotted behind her, hurling curses, as they circled into the street to rush past. Everyone was in such a hurry ... to get where, to do what?

St. Henri was a neighbourhood of old brick factory buildings the colour of burnt cinnamon. Here and there, Aziza passed cement-block warehouses and abandoned lots shielded with razor wire. She spotted rows of attached houses, some falling down, others coming up, as well as shops and restaurants. There was a park, the children bright spots of colour in the snow, as their mothers paced about to keep warm.

Cal called her daily, sometimes more than once a day. At times Aziza suffocated within the bubble of his attention, an echo of what she had felt, both safe and captive in his Valletta flat. How long would he be staying? She had no idea.

Before Cal's arrival, she had enjoyed her spare time, working on her French and English, taking a cooking class with two young women from Fez whom she'd met while waiting in line for their health cards. On long afternoons, off duty, she could almost be a new person without a past—a young woman with possibilities—but with Cal around, she was a near-drowned waif, clinging to a sinking raft, without a tie to the living world.

Despite the cold, Aziza was sweating when she saw the café, Cal waiting at a window booth. She stumbled inside, clumsy and out of sorts. Cal rose from the table; he made her blood quicken, but she resisted him.

"Sorry, it is a busy day for me today. Most days." Her nose and eyes streamed from the cold and she looked for a tissue in the pocket of her parka.

"It's pretty awful out there."

Aziza wiped her nose, dabbed her eyes, then peeled off parka, hat, and gloves, settling opposite Cal. A waitress appeared and he ordered a café au lait and she decided on the same. "Hungry?" he asked.

"A little."

"They have good grilled paninis."

She'd learned what that was: a hot grilled sandwich. Aziza looked at the menu but knew what she wanted: poutine.

"I'll share with you," Cal said, also ordering a veggie and goat cheese panini.

Before their coffees arrived, he pulled out a large leather book. She cleared room, as he spread it open before her.

"This is older stuff. I have photos of my sculptures and installations, they're what I'm doing now, mostly."

Aziza opened the portfolio and slowly turned its pages—charcoal drawings and what he called oil pastels, fixed inside plastic sleeves. Ice pellets blew against the window, like marbles hurled at glass.

Most of his work was of Valletta: he had captured the tiny twisting streets leading down to the sea, the fortress-like museums, and the domed churches, where she had taken refuge during her brief time there. Aziza was startled when she turned a page and saw a close-up of her face, and then turning a half-dozen pages, more sketches of her: eating, reading, even sleeping. She flipped through the rest fast, then slammed the book closed. Furious, she ran into the washroom.

Aziza lingered for ten minutes, splashing cold water on her face. *Why did he think he had the right? Because he'd saved her? He owned her?* When she got back to the table their coffees and food had arrived.

Fries, hot brown gravy, cheese curds—her favourite new food. She ate quickly, mechanically, without tasting, her hands shaking with fury.

"I'm sorry," Cal said. "I didn't mean to upset you. I thought you'd be—"

"I am not being your subject! No art model."

He took a big bite out of the sandwich and talked with his mouth full. "I destroyed most of the sketches I did of you. Then I made more ... okay. I'm sorry, but—"

Aziza put her hands up to stop him. She didn't want to hear what he had to say, she was too angry. Not sure if she could keep down even a spoonful of poutine, she took a sip of ice water, then coffee. She shoved the poutine before Cal, who didn't hesitate to stick his fingers into the bowl, grabbing fry after fry, dripping them into gravy, plucking cheese curds.

"I'm applying to Concordia," he said, between greasy bites, barely looking up.

"You go stop," Aziza said, shaking her head.

"Go stop?"

"Make fun of me all you want."

"What's wrong? Is it just the pictures?"

"Are you being deaf, dumb and blind? Or just plain stupid!" She couldn't believe he dared to draw her while she was sleeping. How easy everything was for him. What did he know of her? Safe, spoiled little boy.

Cal stopped eating and looked up at her.

"You keep yourself away from me." She had to cut her tie to him to survive here.

His lips twitched, like a mosquito darting and teasing, stinging and itching, was trapped inside.

"You always calling, trailing after me and—"

"Because I call you, I'm *trailing* you? You sound a little crazy. Everything's not about you, Aziza."

She laughed at his words, rage making her blood hot. As if she ever thought *anything* was just about her. Her laugh was high and shrill, alien even to herself.

People at other tables looked over and she covered her mouth.

Cal reached out his hand and Aziza snapped hers away, as if from a flame.

Cal got to his feet, paid their check, retrieved his pictures, and left the café.

She was by herself now with all the steamy heat and food, the filthy snow and sooty sky. Her hands shook and her heart thudded. She tried to get a full breath, to calm herself down. Aziza wanted to leave, wished she was inside the underground city wandering and wandering alone in the crowd, but found herself staring out the window as the bitter wind hurled ice chips at the glass. She was doubly alone, severed from her past, unable to imagine her future. She felt as if she were walking a high wire, each step forward a peril of hurtling down, down, and down. Or a tiny victory.

34. ZOE

NOTES: *What was life like for Yael growing up? Muslim by birth, according to her diary, raised by Jews, on tiny Catholic island?*

Zoe arrived in Montreal on a bitterly cold Friday, the temperature minus thirty Celsius, the wind-chill plummeting the "real feel" to minus thirty five. She expected winter, but if weather were animate, the Montreal cold was a whole different species from what she was used to. Hunkering down in her parka, head and hands sheathed in wool cap and mittens, a scarf wrapped around her face, Zoe made her way over to the address Cal had given her in a neighbourhood called Outremont. She'd left home in a rush, not having to worry about Tonio as Cal had kept his promise and found a cat sitter. The wind found its way to exposed patches at the back of her neck and wrists, as ice-coated branches shook with a glassy tinkling. Scattered shards of ice flung here and there were like a shattered mirror. Squinting to see numbers on the houses, Zoe realized that her whole journey was a kind of reflection, looking into her family's past and trying to unearth her own history, putting those broken pieces back together.

Off Laurier, on Workman, she found the townhouse. Icicles hung from the eaves, some three or four feet long. The streetlight made them glitter like white quartz and Zoe found herself mesmerized by one with a tip that resembled a primitive hand, or a devil's pitchfork. Was the hand pointing her in the right direction or was the pitchfork telling her that her quest, all her digging, was wrongheaded, a transgression?

For most of Zoe's life, her aunt hovered in an in-between realm, neither dead nor alive, not here or there, untraceable to any place on a map or accessible through her imagination. Yael's seventeen-year-old voice came alive in her diary, but those thoughts, feelings, and experiences were now decades old. When Zoe strained to envision her aunt, she was the wild sixties child in the old black-and-white photograph that Cal had passed along, frozen in her teenage pose making donkey ears. Until her brother's phone call.

A golden light clicked on in the foyer, and a moment later, a woman opened the door.

"It's Zoe, Cassandra's daughter." The words felt like marbles in her mouth, her lips stiff from the cold.

The door flew open, and in the light stood a tall, slender woman with long salt-and-pepper hair and glowing black skin. "Come in. It's brutal out." Her voice was deep and throaty, as if she'd been awakened or startled out of private absorption. "I didn't expect you till tomorrow." She was wrapped in a green woollen robe, her feet in shearling slippers.

Zoe stepped inside the foyer, her fingers and toes prickling back to life in the sudden heat. A few days after Cal's call, her aunt—how strange the word sounded—had phoned Zoe with an invitation.

She led Zoe into the kitchen, where a wood-burning stove glowed brightly. On the kitchen table were piles of glimmering stones and jewels, like shards of coloured fire.

"Something hot to drink?" She filled a kettle and set it on the stove. "I can offer you tea, or hot cocoa?"

"Cocoa sounds perfect."

"I hope I have fresh milk, let me check." She opened the small fridge. "Voila!"

Zoe glanced about the cosy kitchen with its burgundy

and gold walls, the rich Italian tile and eat-in counter, as the woman heated milk on top of the gas stove. She reached into a high cabinet and took out a thick bar of Belgian chocolate, unwrapped it, and stirred the milk and melting chocolate with a wooden spoon. Her dad had made cocoa the same way. "I hope I didn't wake you. I know it's late."

"I was working on some new designs."

"I'm sorry to show up early, but I wanted to meet you alone before we got together with family. We had no idea you were ... *alive*."

She smiled, her eyes impassive. "Very much so."

Zoe tried to reconcile her image of her mother's sister as a wild mischievous teen, adventuresome enough to break ties with her family and run away never to return, with this calm woman before her. As she moved about her kitchen with definite, fluid gestures, Zoe was impressed by her grace and handsome looks. She hadn't expected it given Yael's self-image in the diary. Zoe had left the book at home and felt a rush of shame. When you were a person who had to know everything, you could quickly become a voyeur. Well, she already was: writer/historian, that was her excuse, but she longed to be good, like her grandpa, or at least, better.

As Zoe watched her aunt, she saw how her large dark eyes, nearly black, the strong nose and chin, might have been ungainly in girlhood ... but she'd grown into her features. The creamy scent of scalding milk filled the kitchen, laced with the aroma of melting chocolate.

"You don't have to go to so much trouble, Yael," Zoe said, still standing. She felt formal and ill at ease.

"I'm Elle now, Elle Yunes. It's rather a long story."

Cal had mentioned something about a name change, which had complicated Zoe's efforts to find her.

"Let me take your wet things. Would you watch the pot?"

Zoe nodded, going to the stove to stir the cocoa.

When the woman returned, she took over. From the fridge,

she withdrew a chunk of aged cheddar and some Oka cheese, then sliced bread on a wooden board.

"I hope you like walnut bread, Zoe. It's my favourite with Québecois cheeses."

Elle poured the cocoa into thick ivory mugs and sat at the counter with Zoe, pulling the sash of her robe more tightly around her waist. Age had not thickened her middle as it did in many women. She cut slices of cheese and arranged them on a plate.

"You look so much like your mother, except that your skin is olive, hers was fair."

"I hear this all the time. But she was so different than me—" Zoe couldn't go on with her thoughts which grew tangled, concentrating instead on the cheese and bread, the cocoa warming her hands, as the image of her mother and aunt as girls swam up unbidden.

"Did my mother ever contact you?" Zoe asked. "I mean, you left at, what, seventeen?"

"My sister, did she speak of me?"

Uncertain what to say, Zoe felt the comforting bulk of her satchel at her feet. Cal's call had been brief, to the point; he figured they would catch up in person.

"Just that you left," Zoe surrendered. "Took off and never came back."

Elle stood, opening the door to the cast-iron stove; kneeling, she piled in logs from the adjacent crib, arranging them with the poker until the fire burned hot and bright in the grate. Beside the stove was a tall walnut cabinet with a glass door. Inside, instead of dishes, were the raw materials of her craft: jewels, stones, wires, silver, gold, a variety of metals.

"It's awkward trying to explain ... my life." She shook her head. "Even to myself."

Zoe leaned down and felt around inside the satchel, her fingers finding the thick brown envelope that had arrived in New Jersey, forwarded from Valletta, from her mother's old nanny

Gisi. She'd been in such a hurry to get up to Montreal—as if her ghostly aunt might disappear again—that she hadn't yet opened the package from Gisi. She'd deal with it later.

"Perhaps Cal told you something about our conversation."

"A bit." She stared at the unhewn stones in the case, which looked like topaz or amber, citrine and amethyst, as well as others that she couldn't identify. "Cal told me you left a message with my father."

"That's right. He offered to give your mother my note, my address; he promised to tell her about my visit."

"What are you saying?"

"Just that I tried." She sounded sad, resigned.

Zoe found it difficult to meet her Aunt's dark eyes and stared into the gem case, just for something to do.

"I hope you'll come by and see my boutique."

The abrupt change of subject jarred Zoe; she didn't know what to think. Had her father told her mother about the visit? He did tend to take over in most spheres: their work, phone messages, the mail, finances. Had her mother chosen to maintain their rift? Zoe felt an ache that she could never know the truth ... and yet here, now, was her mother's sister, her aunt.

"So you didn't tell me, did my mother ever try to get in touch with you?" Zoe needed to understand her mother's hurt, and also who this adventuresome sister had become, her aunt, whom she knew more about than she should.

Elle waited a long time before answering. "Early on, yes, but my heart was in my future. I wasn't ready to return to Malta." She swept back her thick hair. "Later on, not that I'm aware of. Perhaps Cassandra had given up on me by then, on the two of us." She sat at the stool beside Zoe, extending the platter. Zoe reached for seconds.

"I'm always hungry," she said, as much to herself, as to her aunt.

"I was like you when I was younger. Well, not slender and

shapely as you are, but whippet-thin. I didn't like myself much... And yet...."

Zoe couldn't look at her. What she'd read in the diary had touched her to the quick. She understood what it felt like to be an island onto yourself.

"I had a stubborn nature, a hard core, like the pit of a fruit. Not sure where it comes from exactly."

"And my mom?" Zoe's voice was plaintive.

"I thought she had it all when we were young. It's hard for me to think about my sister. I know I failed her."

Zoe's limbs tensed, thinking again of the diary, heat bleeding down her neck onto her chest. She was a thief. How did that fit into her exalted spirituality?

"What is it, Zoe? Are you too warm?"

"You didn't even show up at my parents' memorial service."

Elle glanced into her lap, wrapping her arms around herself. "I was there, but couldn't bear to approach you."

So she had been there. During that service, Zoe was dazed with shock, terrified about how she would manage, Cal hurtling down into delusions. She wouldn't have recognized her aunt anyway. But a shard of ice entered her heart.

"I guess you *and* my mother liked escape." Zoe's words were barbs and she could see how they penetrated her aunt's smooth surface. For the longest time, Zoe had no one to take care of her. She had to take charge, look after everything, even as a child. Bitterness seeped in, an ache of self-pity, an emotion she didn't allow herself often.

She stood suddenly, the stool nearly falling. Quick, nimble, her aunt caught it, her sleeve brushing Zoe's arm. Her robe was plush and warm, perhaps cashmere. She had done well for herself.

"I should go, it's late."

"I know you had it tough, Zoe. Anyway, I see how well you looked after your brother."

"I stayed in one place."

"You're strong."

"Please. You don't know anything about me."

Elle drew back, her lip caught between her teeth.

So they had an aunt, she wasn't missing or dead. Elle. What an affected name! Was she trying to be French now too?

Phrases from Yael's diary drifted back in fragments, out of context: *To be a beauty, even for a day. Alone, I need time to myself. I'm too dark, too skinny. Am I a Jew? Because I was raised by Jews? A spine which sticks out through the skin of my back, a chain Cassandra rubs bone by bone. Her lucky charm. I belong to her.*

"Do you have anything ... stronger?"

Elle smiled. "A sherry?"

Zoe nodded, reluctant to leave, despite herself.

"I'll join you."

She took down two heavy crystal glasses and filled them with sherry. Zoe peeled off her sweater, rolling up her shirt sleeves. They sat watching the stove, then the window, where snow slanted down.

"Were you scared?" Zoe asked her aunt suddenly. "To just take off? Leave your family?"

She smiled to herself, remembering something pleasant and Zoe wondered what it was.

"I was dreaming ahead."

Elle gazed into the wood-burning stove, rose and poked at the burning logs. One tumbled in a puff of glowing cinders. "Zoe, where are you staying tonight? At cousin Zippy's?"

"Not sure."

"Why don't you stay here? You must be tired from your trip."

"I am." Zoe was surprised at how relieved she was by the offer.

"I'll make up the couch. We can talk more over breakfast."

Zoe envied her a little; her aunt did as she pleased, responsible to no one but herself, but Zoe felt *rachmones* for her, too. She hadn't belonged, didn't fit in anywhere, until she made her own niche. They said good night and Zoe lay down on the fold-out couch, her head banked by pillows. Reaching into her leather satchel, she pulled out the manila envelope that Gisi had sent her. Slitting it open, she found a packet of letters tied with ribbon. The dates were erratic and Zoe guessed that wily Gisi had not included them all. Ah well, some were better than none. Zoe took the top letter from the stack and began to read, her mother's voice speaking inside her head.

35. CASSANDRA

May 1, 1978
Northern Italy
  Dear Gisi,
  I'm writing from Portofino, a little fishing village on the Italian Riviera. We've been working non-stop and need a rest. The village is heaven, Gisi, lollipop-coloured houses set into the hills ringing the harbour. You would love it! Yesterday we strolled to the lighthouse, spotted dolphins and starfish. Of course, Lior wanted to scuba-dive. The water was warm, I could see straight to the bottom. Lior planned a special dinner at a restaurant on the quay and we ate looking out.
  We'll have a feast, we're celebrating, he announced to the waiter. (Not to me.)
  It wasn't our anniversary or either of our birthdays. Lior had an odd expression on his face, Gisi, as if he had a secret. He ordered wine, both red and white, made toast after toast, giddy with his own words. (The man is a writer, a talker.) Our waiter kept the wines flowing and I felt happy and relaxed. Something to do with all that wine maybe. We ate sea bass, the fish plucked from the ocean that afternoon, lingering over our wine.
  After dinner, we went up to our room at The Splendido, a sixteenth century monastery turned hotel. Lior poured port. I was on a merry-go-round, the ceiling spun. Lior's words, senseless sounds, syllables. Afterward, I slept as if dead— peacefully dead.

Gisi, I slept for thirteen hours! (You've seen me do it before.) When I awoke, the sun was low. Lior was out.

I found him in a café. Good afternoon Sleeping Beauty. I told him it was nice to have time together without a project.

But we do have a project, Cassya. Gisi, he smiled at me in a really weird way. I asked, so what's the project?

So he tells me he doesn't want to jinx anything.

Gisi, am I going crazy? I think Lior is trying to trick me into getting pregnant.

Love, Cassie

June 17, 1978
Brooklyn, N.Y.

Dear Gisi,

I found out today. Gisi, I was right and I'm terrified. Lior treats me like a fragile vessel, satisfying all my cravings— rare steak and Merguez for breakfast, the hottest curries for dinner, and gelato in the middle of the night. I am hungry and nauseous, full and empty. And I'm not ready to be a mother. Help!

After Abba's death, I floated through life, a sleepwalker, dazed with grief for months, years. It was as if I was watching a woman, Other Cassandra, who looked like me. In such a short space of time, I lost Yael, Abba, then Mum. It was too much. Other Cassandra told me what to do, how to be. I felt eerie and strange, my voice—or was it Other Cassandra—sounded metallic and distant, bouncing off the walls of my echo chamber.

Little by little, I came back to myself. Lior was my lover, father, brother, and friend. He encouraged and believed in me as a photographer, as Abba once did.

Perhaps this child growing inside me—we have no clue if it's a boy or a girl—will ground me.

I'll write again soon. And please write me. I miss you.

With love, Cassie

February 28, 1979
Brooklyn, N.Y.
  Dear Gisi,
  Forgive my silence. I'm just hanging on. You said you wanted
to know everything. You asked for it.
  By the time I was nine days overdue, I could barely stand.
All I could think was: Get this baby OUT!
  Dr. Napolitano induced delivery. The contractions were so
powerful, there was no time for pain relief. I delivered Zoe
"naturally," with coaching from Dr. N, his nurse, and Lior.
  Lior stood at my shoulder. (I don't think he really wanted
to see what was going on down there.) I liked to push; finally
I could do something active. I sat up on my palms, gave it
everything I've got.
  There she was, slithery and purplish: seven-and-a-half pounds,
a scream to match the force of my final oomph.
  Hurrah! I'm not pregnant anymore!
  Though I kvetched about being pregnant, my body took
care of all of the work.
  Now, it's up to me. I enclose here a picture of Zoe. She's a
beauty.
  I'm sorry Lior was short on the telephone; he's not a phone
person. I miss you. I'll talk to him about you coming to help
me. I'll use all my persuasive powers. Can Lalo spare you?
God knows, I could use your help.
  Zoe only takes on that old sage expression in her sleep. The
girl has two modes: sleeping or screaming. I scarcely have time
to shower or button my shirt. Why bother?
  Strangers bother. I mean to say they bother me. When they
hear Zoe scream, they assume I've forgotten to feed her. Or
change her. Or that she's too cold. Or too hot. Suddenly, ev-
eryone's an expert.
  I dress in baggy old sweats and oversized t-shirts and holey
socks. I'm alone days and nights running. Lior is travelling,
while I stay home with the baby. (I often sing and speak to

Zoe in Maltese, it calms her and I want her to learn my mother tongue.) I miss my work. When she cries, I cry. When she screams, I feel an inside scream, throttled before it escapes.

If you saw our cluttered top-floor flat, Gisi, you'd kill me! It looks like a squat a group of bums hung out in for a while, then abandoned. Our home smells of dirty diapers and spit-up. My day is a rondo of calming feeding changing calming feeding changing....

This morning when I picked Zoe up, she smiled her first smile. A wide-open big grin. She smiled at me.

Love, Cassie

June 3, 1979
Brooklyn, N.Y.

Dear Gisi,

I have news. We have to move end-summer. The plumber who owns our brownstone died and the townhouse is sold. Lior wants to leave the city; I want to stay. We'll see what happens.

Yesterday, Lior was home all day and cared for Zoe while I had the day free. A gift!

Last night he surprised me with a tiny Minox 35 mm camera. Small, light. He still sees me as a photographer, Gisi. I'll carry it everywhere. On long walks with Zoe, wherever we are. I want to do more personal work, now. Something all my own.

Love, Cassie

July 2, 1979
Lake Isle, N.Y.

Dear Gisi,

While you're having a lovely summer on Gozo, we're dodging thunderstorms, sweating out hellish heat and humidity, between downpours. I know you want me to bring the baby to Malta. Right now, I can't, it's impossible, Gisi. I hope you'll come to us. I'm working on Lior, will keep you posted.

Yesterday he came home and told me he had a surprise for

me. (You know him and his surprises.) Well, I'd had one hell of a day with Zoe. She screamed from dawn to dark, like a dying cat, an out-of-tune violin, an ambulance coming. I figured I could do with a treat.

Of course, the baby stopped crying as soon as she heard her daddy. He picked her up, threw her in the air (nearly giving me a heart attack), catching her just in time.

I want this to be a real surprise, he said, putting the baby down for a moment—on the floor—where she was quiet, staring at the pattern of light on the ceiling.

Close your eyes, he told me, slipping a sleep mask over them.

He smelled of smoke and sweat. A warm wind blew through the window. The surprise I craved was a break. I wanted you, Gisi! Maybe you were hiding in the next room.

I hope it's not jewels, I said.

Lior laughed, a gruff sound that made me anxious.

He led me out to our battered jeep and helped me in, buckling Zoe into her car seat. Lior rolled down the windows and the air blew my hair wild around my face. At first the baby squirmed and whined, but as Lior built up speed, she slept. With my eyes masked, my sense of time was confused and the ride felt long and peaceful.

Not much longer now, love, Lior said, as if reading my thoughts.

I heard the crunch of gravel as Lior slowed to a stop and pulled out the parking brake. I smelled water, a briny scent. As I moved to take off the blindfold, Lior stopped me, placing his palm firmly over my eyes.

Zoe was quiet and I whispered to Lior, never wake a sleeping baby.

Especially ours. Come.

I tripped on what felt like some rocks and Lior steadied me, leading the way down a steep hill. I felt a breeze, heard waves lapping. Lior pulled off the blindfold.

I stood before a lake, waves ruffling softly, sun on the water.

Take off your shoes, Lior said, kicking off his own. Feel this sand.

I froze, unable to move. I'm not sure what I felt, Gisi, but I shivered.

"What is it?" Lior's voice was clipped, anger at its edges. "I'm taking a swim."

I went to check on Zoe, while Lior stripped and swam out so far, I could barely see him.

When he came back to the car, Zoe opened her eyes.

Let me have her, Lior said. I'll take her into the water.

No. I wouldn't let him touch her. Instead, we left the car and walked down a trail that led to a brick U-shaped apartment complex. Children were playing. Mothers lolled on stoops, flipping through glossy magazines, or trying to read a paragraph from a book.

Lior felt in his pocket and pulled out a key, opening the door to our new place, railroad style, with boxy rooms and little character. The kitchen was small with a lino floor, but it looked out on a garden. There was a "master" bedroom and two tiny rooms that could be offices or darkrooms, or children's bedrooms. The living room was a larger square and there was a den with faux wood panelling. I hate those fake wood walls. In fact, I hate the whole place. Out in the boondocks, hours away from Brooklyn and all of my friends.

He might have discussed it with me!

I felt a terrible dread, Gisi, standing there alone holding Zoe. And that's where I am now, piled into the box with our boxes. Lior is on assignment, in Bombay. Here I am alone with my little girl.

Love Cassie

August, 14, 1979
Lake Isle
  Dear Gisi,
  Zoe's first word: Da-Da. Wouldn't you know? She calls me

Dat. Which is also her word for thing. I am Dat. Shah-Dah means help me, Di-do is thank you.

Love Cassie

October 3, 1982
Lake Isle
   Dear Gisi,
   I always feel better after we have a good talk. Lior built me a darkroom in one of the small bedrooms. Did I already tell you on the phone? I can't remember. My brain is Swiss cheese ... but I am working again. Zoe and I stroll the lake and I always take my Minox. Lior pores over my pictures ... when he's around.
   Today Zoe and I were sitting on the beach. She made up a story in pictures, which she finger-traced on my back. Sometimes her fingers tickled, or they gave me a back scratch, or soothing massage. Her story had to do with a baby, it seemed, but I wasn't sure. A tall woman with a baby in a sling and a toddler running beside her came over and asked me to take their picture. Then she yelled at her son who was dashing toward the water without anyone watching him.
   I admit, Gisi, I liked the way she spoke to her kid. I've heard too many mothers showing off their infinite patience (even when their children are being monsters) in front of other mothers as if trying to win MOTHER OF THE YEAR AWARD! *In truth, it sickens me, this crazy competition. I long to find a friend I can really confide in, about my low moments, where I have to sit on my hands to avoid smacking Zoe, when I am all sucked out, a zombie, a No-Am.*
   Zoe was staring at this woman's baby and said, I want dat.
   You mean Mama? I asked. Though she knew to call me Mama by now, Gisi, she sometimes reverted to dat.
   No, dat. Zoe pointed at the baby and the woman and I looked at each other, laughing.
   We introduced ourselves, Gaia and I, while her son touched

my camera. Careful buddy, Gaia warned.

I'll take a shot of you and the kids, no problem, I offered.

She asked if I could get the lake and the trees into the shot and I had them sit in the sand, hoping it wasn't too cold. Gaia had to nearly tackle her boy to get him into position. She trapped him within her spread legs, the baby in her lap. We tried another on a boulder with her son aiming a stick. I shot a roll of film. Gaia thanked me and gave me her number.

We plan to meet for walks and coffee; it turns out she lives in the same complex, one floor down, alone with her children.

I'll write more soon, or call.

Love, Cassie

November 11, 1982
Lake Isle
   Dear Gisi,
   I'm glad Lalo is out of hospital. I'm sure you are taking good care of him. Zoe is happy he loved her drawings.

Having another mom to talk to makes all the difference. Remember I told you about Gaia? Honestly, her friendship has really cheered me up.

Zoe is crazy about her baby, Luciana. Gaia took Zoe into her lap and let her hold Luci! Zoe likes to stroke the baby's hair and wants to feed her, though Gaia is still nursing.

Zoe's like a mini-mom. I can't let Lior in on this. He wants another one. Gisi, I can barely write the word, b a b y.

Love, Cassie

December 15, 1982
Lake Isle
   Gisi,
   Big news: We've gotten an assignment for a piece on Andalucía. I plan to go to Spain with Lior and Gaia will look after Zoe. I'll call you at the holidays.

Love, Cassie

January 21, 1983
Lake Isle

The trip to Spain was great, Gisi, and it felt good to be creative partners with Lior again. Drenching sun mid-winter. We soaked it up. I'll send pictures, as well as our piece when it's published in Arrive.

When we got home, we found Zoe with Gaia, her little assistant. Zoe looked up at me, as if she couldn't quite place me. That hurt.

You here from long? she asked, gazing up at me. Interesting phrase. Well, Gisi, I'd gone from dat to you. A step up.

Love always, Cassie

August 16, 1983
Lake Isle

Dear Gisi,

I miss you every day. I didn't realize you tried to call me until I got your letter. Lior often "forgets" to give me my messages.

I'm so glad Lalo is better and that you can enjoy the beach. The three of us had an evening outing to the lake last Sunday. The heat and humidity were terrible—typical for August—like you were walking through steam.

We set out after supper. Zoe wore the little red and white gingham bathing suit you sent her and I stayed in shorts since I only intended to dip my feet in. I brought my Minox with me and will send photos soon. We were building Valletta in sand—Zoe always asks about home—complete with lake water for the Mediterranean. It was a big project and we spent nearly two hours on our masterpiece. Before we finished, Lior tried to coax Zoe down to the water.

Not now, Daddy.

No time like now! He lifted Zoe into his arms, flipping her over his shoulder.

Lior walked into the water. He lifted Zoe high above his

head, then hurled her into deep water. I ran into the lake, Zoe's cries in my ears, and then silence.

Lior got to her before me.

Once she caught her breath, she cried hysterically, then screamed, I hate you, Daddy!

I wrapped a blanket around her and carried her back to the apartment, swaddling her in warm jammies and giving her supper in bed. Zoe fell asleep in my arms. Stroking her hair, I felt an ache of love. All night I lay awake listening to her breathe.

Lior is a bully, Gisi. But then he changes, beams his warmth on me and Zoe. We fall in love again. Stupid, stupid.

The next morning while Zoe was at Gaia's, Lior and I fought.

She has to learn to swim. For safety, he tells me.

So you nearly drown her, idiot.

She'll learn to love the lake.

Great aversive therapy, Lior. And why does she have to love the fucking lake? (Sorry, Gisi, I know you hate profanity.) Anyway, she did love the lake until yesterday.

I threatened Lior: Don't you ever throw my baby girl into the water again. You hear me? You schmuck! Or I'll drown you.

P.S. I'll call you when he's out, Gisi.

Love, Cassie

February 4, 1984
Lake Isle
Dear Gisi,

I'm sorry it's been just postcards, but today I have time to write you a proper letter, though it's short. I saw Dr. Napolitano last week because I still have abdominal pain and hellish periods, which are never regular. He thinks I have fibroids. It's unlikely that I could have another child, even if I want to. I'll write more later, better yet, I'll call.

Love Cassie

July 11, 1987
Lake Isle
  Dear Gisi,
  Dr. Napolitano was WRONG! *I'm pregnant. Again. Lior is over the moon. So is Zoe, who can't wait to be an official little Mommy. I can't believe I'm to be the mother of two, Gisi. I hope I can be a good mother, or a good enough one, to use the jargon. My due date is March, '88. Let's talk each week. I need your encouragement. Zoe and Lior both want a boy, a little brother for Zoe to pamper, for Lior, an heir.*
  Love Cassie

36. ZOE

NOTES: *Thinking about Hebrew words for brother and sister: ach and achot. Ach related to Hebrew verb: to join, stitch. Debate among scholars: did the verb derive from the noun or the noun from the verb?*

Zoe sat across from Cal on the train from Montreal to New York City, eleven hours more or less, depending on delays at Customs. As the train rocked back and forth, rocking her with it, Zoe closed her eyes, remembering Cal as a baby. Her mother let Zoe hold Cal soon after he emerged, his skin peely as bark. She stroked his warm smooth head, surprised by its soft spot, smelling his milk-fresh skin. She loved to watch her baby brother sleep.

At home when Cal cried, Zoe often got to him before their mother did, his face scrunched up purply and wet. She loved the unexpected weight of his body, plush yet dense, as she drew him into her chest. Zoe had no need for dolls, she had the real thing.

On summer nights she opened the window while their parents slept and she and Cal both listened—crickets, birds, the lonely whooshing of a car, wind through leaves, the lake lapping—as they watched the mysterious dark silhouettes of trees moving against the slightly paler sky.

The train jolted to a stop and Cal gave her a slight smile, his legs extended, their feet touching.

"So what did you think of Yael?" Zoe asked.

"You mean *Elle*." Cal took out his sketchpad and began to draw in brisk, fluid strokes.

"Yeah, Yael/Elle, Elle/Yael." She pushed against his feet and he pushed back, a game of theirs from childhood. "You know when I went away, I learned more about her and Mom."

Cal let his legs go slack. "What?"

Zoe let the air out of her chest, waited awhile before speaking. "I found some things of Mom's that she left with ... a close friend in Mexico. There were some personal belongings of Yael."

"Why did she have Yael's things?"

Zoe didn't know quite how to answer. "Yael left things behind when she fled as a teen. Mom ended up with some of them and kept the important—"

"You and Mom were close, you had something special. I feel I hardly knew her. There were moments, but—"

"I know her better now." Strange, to get to know someone after death and yet a necessary continuation. "Callie, I don't think Mom was happy." Zoe had needed to pretend that her parents were okay together, but her encounter with Luz and what she'd learned about Yael's abortive visit to their home cast all that into question. And marrying so young after Yael took off and then losing her dad—she'd probably rushed into marriage as so many women did at that time.

"Maybe Dad wasn't happy—with Mom." He kept drawing, not looking up at her.

"Now, you're the one who really had a bond with Dad. Swimming together, all those evenings in the inner sanctum, listening to the blues. I was really jealous."

Cal reached across the aisle and took her hand. "Well, he threw you into the water."

"Damn right. And look what happened." Zoe turned Cal's sketchpad around so she could see what he was drawing. "It's her, not bad."

"She's got an interesting face, Elle/Yael."

Their lost and found aunt did indeed. Zoe and Cal had so much to talk about during their long ride, suspended and out of time, while they were moving and going and hadn't yet arrived. What did he think of Yael—no, Elle? Did Mom know she'd tried to reconcile? Had Cassandra ever reached out to her lost sister, beyond her early attempts? Such sadness for their mom and her sister, this estrangement that never healed. Could she and Cal forge any kind of real bond with her? What was she all about, this Aunt Elle, the only bridge from past to present. And her appearance through the void of so many losses, *beshert*, a small miracle.

Zoe had liked Elle, in a way, she was just so much herself, self-sufficient. Maybe she and Elle could find common ground.

Zoe thought about herself and the life she'd built. Many women her age were already married, some had children, but Zoe felt no urge to be a mother now or in a few years, or ever, those maternal stirrings had spent themselves when she was just a girl. She wanted something different from life now, and imagined being loose and weightless, a different way to breathe.

37. AZIZA

Aziza had never taken an overnight trip just for pleasure. When she was a young girl, her family often spent a day at the beach enjoying a leisurely picnic. Amah packed a basket with fresh bread, chunks of tuna and *harisa*, oranges, plums, date cookies, and a thermos of tea, while Baba slipped in her favourite sesame sticks wrapped in wax paper. As the day dwindled into twilight they watched the sunset, lingering into dark, when they could only hear the waves.

When Dr. Fortier invited Aziza to join the family on a trip to New York City for a medical conference, she was fearful—any type of travel sparked terror—though David, Patrick, and Caroline distracted her on the long drive from Montreal playing a game where one person started a story, then passed the "mic," so another one of them could invent what happened next. The stories that came out were wild and funny. Anne and Roger had an assortment of music—rock, jazz, blues, and classical—depending on whose turn it was to choose, so the time passed quickly.

Aziza missed the radio from home, listening to folk music with Baba, the TV full of threats and images of torture. They came unbidden and now she tried to force those pictures out of her mind.

Aziza planned to visit Cal in Montclair, which was apparently quite close to New York City by train. She had no idea whether she would feel at ease with him, an ordinary traveller visiting a friend, or like the half-dead waif he'd saved from the sea. She was growing stronger and sometimes that drowning girl seemed like a different person.

On the short train ride from Manhattan to Montclair, Aziza couldn't help thinking about their last meeting in Montreal, how Cal had left her at the café after she'd yelled at him for the portraits. For a moment, she was stunned, then relieved. She had not directly expressed rage in her life—though she'd felt it—and lashing out was a release, if only for a moment. At last she was free of him, able to start fresh without the shadow of her history.

A few days later, she felt bad about it and tried to contact Cal, but heard that he and his sister were gone. Cal didn't say goodbye, they'd made no future plans, neither of them had apologized. He simply vanished. Again, he took Aziza by surprise.

Though Aziza resumed her routine at the Fortier's, she thought of Cal as often as breath, the breath she'd accused him of suffocating. She considered calling or emailing him, but had no idea what to say, so they lived their lives separately for several months.

During the long Montreal winter, Aziza sought news of her father, Idir. She wrote her old neighbours, the Hadads. Ammar had played dominoes and cards with Baba and owned the spice stall beside Baba's in the souk. His wife, Jarita, visited Aziza's mother during her long illness, bringing home-baked sweets and the latest gossip. Aziza asked Anne and Roger for help tracing what had happened to her father and they wrote to their own contacts in Libya.

In March, at last a letter came from Ammar and Jarita. Idir's body had been found at the side of the road near Gergarish, the street that follows the sea. He'd been stabbed, then strangled with the cross he wore around his neck. They suspected that when Idir disappeared, he'd been taken to a compound Qaddafi used as a jail, but they couldn't be certain. The Hadads wrote that they had seen to a secret burial beneath the plum tree in Aziza's backyard and said prayers for him and for Aziza's future.

After receiving this news, Aziza took to her room. She was unable to get out of bed, her legs and arms like the stone limbs of a statue. The uncertainty she'd hovered in was gone.

Aziza couldn't bear to think of the torture Baba had endured. Nights, she lived and re-lived it in dreams, awakening to terror. She wanted Qaddafi killed. Not once, but to die every minute, every hour.

Anne and the children looked after her, made sure that she had enough to eat, and at least tried to rest. Aziza became too aware of the fact that she was alive: every breath she took in and let out, the monotonous beats of her heart, her basic animal needs which seemed unending, absurd. Roger prescribed a sedative that pulled her just under the surface of sleep and kept nightmares at bay.

Slowly, little by little, she found a small comfort in her old routine. Relief at the news of Baba's burial, the kindness of their Libyan friends, the generosity and goodness of the Fortiers, and her new friends here in Montreal glimmered like the heart of a small flame.

Aziza thought of Cal and wrote to him with news of her father. He sent back a beautiful letter in which he reminded her of the good family memories she'd shared with him. She saved Cal's letter, taking it out and reading it over and over. On his birthday, Aziza sent Cal a card. Once she'd broken the silence, they began to talk on the phone every few weeks, and when Aziza told him that she was coming to New York City, he invited her to visit.

When the train pulled into Montclair, New Jersey, Aziza saw Cal looking out for her on the platform. Before he spotted her, she enjoyed watching him leaning against a post, squinting against the sun.

Aziza approached him, her belongings bundled into a knapsack she'd borrowed from Caroline.

"You made it." Cal stumbled on a nail protruding from the platform and she steadied him. "I wasn't sure you'd come."

"Let us have a do-over." Aziza laughed, touching the tip of his nose lightly with her index finger.

"Where did you get that one?"

"The kids, who else? They give me my best expressions."

Cal tried to loop her backpack off her shoulder, but Aziza stopped him

"Feel like stretching your legs?" he asked, gently swinging his arm around Aziza's shoulder.

"Yes, the day is beautiful."

"A bit hot for me ... but we don't have far to go."

Aziza felt the sun everywhere, like mercy. "I am used to heat," she said softly. "I like it."

After a walk through the village, Cal stopped before a worn house with peeling blue paint. He fiddled with the lock, hair falling into his eyes, and then let them in. Aziza entered the dark foyer, the quiet of the old house drawing in around them.

"We're upstairs. Zoe doesn't believe in AC," Cal said, "but I have one in my window."

"What is this AC?"

"Air conditioning."

"Oh, yes. I don't like it. It makes me too cold."

The upstairs apartment was arranged like the cars of a train. Aziza passed a living room cluttered with books and CDs, several bedrooms, a washroom, and at the back of the house, they entered a kitchen that led out to a back porch.

"Is your sister at home?"

Cal nodded. "Deep in. She's working on her thesis. Let me take your stuff."

Aziza carefully slid the straps off her shoulders and handed Cal her backpack, which he put on the floor in a cluttered corner of the living room.

There he was, that cat he'd had back in Valletta. He came over to Aziza and rubbed back and forth against her legs. So many memories came back in a rush and she squeezed her eyes shut.

"Tonio remembers you."

Aziza stooped and petted him, his fur unbearably soft. "He's so fat!"

Cal laughed. "Obese. I spoil him. I've got him on wet food, my vet's orders, so he'll lose some weight. But if I don't give him enough, he taps my arm three times with a paw, then bites me."

Aziza laughed, scratching Tonio's forehead where he had a white marking like the letter *M*.

"When I first put him on his diet, he started in on the plants again. What a nightmare! I'll get us something cold to drink."

Aziza nodded, as Tonio slunk away, lolling in a patch of sun. She did not know what to do with herself. She had never visited a man's home unless she was accompanied by Baba or with friends. (Staying at Cal's flat in Valletta was hardly a visit.) Still, it felt good to be here; she wasn't a little girl anymore.

"Go on out to the porch," he offered, "there's always a breeze there."

Aziza walked through the kitchen onto the back porch, the screen door slamming behind her. She sat in a wooden rocker gazing onto the untended garden, and beyond to the tracks, as a train roared past. At last Cal came out with iced drinks and handed her one.

Aziza took a sip; it was sweet and tart, refreshing.

"I mixed ice tea and lemonade."

"It's good," she said, as Cal sat in the other rocking chair and stretched out his long legs. As Aziza watched him, Cal picked at his nails and cuticles, jiggling his foot, sweat darkening the underarms of his t-shirt. She had never seen him so nervous; for once, she could be the strong one.

"So, what do you want to do?"

Aziza was close enough to touch his knee, felt sharp bones

and tendons, the dampness of sweat. "Cal, we do not have to do anything."

He laughed. "So what did you see in the city?"

"We went to Central Park and did the rollerblaking."

"Blading."

"I love that thing! The children went out on a boat, but I stayed with Anne. She wanted to take me to the museums, so we went to Natural History, but I wanted to save The Metropolitan and the one of modern art ... to go with you. A welcome breeze rustled through the trees, cooling the back of her neck.

"I'm so sorry about your father, Aziza. Thanks for telling me."

She nodded, silence yawning between them.

"So what's happening in Montreal?" Cal asked finally, "since we talked?"

"The routine does not change much. The children have school, and then camp for part of the summer, and I have my activities—my work in the home, my study of French and English, my cooking—"

"What are you cooking?"

"I've been missing food from home. So I am making it for the Fortiers."

"Like what exactly?"

"Oh, *shashokva,* which is a roasted lamb in a tomato sauce or *mouloqiyah*, steamed vegetables with peppers and cilantro. These are some of my family's specialities. Eating them makes me happy and homesick." She looked away from him for a moment, then went on. "My friend who is from Fez sometimes cooks with me. We have a plan to do a side-business, selling our best dishes to some of the food shops." It was an idea that pleased and excited her, doing something of her own, a link between past and present, old life and new. Having a goal, a dream, gave her hope. "In Montreal the people are nearly obsessed with eating good."

They shared a laugh. "Sounds like my kind of place."

"And what is your news?"

Before he could answer, Zoe came out to the back porch, a pair of glasses on her nose, dressed in pyjamas and an underwear top ... what did Caroline call it ... a tank top. Yes! That was it. Aziza rejoiced when she found the right word in French or in English.

"Aziza!" Zoe bent down and kissed her on both cheeks, Montreal style. "Did Cal get you settled?"

"We are making a start."

"You can have a room to yourself," she raked fingers through her hair, "if you like."

"Thank you. How is the writing?"

"It's ... going. Or coming. What are you guys doing for dinner?"

"Don't know," Cal said, "it's almost too hot to eat."

"Well, I'm heading into the city, overnight."

Cal lurched into an upright position. "That British guy you met in Mexico? The antiques man?"

Zoe nodded. "So you two are on your own. I shopped so there's plenty of dinner fixings in the fridge."

"Why not bring him home," Cal teased, "so he can meet the fam."

Zoe gave his shoulder a push. "Such as it is. Well, I need to change and take off."

"Be good!"

"Likewise."

In the kitchen, they made a big salad with tuna, hard-boiled eggs, and black olives, and Aziza tried out a recipe she found in a cookbook for a cold cucumber soup. Cal opened a bottle of Chardonnay and they sat outside on the porch, where it was cooler.

They shared the wine and talked in drifts, Aziza sharing memories of her Amah and Baba. "And so you were telling me your news," she said, "when Zoe came in."

"Oh, yeah. I was accepted by a couple art schools—Concordia and one in the city." He gazed up at Aziza.

"And so have you made a decision?"

He nodded.

"You are keeping me in the suspense."

"I'm going to Concordia."

Aziza felt a rush of pleasure. "You have found your family there."

"As Zoe said, such as it is."

"It? Don't you mean, they?"

"Z, so now you're correcting my English?"

She laughed, thinking of Cal and Zoe, Zoe and Cal, the two of them, a family. It was hard for her to imagine how Cal could leave his sister. "What is Zoe's opinion?"

"She's happy for me. Time to be on my own, *finalement.*"

"Is that your only French word?" She slung her legs over his thighs, wrapping her arms around his neck. All at once the posture felt painfully familiar, how he'd carried her from the sea, but now she felt a strength in her limbs and a quickening.

"You can help me warm up my *français.*"

They sat outside a while longer and then did the washing up. Aziza retreated to the bathroom, and when she emerged, Cal drew her outside onto the back porch once again where he had placed a camping mattress and a bag for sleeping. "What do you think, the breeze is amazing out here."

Aziza stretched out on the cool sleeping bag. She had seen similar ones rolled up and tied with twine in the Fortiers' basement, which the children used for camp. Though she tried to identify the stars, the summer sky was too cloudy.

Cal turned and stroked her bare arm, and Aziza could feel his hand trembling. She rolled onto her side, caressing his face.

"I don't know what to do." She had no experience with men, never had time for a boyfriend. Living so closely with Baba, there was no room for desire. Nights in Libya, trying to sleep, she felt as if she were falling, the bed slipping away beneath her.

"It's not like I'm the world's expert."

Aziza leaned into him, brushing her lips against his neck, the skin surprisingly soft. She found a mole a few inches below his left ear, a deep hollow at his throat.

He pulled his t-shirt over his head and threw his jeans into a heap. Slowly, he undressed her. For a second, she was back in Detention, stripping off clothes to barks and commands, cold and shamed ... but the image flashed through and away. She breathed a deep sigh of relief.

"Are you okay?"

She kissed him on the mouth, exploring every corner of his full, wide lips with hers, stroking his arms that were lean and strong, with a raised network of greenish veins. Cal lay over her, moving his lips over her body and she shivered with pleasure. There was an awkward pause, when he grabbed his jeans and searched through his pockets, cursing. At last he drew out the small shiny plastic square, ripped it open with his teeth, and slid on a condom, as she turned away, relieved.

Aziza slid her hands lightly over his, moving them over her breasts and hips, then grasped him and guided him inside of her. The pain was sudden and sharp, like a puncture, and soon she felt the warmth of blood between her legs.

He stopped suddenly. "Am I hurting you?"

She was very still; they both froze.

Aziza lifted her hips to meet his, and he began to move again. Cal rolled her on top of him and she held him fast with knees and thighs, as they moved together, slowly building speed and force until the rawness faded into an ache and burst rippling into blinding pleasure.

She breathed hard and fast, a calm spreading through her limbs. So this is what it felt like. The strength of her desire was pure joy.

Soon Cal cradled her head, as she lay on his chest and Aziza dozed buoyant on the sea that linked Libya and Malta, where he had first found her and she had found him.

38. ZOE

NOTES: *Rosh Hashanah, 1969. Nannu, you write, One mystery closes and another one opens. Today the world is born again. This day is the beginning of your works.*

That fall, Zoe travelled to Montreal with Cal to celebrate Rosh Hashanah with their newfound relatives who were gathering at cousin Zippy's house. Elle was there, Cal brought Aziza, and Zippy's son and daughter-in-law arrived with their twin toddlers. Zoe had considered inviting Bertram, but wasn't ready to plunge him headlong into the chaos of her lost and found family, though she was seeing more and more of him in New York, with no urge to run away. This was new, possibility.

The family all attended Rosh Hashanah services at Zippy's shul, one of the longest services of the year and unique enough to merit its own prayer book. As she chanted and sang with relatives and strangers, Zoe thought of what Nannu had written about the mysteries of their family history and of Judaism, strings and knots each unravelling to reveal a discovery and another mystery. Those beautiful words in the Torah: *It will be a day of sounding for you.*

When they returned to Zippy's house, Zoe helped her cousin in the kitchen baking round loaves of challah, tossing salad, checking on the roast chicken and brisket. Dinner was a chaotic affair, as the twins tore around the living room in a game of tag, crashing into furniture, toppling vases and candy bowls, Aziza and Cal dipped apples in honey, snogging or trying to catch and contain the boys, while Zippy and Elle argued about Quebec's language laws and sovereignty. Elle supported both, while Zippy was opposed.

Zoe wasn't used to the heat, bustle, and pandemonium of family life and felt as though she had gone from a cool quiet room into colourful chaos. It was hard to hear one's own thoughts, let alone have a conversation, so Zoe asked Elle if she could speak to her in private.

Elle led Zoe to a sitting room overlooking a small park, blanketed in scarlet, orange and gold leaves and sat in a brocade love seat as Zoe settled across from her. Having an aunt and some extended family up here, with Cal now living in Montreal was another opening. Zoe could work twelve hours straight if her project was going well, eat what and when she liked, sleep ... or not.

"I think of my father during the High Holy Days, and my sister, too," Elle said. "We walked to the edge of the Mediterranean after services, to do *Tashlich*. Boy, did I have sins to cast off! We'd empty our pockets, turn them inside-out. I loved that ritual."

Zoe nodded. "You feel cleansed."

Immersed in writing her thesis on the nearly lost Jewish community and history of Malta, which now included her grandfather's writings and her mother's photos, Zoe felt deeply bound to them both. Nannu's voice had saved her through so many lost and lonely years.

"You know, my father talked about forgiveness at this time of year," Elle was saying. "I was bad! If you want, we can walk along the Lachine Canal, empty our pockets.... Ask for ... forgiveness."

She seemed to choke on that last word. Who wouldn't? Where to start?

Could Zoe forgive Elle her affected self-naming? For abandoning the family? For never contacting her and Cal, though she knew they existed?

Could she forgive her parents their absence, dead and alive, alive and dead?

Could she forgive herself her stupid fears of water and little bitty kitty cats? For going where others feared to tread, to places that were none of her damned business? For being light-fingered when it suited her purpose?

Zoe was weary of being all bunched up, how light she might feel, if only. She and her aunt sat together for awhile, each in their own thoughts.

"I'd like to walk along the Canal," Elle said. "How about you—and Cal?"

"Good luck there; clearly, he's got other priorities."

Elle chuckled and Zoe realized how much she liked her laugh, deep and from her chest, unfettered. What a relief not to have to nag her brother about everything.

"Do you see much of Cal?"

Elle smiled. "I check in with him every couple of weeks, suggest things to do and see. He and Aziza went with me to a gallery in the Old Port this summer."

"Thanks for that," Zoe said. "Not that he really needs looking after, but—"

There was a thunderous crash from below and some shouting. After a few beats of silence, Zoe asked, "Is it always like this?"

"Just wait," Elle said. "Zippy has four children and they all have children. You'll meet everyone … eventually."

They heard Zippy calling out for Elle. "You know, I should get downstairs." She stood. "You said you wanted to talk about something. Can it wait?"

She started to walk away and Zoe grasped her arm. She had waited too long and didn't want to wait any longer; if she did, she might wait forever. Zoe shook her head.

"Okay, give me a minute. I'll get your brother and Aziza to take charge, Zippy is getting on."

While Elle was downstairs, Zoe braced herself. At last, her aunt appeared, harried and out of breath.

"Sorry," she said. "The little perishers are asleep. Finalement."

Zoe barely seemed to hear her, as she dug around in her satchel until she felt the edges of the fat little diary and tugged it out, handing the book to Elle.

Her aunt looked stunned, as she took the book and turned it over in her large, strong hands, running her fingers over the worn and fraying marbleised cover of mauve, pink and purple, faded but still lovely after all this time.

"I should have returned it, but I didn't know anything about you, your whereabouts, even if you were alive." Zoe's voice came out thin and rushed. "I'm sorry."

Elle sat up straight, her spine rigid, her regal head extended toward Zoe. "How did you get this?"

"I met a friend of my mother's last summer when I was trying to find out more about what happened to my parents in Mexico. She had it."

"I don't understand."

"They were close--she had some of Mom's things saved."

Elle shook her head hard. She frowned, puzzled, and for the first time looked older than her years.

"Maybe when you fled Valletta, you left your diary behind."

"Actually, I packed it. But I think our old nanny Gisi stole it while I caught a few hours of sleep the night before I left. I wouldn't put it past her. Cassandra could have found my diary and saved it."

"I'm sorry," Zoe said again. "But I didn't know where you were ... or even if you were alive." She knew she was repeating herself but had nothing else to say.

"Sorry does not cover it, Zoe." Her voice was unnervingly quiet. "You knew I was alive this past winter and exactly where to find me. You stayed at my flat."

"I know, but I ..." Zoe was ashamed. She'd wanted to keep the diary.

As if reading her thoughts, Elle enclosed the diary between both hands, shielding it. "Did you...?"

Zoe's silence was answer enough.

"You know, I like to think of myself as a private person."

"Last spring while I was in Valletta, I heard from that former nanny of yours and Mom's, Gisi—"

Elle groaned. "She makes *Rebecca's* Mrs. Danvers look like a saint."

Zoe laughed, despite herself. "Well, she was very devoted to Mom. She thought she was really distraught before her death, that—"

"What?"

Zoe didn't know what to say, what not to say. "I went to Mexico, the town where my parents drowned, Zícatela, in Puerto Escondido, to see if I could find out anything more. I just needed to be at that place, I guess, where they'd last been. I met a woman there, like I was saying, who was quite close to Mom and she gave me an aluminium case with many of Mom's things, as well as—"

"My case. What else was in there?"

"Letters, photographs. Notes for a project Mom was doing with her father. My Dad's watch." Zoe felt a stab of guilt remembering how she'd hocked her father's jewellery to rustle up some cash, a watch which would have rightfully gone to Cal.... "A beautiful pendant of gold with a charm shaped like a menorah, studded with stones."

Elle made a sound, a cross between a murmur and moan.

"What is it?"

"Can you bring that pendant tomorrow, I'd like to see it. And I'd like to have my aluminium case returned."

"Of course." Shame heated her face.

"The pendant you mention, I designed it. I thought of giving it to your mother as a gift, but never did."

Zoe didn't need to ask why.

"I'm sorry," Zoe said. "I don't know if you can forgive me. But if you can, now—"

"Is the time." Elle emitted a sad laugh, with an edge of bitterness. "That's what your Nannu would have said. He needed forgiveness, too. He was far from perfect."

Zoe felt a charge of fear, like mercury in her veins. In truth, she didn't want to know about Grandpa's flaws, she still needed him. "Oh, in the case, there were some letters from a Bakka Yunes to my grandfather."

"Why didn't you say so?"

"I couldn't read them. There's a good deal of water damage and they're written in Arabic with some French here and there. Is she a relation of yours?"

"Please bring those tomorrow."

"You already have them, I tucked them into the flaps of the diary." Her aunt didn't answer her question, but there would be time now, or later, to ask again.

"I still miss my sister, you know, and I imagine you—"

"What, tell me."

"Well, I want my private possessions returned—but I'd like you to keep the necklace. I couldn't give it to Cassandra."

"You're not mad?"

Her aunt didn't answer right away. Then she said, "You can feel anger along with a bunch of other things."

Zoe didn't know what to say.

"The necklace has an inscription on the back," her aunt said.

"Yes, I read it. 'To the love of our Father Jahwe.' The two-line inscription on the floor of the southern temple of Ggantija in Xaghra. Sign of the first Jews who landed on Gozo. I visited the site with an old friend of yours."

"Yes?"

"Max Ellul."

"Oh my God." Yael's hands flung to her face. "How is Max?"

"Well. You know, he wanted to thank you for those cufflinks

you sent him so many years ago, but had no way to track you down."

Elle nodded slowly. "I didn't want to be found, then."

"Could we talk...just the two of us? I'd love to know more about your childhood in Valletta, your life since. My grandpa. You see, he helped me find out who I am."

Elle looked up, startled.

She'd said too much. "Can we talk at a quieter time?"

"It's tough for me to look back. Are you in town for long?"

"No."

"Come by my place tomorrow around four. I've got questions for you, too. I want to know more about my sister and her life. We'll commune with ghosts."

Zoe had weathered so many losses, absence had become a kind of presence, even present. She nodded.

"I don't know if I'll ever feel like your aunt, being absent so long."

Zoe thought of the phrase Elle had used on their first meeting. We can dream ahead, but she didn't say anything.

They sat for a while longer and when they joined the others in the living room, the diary was nowhere in sight. Zoe dipped an apple in honey and looked around the table. Zippy had laid out pomegranates.

According to legend, pomegranates contain 613 seeds, one for each of the 613 mitzvot, Nannu said. Zoe mouthed his words, a kind of prayer: *May our good deeds in the coming year be as plentiful as the seeds of the fruit.* Well, she could try anyway, that's all anyone could do.

So her quest hadn't yielded what she was looking for, an answer or explanation for her parents' sudden deaths; instead she'd learned that certain aspects of her parents' lives would remain unknowable, a palpable vacancy.

In truth, her journey had enabled her to solve a different mystery than the one she'd set out to unravel and led her to her aunt, a link to her past, and a possible presence in her and

Cal's lives. Tomorrow, Zoe would learn more about Nannu and Mom when she was just a girl, questions she'd been saving up for a lifetime.

EPILOGUE: SKYWATER

ZÍCATELA, MEXICO, OCTOBER 2000

Cassandra brought toast and *café con leche* out to the back deck of the cottage overlooking the sea. Lior mumbled thanks and bit into a crusty triangle, a runnel of melted butter trickling down his chin. The sun was a filmy, yellowish-white yolk in the sky and made Cassandra think of a poached egg. Already the day was hot, a wet wind off the water. They were on the Oaxaca Coast for a cover story for *Arrive*, a plum assignment. Yet Cassandra was eager to get back home: Cal's drawings and paintings were being featured in a school art show, and over the years, Cassandra had missed too many of her children's milestones.

She watched Lior as his pen scratched furiously filling a legal pad with his large, dense handwriting. Without glancing up, he consumed the rest of his breakfast.

"Got to lose a few pounds," he mumbled *sotto voce*, swallowing the last bite. "Get down to my fighting weight."

"So do it."

"But there are so many different kinds of food."

Lior had put on weight during the past decade, as much as fifty pounds, burgeoning from a lanky, well-proportioned man into a bulky middle-aged one with a barrel chest and insistent paunch. His leonine hair was still thick, black shot through with silver.

"Lior—"

"Give me a minute."

He wrote for another fifteen, a faint gleam of sweat on his forehead.

"Yes."

Zícatela was a forbidding place, the sea the colour of dirty dishwater, waves as high as walls, black and white signs jabbed into the greyish sand warning of the perils of swimming. Cassandra listened to the surf sizzle, surprised by how it made her want to get out there with her board. She'd surfed nearly every day of this trip; even though it had been a few years since she'd been out on a board, her body remembered.

"Well, what is it? I need to finish this chapter, then I've got a surfing lesson with Ricardo. Join me. You'll be great, C."

He made this a statement: no, a command.

"I don't need to be great, but I'll have fun, take plenty of good pictures. That's good enough for me."

"You need experience ... and practice."

Cassandra had learned to surf in the calmer waters on the lovely Playa Carrizalillo during their first visit to Puerto Escondido two decades ago. She was in her early twenties, then, and took lessons with a master named Luis. On her first try, she managed to get up for a few seconds before a wave knocked her down. She enjoyed lying on her belly on the board and paddling around, buffeted by the sea. During her second lesson, she really took a ride. The rush was like nothing she'd ever experienced, shooting out of a crescent of furling sea, radiant, buoyant. Luis called her a natural. She'd kept it up erratically over the years, but she was still lithe and agile.

"I had a long chat with Gaia last night."

"Who?"

Cassandra clattered her cup back into its saucer, sloshing milky coffee onto her white shorts. "My friend, Gaia. Lior, you remember perfectly well. My friend who ran the homecare in Lake Isle, where Zoe virtually lived for awhile, helping her out as little mommy."

"So?" Lior lit a corncob pipe and puffed, then hurled it into the bin, making a clattering basket.

"For God's sake, Lior."

"Got to quit."

Cassandra smoothed her white shirt over her hips, then rolled down the cuffs to protect herself from the sun. Her phone call with Gaia was heartening; in truth, she'd become more and more isolated each year with Lior. "We caught up with each other, spoke about many things. Gaia is well, by the way."

"Good."

"Apparently, she'd written me several letters this past year, since she moved down south—she's in Charlottesville now, Lior—not to mention cards, photos of her kids. I never got them. Lior?"

For the past five years, perhaps longer, Cassandra suspected that Lior was going through her mail and their professional correspondence confiscating anything that he didn't want her to read, though she couldn't prove it. He also erased phone messages, or forgot to tell her about them.

Lior kept on writing, head bent.

"She's my best friend, Lior. Gaia had my address, zip code, everything."

When Zoe was eleven and Cal two, they'd moved to that ramshackle house on Valley Road, roomy, but in need of work. It was close enough to Lake Isle that Cassandra and Gaia arranged to visit back and forth twice a month, or they'd meet in New York. They enjoyed leisurely conversations when Lior was out of the house or away on assignment. That's when Cassandra called her old nanny, Gisi, longing to hear the sound of her voice. Zoe and Cal still asked her about Valletta, what it was like to grow up in Malta. For years, they'd begged to visit. Even though it would be painful to go back home with her children, who weren't little kids anymore, Cassandra could see Gisi. That would be a comfort. Who knew how long Gisi would be around, she was getting on.

"You were talking in your sleep again." Crumbs littered Lior's bright green Lacoste shirt, nestling inside the creases of his crotch, where his khaki shorts bunched up as he worked.

Cassandra felt herself recoil; it was hard to remember how much she'd wanted him once.

"You were wailing, Ya-ya-ya-ya-ya!"

Cassandra's dream swam up whole. Yael spooned around her, knees pressed into Cassandra's calves, the warmth of her sister surrounding her, Yael's smell, a whiff of sweat, bite of peppery paprika. The swath of black hair, coarse and heavy, brushed Cassandra's back with its itchy warmth. Cassandra relaxed within Yael's arms but with each breath her sister re-ceded, swathes of white bleeding between pointillist dots until she vanished altogether.

Cassandra awoke, her grief almost new. Hollow, she would have to endure it. Still.

"Was it your sister?" Lior put a heavy arm around her shoulder. Cassandra stiffened, drawing away.

Lior looked at Cassandra in a slow steady gaze roving from her head down to her toes, probing. He began to scribble again, fast and furiously.

"What are you writing, Lior?"

"I want to see if I can make up something from scratch. Create a world."

"Are you going to share it with me?"

"Not yet."

Lior put down his pen and stood up; standing above and behind her, he held Cassandra within his embrace. "Tell me, Cassya. About you and Yael."

Cassandra broke free of Lior's hold, though he tried to constrain her. "Let me breathe!" She leapt to her feet. "Leave me. Or I will leave you."

"Is that a threat?"

"A promise."

He reared back, a histrionic pose. She should have left him

years ago, but they made a good photographer/writer team, had done well for themselves. He was one of the first people who believed in her and did still; Lior was a believer. Perhaps that was the quality that drew her and made her stay. He was devoted to their children in his way and had a strange hold over her heart, but boy, did he piss her off.

"And stop going through my fucking mail! For all I know—"

"What do you know? Tell me."

Cassandra retreated to their room and slammed the door, bolting the latch and throwing herself face down on the bed. Her chest ached. Three times she'd gone to look for Yael, shortly after her marriage, and later, about fifteen years ago, and then more recently, was it seven years now, since she'd tried? The first time, they'd been on assignment in Morocco and she looked for Yael in Marrakesh, going to the address of the Ryad on her last postcard. No luck and she was on deadline, had to return home quickly. The last two times, Cassandra didn't get very far before Lior came after her and put a stop to it. Now Cassandra thought about searching for Yael again. Today, there was always a way to find someone, to contact them; she hadn't been persistent enough. In truth, she was petrified. Both by Lior *and* Yael. She could only imagine what Lior was capable of ... and what if Yael didn't want anything to do with her? To be abandoned again would be too much to bear.

Cassandra was often afraid, bits of her eroded over the years so she scarcely recognized herself. Reaching for the phone, she dialled Zoe's number in New Jersey, her heart contracting when she heard her daughter's voice.

Lior was right outside the door, shouting, "Cassya, let me in!"

"What's going on there, Mom? Are you okay?"

There was a long silence on the line, crackling with static. For a few moments, Cassandra couldn't form words, then whispered, "I will be. How are you, love?"

"I'm okay. Juggling two papers, neither of which is tracking. Honestly, Mom, I've got too much to deal with."

"And Cal?"

"I have to hassle him to do any homework. Or to help me with the all the crap that needs doing around here. The house is falling down around us and the bills are piling up. Collection people call me nonstop, what do you want me to say to them, Mom? I need to head into the city in a minute. Shit. Mom! I'm late. Can we talk later?"

"Darling, I'm afraid I've been a poor excuse for a mother."

There was a beat of silence.

Cassandra knew Zoe couldn't stand self-pity. She heard the click of the line, had her daughter hung up already, or was it just a poor connection?

"I love you, Zoe."

Slowly, Cassandra replaced the phone in its cradle, soundlessly, as she heard Lior in the bathroom. When he emerged, he called out, "I'm going out for my lesson with Ricardo!"

Cassandra didn't answer, but when she heard him leave, she fled to Luz's cottage. Her friend was waiting for her. Luz took her into her arms and stroked her back in circular motions. She had delicate brown hands, quick and graceful, with perfect scarlet nails.

"Cassita, *mi amor*, what is happened?"

"My children—"

"They are not babies, Cassita, and they are doing fine."

"Better without me—" Zoe and Cal were cool when they saw her, aloof and contained. Well, what did she expect? There were moments, though. Last month Zoe suggested lunch in the city—she needed to talk about everything—why hadn't Cassandra asked what she meant by "everything." Then Zoe postponed lunch, but they would do it when Cassandra returned home, they'd have a real talk, a long, leisurely one. Cal handed her the invitation to his school's art show, "Will you be home, Mom?" a plaintive tone to his voice, which was just beginning to change. They both needed her.

"Stop this now, Cassita."

"Luz, they hardly even consider me their mother." It haunted her. She didn't know how to wend her way back in, or even if she was capable of sustaining contact with her children; there was something missing in her, broken.

"Of course, it's my fault." Enough with self-pity. She was pathetic. It did no good.

"What is happened?"

"Lior is writing something—"

"And this is news?"

Luz looked at Cassandra and then did an uncanny imitation of Lior's writing face, lips puckered and thrust out, brow lowered in concentration, one hand scribbling, the other ruffling his hair. They cracked up, laughed and laughed, though Cassandra's laugh sounded like a yell.

Luz stroked Cassandra's face that was damp, drying it with her hands. Then she held Cassandra's head and kissed her, softly at first, then harder.

"Not now."

"Okay, *mi amor.* Are you hungry? I've made fish tacos and guacamole."

They sat in the kitchen and enjoyed their meal. Luz had stirred up a sangria with plenty of fresh fruit and she poured them each glasses. They spread out photographs Cassandra had taken and a few which Luz had shot, all of the two of them, then secreted them in a box.

After they cleared the table, Luz took Cassandra into her arms as they stood in the foyer. They were just about the same height and build, small, slender and shapely, with delicate womanly curves. As they embraced, Cassandra felt a leap in her belly, an answering completeness in the twinness of their bodies.

"I want to go where we can't hear the waves."

Luz shut the windows, put on the fan, then a CD of Andre Segovia, Estudio Sin Luz. "You see how cosy we are."

"He won't be long."

"At least an hour."

Cassandra couldn't hear the waves, what a relief that was, but she was on edge, and let Luz massage her with soothing oils. Slowly, she began to melt under Luz's touch, and though she couldn't see Luz' eyes, she felt her gaze warm her from her skin to her core. Her life with Lior was not her own, though it was of her own making. Sometimes she feared that the sum of her life was a reaction to Yael's abandonment. She longed to step out of it and start fresh. She was only forty-six, she had time. Perhaps that was what Yael had felt and longed for years ago; Cassandra understood it now all too well.

For the next few days, Cassandra and Lior lived side by side, not speaking, tension a taut line between them. And then one night, Cassandra dreamt deeply. Lior caressed her face; he looked at her with calm grey eyes, serene and beautiful. She loved the touch of his hands, his gaze.

Opening her eyes he was there at her bedside stroking her hair. Surfacing, she drew back fast, sitting up against the headboard.

"I startled you."

"A bit." Cassandra tried to free herself from the gauzy web of her dream.

"Cassya, I'm a schmuck."

"You said it."

She willed herself not to laugh, or even smile at him. She was still angry, but less afraid.

"You'll forgive me, Cassya."

Only he would make that phrase a statement. She removed his hand from her hair and lay it in his lap. "I've been doing a lot of thinking these days." These years, she thought to herself. "I want to separate."

Lior's chin drew inward, he held his face in his hands.

"This can't be a surprise, Lior."

"I'm no good without you."

"You're no good with me." They had a laugh together, despite everything.

"Can we finish this trip, do a bang-up job on the project? Give me at least that, Cassya."

"I'm not going anywhere," she said coolly. "Not yet."

"We've got to think this through. I'll be better, our kids—"

"They're not kids."

"Cal is twelve, in case you've forgotten."

"There you go."

Cassandra rose from the bed and wrapped a robe around herself, feeling too exposed. She paced the room, talking to herself, as much as to Lior.

"I've never lived on my own. Ever. I went from my parents' house in Valletta to ours in Brooklyn. Maybe it's late, but I want to see what it's like—"

"What we had, then, we can have back, Cassya. It's not too late."

"You sound like a cheesy love song."

It wasn't too late for her to begin again on her own, to find Yael. Alone, it might be possible. With Lior, her world constricted. He was jealous of anyone who had a hold on her time or heart.

"I remember seeing you in the Upper Barrakka Gardens for the first time. You were—still are—a goddamn beauty. I felt it, our fit."

She didn't answer or reassure him; how could she?

"Cassya, it's *beshert*. We're meant to be."

"Zoe and Cal have always wanted to see Valletta. Before, it was too painful for me, but so much time has passed. I want to take them, I need to see Gisi."

"We'll go! As a family."

He came up behind her and put his arms around her waist; she stiffened. "We can start planning the trip."

Cassandra wanted to go alone, with Zoe and Cal, not with Lior.

"Can I get you a coffee C, some breakfast?"

"Sure," she said, her thoughts elsewhere. Cassandra wondered if seeing Yael at last would heal the sadness she carried with her everywhere.

Lior stopped and turned toward her. "Can we wait until we get back to talk things through?"

"Okay." She would give him that small concession; it wasn't long to wait.

"And we'll go out for a surf together tomorrow."

She gave him a wan smile. *It helps me forget,* she thought to herself, *when I manage to catch a wave.*

He went to her and kissed her lightly on the forehead. She didn't resist or respond.

The following afternoon, Cassandra set out with Lior for the beach, each of them carrying a bright yellow surfboard. Lior trod heavily in the dark, gritty sand, walking on the balls of his feet like a prize-fighter, thrusting out his belligerent chest and paunch, as if they were badges of honour. Cassandra felt a strange lurch of love and pity for him, a messy knot in her gut. They waited ten, fifteen minutes for their coach, Ricardo, and then got a call on Lior's mobile that he was sick, sorry, but couldn't make it.

For Zícatela, the sea was calm, only a handful of surfers out. Cassandra waded into the water and then she and Lior paddled out together toward the break.

As she stretched out on her board, Lior grinned, and she managed a smile for him. Together, they had a few good runs, riding fluidly into shore.

They lolled out by the break for a good twenty minutes, bobbing and swaying, no big waves in sight. At last they caught a good one and Cassandra felt the rush, shooting out of a tube of furling, glistening sea.

Little by little, the other surfers knocked off and the shoreline was desolate. Dusk came quickly, the sun lowering in the sky like a pale, carelessly tossed disc.

All at once, the break turned choppy, as waves careened in,

building speed and height; the sea now looked frigid as the Arctic. Was that Lior out among the waves, more like foamy glaciers? She shouted into the cold mist that they should go in, call it a night. He didn't answer or she couldn't hear him; it was hard to make out anything above the sea's roar. Cassandra called out again, struggling to get into shore on her own.

Panicked, she couldn't spot Lior and was making little progress toward the beach, as a wave slapped her off her board and the current pulled and bounced it out of her reach.

Cassandra treaded water, faced longingly toward shore, alone out there at sea.

All at once, she heard Lior's voice behind her—a seagod— lifting her at her waist and hips and dragging her backward onto his board in a bellyflop. Cassandra lay on her stomach, panting, as Lior slid behind her, his chest heavy and hard against her back, pinning her to the board.

Cassandra felt Lior paddling furiously parallel to shore, whispering something in her ear again and again that she couldn't quite make out but sounded like *beshert,* meant to be. As she squinted out to sea, clinging to their board, a huge breaker approached. It raged up—the height of a two-story house—in shock, she felt its speed and rumble in her bowels, its pure force, as the wave's hump back curled, then broke, spray smashing and sloshing, shaking her like a child's rattle inside a vortex so deafening it was a kind of silence.

Where was Lior now, inside the wave with her?

Water stung Cassandra's eyes, burned the lining of her nose, filled her mouth, ballooned her lungs. She was in a mammoth washing machine, kicking and flailing. Unsure which way was up—to light, air—which way down to the bottom of the sea.

She stroked and kicked, held and held her breath....

Now, she is breathing underwater.

Cassandra pushes Cal high, hears his happy shriek, as he sails into the air on a swing and she catches him, then lets go. Zoe writes on her back. What is it that her daughter is saying?

Cassandra cannot decipher it. Zoe traces slowly, then lifts her hand from her mother's back until there is no touch at all.

Cassandra kicks and strokes, glides up and up toward Zoe and Cal, back to Yael—how it hurts to mouth their names. At last a stealthy calm engulfs her. Air, light, floating toward skywater. Drowned, not saved.

ACKNOWLEDGEMENTS

I'm grateful to The St. James Cavalier Centre for Creativity in Valletta, Malta for a generous residency fellowship. My stay in Valletta was life-changing and inspired much of this novel. Chris and Carmen, you made me most welcome, as you shared your island's history, treasures, and secrets. Josette, your warmth and presence made me feel at home, when I could so easily have been a stranger in a strange land.

Heartfelt thanks to The Virginia Center for the Creative Arts (VCCA) for time and space in which to work. I completed much of *In Many Waters* during residency fellowships at VCCA, my home away from home.

Angie Chuang was generous in reading several drafts of this novel as it took shape and offering trenchant comments, as well as encouragement and belief. Zsuzsi Gartner provided invaluable critique and suggestions which helped me hone the novel into its final form.

I am both inspired by, and indebted to, the extraordinary writer Hisham Matar who read and spoke in Montreal. His work, particularly *The Return: Fathers, Sons and the Land In Between* and *In the Country of Men* transported me on indelible journeys.

Grateful thanks to powerhouse, Luciana Ricciutelli, Renée Knapp, and the wonderful team at Inanna Publications.

The love, support and belief of Gabriel, Tobias, and Michael has made it possible for me to wake up each day and to do the work I am passionate about, to pursue my writing dream.

Finally, to the millions of refugees around the globe: may you find safe haven.

Photo: Monique Dykstra, Studio Iris

Ami Sands Brodoff is the award-winning author of three novels and a volume of stories. *The White Space Between,* which focuses on a mother and daughter struggling with the impact of the Holocaust, won The Canadian Jewish Book Award for Fiction. *Bloodknots,* a volume of thematically linked stories about families on the edge, was a finalist for The Re-Lit Award. Her debut novel, *Can You See Me?* was nominated for The Pushcart Prize and is a recommended book of NAMI (The National Alliance for the Mentally Ill). Ami contributes essays, articles and reviews to such diverse publications as *Tablet, Vogue, The Globe and Mail, The Montreal Review of Books,* and *Quill and Quire.*